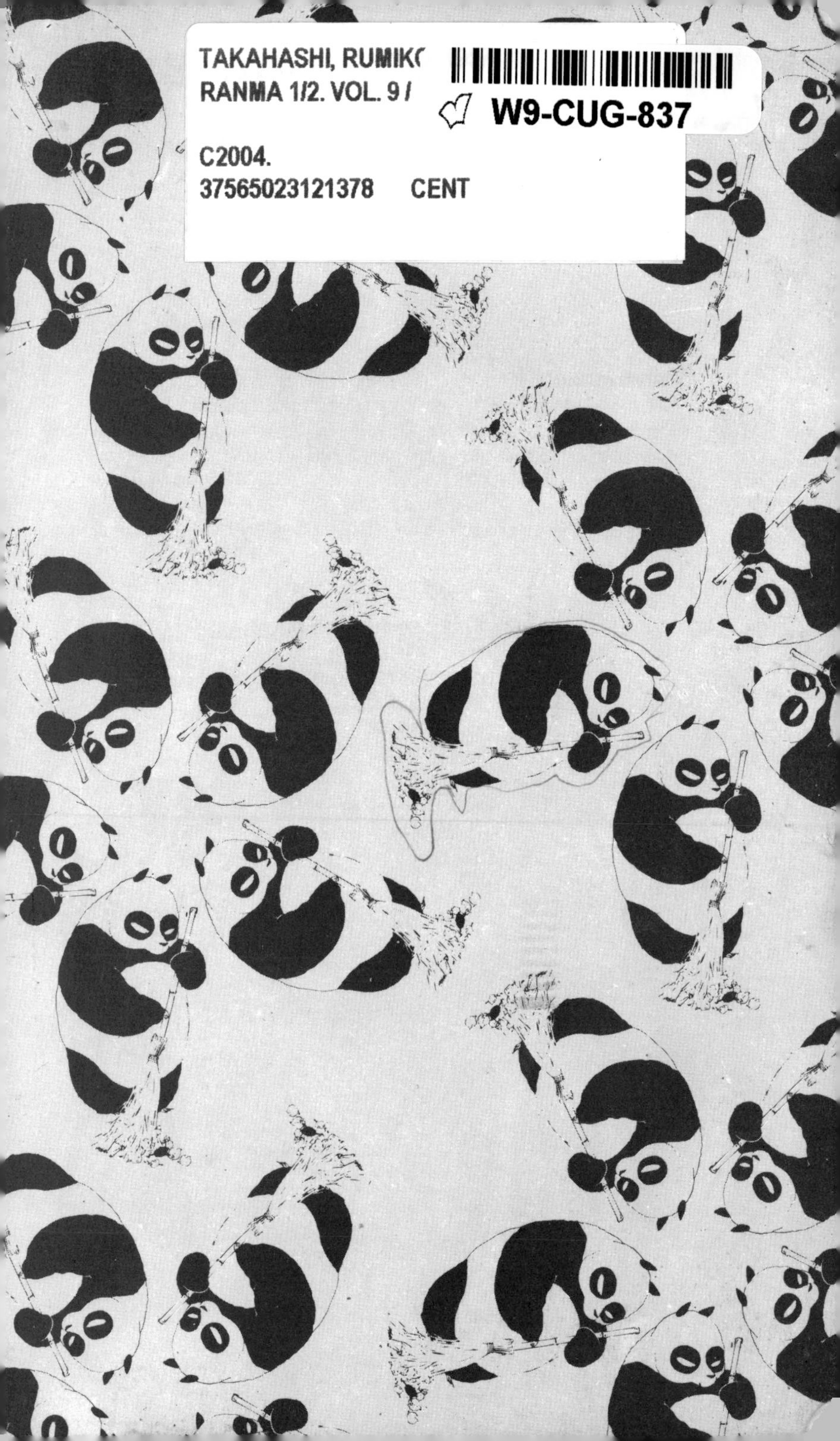

"**Rumiko Takahashi** doesn't miss single farcical opportunity as every volume is crammed with raging hormones, romantic entanglements, gender-swapping, and martial-art silliness. Boy changes to girl, man to panda, girl to cat -- and everybody's kung fu fighting."

Anodyne Magazine

"**Ranma 1/2** is a must see for anyone who likes a wicked sense of humor."

Gamers' Republic

OTHER TITLES BY RUMIKO TAKAHASHI

RANMA 1/2
MAISON IKKOKU
LUM*URUSEI YATSURA
INU-YASHA
RUMIC WORLD TRILOGY
RUMIC THEATER
ONE-POUND GOSPEL
MERMAID SAGA

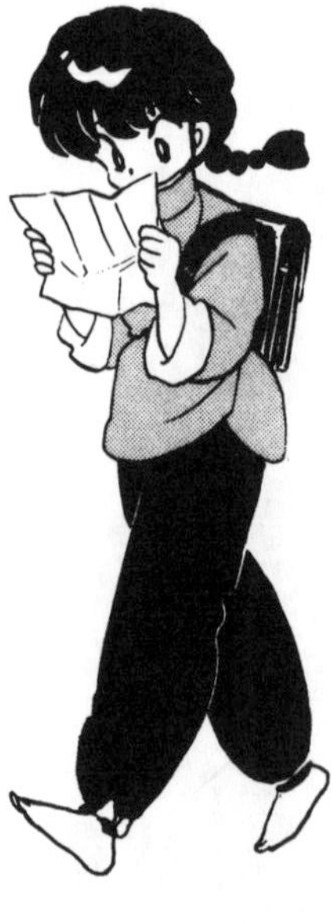

VIZ GRAPHIC NOVEL
RANMA 1/2™

9

This volume contains
RANMA 1/2 PART FIVE #7 through #12 in their entirety.

Story & Art by Rumiko Takahashi

English Adaptation by Gerard Jones & Toshifumi Yoshida
*

Touch-Up Art & Lettering/Wayne Truman
Cover Design/Viz Graphics
Editor/Trish Ledoux
Managing Editor/Annette Roman
*

Sr. V.P. of Editorial/Hyoe Narita
Sr. V.P. of Sales & Marketing/Rick Bauer
Publisher/Seiji Horibuchi
*

First Published by Shogakukan, Inc. in Japan
*

Printed in Canada
*

Published by Viz, LLC.
P.O. Box 77010
San Francisco, CA 94107
*

10 9 8 7
First printing, June 1997
Fifth printing, December 2001
Sixth printing, September 2002
Seventh printing, June 2003

www.animerica-mag.com

VIZ GRAPHIC NOVEL

RANMA 1/2

STORY & ART BY
RUMIKO TAKAHASHI

CONTENTS

PART 1
AKANE BECOMES A DUCK

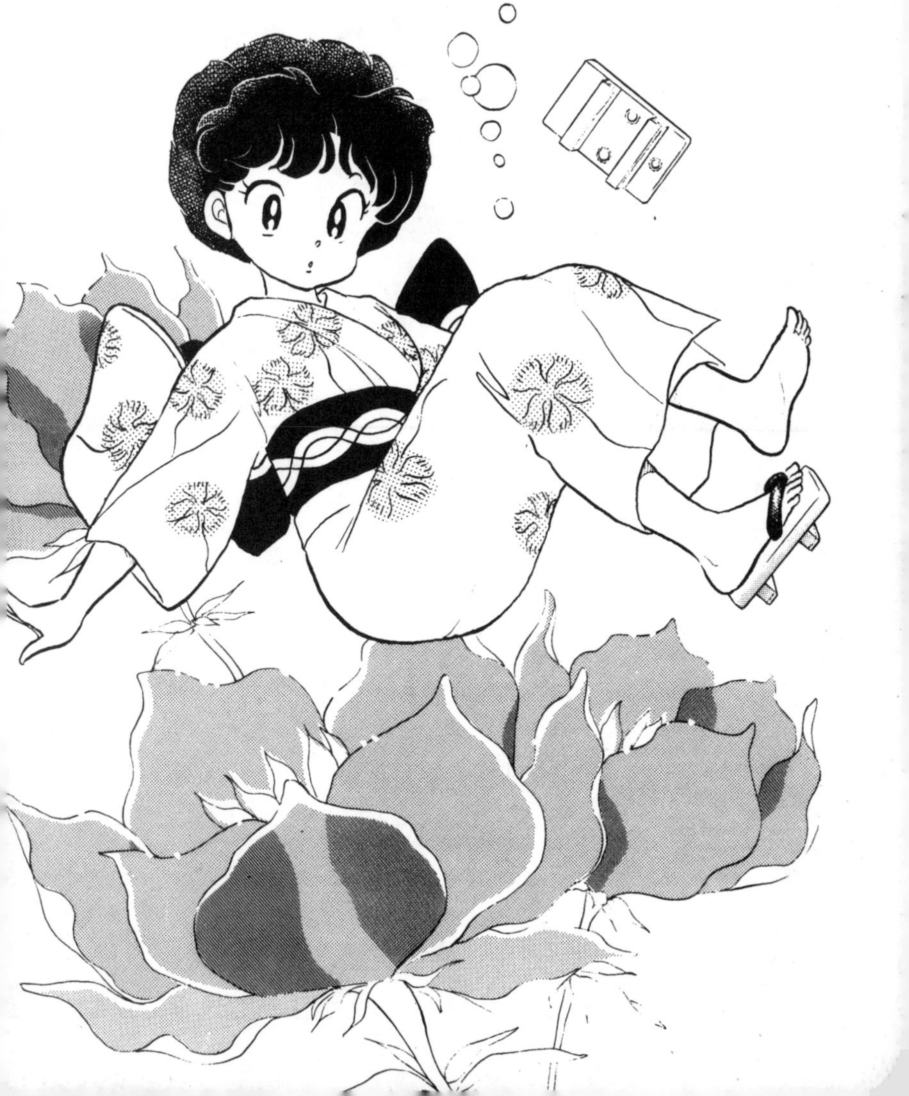

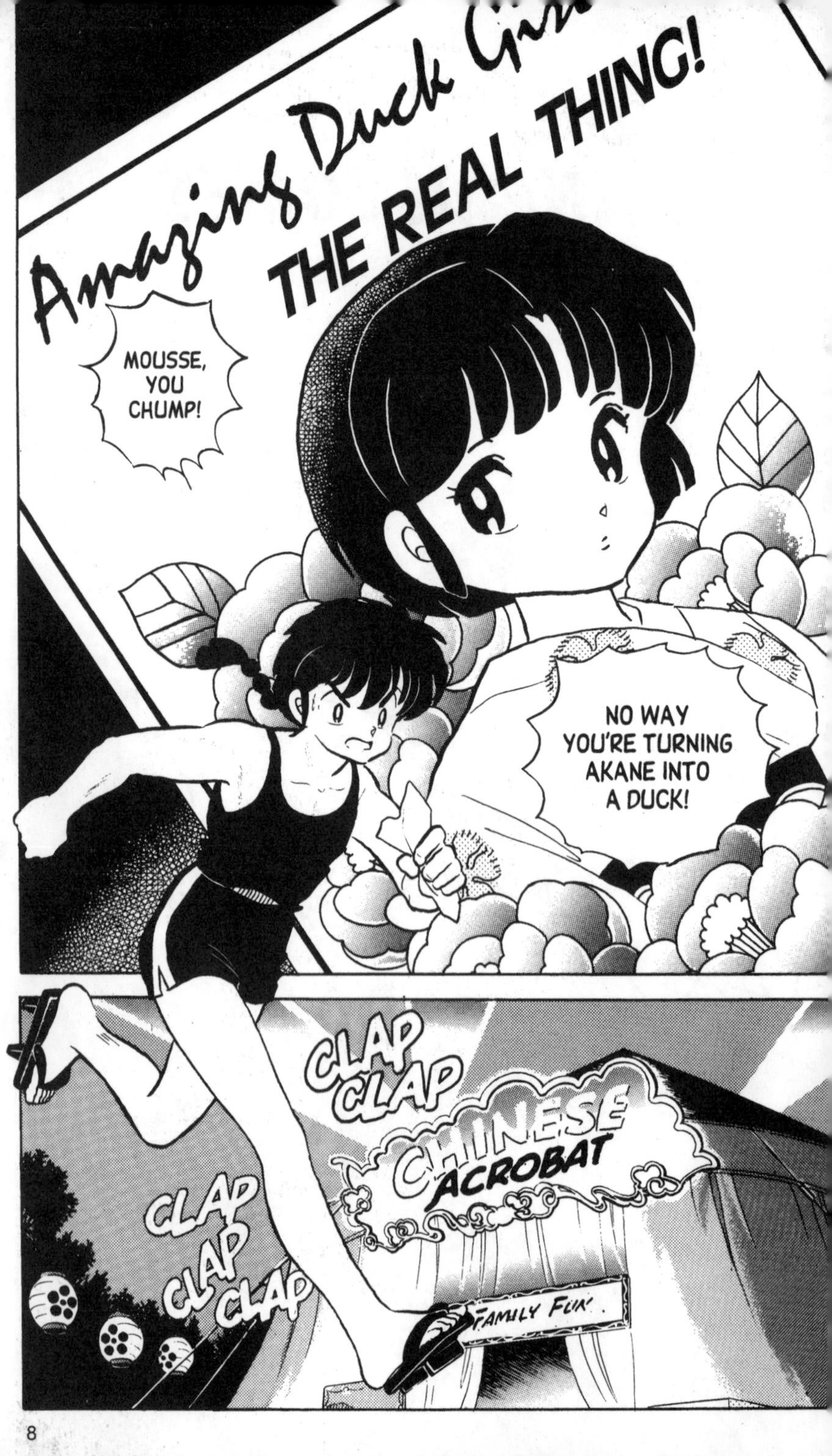
Amazing Duck
THE REAL THING!
MOUSSE, YOU CHUMP!
NO WAY YOU'RE TURNING AKANE INTO A DUCK!
CLAP CLAP
CHINESE ACROBAT
CLAP CLAP CLAP
FAMILY FUN

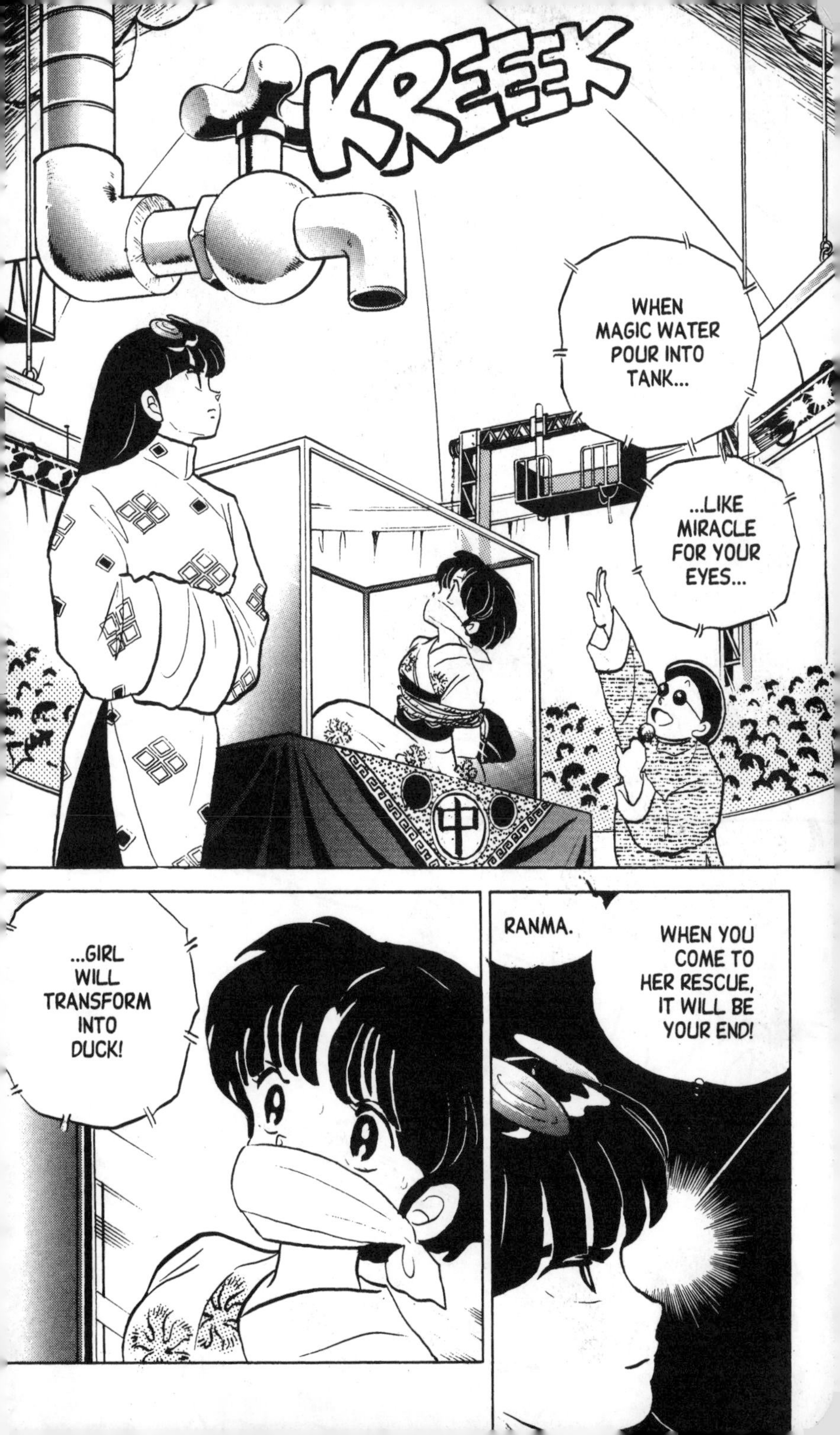
KREEEK
WHEN MAGIC WATER POUR INTO TANK...
...LIKE MIRACLE FOR YOUR EYES...
...GIRL WILL TRANSFORM INTO DUCK!
RANMA.
WHEN YOU COME TO HER RESCUE, IT WILL BE YOUR END!

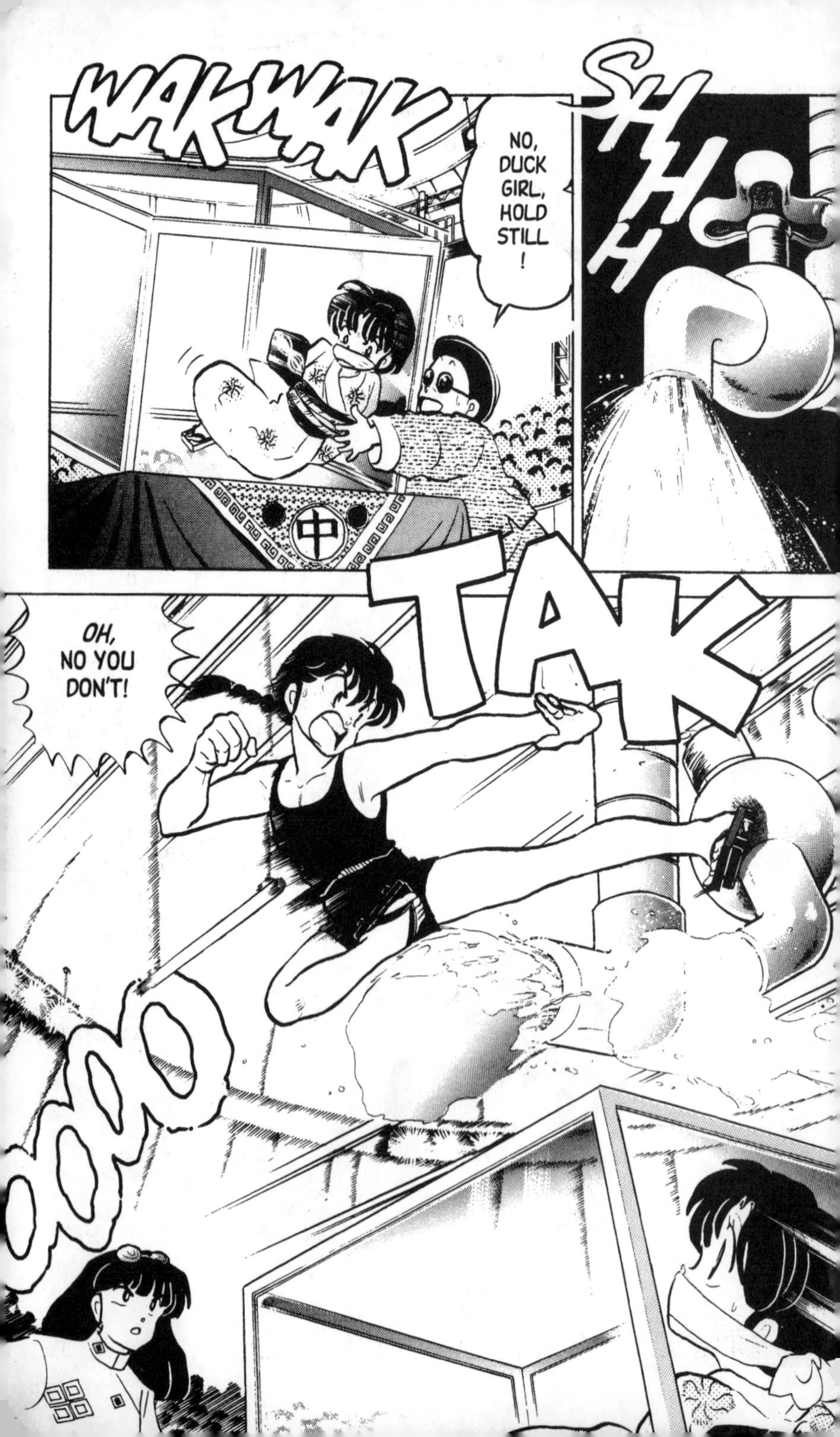
WAK WAK
NO, DUCK GIRL, HOLD STILL!
SHHH
TAK
OH, NO YOU DON'T!
OOOO

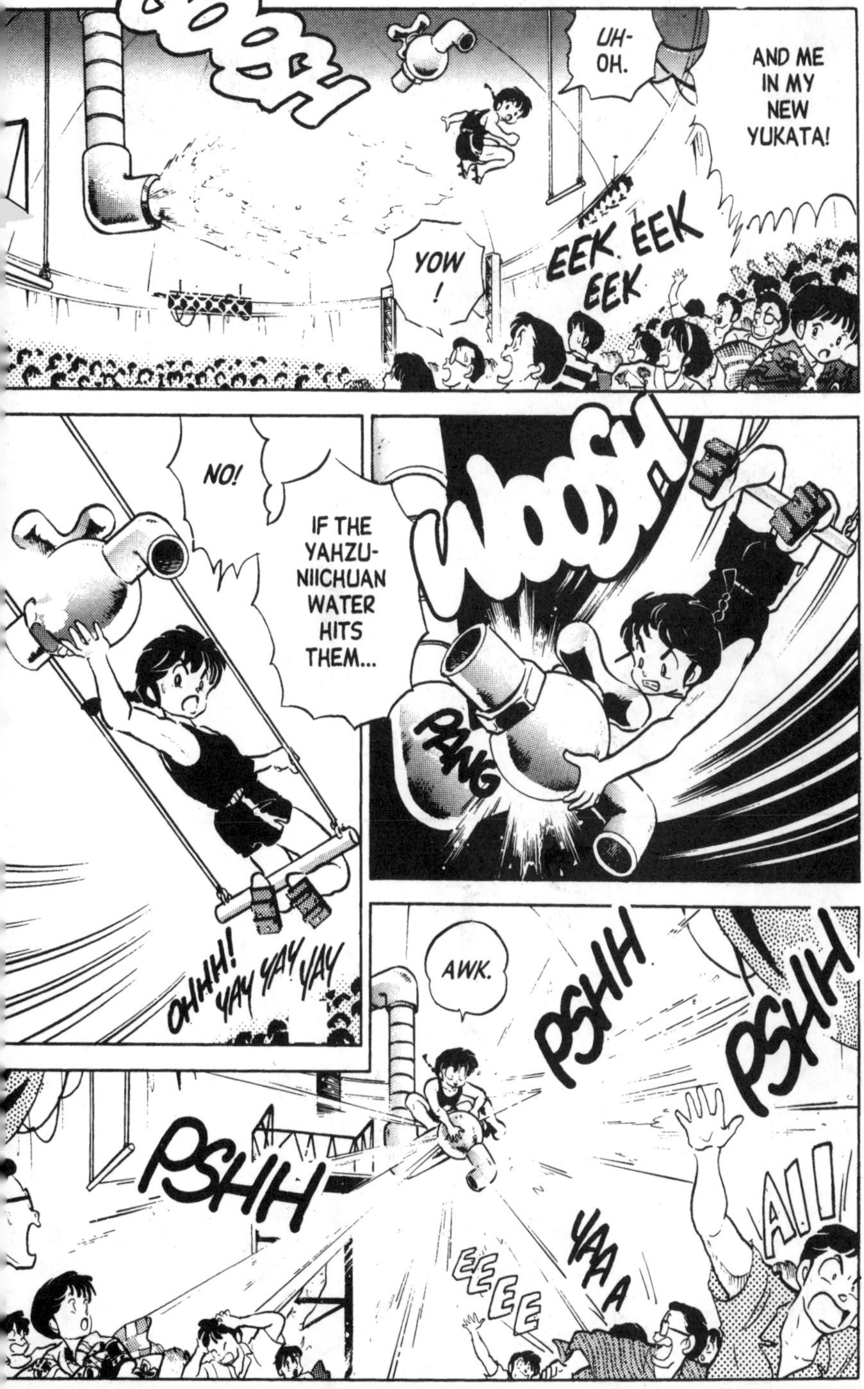
COOOH
UH-OH.
AND ME IN MY NEW YUKATA!
YOW!
EEK EEK EEK
NO!
IF THE YAHZU-NIICHUAN WATER HITS THEM...
OHHH! YAY YAY YAY
WOOSH
PANG
AWK.
PSHH
PSHH
PSHH
AII!
YAAAA
EEEEE

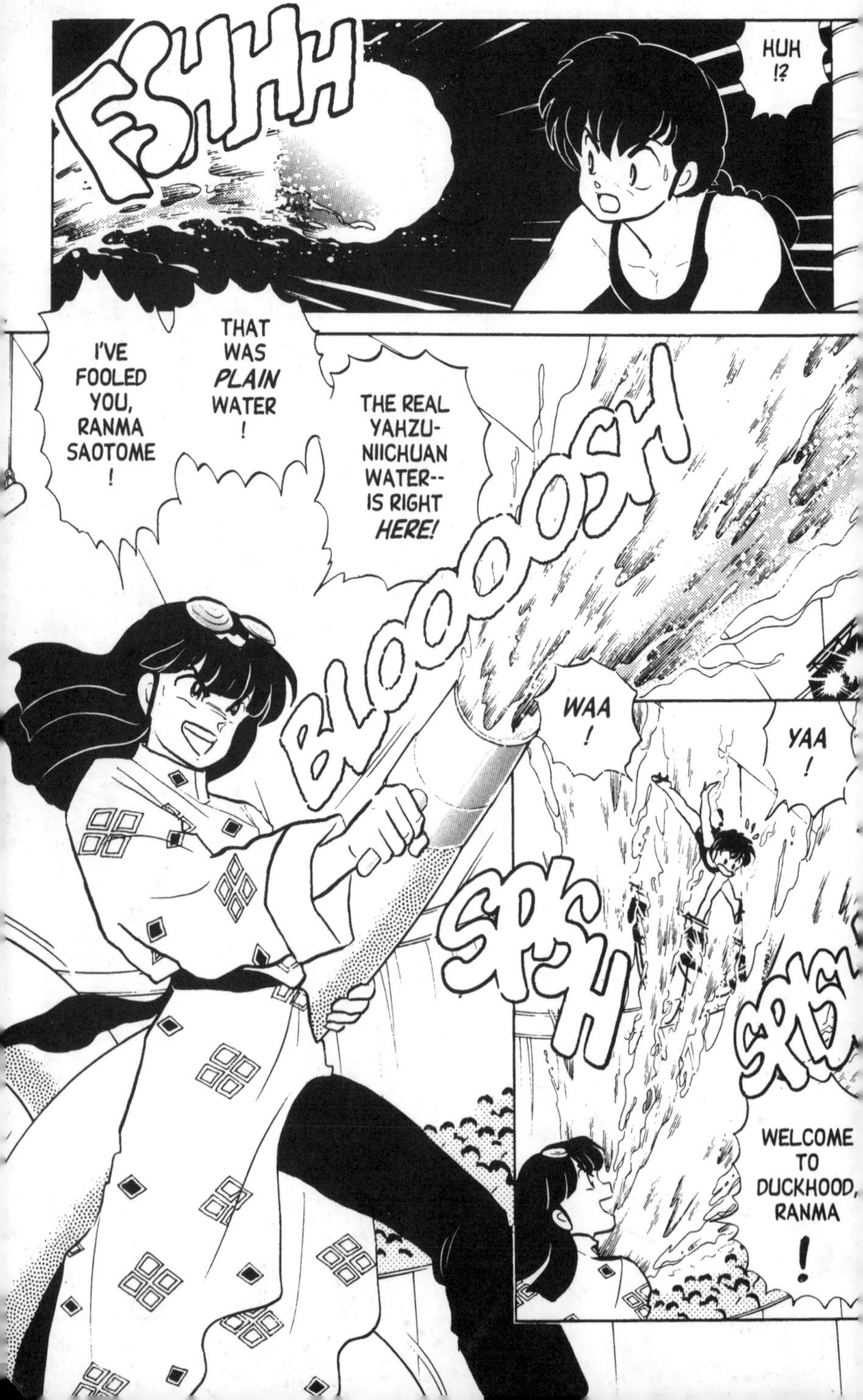

FSHHH
HUH !?
I'VE FOOLED YOU, RANMA SAOTOME !
THAT WAS *PLAIN* WATER !
THE REAL YAHZU-NIICHUAN WATER-- IS RIGHT *HERE!*
BLOOOOOSH
WAA !
YAA !
SPLSH
WELCOME TO DUCKHOOD, RANMA !

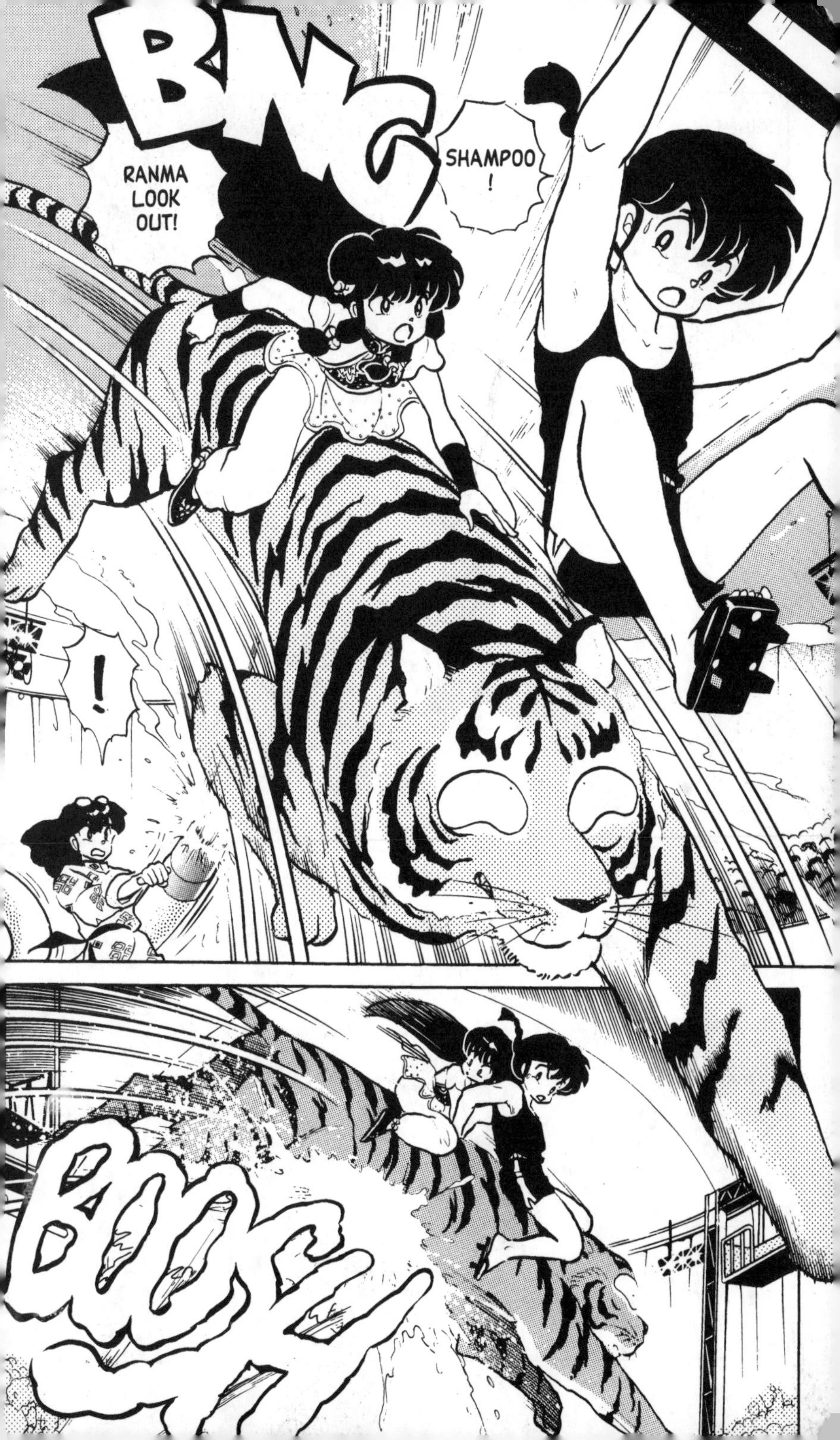
BANG
RANMA LOOK OUT!
SHAMPOO !
!
BAM

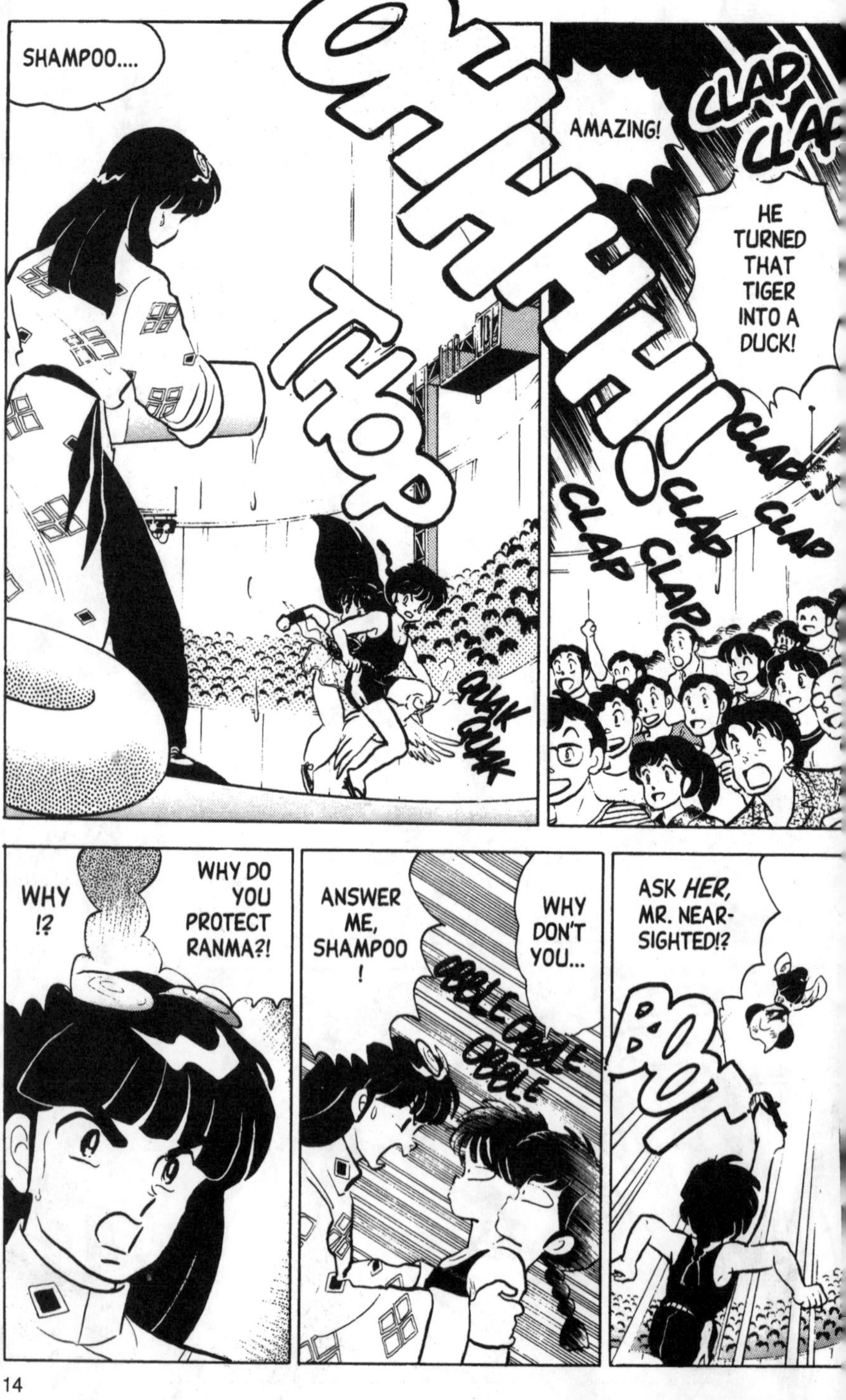
SHAMPOO....
OHHHHH!
THOP
QUAK QUAK
AMAZING!
CLAP CLAP
HE TURNED THAT TIGER INTO A DUCK!
CLAP CLAP CLAP CLAP CLAP
WHY !?
WHY DO YOU PROTECT RANMA?!
ANSWER ME, SHAMPOO!
WHY DON'T YOU...
GOBBLE GOBBLE GOBBLE
ASK *HER*, MR. NEAR-SIGHTED!?
BOP!

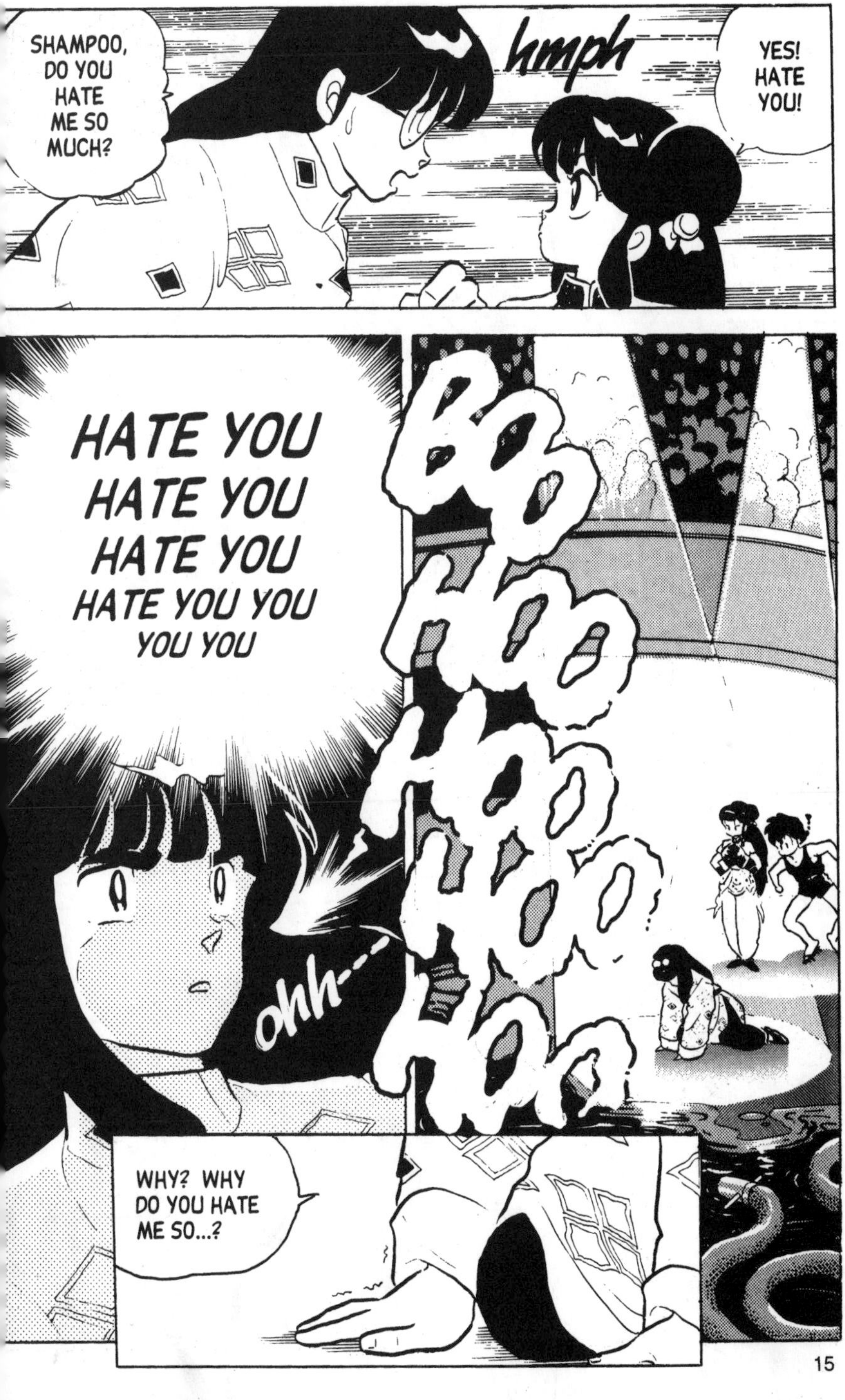
SHAMPOO, DO YOU HATE ME SO MUCH?
hmph
YES! HATE YOU!
HATE YOU HATE YOU HATE YOU HATE YOU YOU YOU YOU
ohh...
Boo hoo hoo hoo hoo
WHY? WHY DO YOU HATE ME SO...?

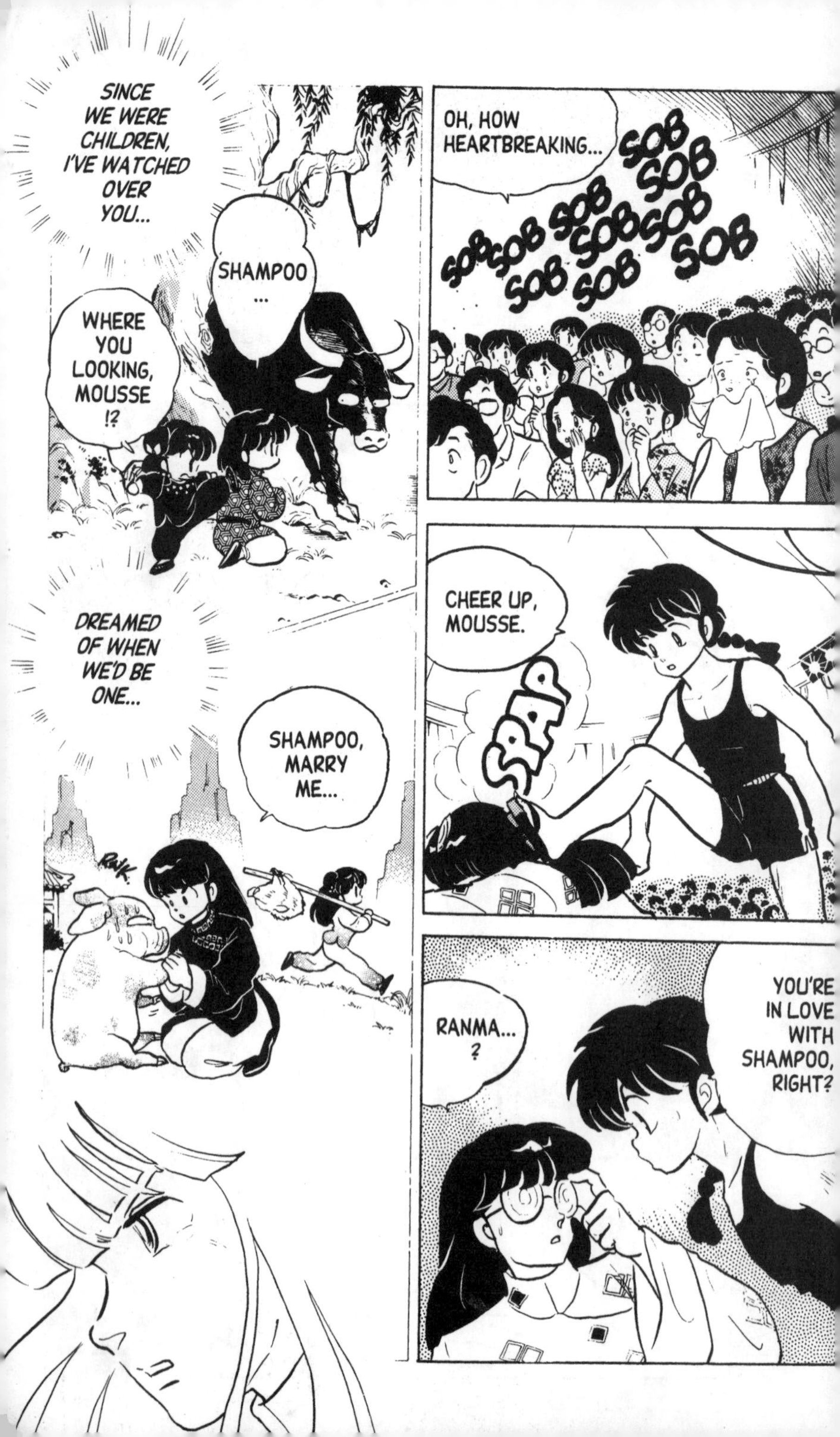
SINCE WE WERE CHILDREN, I'VE WATCHED OVER YOU...
SHAMPOO ...
WHERE YOU LOOKING, MOUSSE !?
DREAMED OF WHEN WE'D BE ONE...
SHAMPOO, MARRY ME...
RNK
OH, HOW HEARTBREAKING...
SOB SOB SOB SOB SOB SOB SOB SOB SOB SOB SOB SOB
CHEER UP, MOUSSE.
SPAP
RANMA... ?
YOU'RE IN LOVE WITH SHAMPOO, RIGHT?

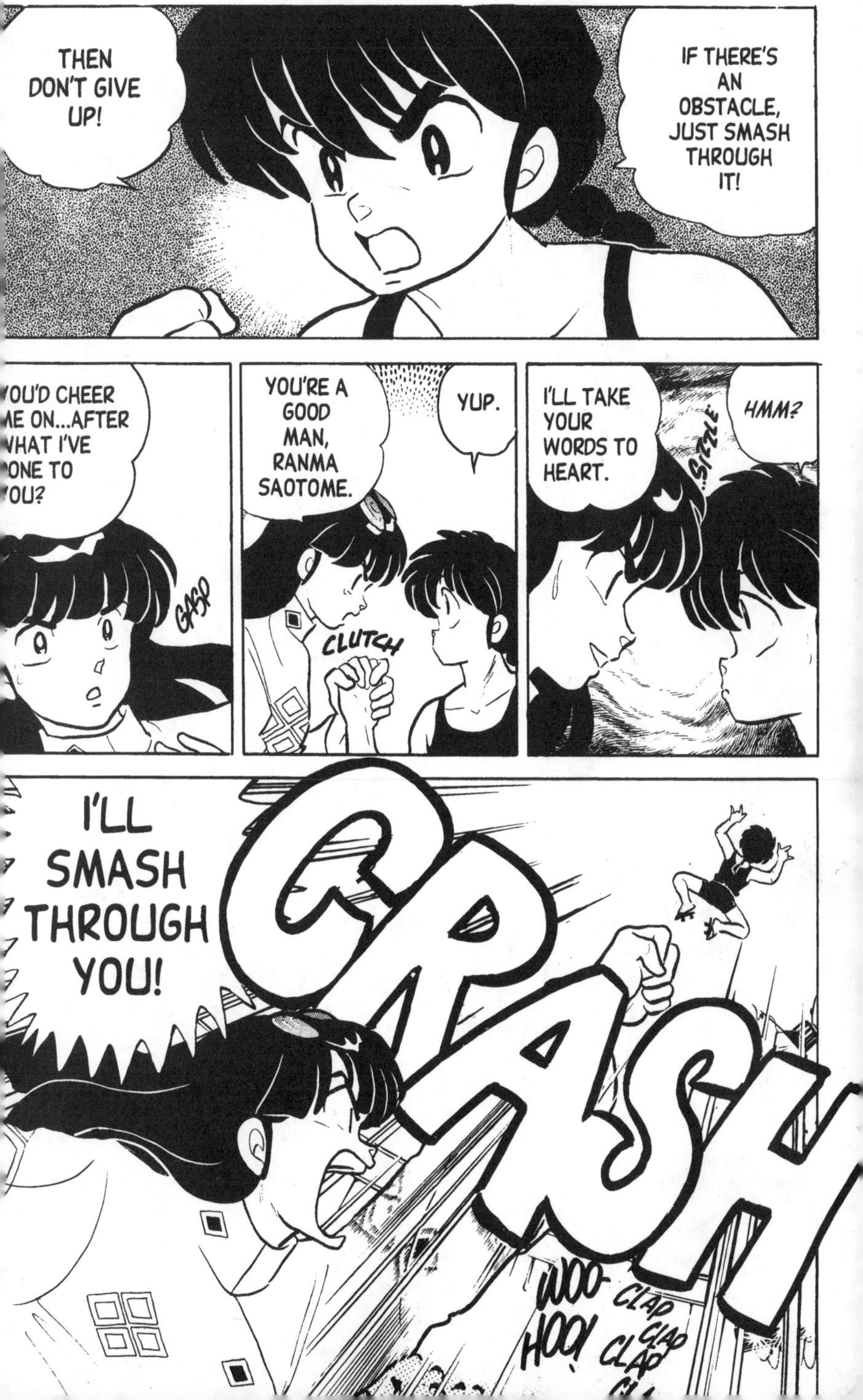
THEN DON'T GIVE UP!
IF THERE'S AN OBSTACLE, JUST SMASH THROUGH IT!
OU'D CHEER
E ON...AFTER
HAT I'VE
ONE TO
OU?
GASP
YOU'RE A GOOD MAN, RANMA SAOTOME.
YUP.
CLUTCH
I'LL TAKE YOUR WORDS TO HEART.
SIZZLE
HMM?
I'LL SMASH THROUGH YOU!
CRASH
WOO-HOO!
CLAP CLAP CLAP

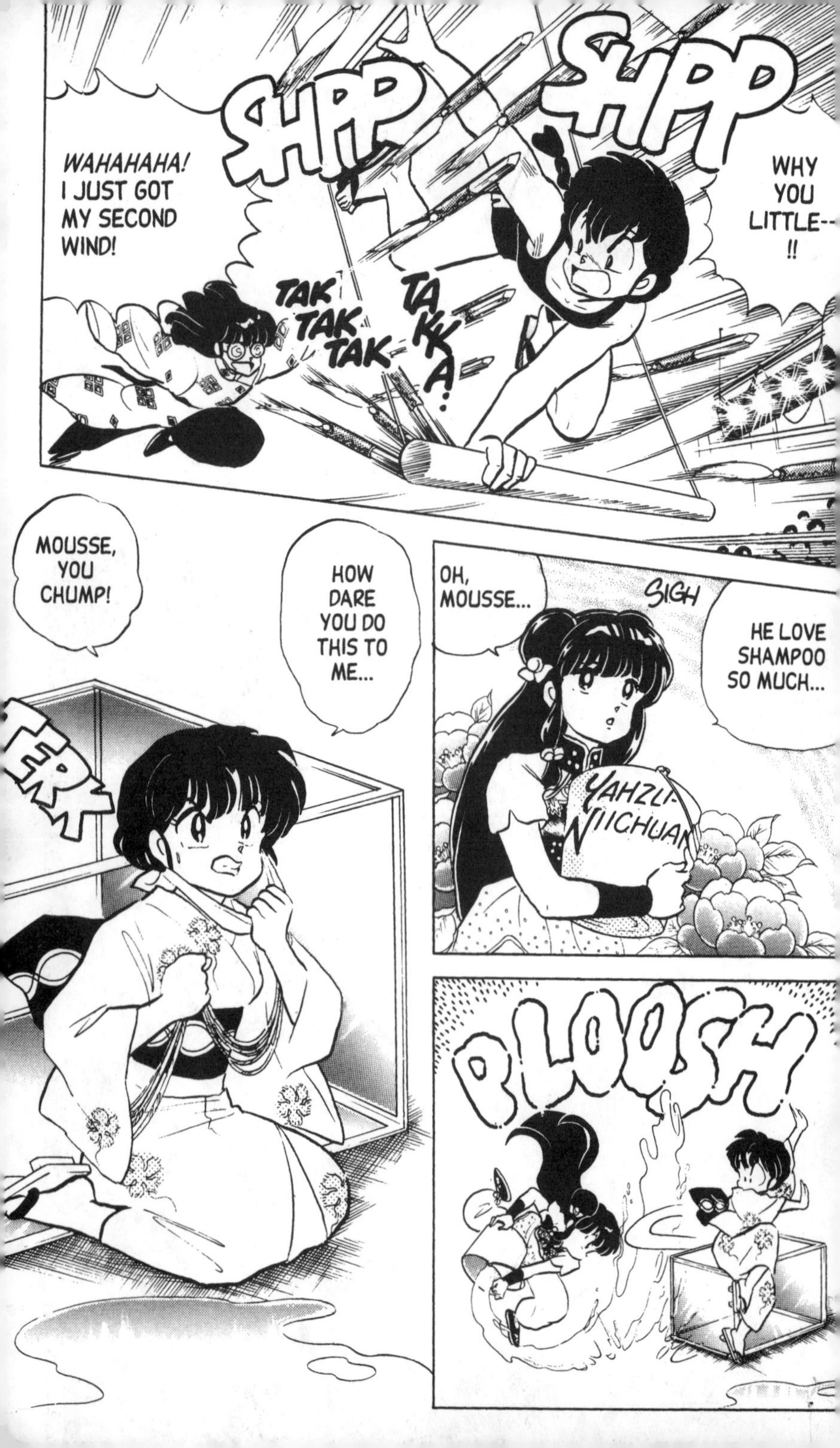
SHPP
SHPP
WAHAHAHA! I JUST GOT MY SECOND WIND!
TAK TAK TAK
TAKKA
WHY YOU LITTLE-- !!
MOUSSE, YOU CHUMP!
HOW DARE YOU DO THIS TO ME...
OH, MOUSSE...
SIGH
HE LOVE SHAMPOO SO MUCH...
YAHZLI-NIICHUAN
PLOOSH

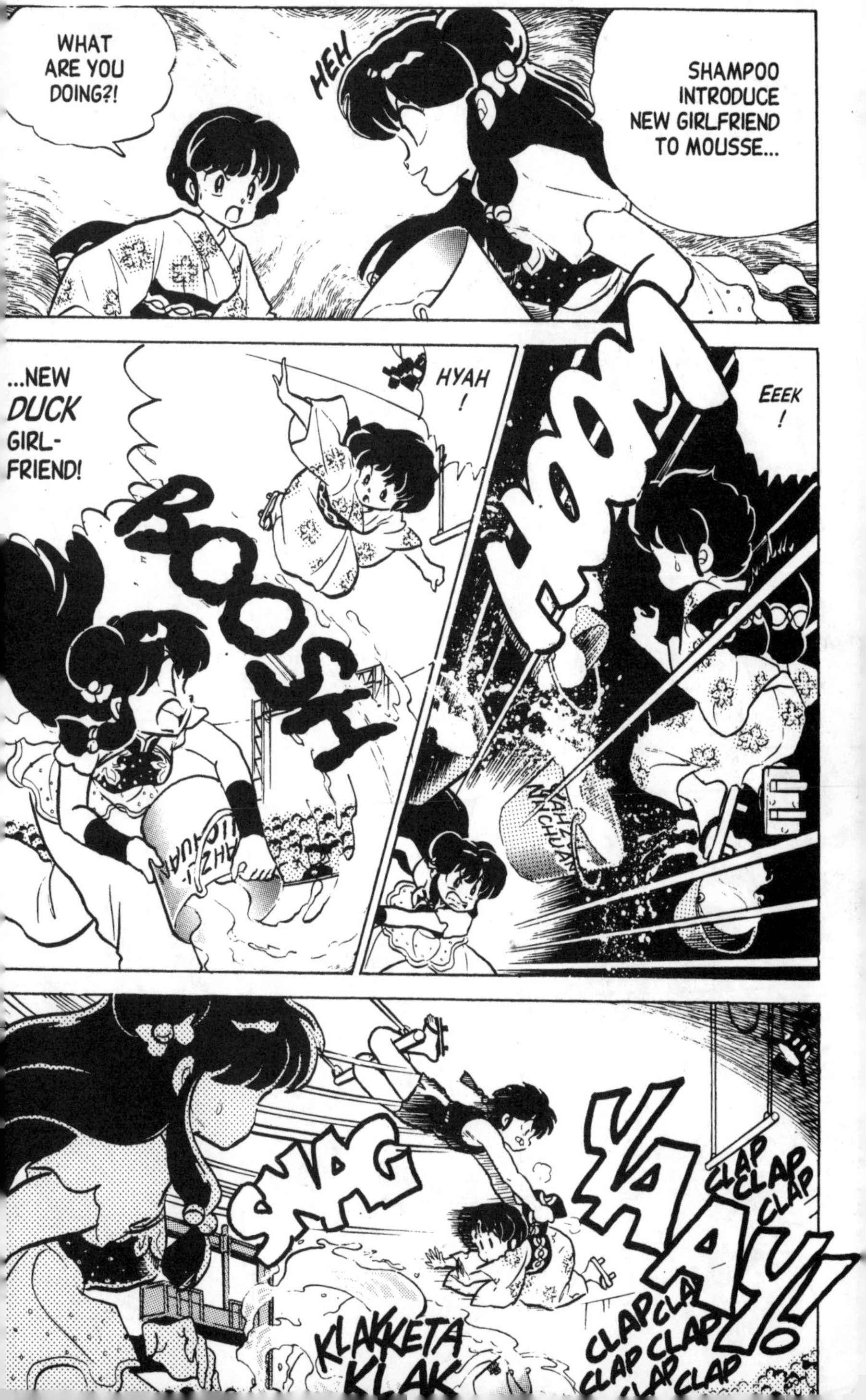
WHAT ARE YOU DOING?!
HEH
SHAMPOO INTRODUCE NEW GIRLFRIEND TO MOUSSE...
...NEW DUCK GIRL-FRIEND!
HYAH!
BOOSH
EEEK!
YAAAY!
CLAP CLAP CLAP CLAP CLAP
CLAP CLAP CLAP CLAP CLAP CLAP CLAP
KLAKKETA KLAK

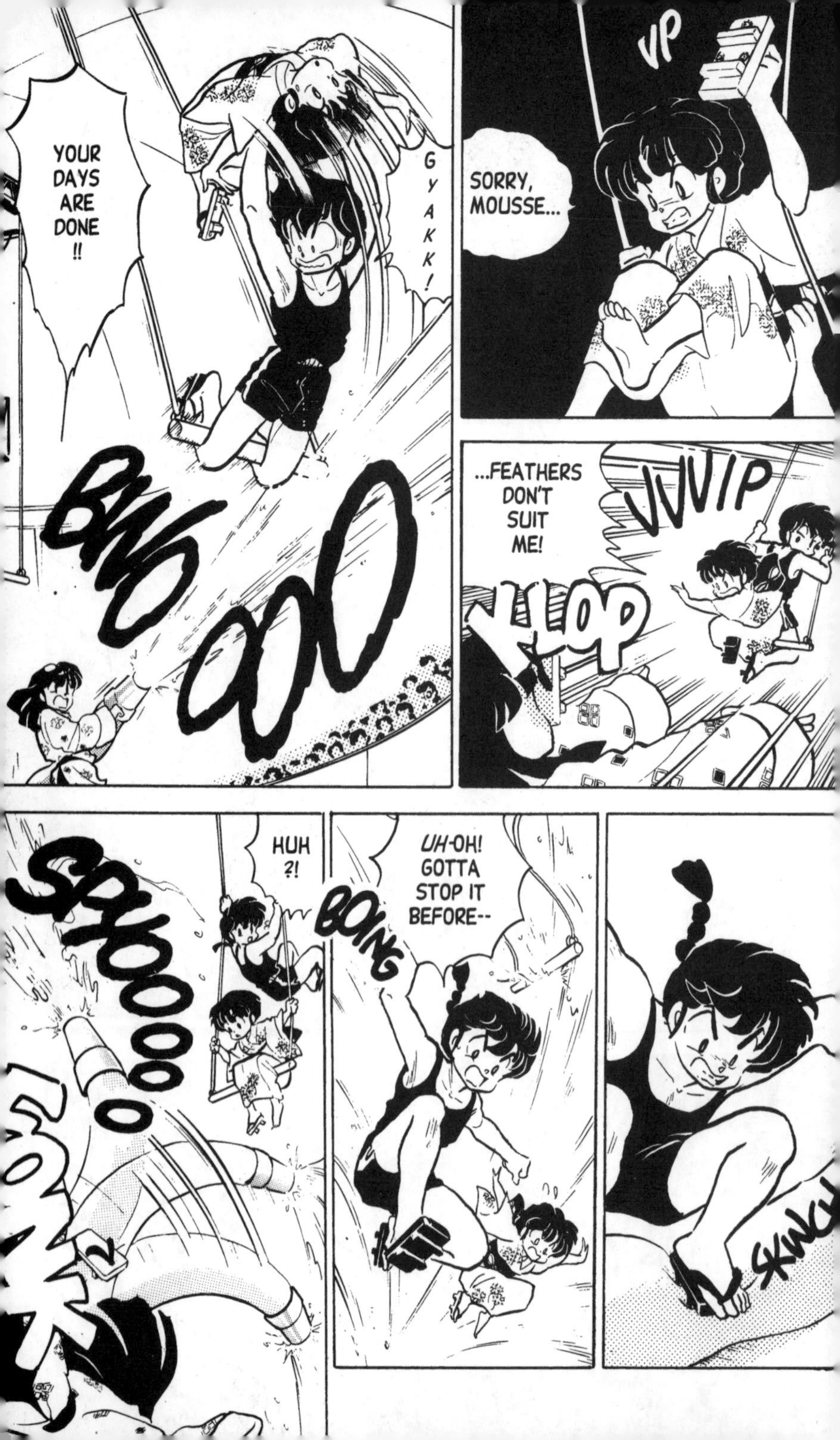

YOUR DAYS ARE DONE !!
GYAKK!
VP
SORRY, MOUSSE...
...FEATHERS DON'T SUIT ME!
VVVIP
FLOP
HUH ?!
BOING
UH-OH! GOTTA STOP IT BEFORE--

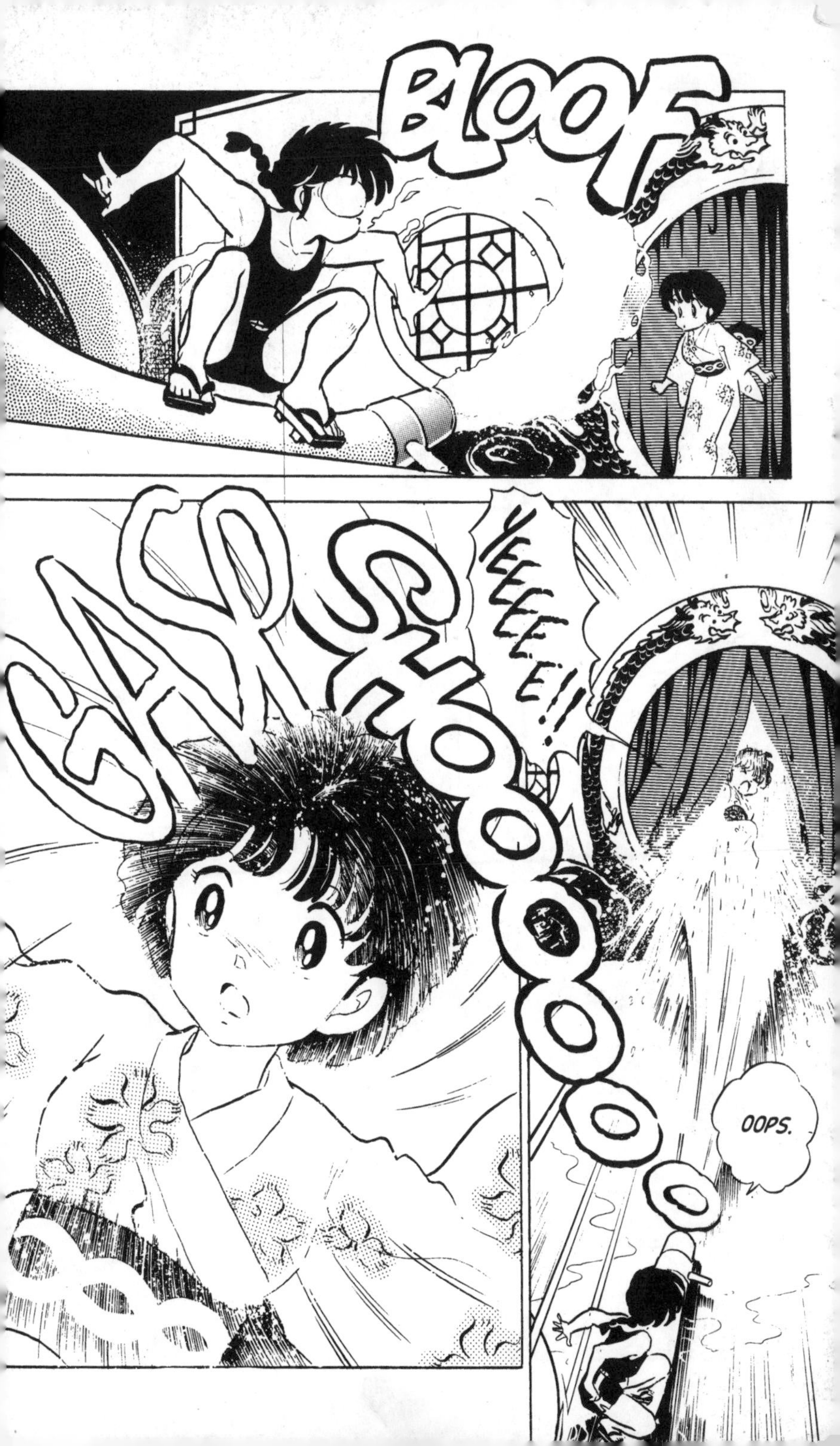
BLOOF
GASH
SHOOOOOOOO
YEEEEE!!
OOPS.

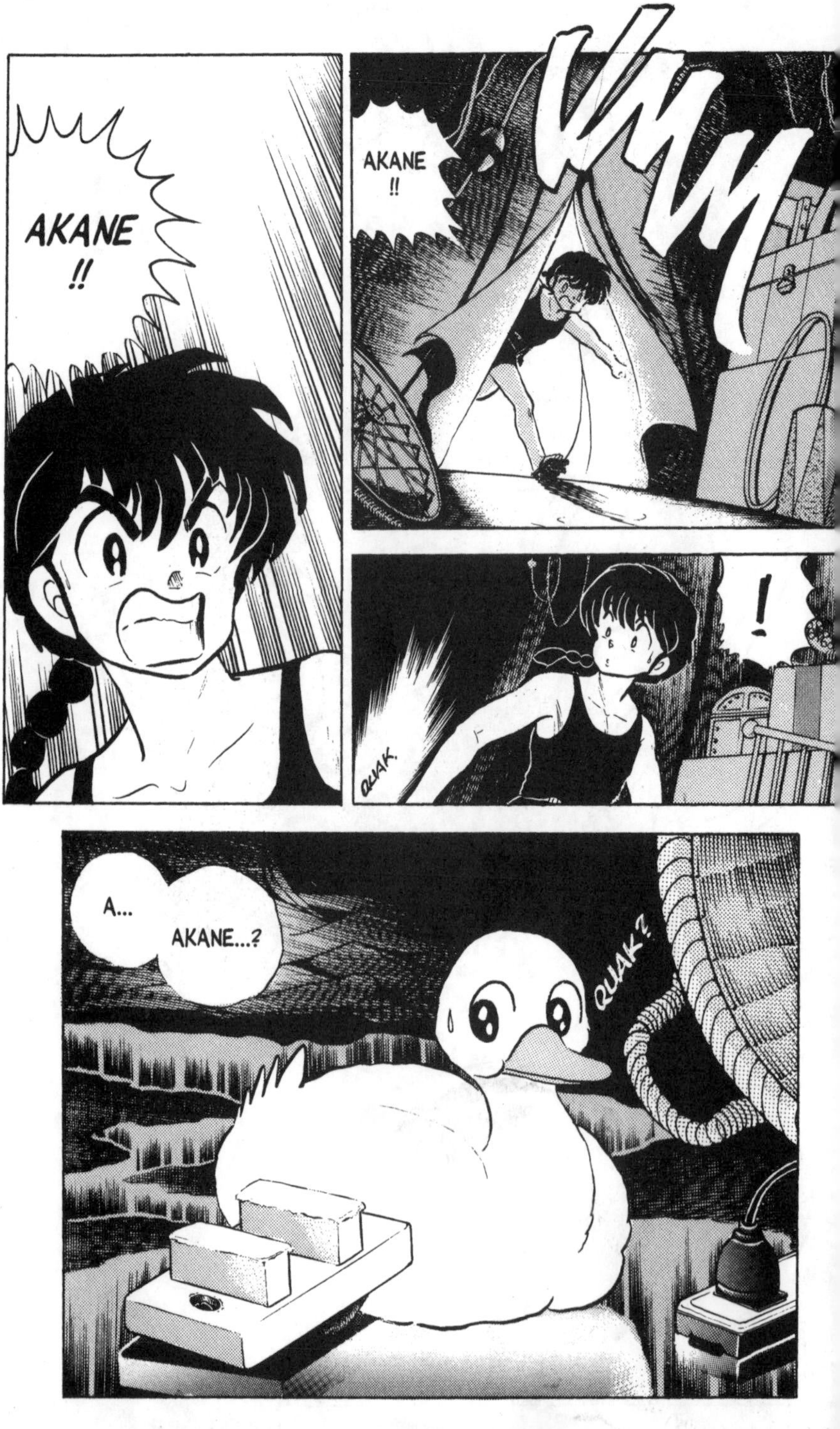
AKANE !!
AKANE !!
!
QUAK.
A...
AKANE...?
QUAK?

PART 2
FOWL PLAY

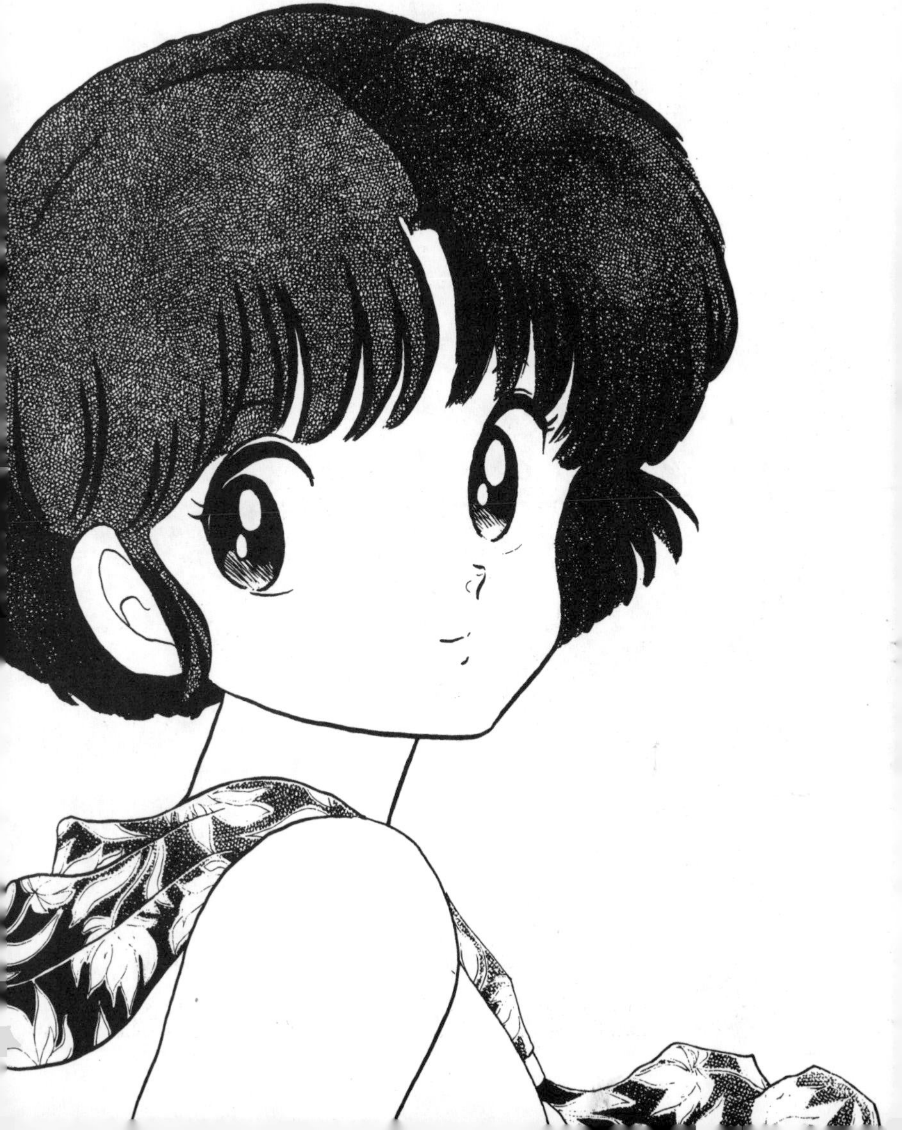

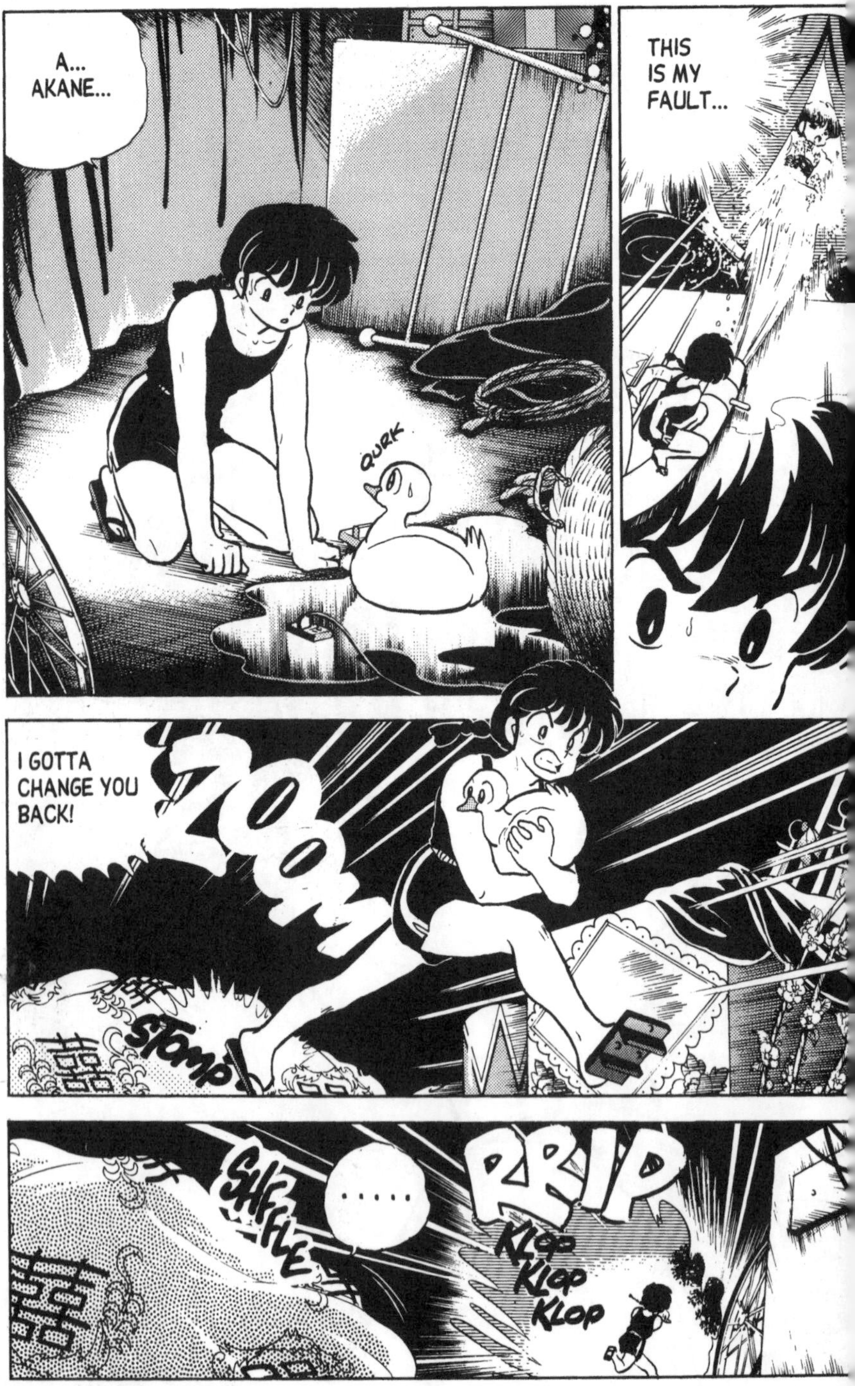
A... AKANE...
QURK
THIS IS MY FAULT...
I GOTTA CHANGE YOU BACK!
ZOOM
STOMP
SHFFLE
.....
RRIP
KLOP KLOP KLOP

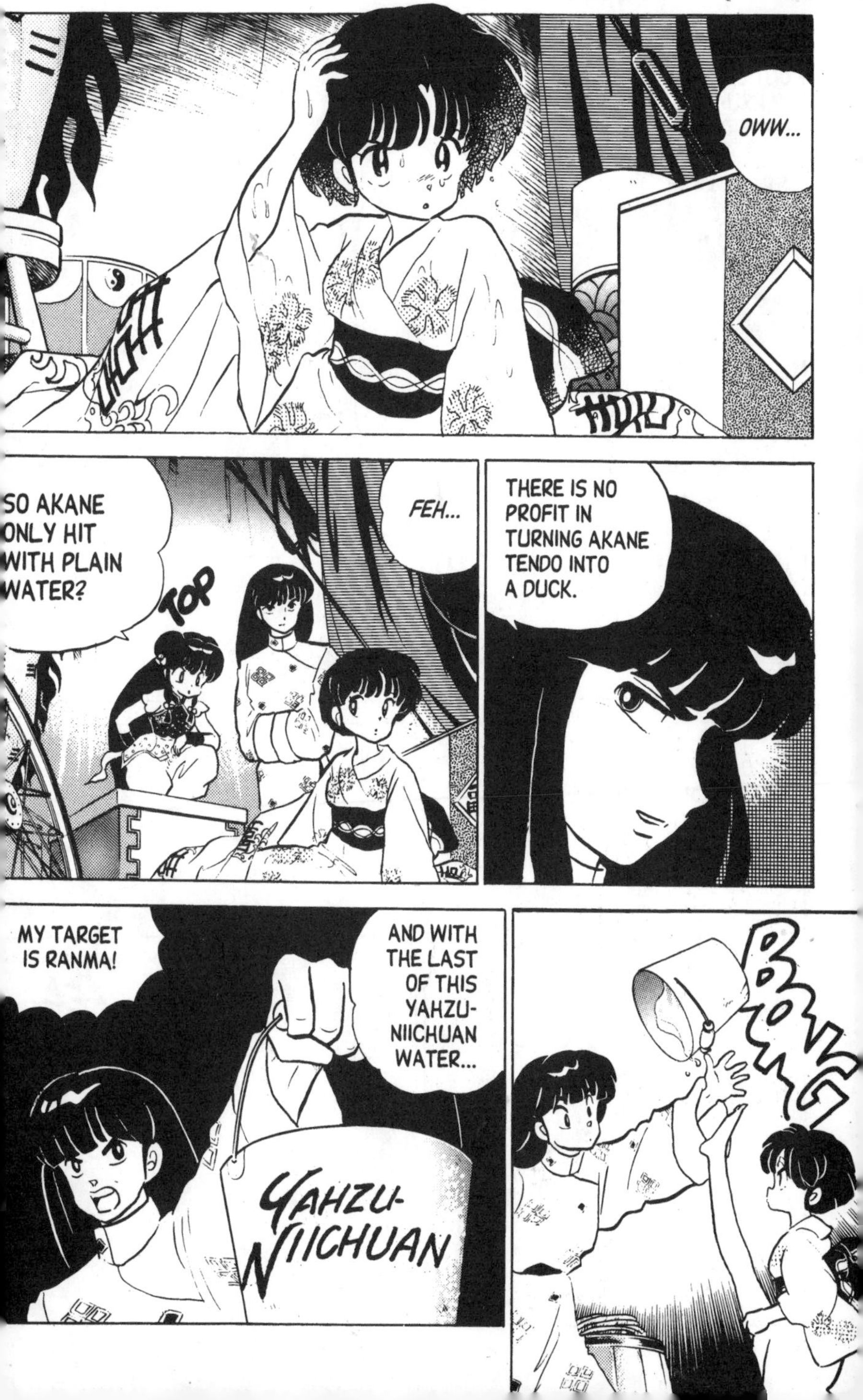
OWW...
SO AKANE ONLY HIT WITH PLAIN WATER?
TOP
FEH...
THERE IS NO PROFIT IN TURNING AKANE TENDO INTO A DUCK.
MY TARGET IS RANMA!
AND WITH THE LAST OF THIS YAHZU-NIICHUAN WATER...
YAHZU-NIICHUAN
BONNG

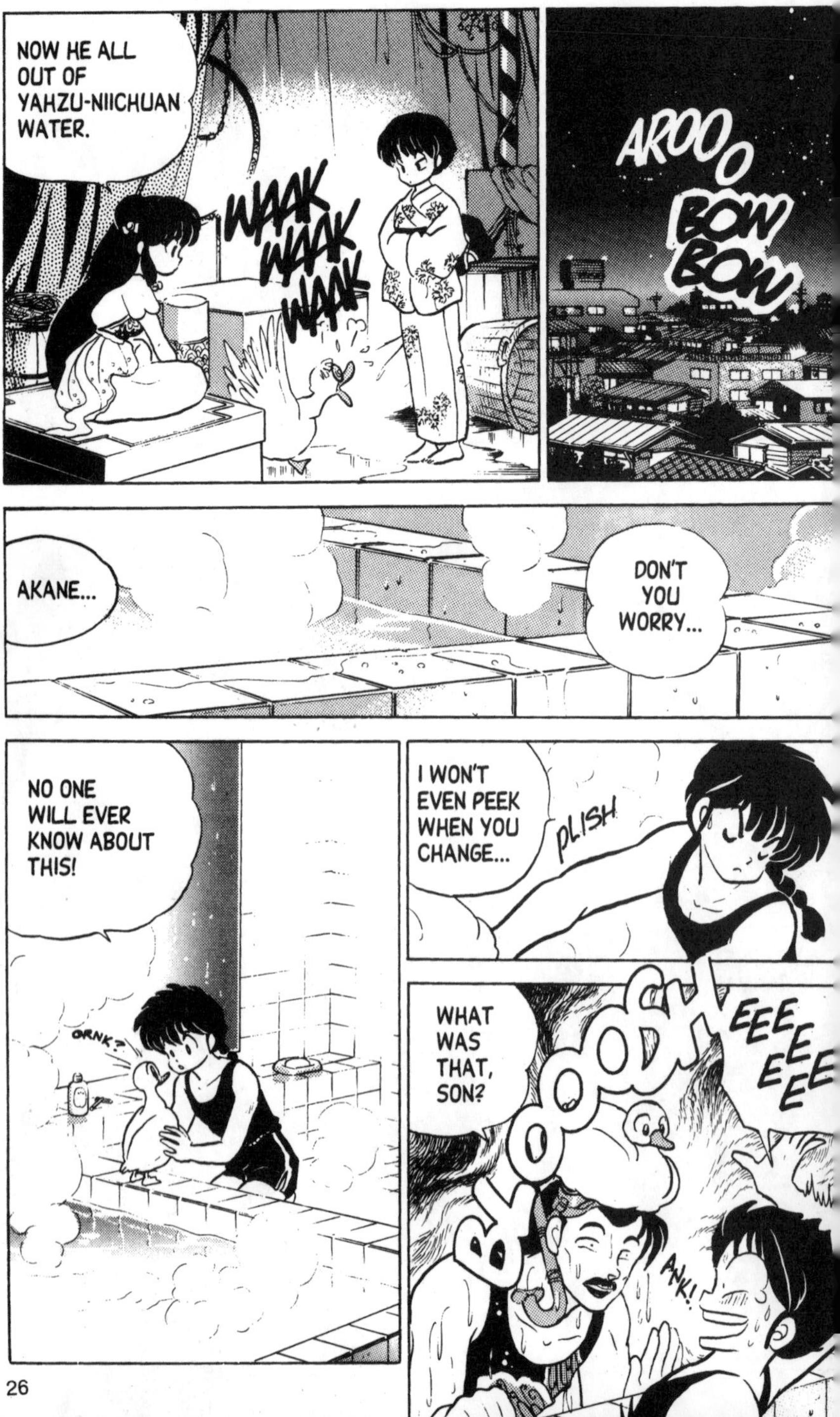
NOW HE ALL OUT OF YAHZU-NIICHUAN WATER.
WAAK WAAK WAAK
AROOO BOW BOW
AKANE...
DON'T YOU WORRY...
NO ONE WILL EVER KNOW ABOUT THIS!
ORNK?
I WON'T EVEN PEEK WHEN YOU CHANGE...
PLISH
WHAT WAS THAT, SON?
BLOOOOSH
EEEEEEEE
ANK!

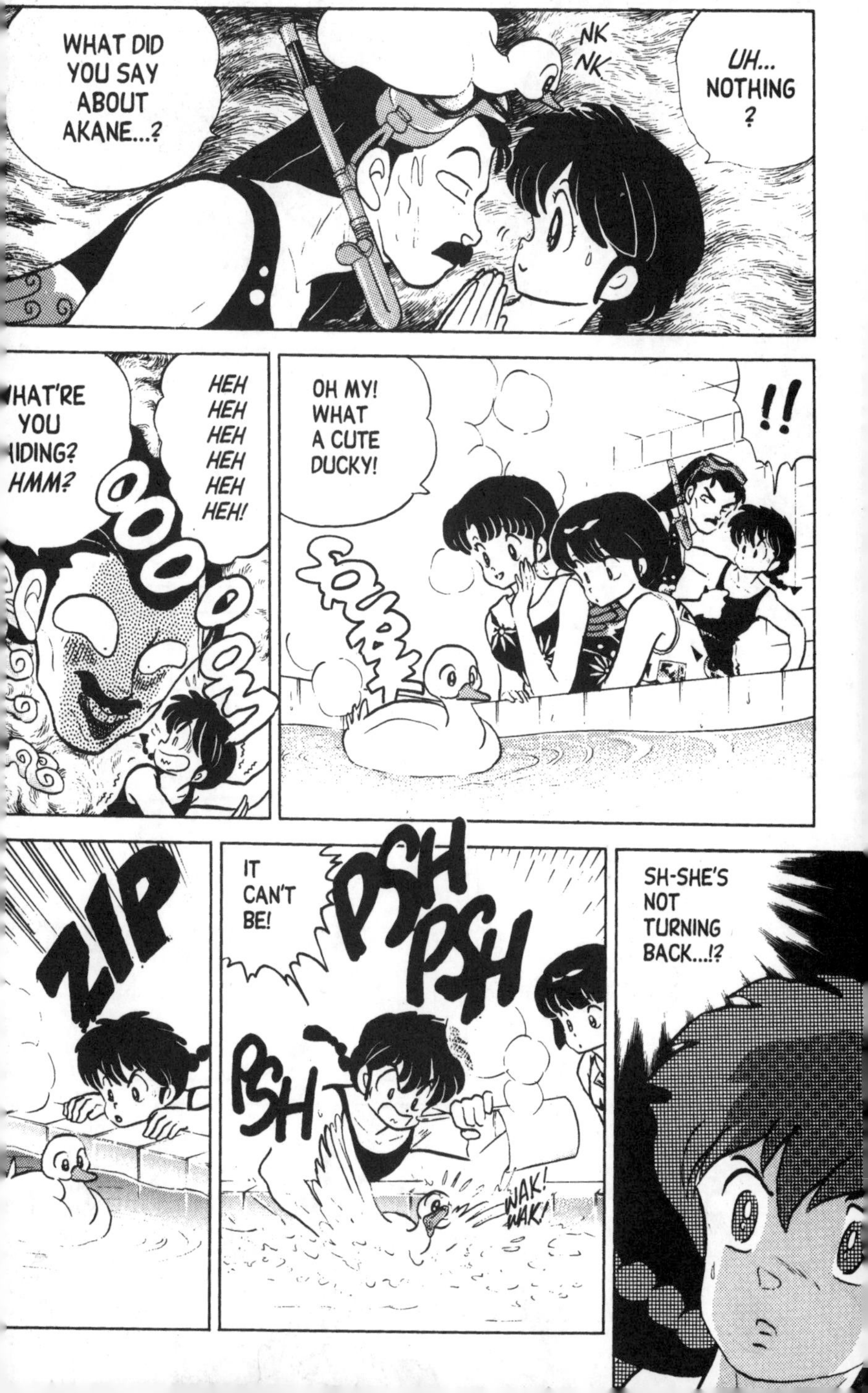
WHAT DID YOU SAY ABOUT AKANE...?
NK NK
UH... NOTHING ?
WHAT'RE YOU HIDING? HMM?
HEH HEH HEH HEH HEH HEH!
OOOOOOOM
OH MY! WHAT A CUTE DUCKY!
SQUEAK
!!
ZIP
IT CAN'T BE!
PSH PSH
PSH
WAK! WAK!
SH-SHE'S NOT TURNING BACK...!?

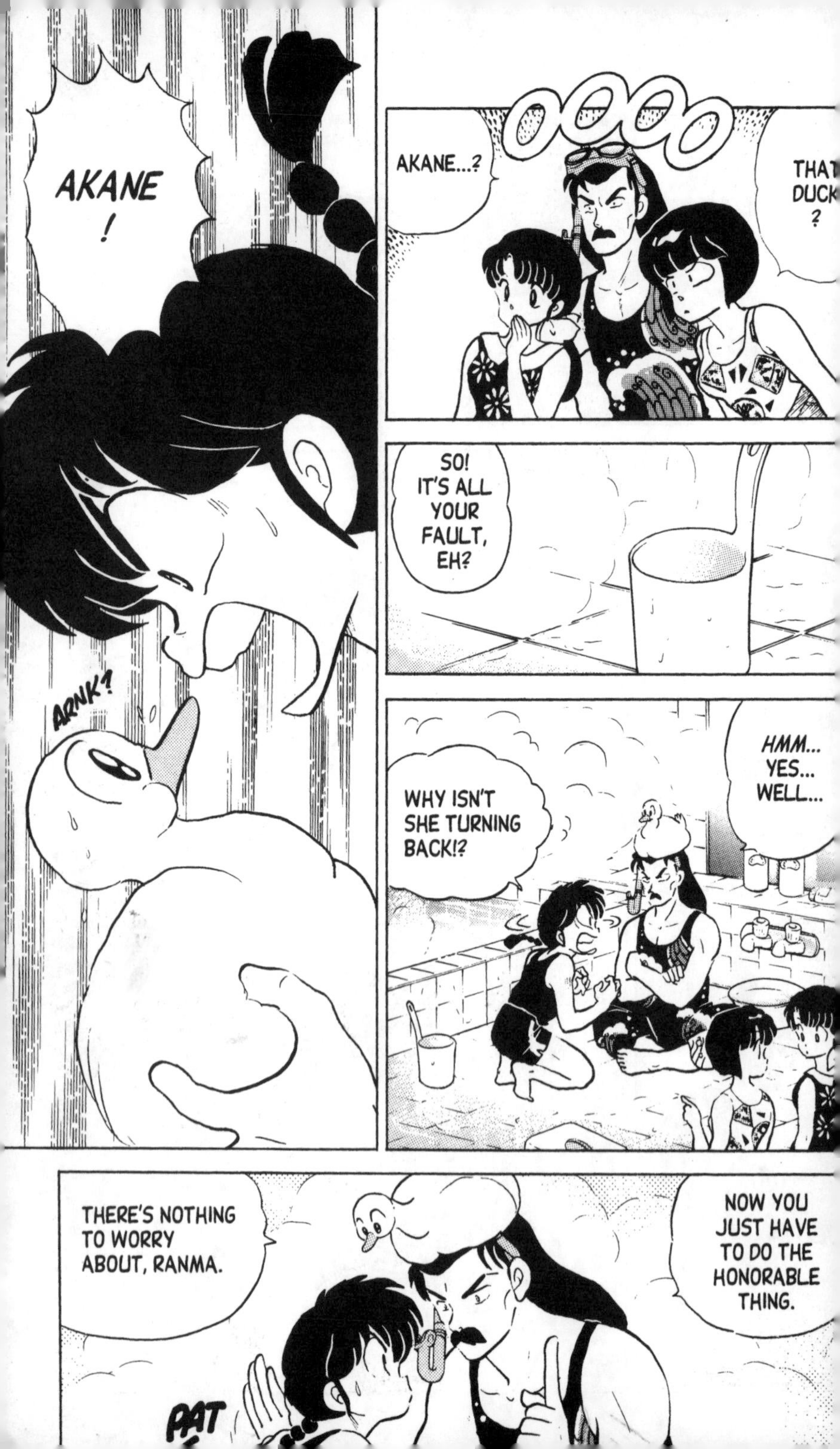
AKANE !
ARNK!
AKANE...?
THAT DUCK ?
SO! IT'S ALL YOUR FAULT, EH?
WHY ISN'T SHE TURNING BACK!?
HMM... YES... WELL...
THERE'S NOTHING TO WORRY ABOUT, RANMA.
NOW YOU JUST HAVE TO DO THE HONORABLE THING.
PAT

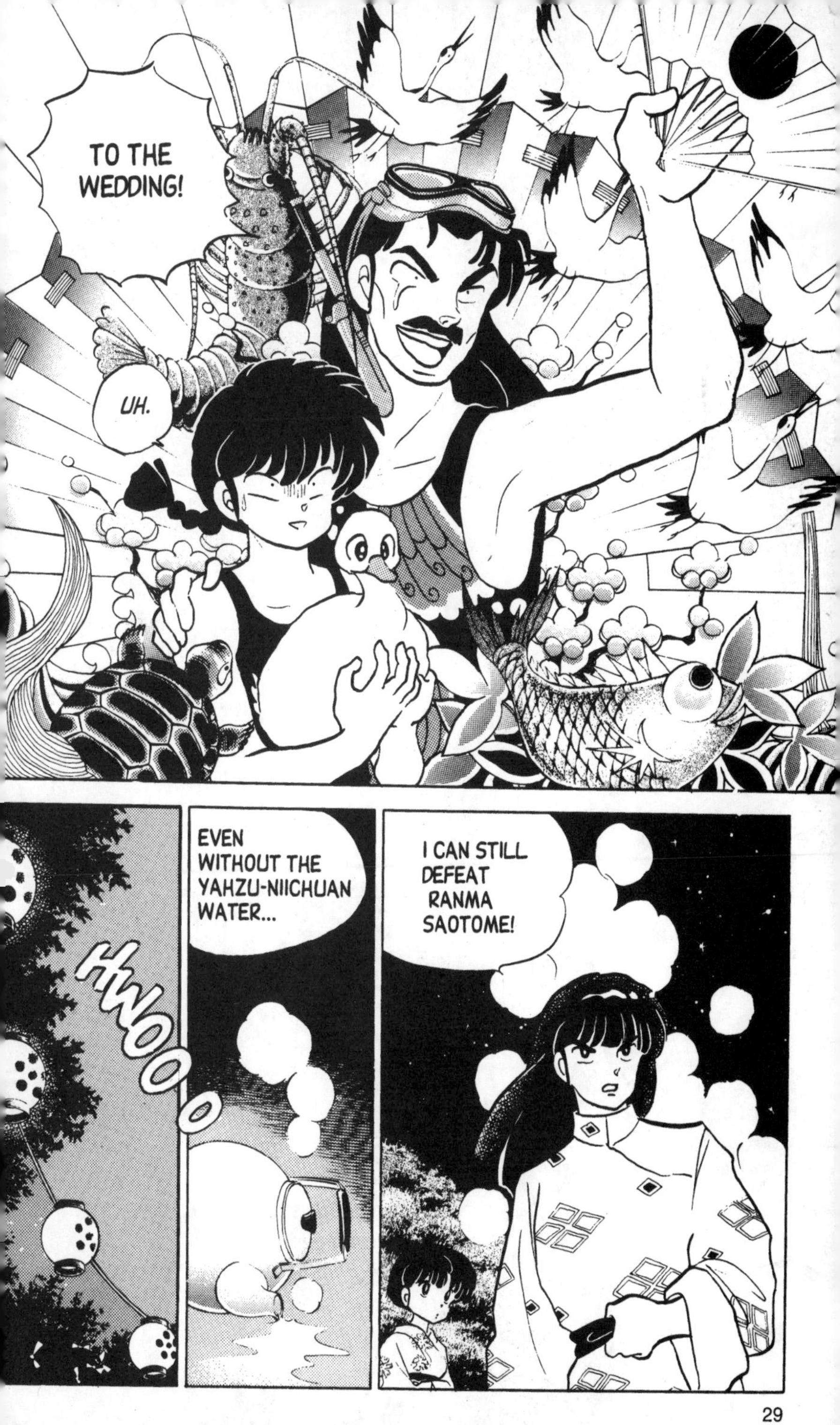
TO THE WEDDING!
UH.
HWOOOO
EVEN WITHOUT THE YAHZU-NIICHUAN WATER...
I CAN STILL DEFEAT RANMA SAOTOME!

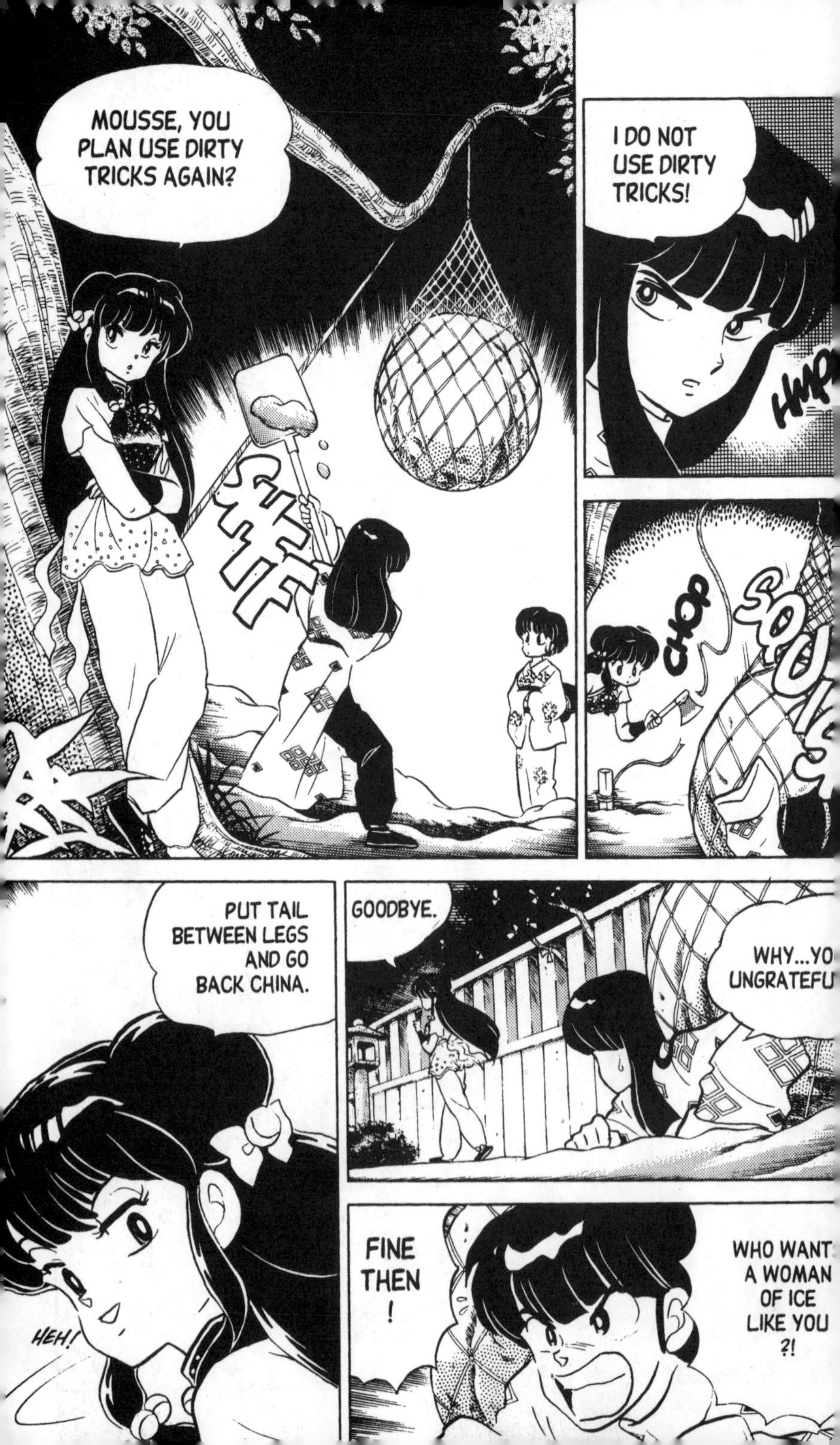
MOUSSE, YOU PLAN USE DIRTY TRICKS AGAIN?
I DO NOT USE DIRTY TRICKS!
CHOP
PUT TAIL BETWEEN LEGS AND GO BACK CHINA.
HEH!
GOODBYE.
WHY...YO UNGRATEFU
FINE THEN !
WHO WANT: A WOMAN OF ICE LIKE YOU ?!

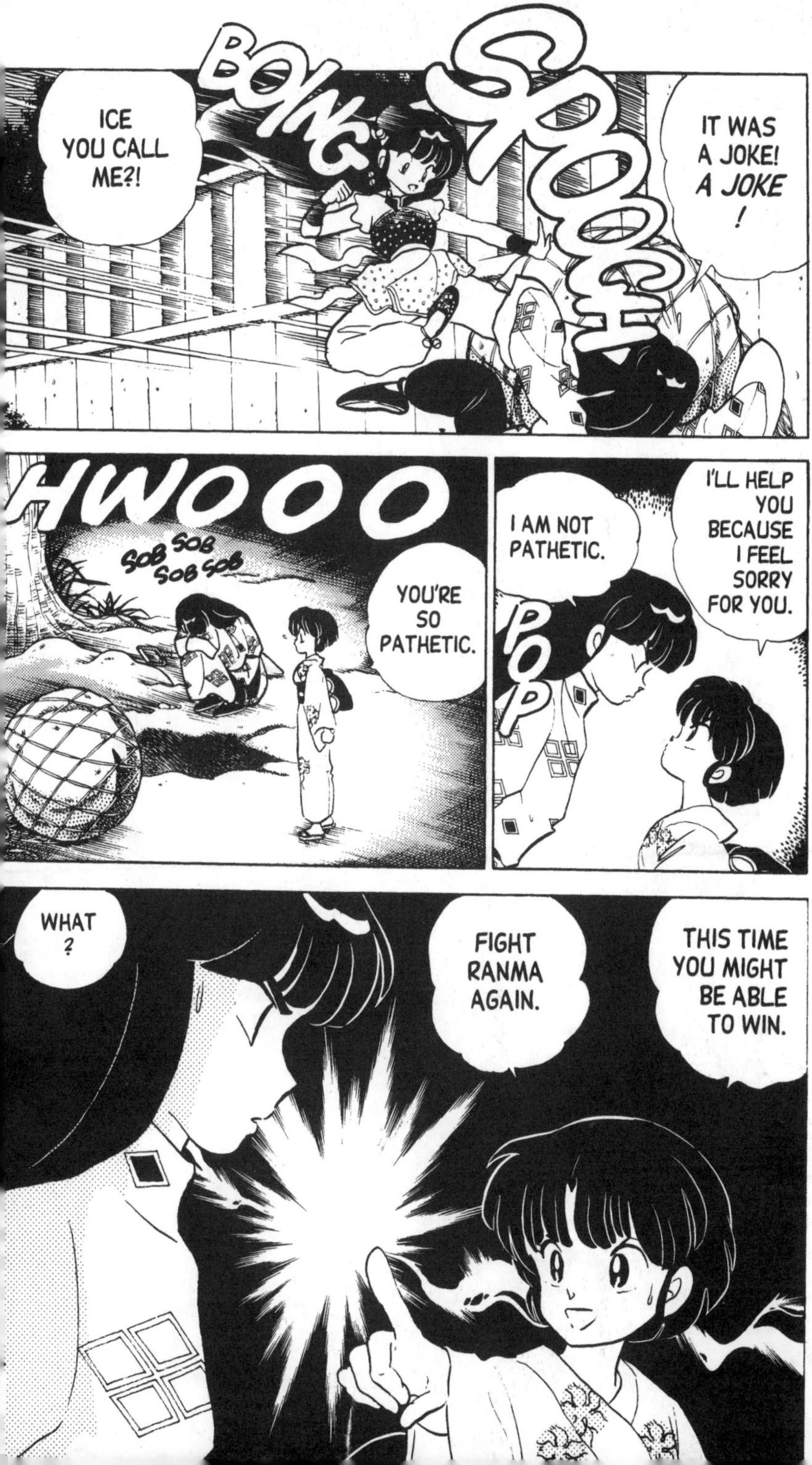
BOING
ICE YOU CALL ME?!
SPROOCH
IT WAS A JOKE! A JOKE!
HWOOO
SOB SOB SOB SOB
YOU'RE SO PATHETIC.
I AM NOT PATHETIC.
POP
I'LL HELP YOU BECAUSE I FEEL SORRY FOR YOU.
WHAT?
FIGHT RANMA AGAIN.
THIS TIME YOU MIGHT BE ABLE TO WIN.

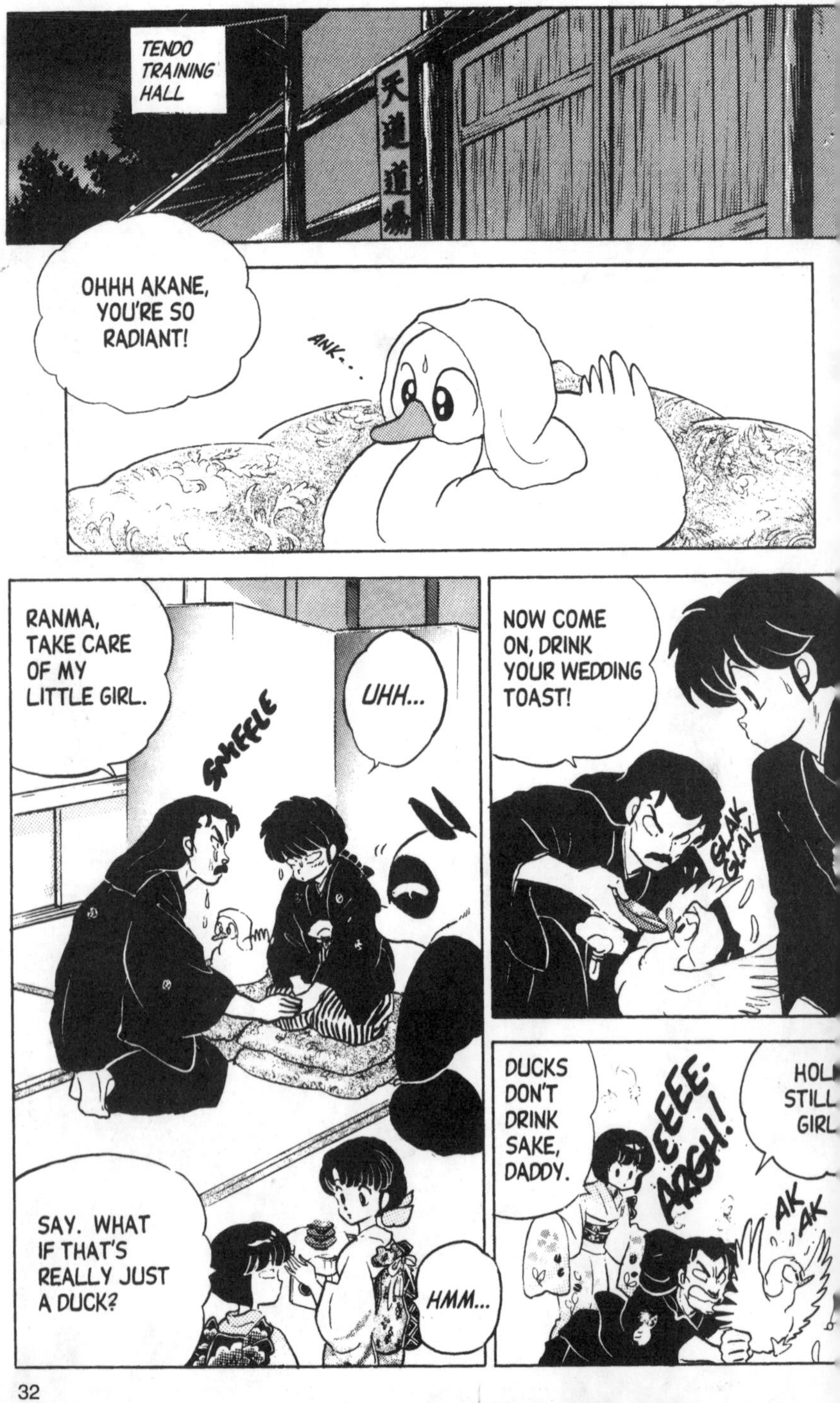
TENDO TRAINING HALL
天道道場
OHHH AKANE, YOU'RE SO RADIANT!
ANK...
RANMA, TAKE CARE OF MY LITTLE GIRL.
SNIFFLE
UHH...
SAY. WHAT IF THAT'S REALLY JUST A DUCK?
HMM...
NOW COME ON, DRINK YOUR WEDDING TOAST!
GLAK GLAK
DUCKS DON'T DRINK SAKE, DADDY.
EEEE ARGH!
HOL STILL GIRL
AK AK

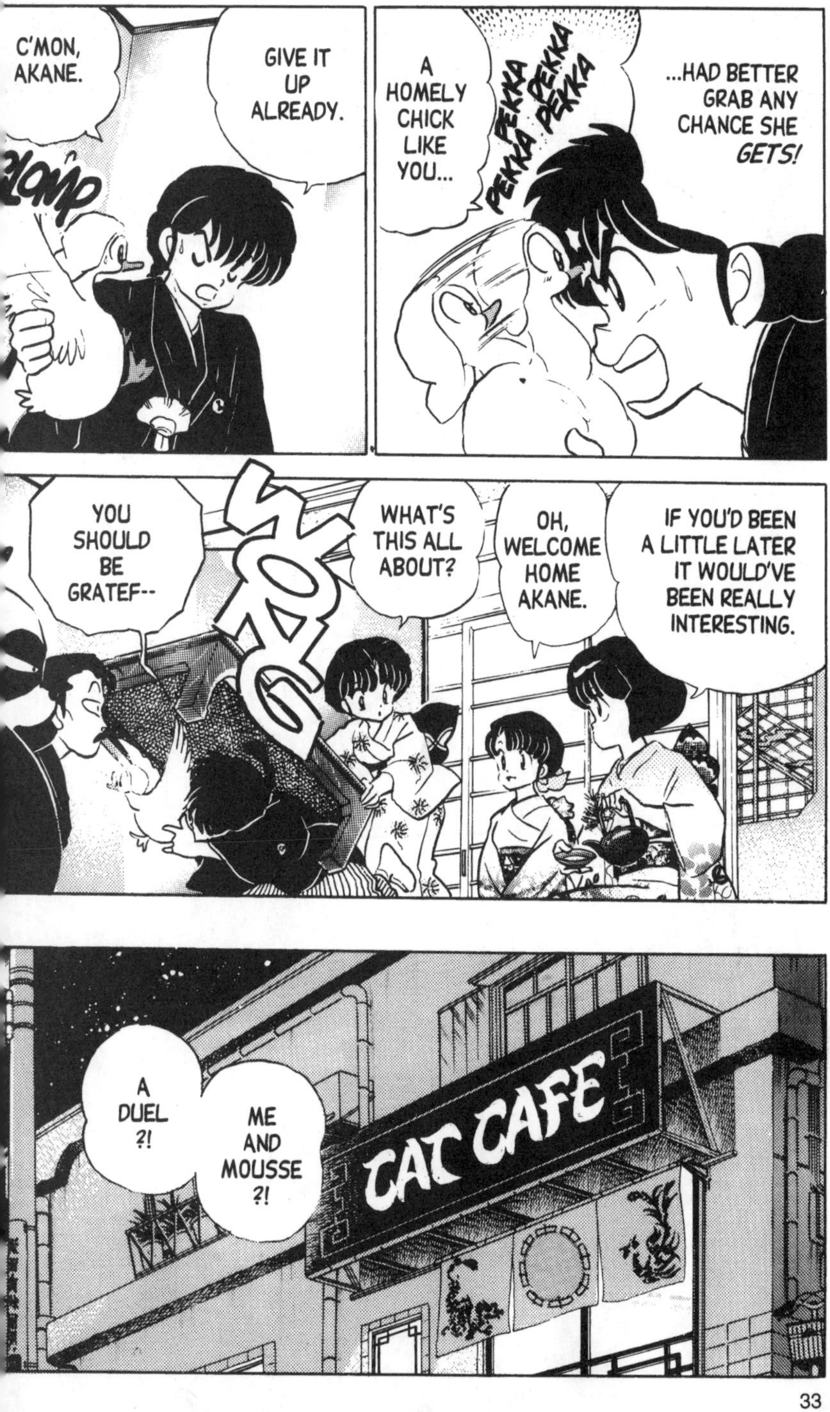
C'MON, AKANE.
GIVE IT UP ALREADY.
A HOMELY CHICK LIKE YOU...
PEKKA PEKKA PEKKA PEKKA
...HAD BETTER GRAB ANY CHANCE SHE *GETS!*
YOU SHOULD BE GRATEF--
WHAT'S THIS ALL ABOUT?
OH, WELCOME HOME AKANE.
IF YOU'D BEEN A LITTLE LATER IT WOULD'VE BEEN REALLY INTERESTING.
CAT CAFE
A DUEL ?!
ME AND MOUSSE ?!

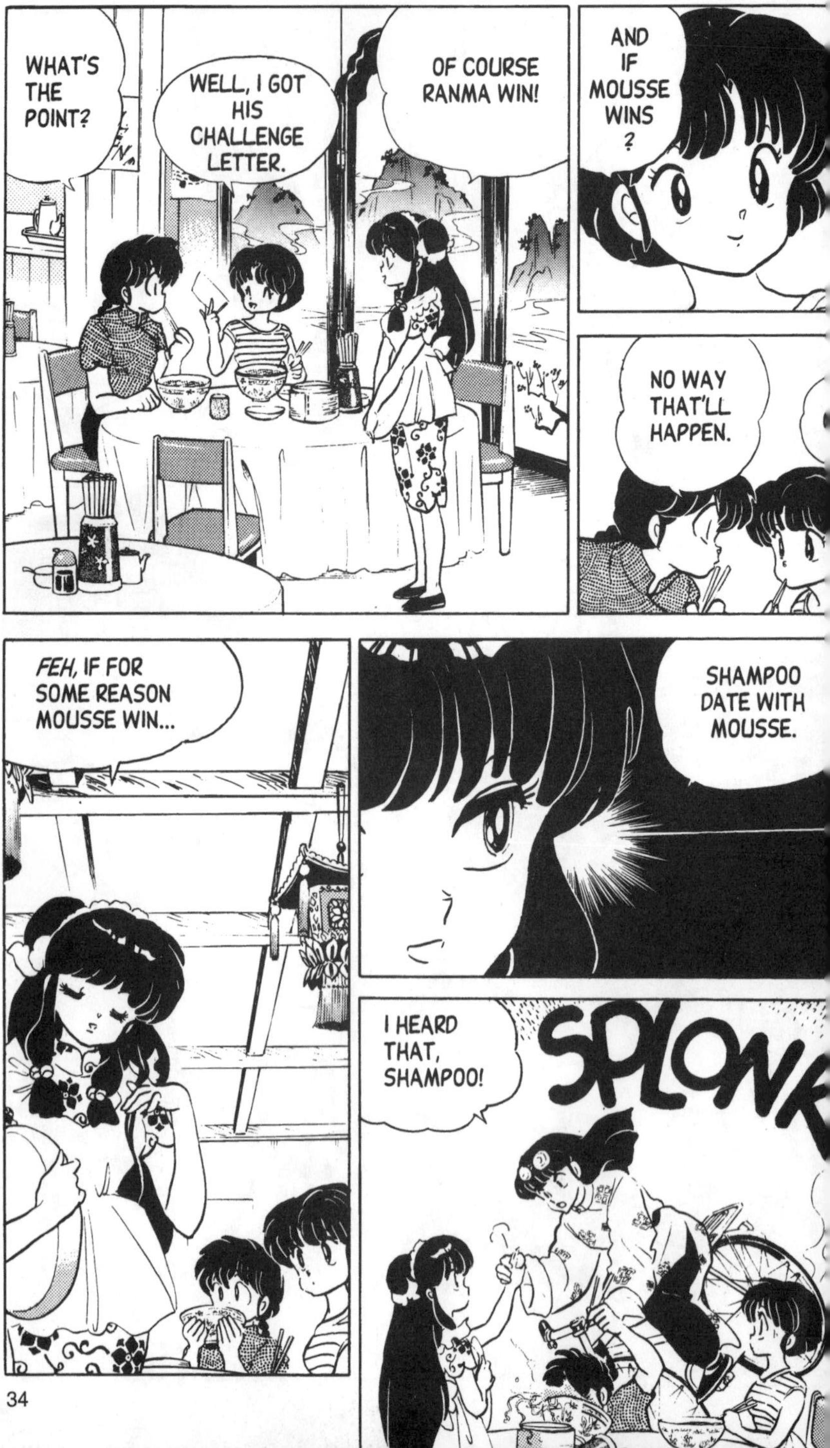
WHAT'S THE POINT?
WELL, I GOT HIS CHALLENGE LETTER.
OF COURSE RANMA WIN!
AND IF MOUSSE WINS ?
NO WAY THAT'LL HAPPEN.
FEH, IF FOR SOME REASON MOUSSE WIN...
SHAMPOO DATE WITH MOUSSE.
I HEARD THAT, SHAMPOO!
SPLONK

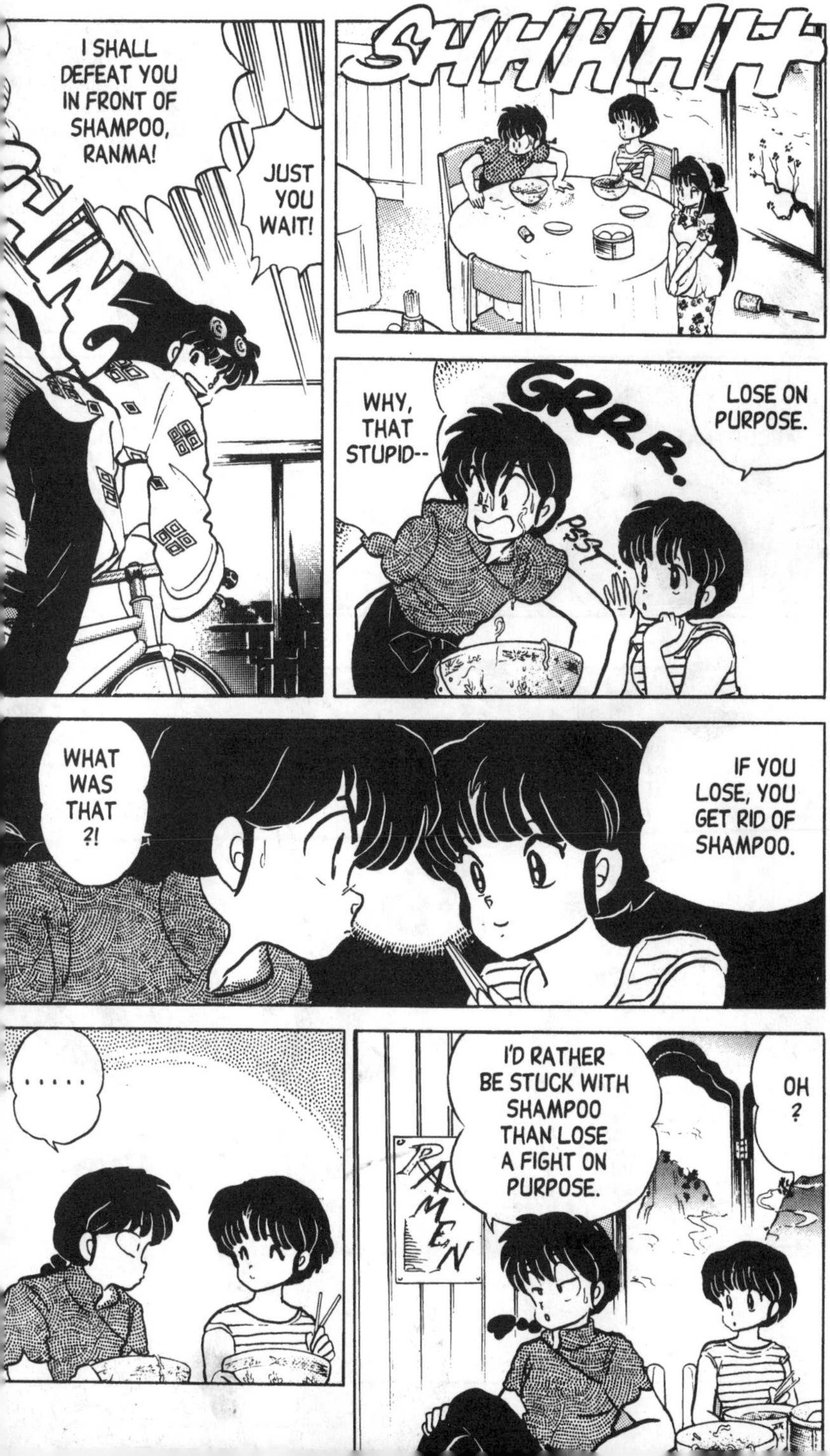

I SHALL DEFEAT YOU IN FRONT OF SHAMPOO, RANMA!
JUST YOU WAIT!
SHHHHHH
WHY, THAT STUPID--
GRRR
LOSE ON PURPOSE.
PSST
WHAT WAS THAT ?!
IF YOU LOSE, YOU GET RID OF SHAMPOO.
......
I'D RATHER BE STUCK WITH SHAMPOO THAN LOSE A FIGHT ON PURPOSE.
RAMEN
OH ?

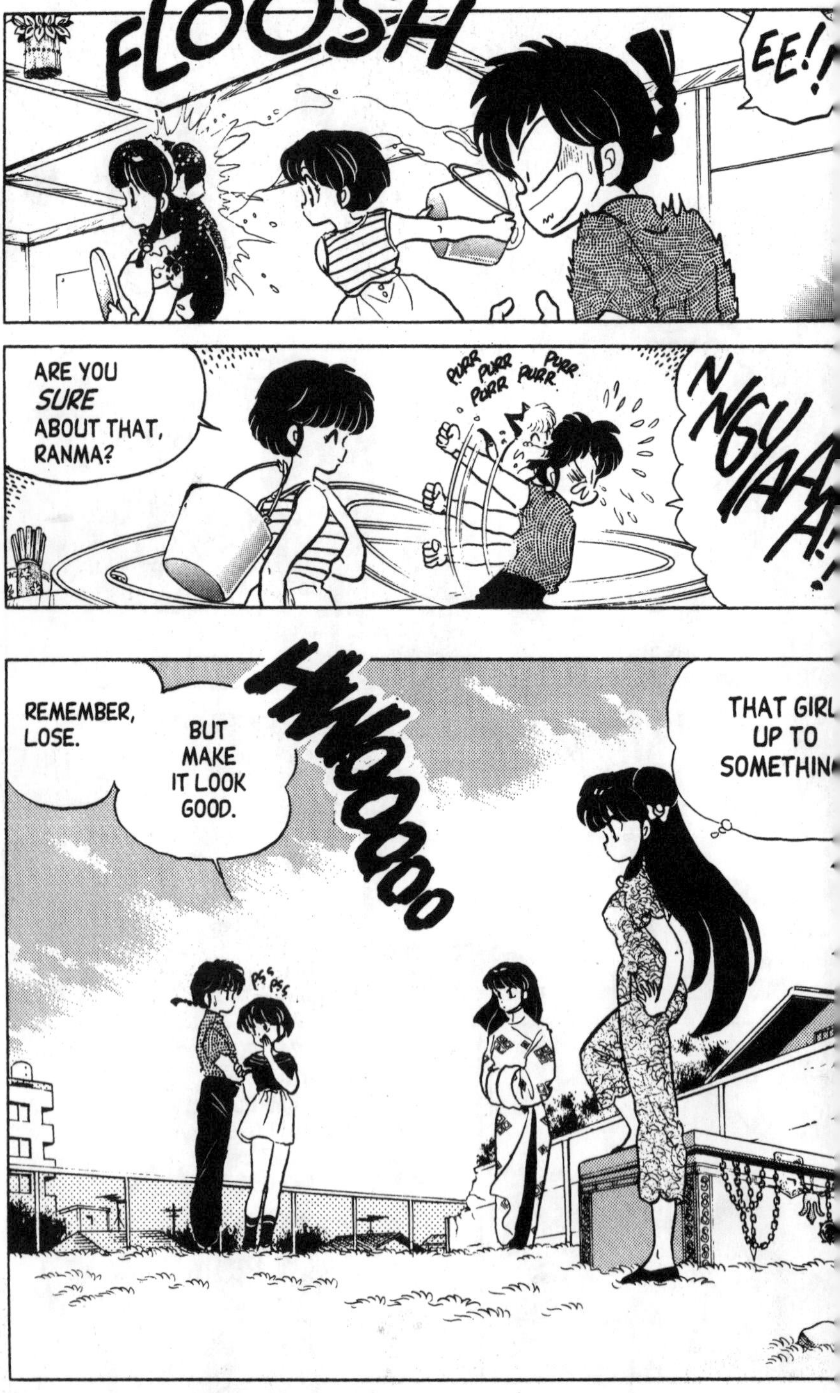
FLOOSH
EE!!
ARE YOU SURE ABOUT THAT, RANMA?
PURR PURR PURR PURR PURR
NNGYAAAA!!
REMEMBER, LOSE.
BUT MAKE IT LOOK GOOD.
HWOOOOOOO
PSS PSS
THAT GIRL UP TO SOMETHIN

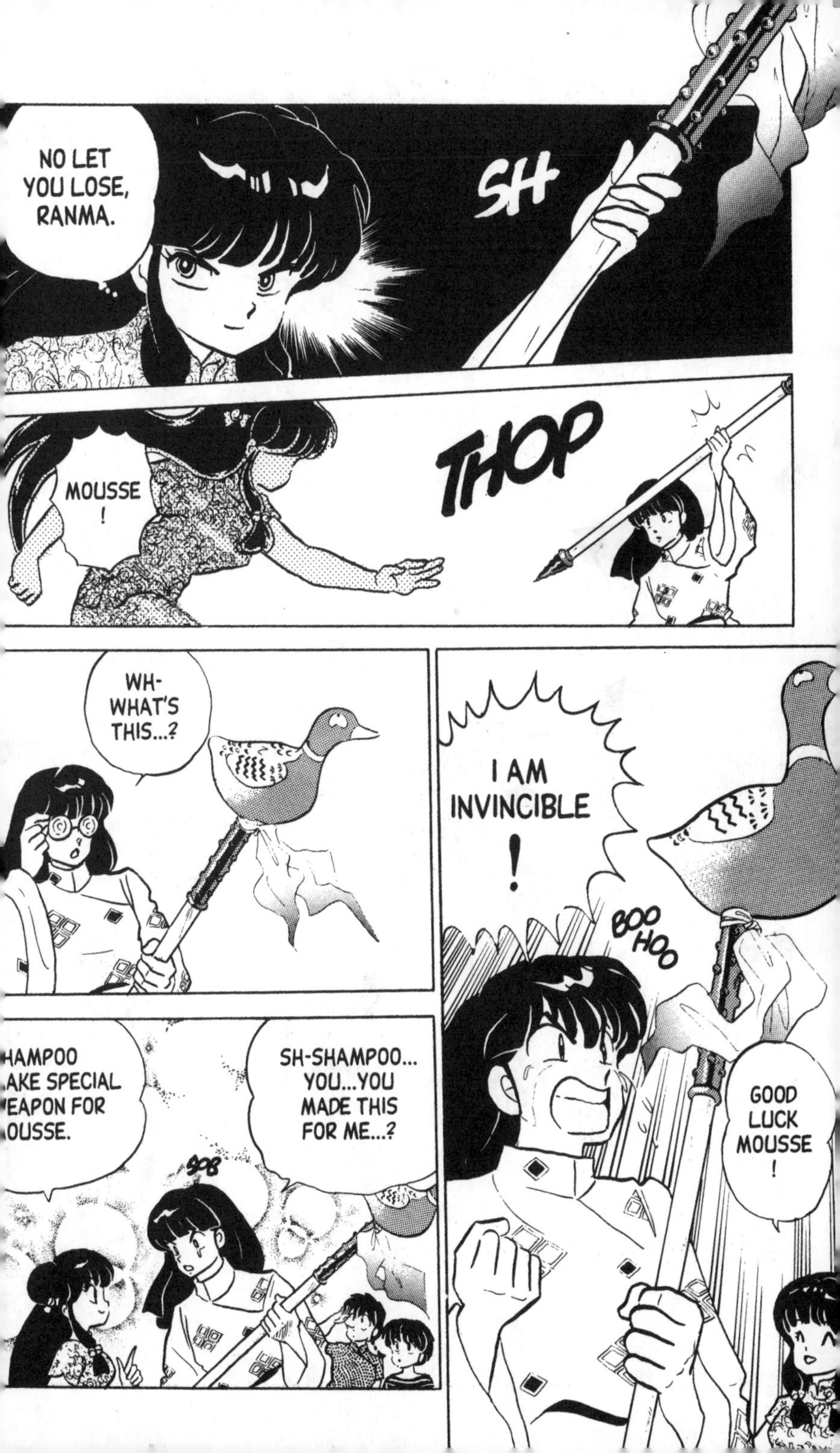
NO LET YOU LOSE, RANMA.
SH
MOUSSE !
THOP
WH- WHAT'S THIS...?
I AM INVINCIBLE !
BOO HOO
GOOD LUCK MOUSSE !
HAMPOO AKE SPECIAL EAPON FOR OUSSE.
SH-SHAMPOO... YOU...YOU MADE THIS FOR ME...?
SOB

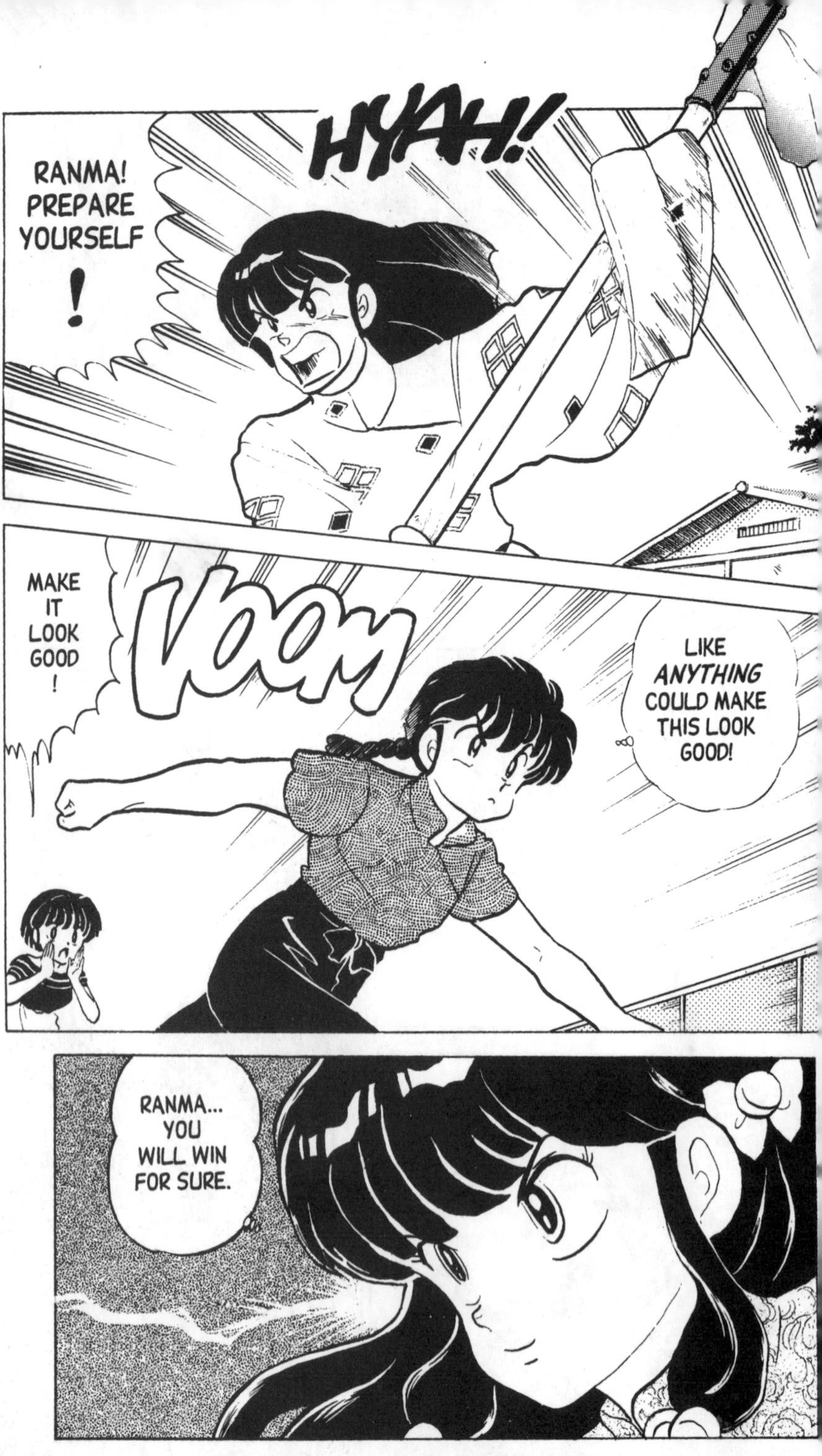
RANMA! PREPARE YOURSELF !
HYAH!
MAKE IT LOOK GOOD !
VOOM
LIKE ANYTHING COULD MAKE THIS LOOK GOOD!
RANMA... YOU WILL WIN FOR SURE.

PART 3
THE HAPPIEST MOUSSE

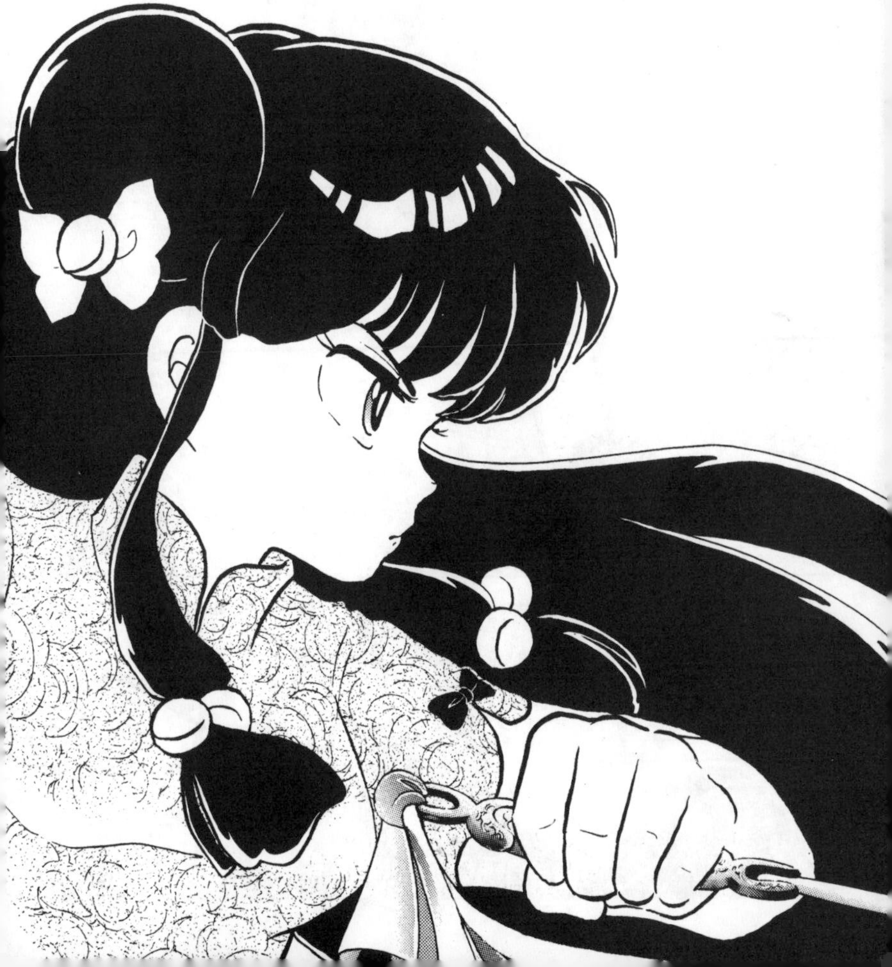

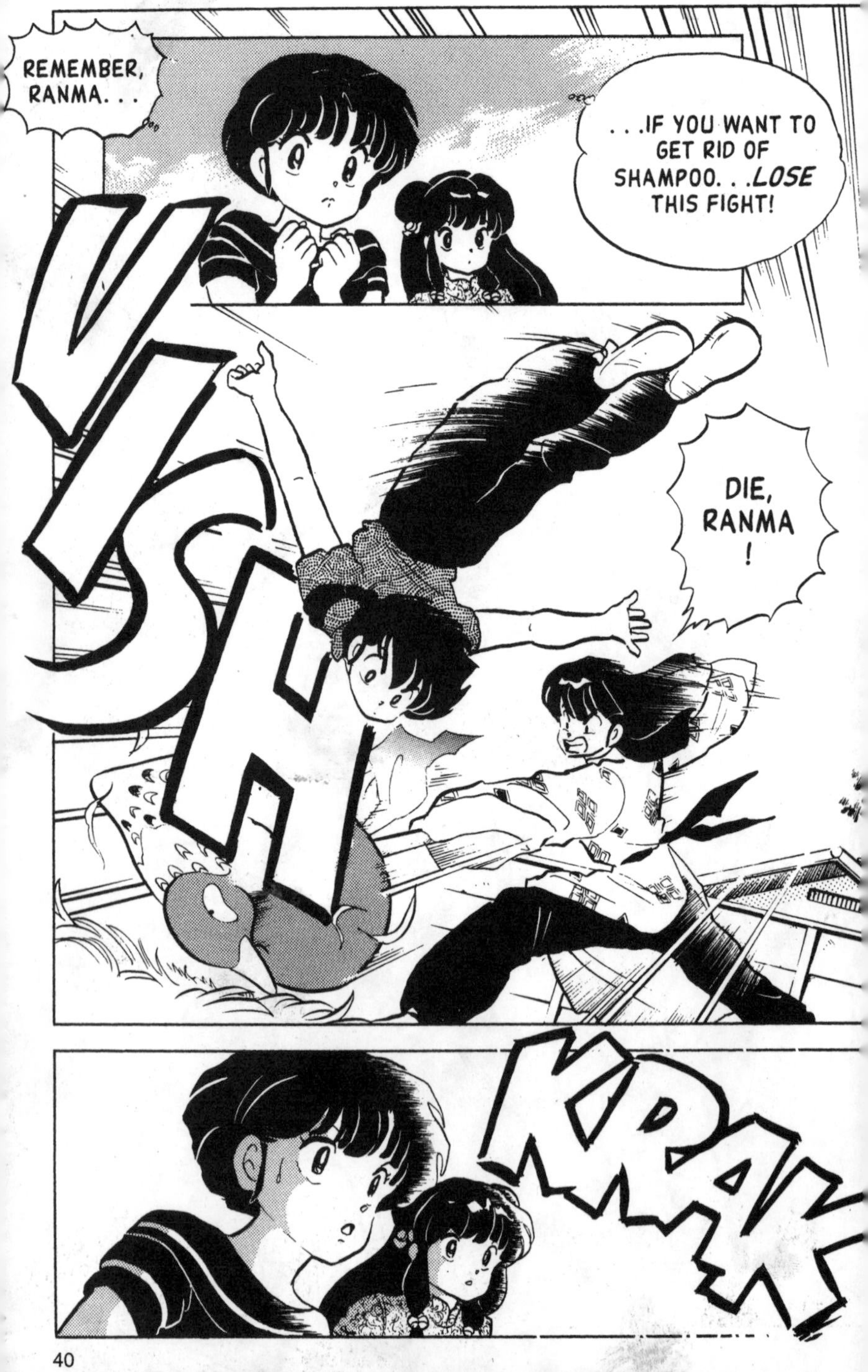
REMEMBER, RANMA. . .
. . .IF YOU WANT TO GET RID OF SHAMPOO. . .*LOSE* THIS FIGHT!
VSSH
DIE, RANMA!
KRAK

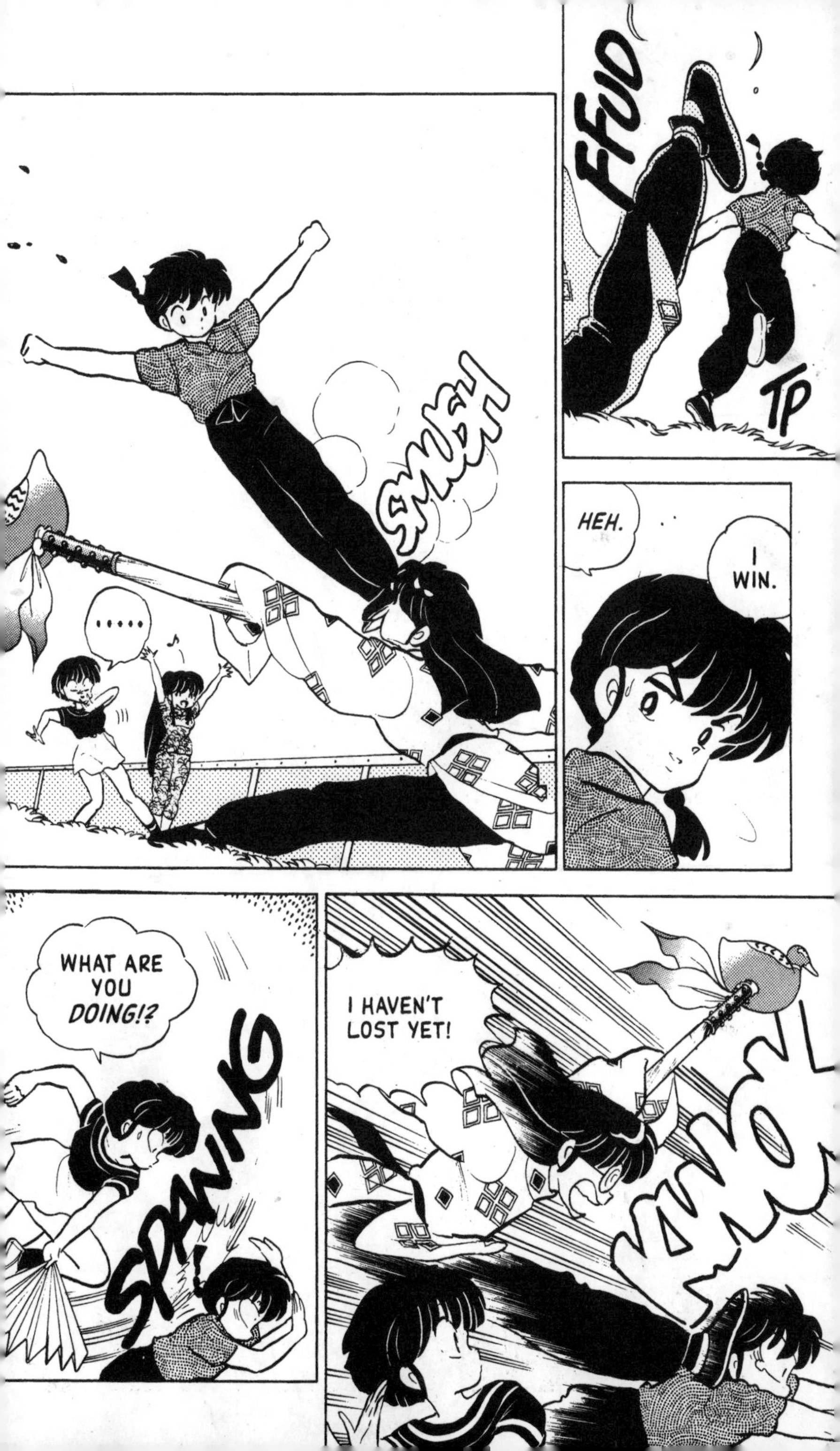
FUD
TP
HEH.
I WIN.
SMASH
.....
I HAVEN'T LOST YET!
WHAT ARE YOU DOING!?
SPANNG

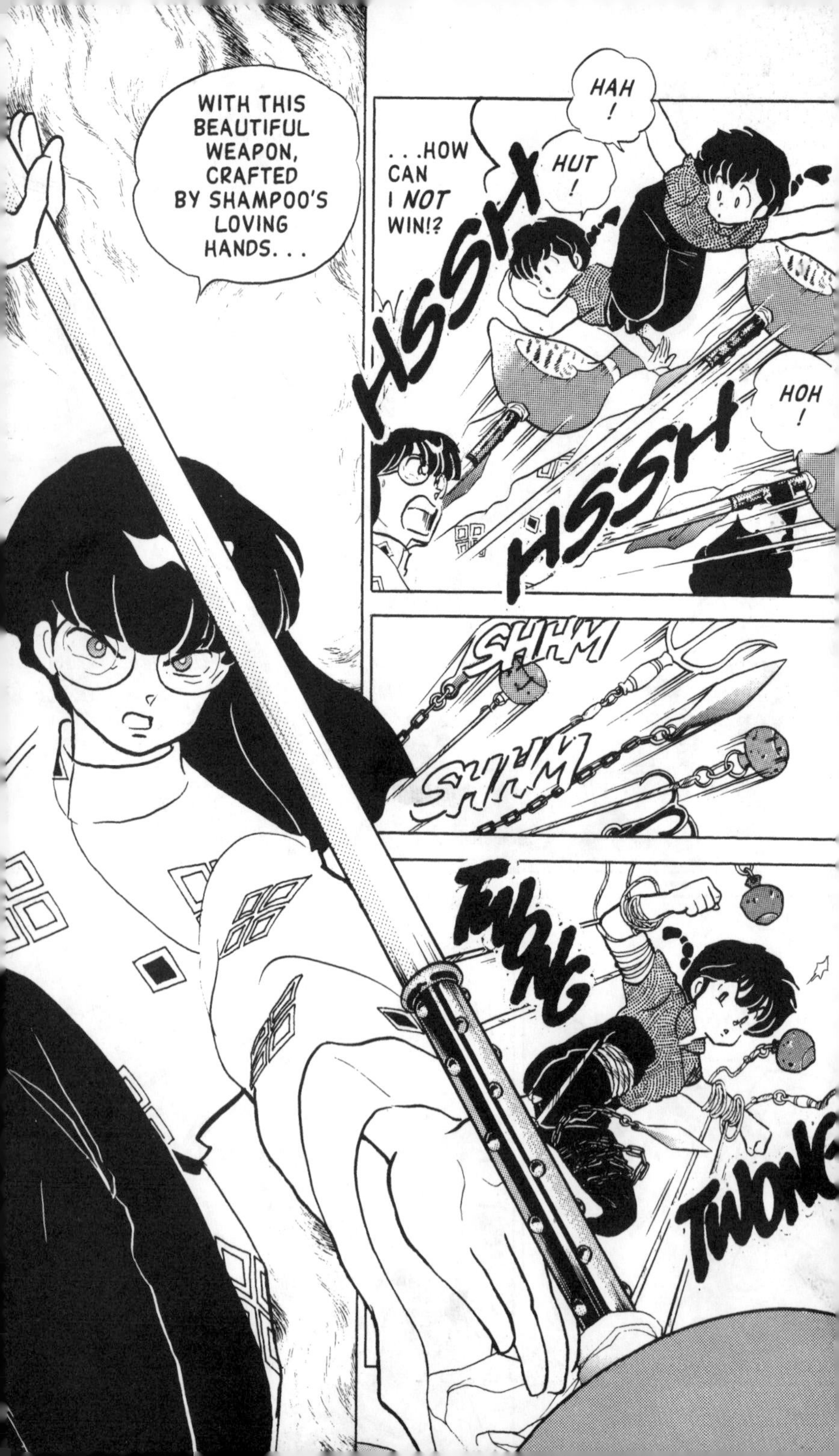
WITH THIS BEAUTIFUL WEAPON, CRAFTED BY SHAMPOO'S LOVING HANDS. . .
. . .HOW CAN I NOT WIN!?
HAH!
HUT!
HSSH
HSSH
HOH!
SHHM
SHHM
TWONG
TWONG

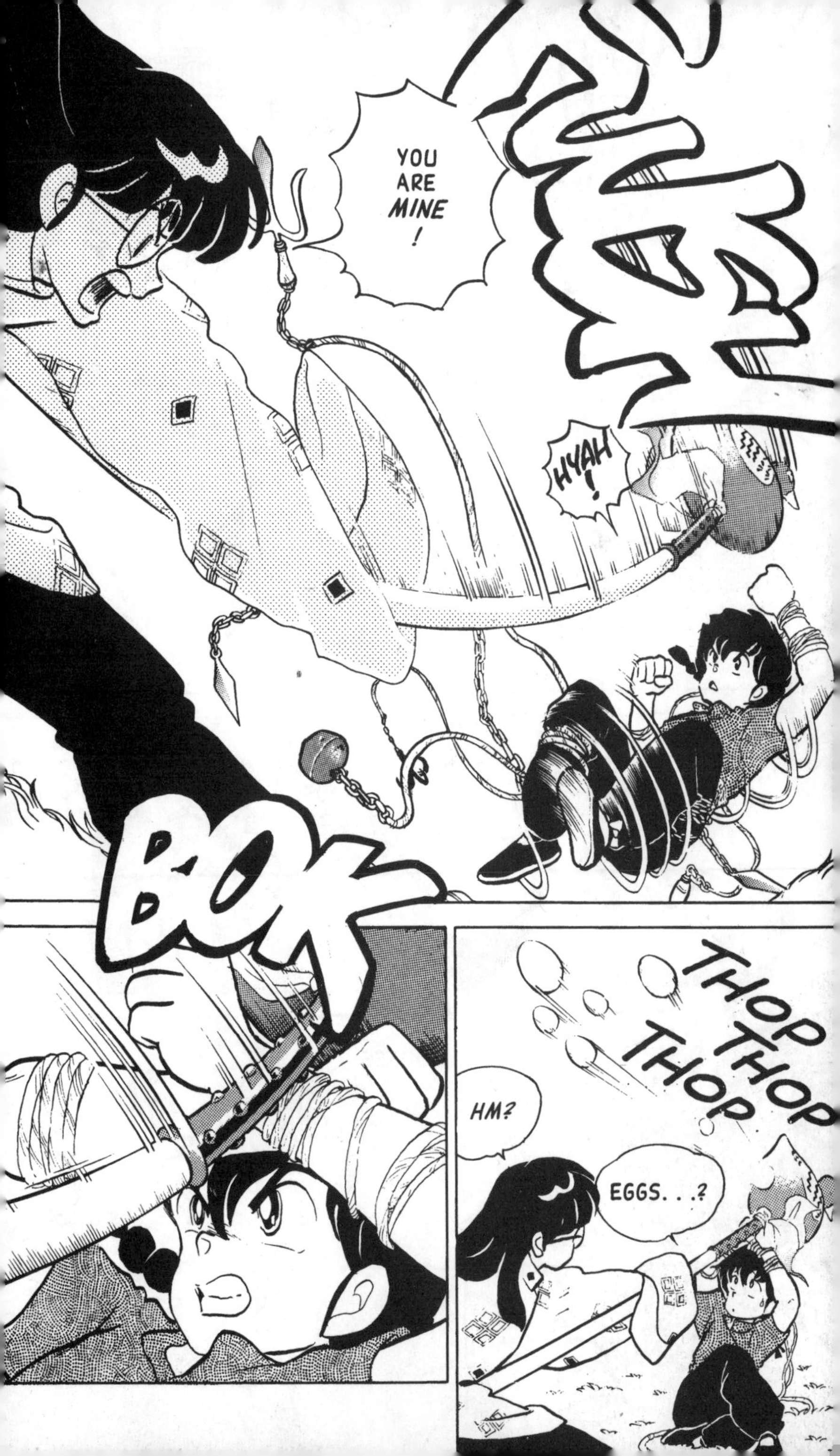
YOU ARE MINE!
HYAH!
BOK
THOP THOP THOP
HM?
EGGS. . .?

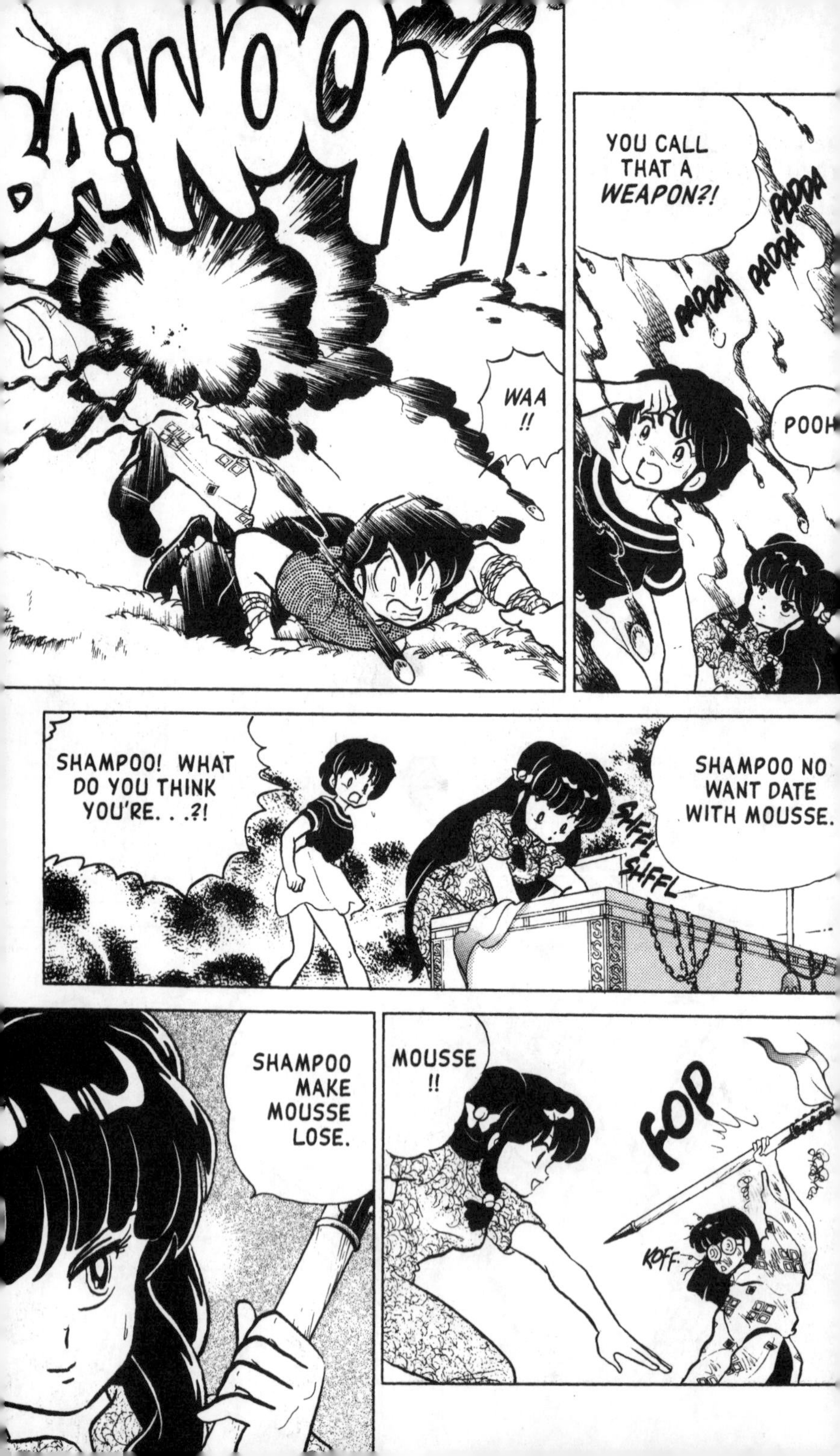
BAWOOOM
WAA !!
YOU CALL THAT A WEAPON?!
PADDA PADDA PADDA PADDA
POOH
SHAMPOO! WHAT DO YOU THINK YOU'RE. . .?!
SHAMPOO NO WANT DATE WITH MOUSSE.
SHFFL SHFFL
SHAMPOO MAKE MOUSSE LOSE.
MOUSSE !!
FOP
KOFF

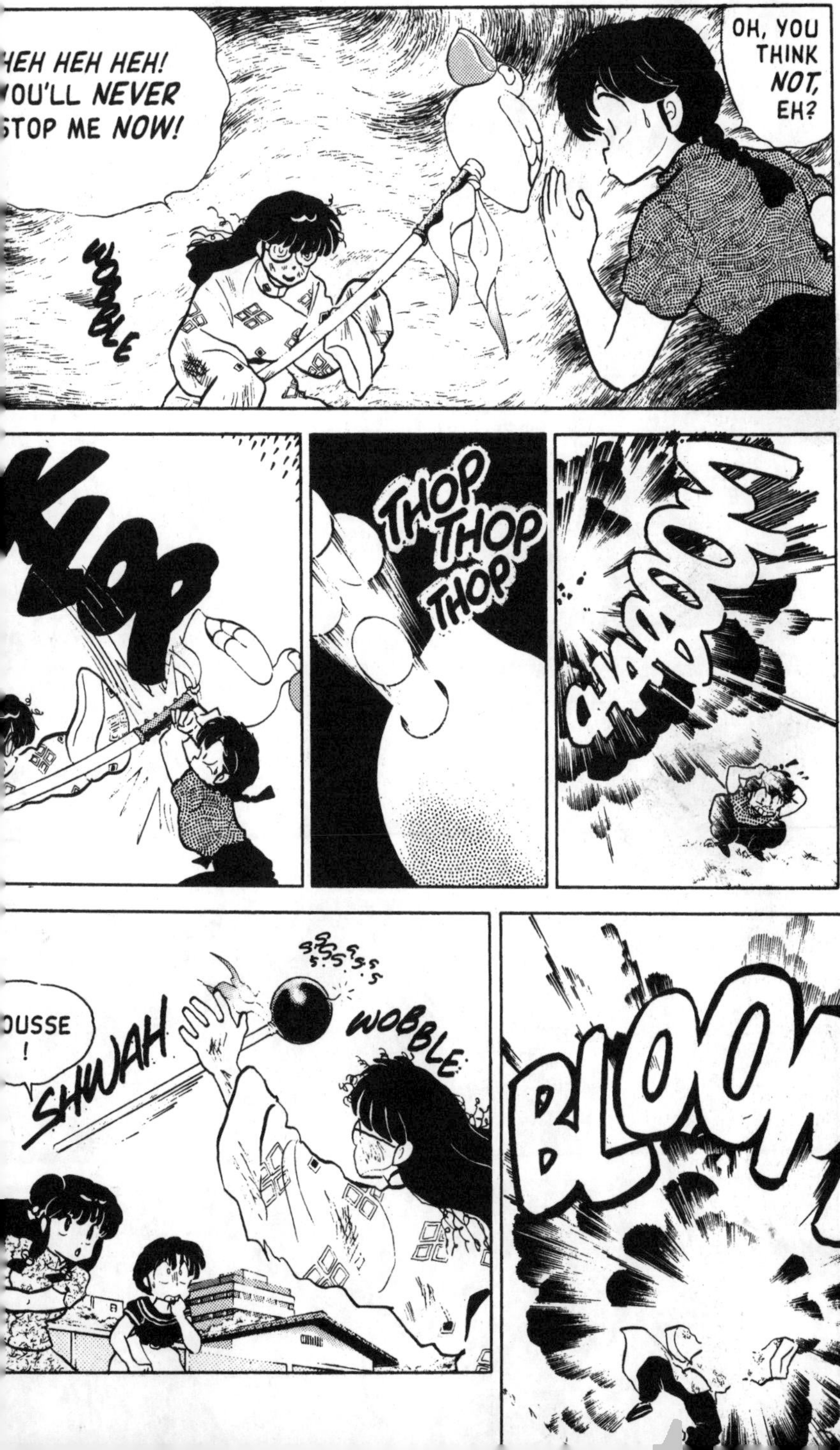
HEH HEH HEH! YOU'LL NEVER STOP ME NOW!
WOBBLE
OH, YOU THINK NOT, EH?
KLOP
THOP THOP THOP
CHA-DOOM
OUSSE !
SHWAH
WOBBLE
BLOOM

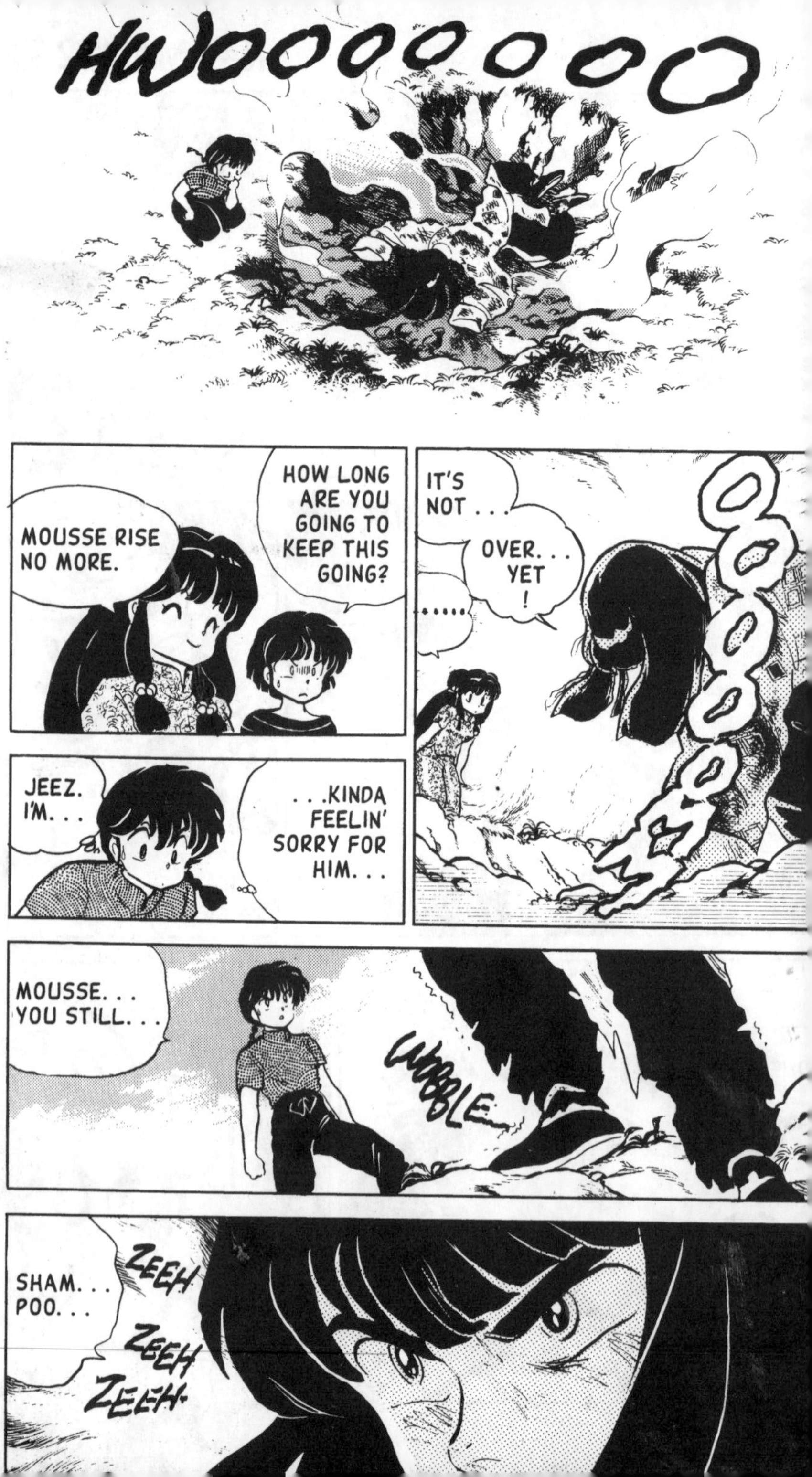
HWOOOOOOO
MOUSSE RISE NO MORE.
HOW LONG ARE YOU GOING TO KEEP THIS GOING?
JEEZ. I'M. . .
. . .KINDA FEELIN' SORRY FOR HIM. . .
IT'S NOT . . .
OVER. . . YET !
......
OOOOOOOM
MOUSSE. . . YOU STILL. . .
WOBBLE
SHAM. . . POO. . .
ZEEH
ZEEH
ZEEH

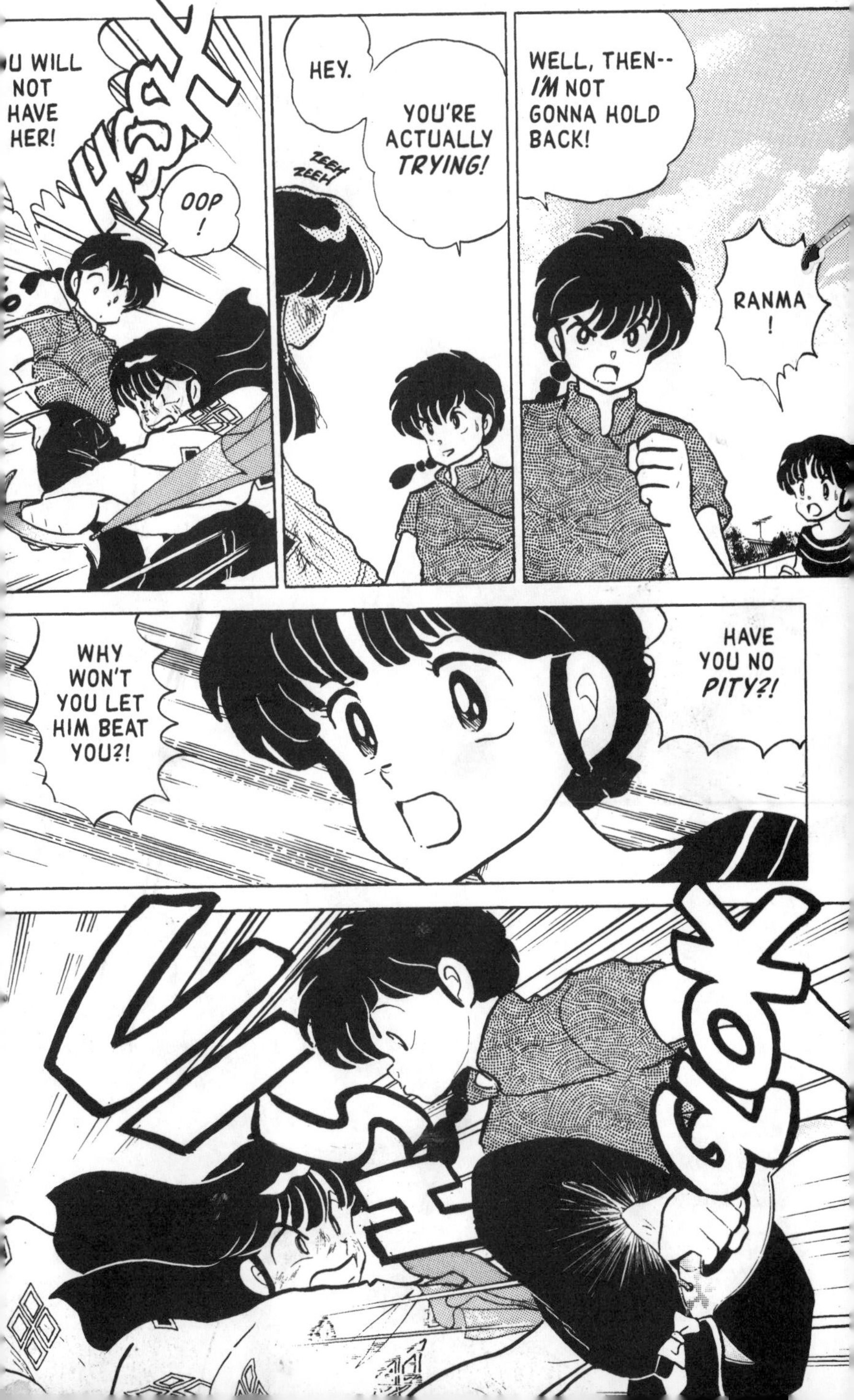
U WILL NOT HAVE HER!
OOP!
HEY.
YOU'RE ACTUALLY *TRYING!*
ZEEH ZEEH
WELL, THEN-- *I'M* NOT GONNA HOLD BACK!
RANMA!
WHY WON'T YOU LET HIM BEAT YOU?!
HAVE YOU NO *PITY?!*

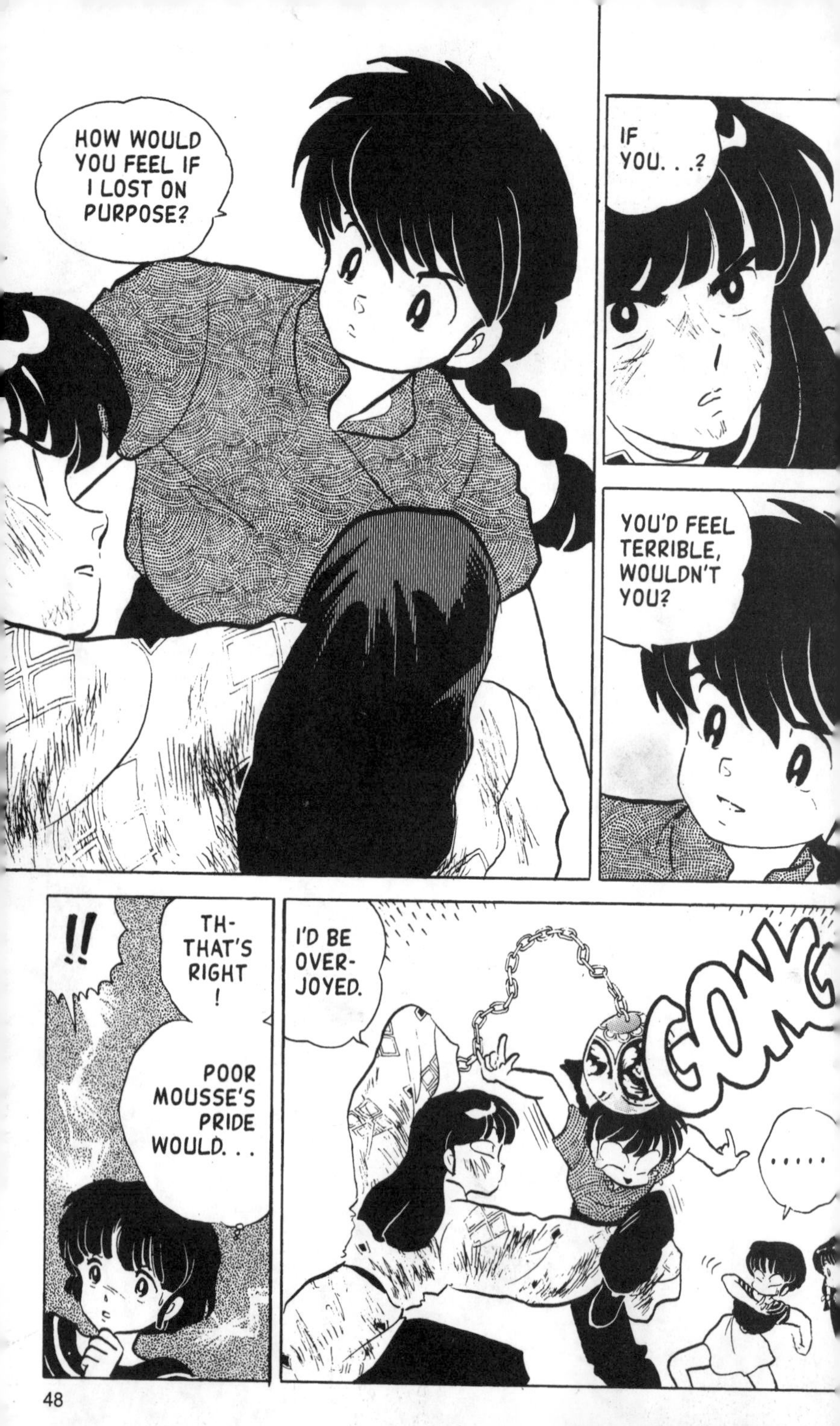
HOW WOULD YOU FEEL IF I LOST ON PURPOSE?
IF YOU. . .?
YOU'D FEEL TERRIBLE, WOULDN'T YOU?
!!
TH-THAT'S RIGHT!
POOR MOUSSE'S PRIDE WOULD. . .
I'D BE OVER-JOYED.
GONG
. . . . .

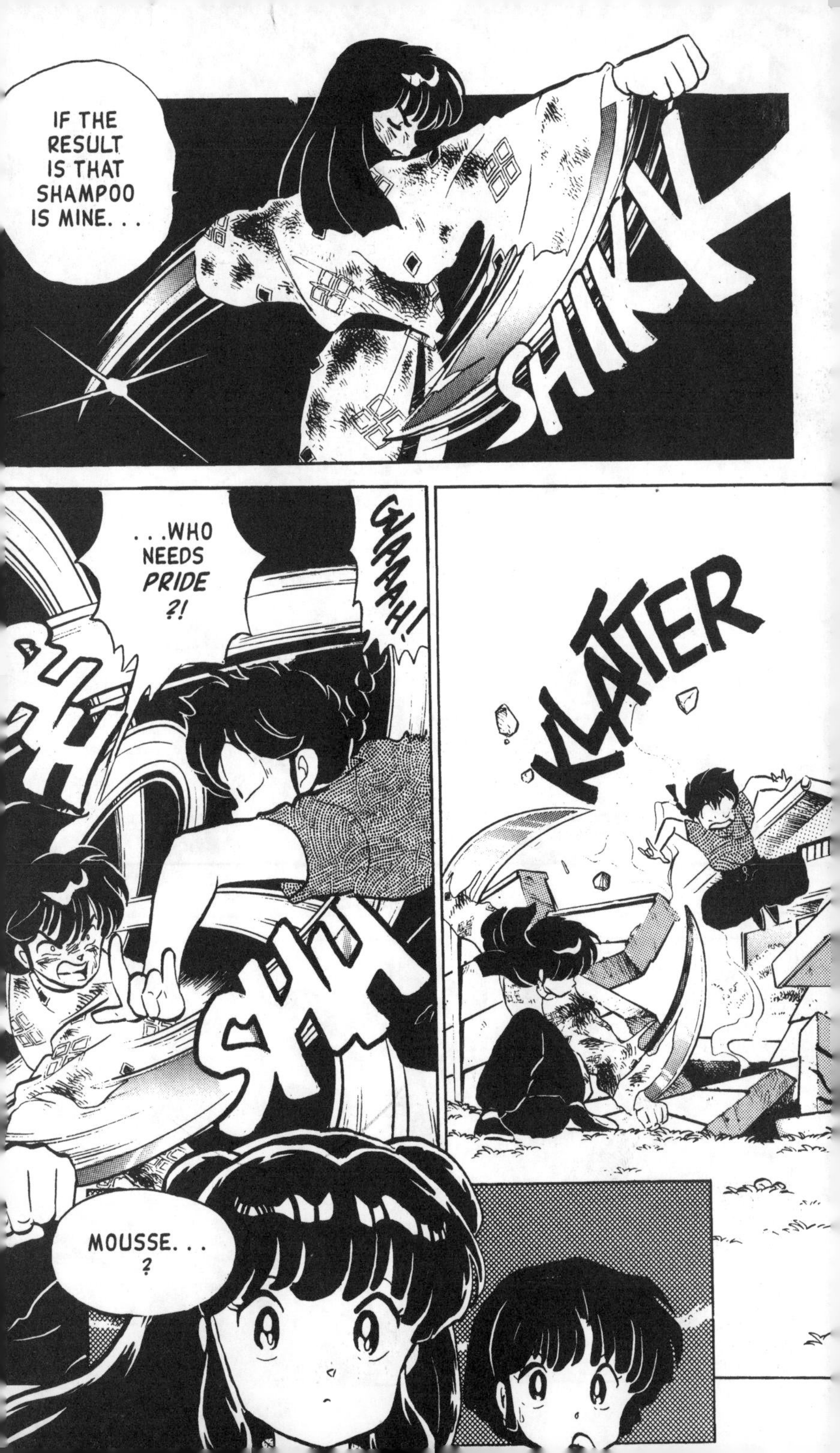
IF THE RESULT IS THAT SHAMPOO IS MINE. . .
SHIKK
. . .WHO NEEDS PRIDE ?!
GWAAAH!
KLATTER
MOUSSE. . . ?

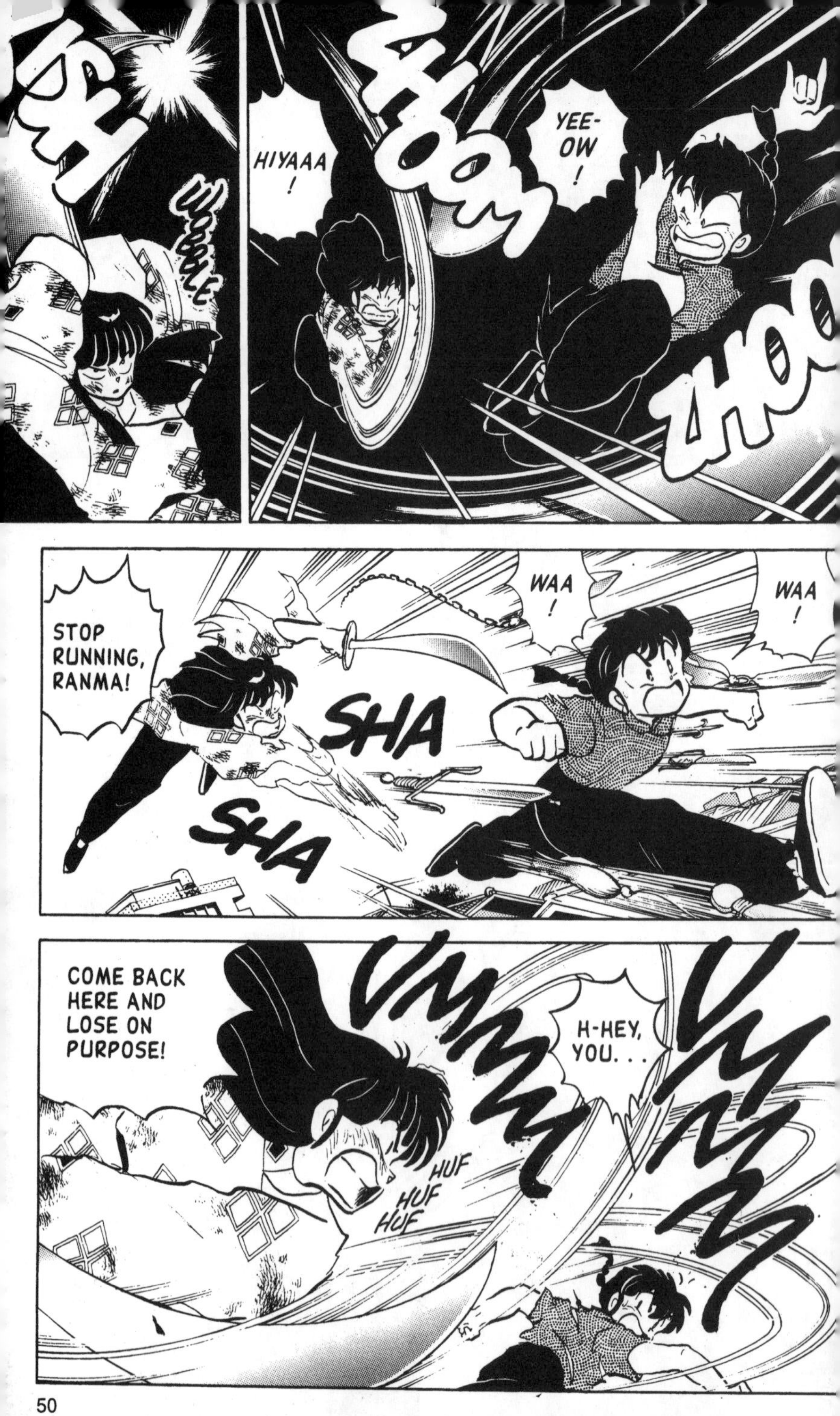
HIYAAA!
YEE-OW!
ZHOO
STOP RUNNING, RANMA!
SHA
SHA
WAA!
WAA!
COME BACK HERE AND LOSE ON PURPOSE!
HUF HUF HUF
H-HEY, YOU. . .

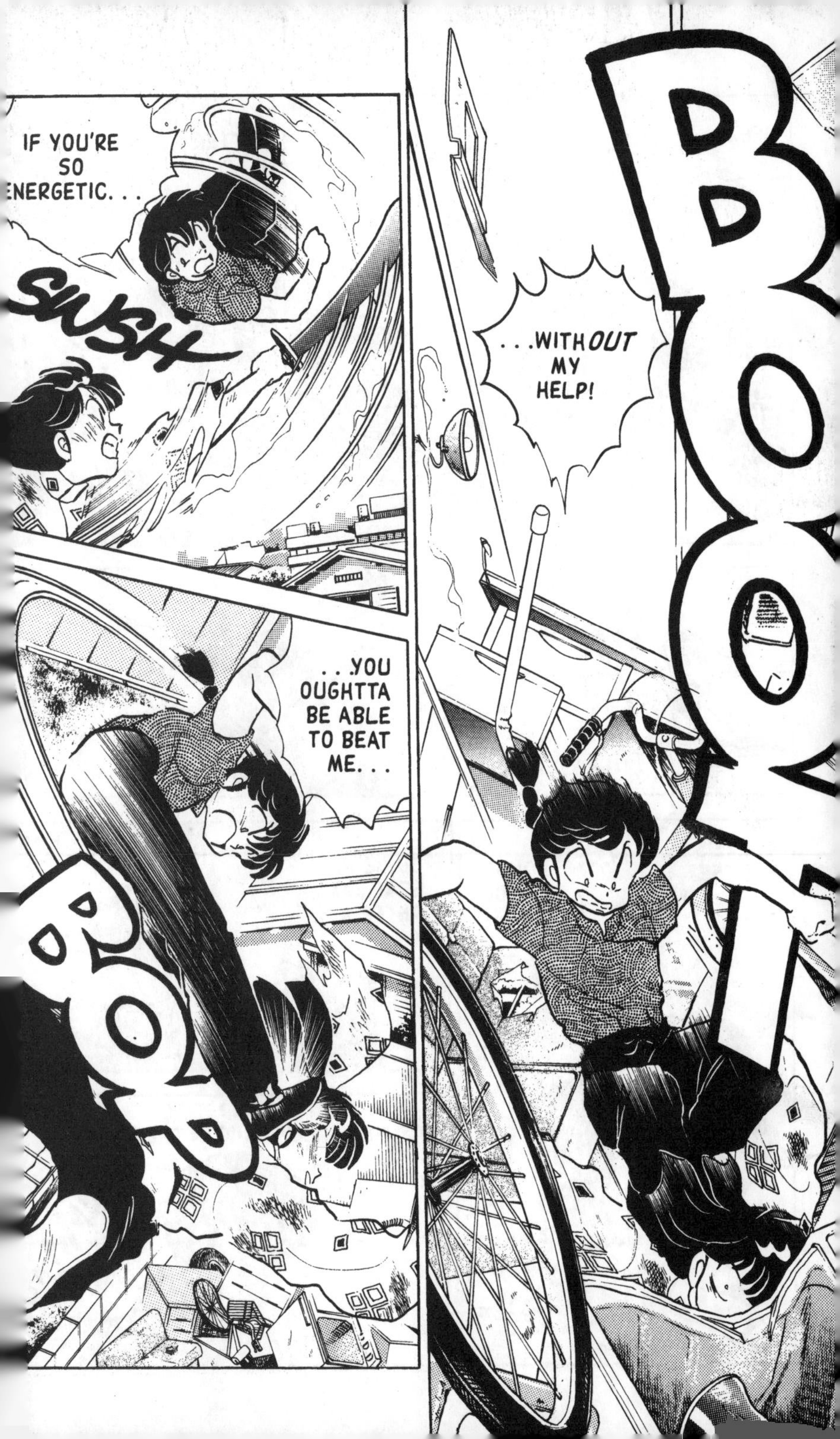
IF YOU'RE SO ENERGETIC. . .
SWISH
. . .YOU OUGHTTA BE ABLE TO BEAT ME. . .
BOP
. . .WITH*OUT* MY HELP!

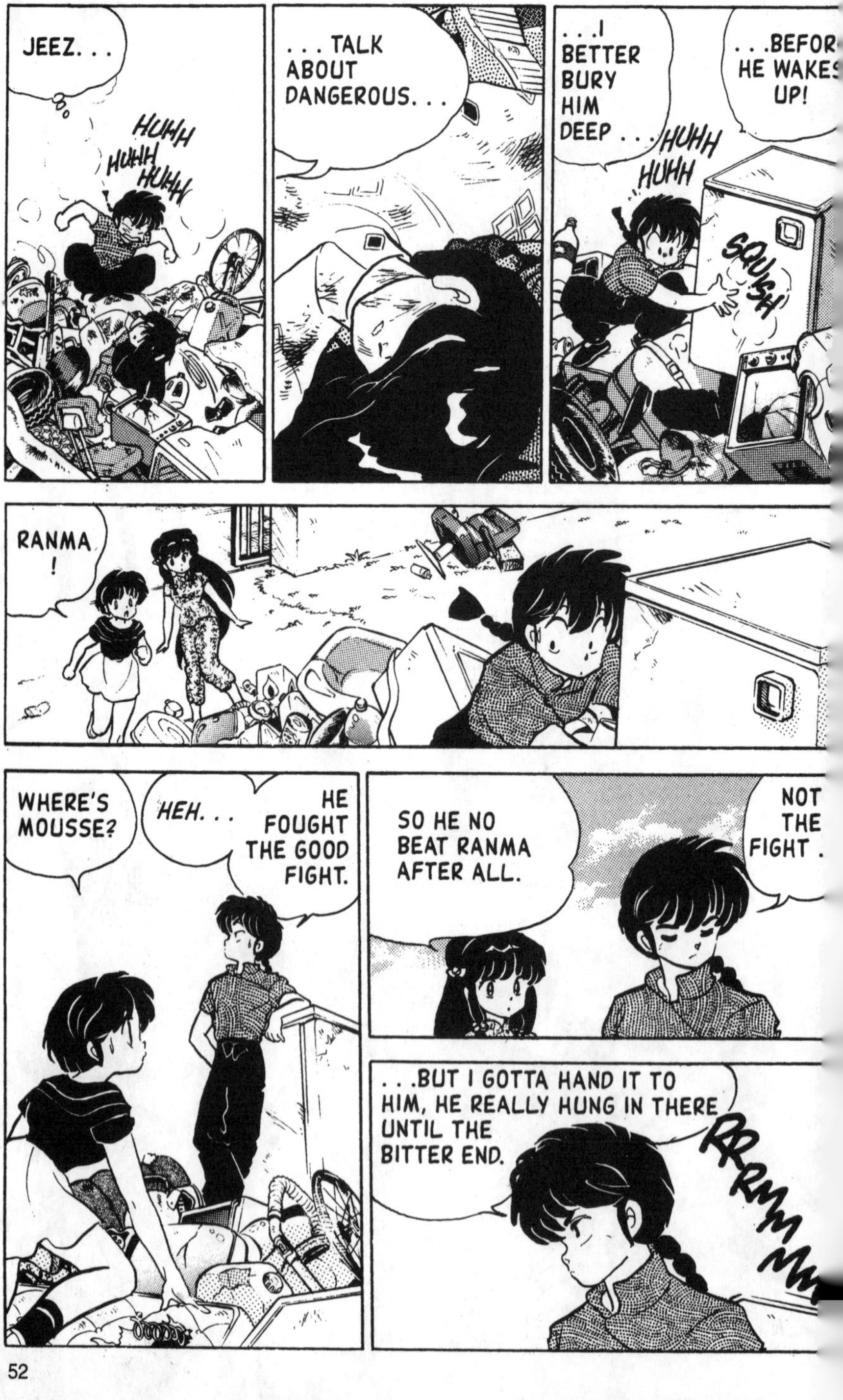
JEEZ. . .
HUHH HUHH HUHH
. . . TALK ABOUT DANGEROUS. . .
. . .I BETTER BURY HIM DEEP . . .
. . .BEFOR HE WAKES UP!
HUHH HUHH
SQUISH
RANMA!
WHERE'S MOUSSE?
HEH. . .
HE FOUGHT THE GOOD FIGHT.
SO HE NO BEAT RANMA AFTER ALL.
NOT THE FIGHT .
. . .BUT I GOTTA HAND IT TO HIM, HE REALLY HUNG IN THERE UNTIL THE BITTER END.

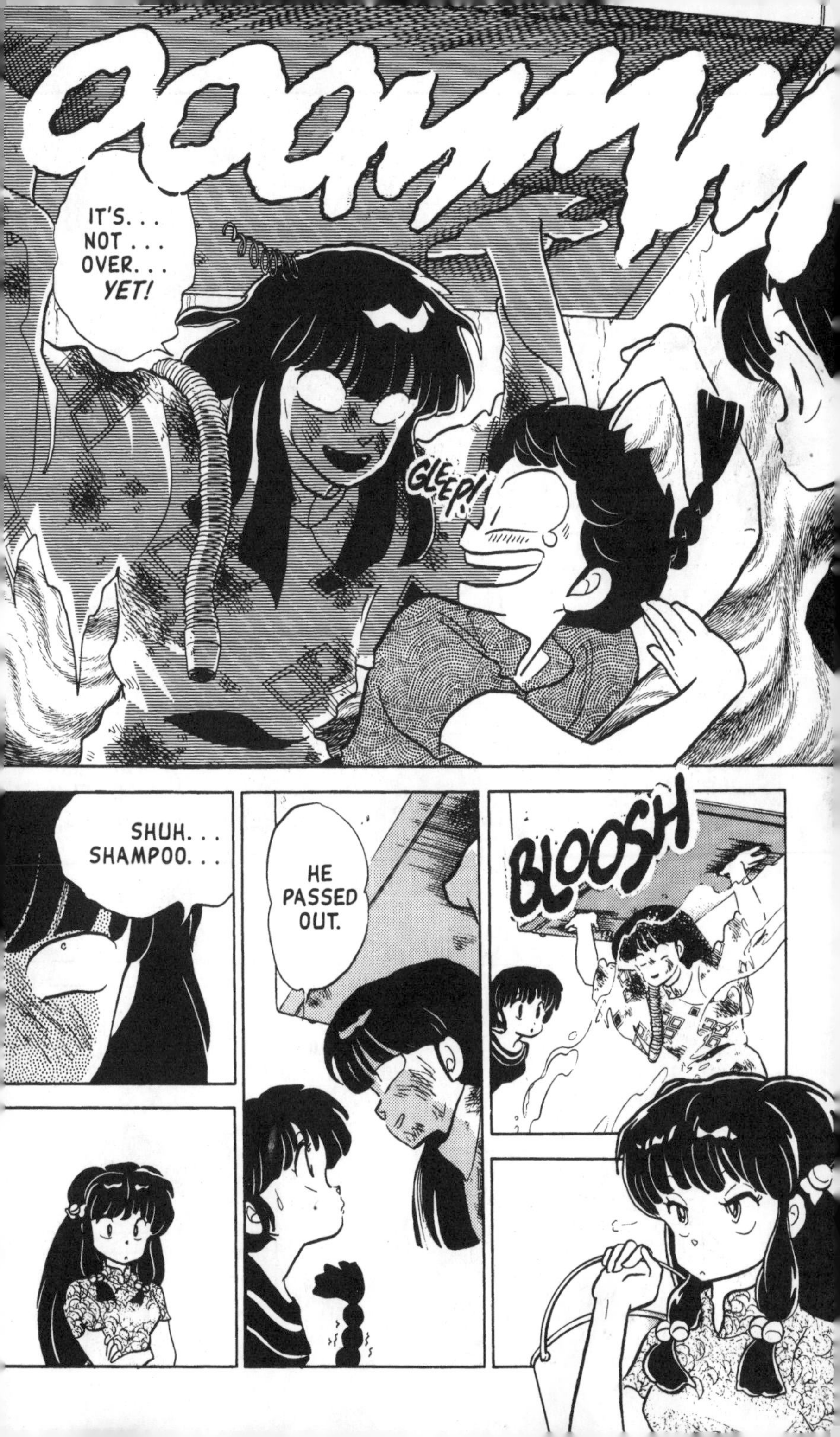
OOMM
IT'S... NOT... OVER... YET!
GLEEP!
SHUH... SHAMPOO...
HE PASSED OUT.
BLOOSH

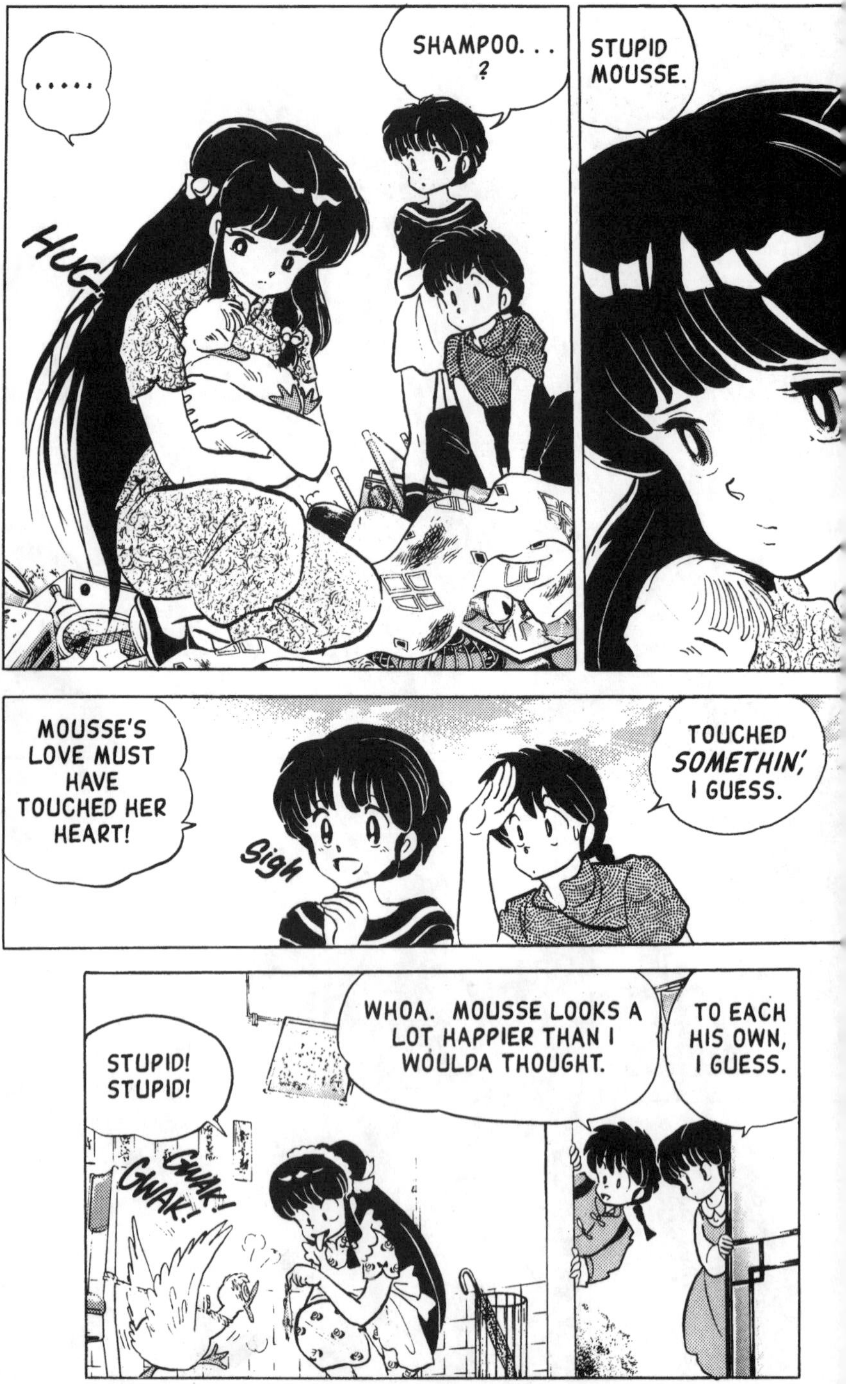
. . . . .
HUG!
SHAMPOO. . . ?
STUPID MOUSSE.
MOUSSE'S LOVE MUST HAVE TOUCHED HER HEART!
Sigh
TOUCHED *SOMETHIN',* I GUESS.
STUPID! STUPID!
GWAK! GWAK!
WHOA. MOUSSE LOOKS A LOT HAPPIER THAN I WOULDA THOUGHT.
TO EACH HIS OWN, I GUESS.

PART 4
TSUBASA KURENAI BUSTS LOOSE!

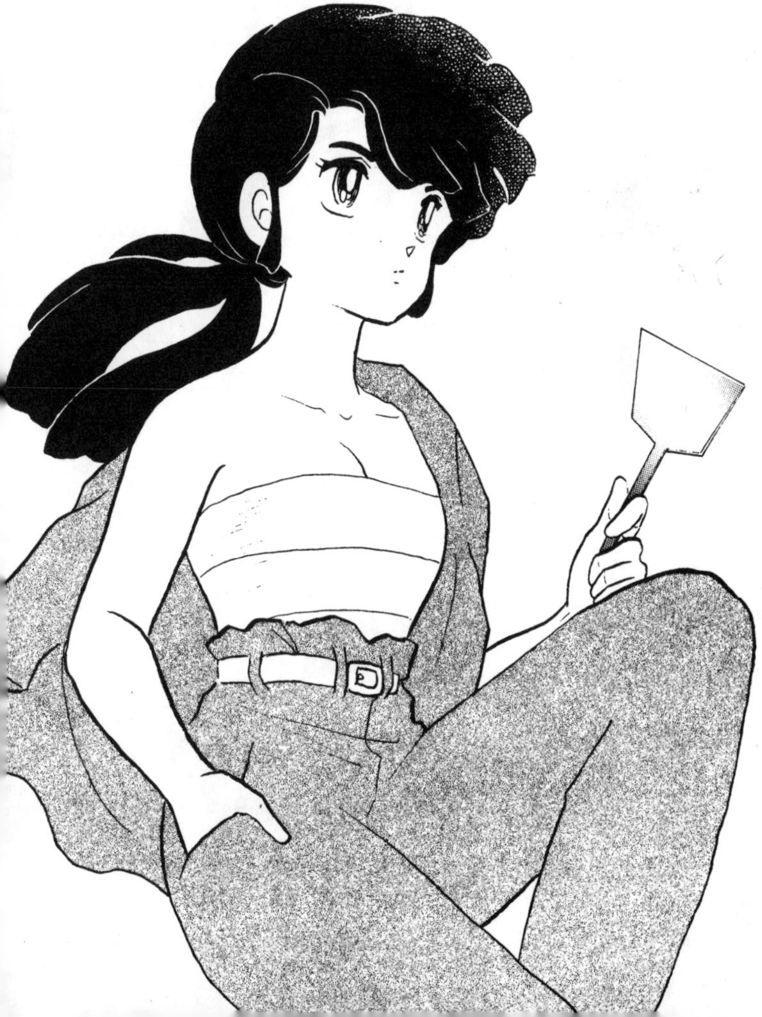

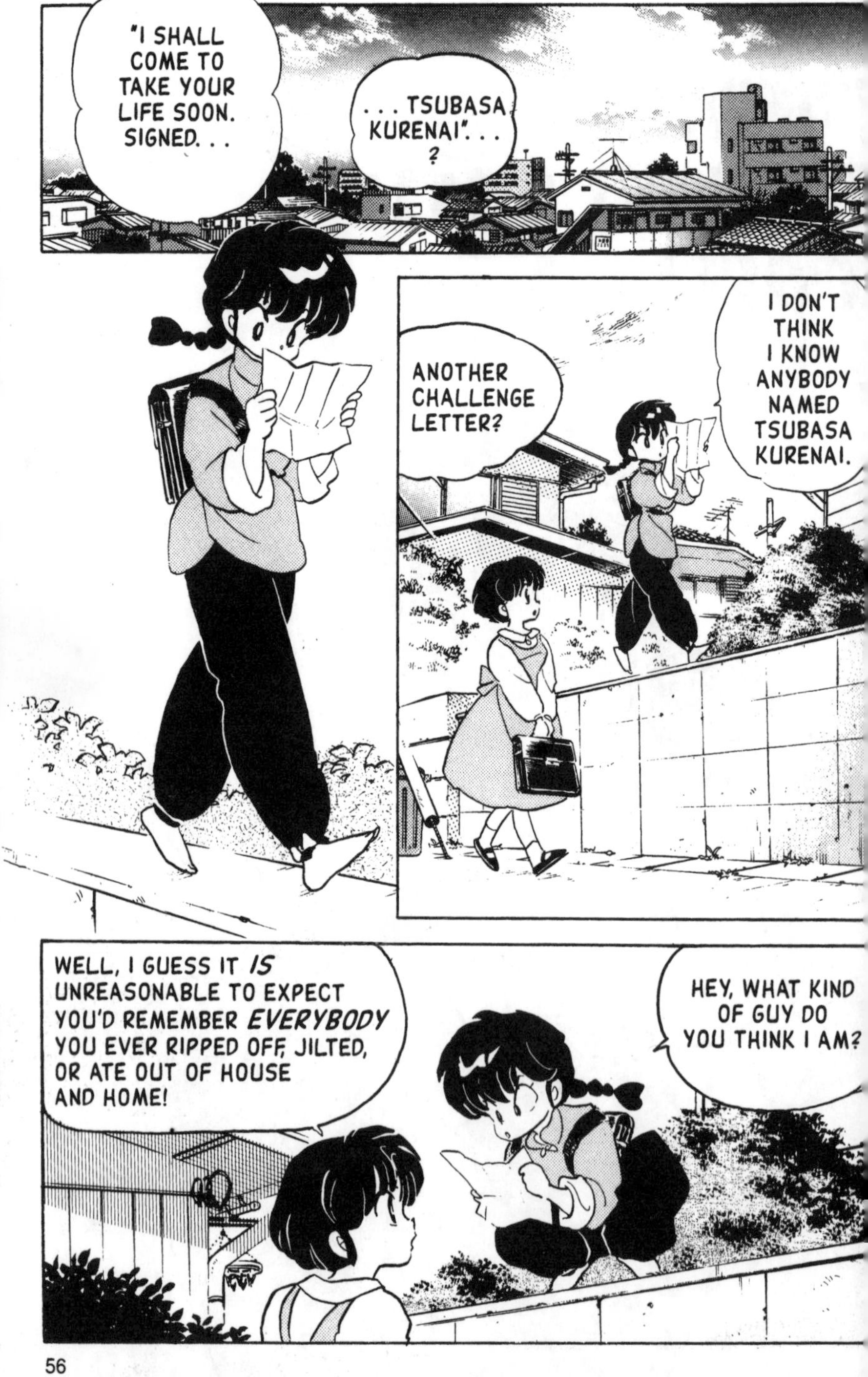

"I SHALL COME TO TAKE YOUR LIFE SOON. SIGNED. . .
. . . TSUBASA KURENAI". . . ?
ANOTHER CHALLENGE LETTER?
I DON'T THINK I KNOW ANYBODY NAMED TSUBASA KURENAI.
WELL, I GUESS IT *IS* UNREASONABLE TO EXPECT YOU'D REMEMBER *EVERYBODY* YOU EVER RIPPED OFF, JILTED, OR ATE OUT OF HOUSE AND HOME!
HEY, WHAT KIND OF GUY DO YOU THINK I AM?

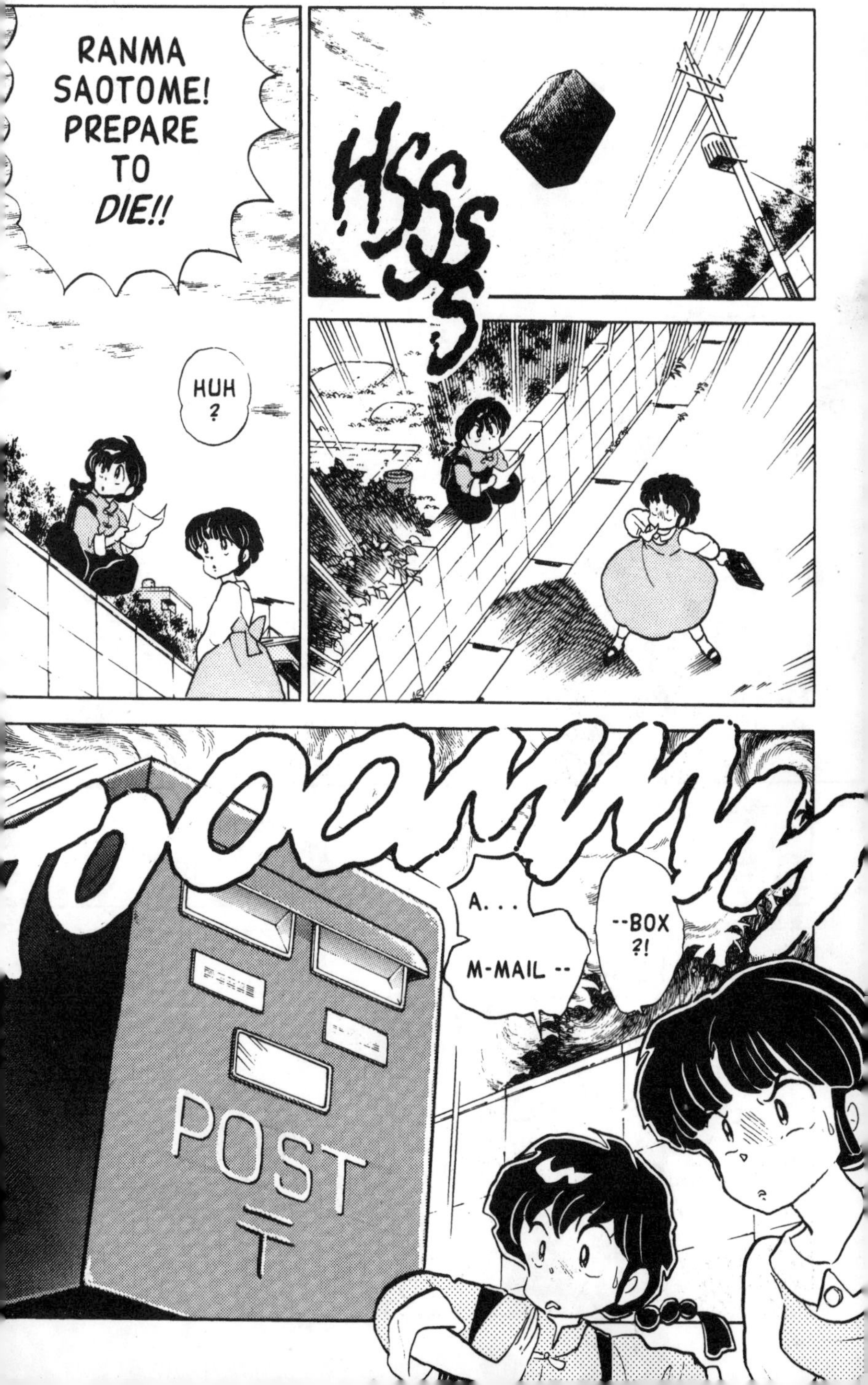
RANMA SAOTOME! PREPARE TO *DIE!!*
HUH ?
HSSSS
A. . . M-MAIL --
--BOX ?!
POST
〒

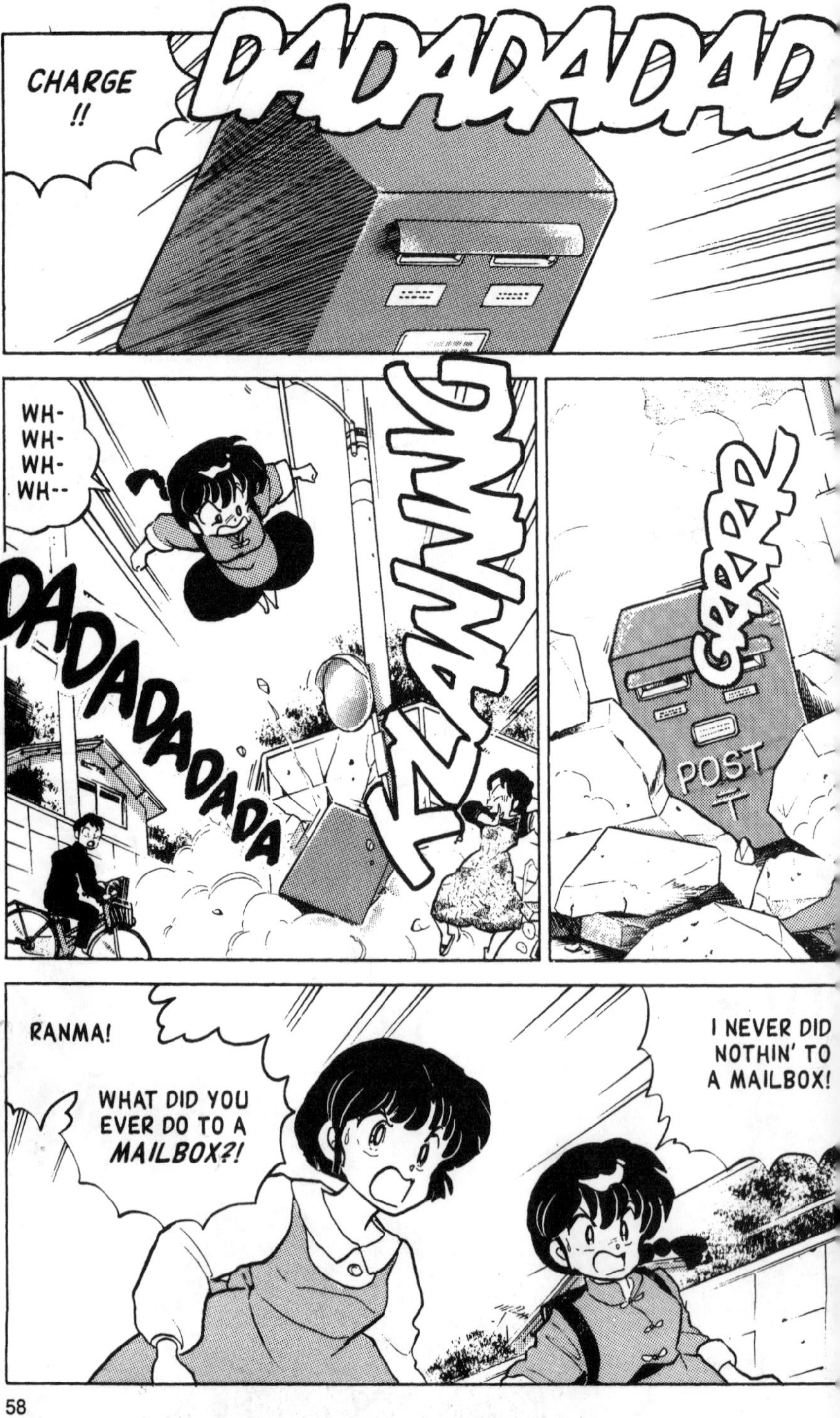
CHARGE !!
DADADADADAD
WH- WH- WH- WH--
DADADADADADA
KZANNNG
GRRRRR
POST 〒
RANMA!
WHAT DID YOU EVER DO TO A MAILBOX?!
I NEVER DID NOTHIN' TO A MAILBOX!

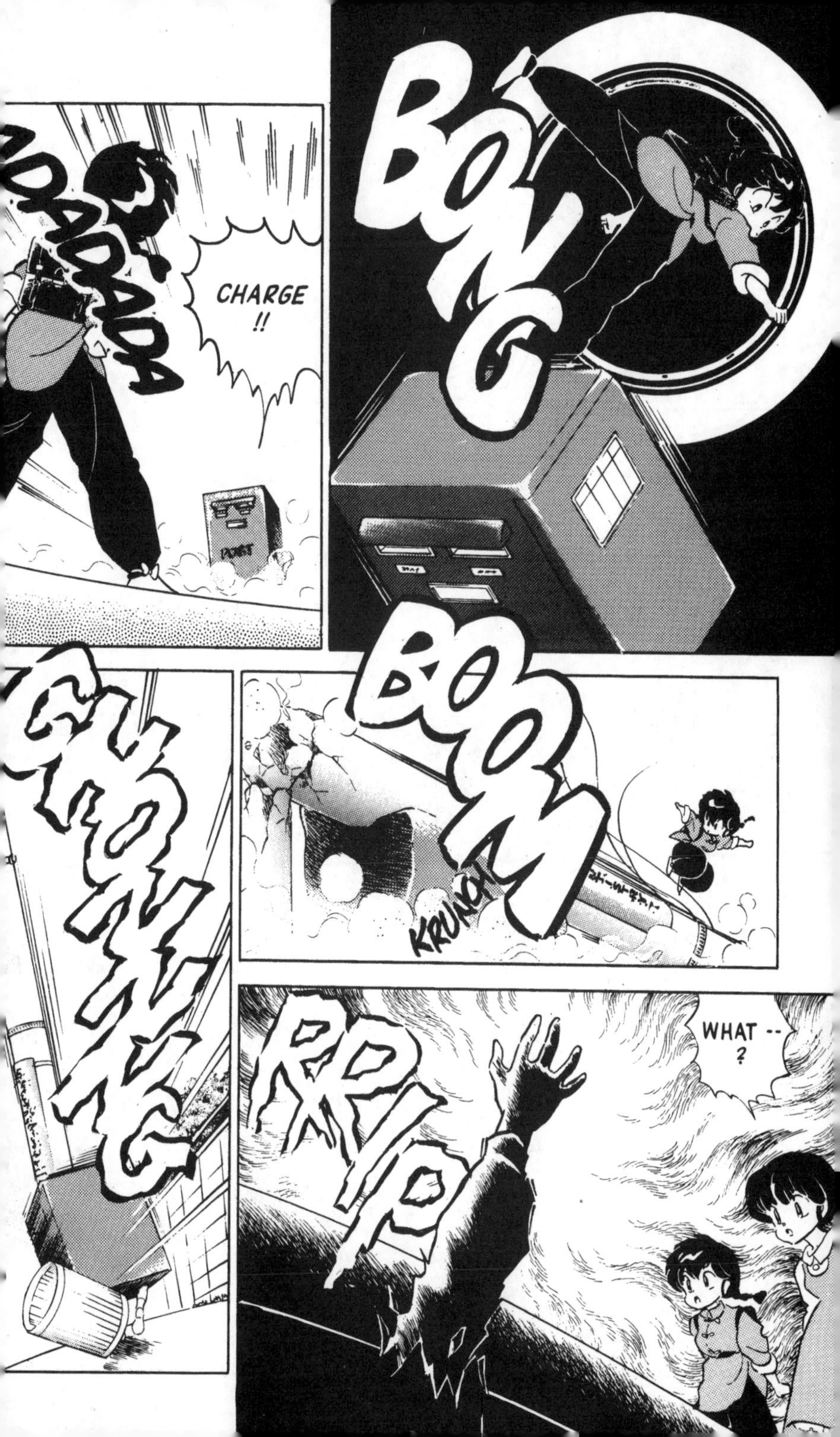
CHARGE !!
BOING
BOOM
KRUNCH
RRIP
WHAT -- ?

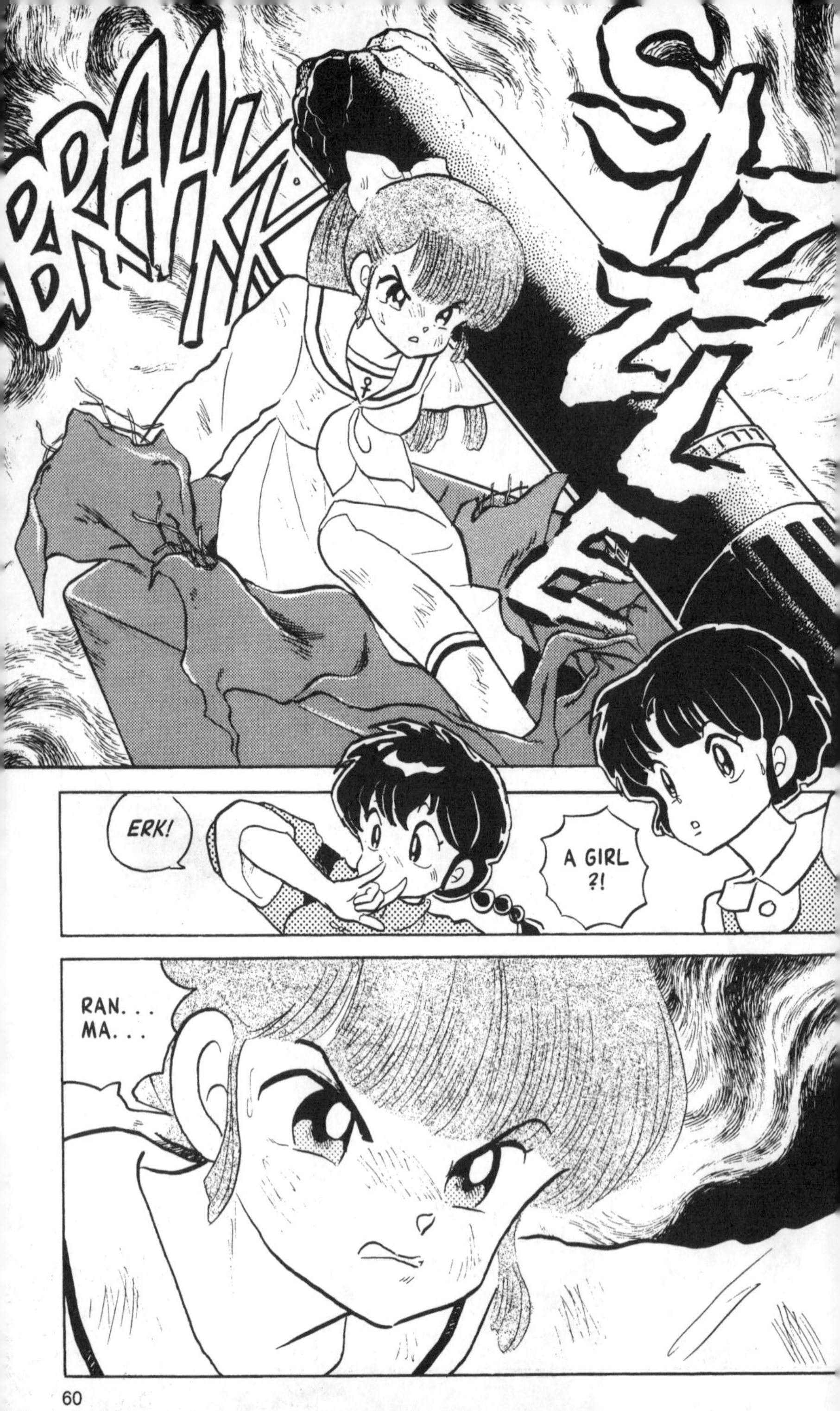

ERK!
A GIRL ?!
RAN. . .
MA. . .

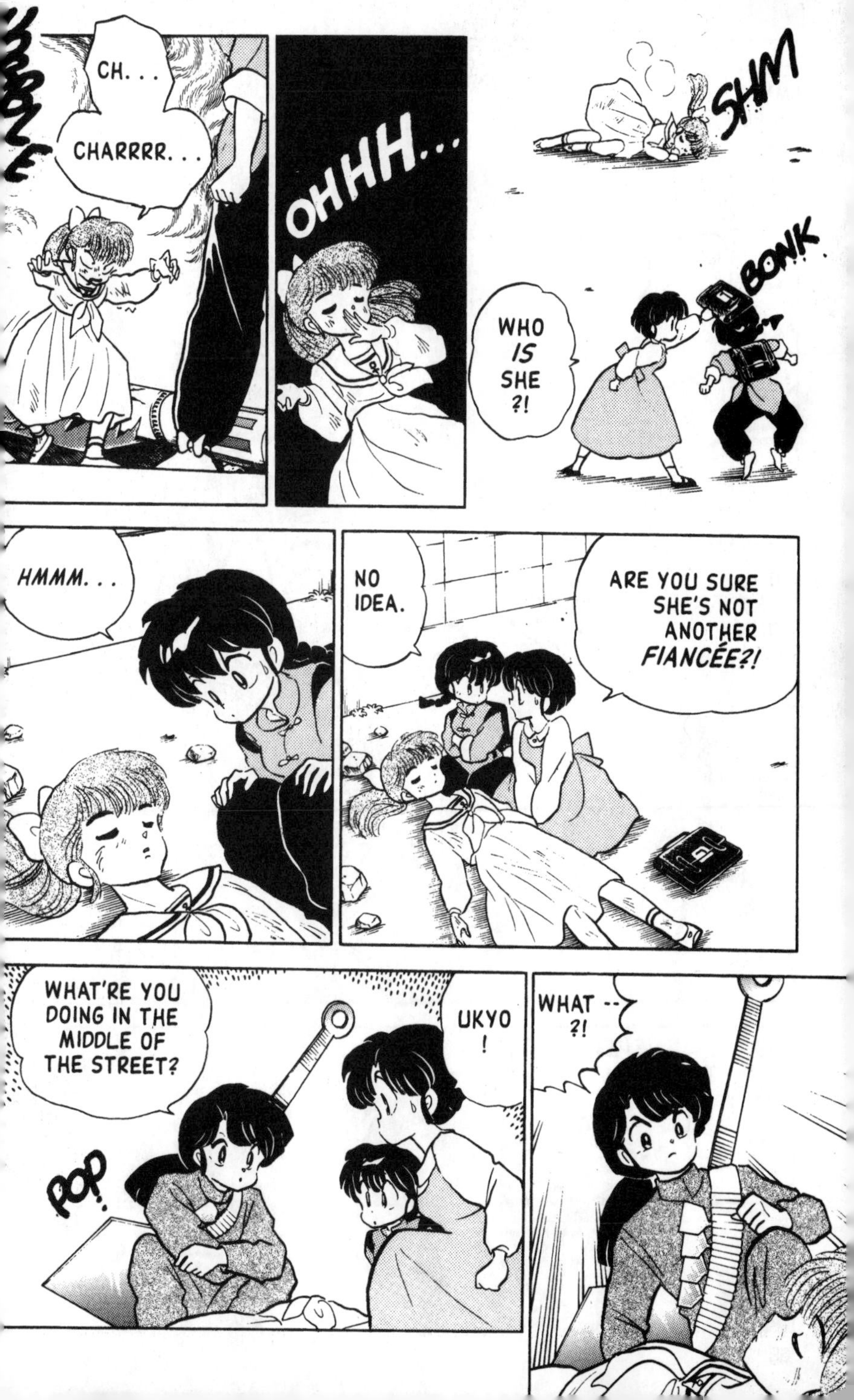
CH. . .
CHARRRR. . .
OHHH. . .
SHM
WHO IS SHE ?!
BONK
HMMM. . .
NO IDEA.
ARE YOU SURE SHE'S NOT ANOTHER FIANCÉE?!
WHAT'RE YOU DOING IN THE MIDDLE OF THE STREET?
POP
UKYO !
WHAT -- ?!

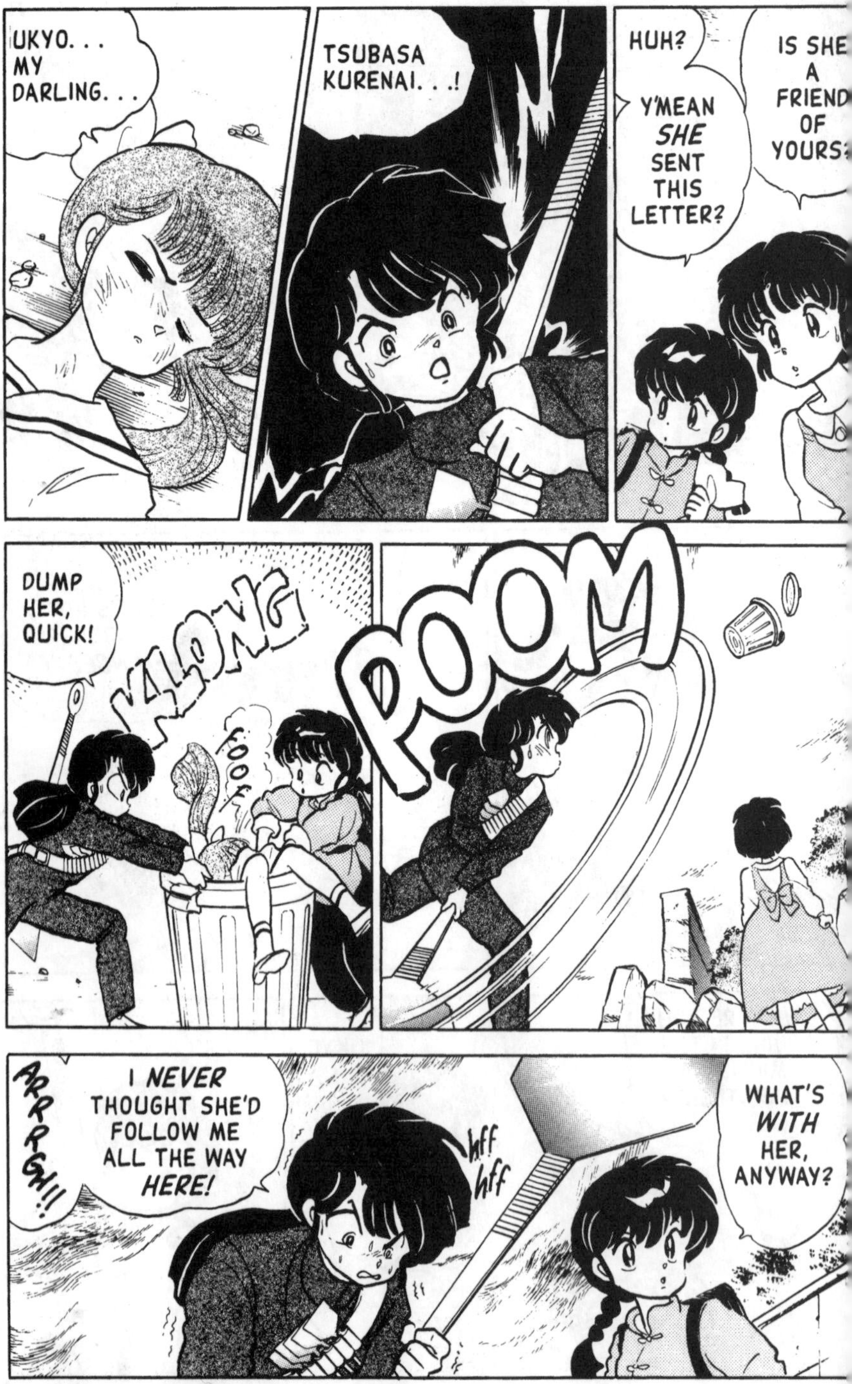
UKYO. . . MY DARLING. . .
TSUBASA KURENAI. . .!
HUH?
Y'MEAN SHE SENT THIS LETTER?
IS SHE A FRIEND OF YOURS?
DUMP HER, QUICK!
KLLONG
FOOF
POOM
ARRRGH!!!
I NEVER THOUGHT SHE'D FOLLOW ME ALL THE WAY HERE!
hff hff
WHAT'S WITH HER, ANYWAY?

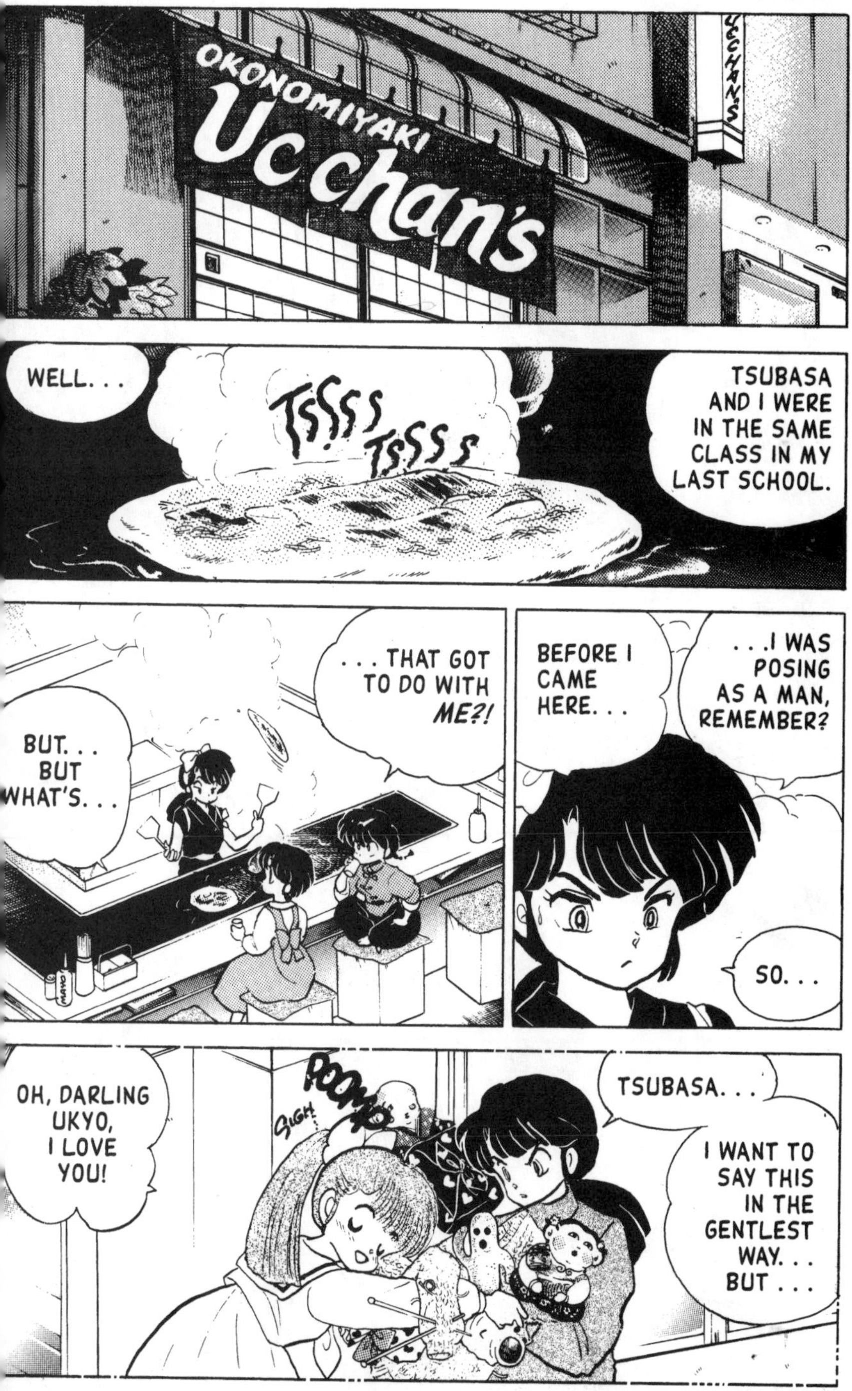
OKONOMIYAKI
Ucchan's
UCCHAN'S
WELL. . .
TSSSS TSSSS
TSUBASA AND I WERE IN THE SAME CLASS IN MY LAST SCHOOL.
BUT. . . BUT WHAT'S. . .
. . . THAT GOT TO DO WITH ME?!
BEFORE I CAME HERE. . .
. . .I WAS POSING AS A MAN, REMEMBER?
SO. . .
OH, DARLING UKYO, I LOVE YOU!
POOMP
SIGH. . .
TSUBASA. . .
I WANT TO SAY THIS IN THE GENTLEST WAY. . . BUT . . .

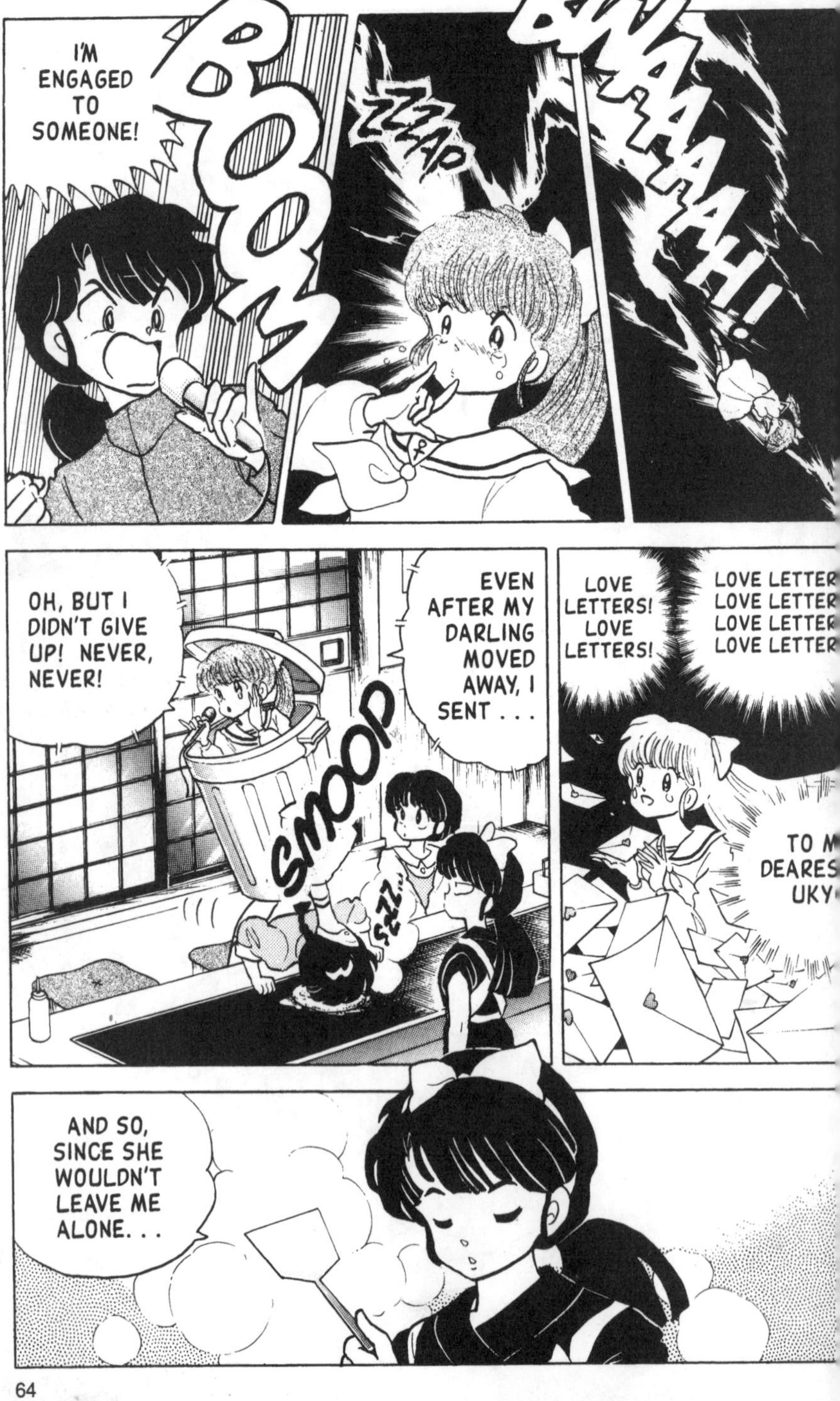
I'M ENGAGED TO SOMEONE!
BOOM
ZZZAP
BWAAAAAH!!
OH, BUT I DIDN'T GIVE UP! NEVER, NEVER!
EVEN AFTER MY DARLING MOVED AWAY, I SENT . . .
SMOOP
ZZZ..
LOVE LETTERS! LOVE LETTERS!
LOVE LETTER
LOVE LETTER
LOVE LETTER
LOVE LETTER
TO M
DEARES
UKY
AND SO, SINCE SHE WOULDN'T LEAVE ME ALONE. . .

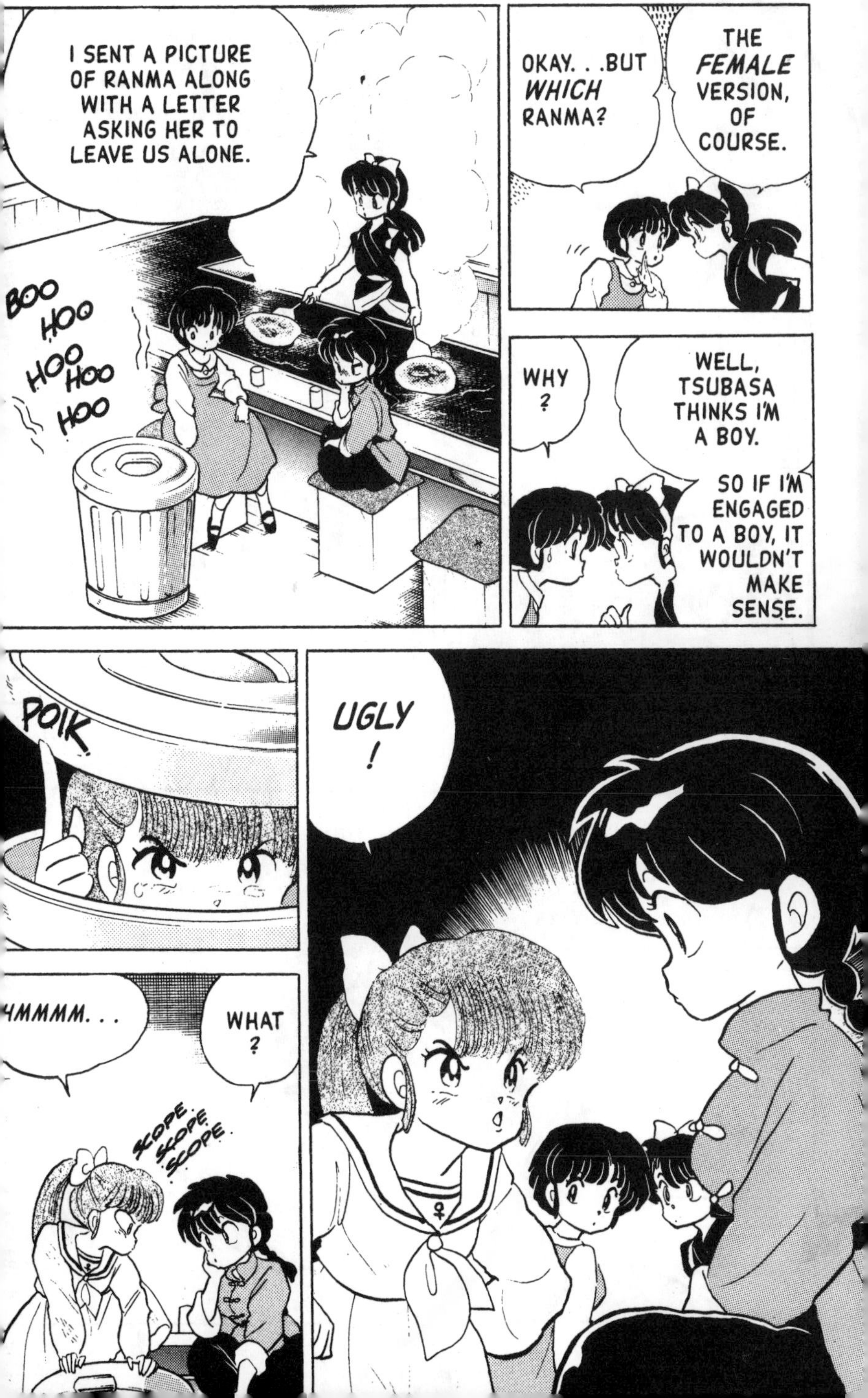
I SENT A PICTURE OF RANMA ALONG WITH A LETTER ASKING HER TO LEAVE US ALONE.
BOO HOO HOO HOO HOO
OKAY. . .BUT *WHICH* RANMA?
THE *FEMALE* VERSION, OF COURSE.
WHY?
WELL, TSUBASA THINKS I'M A BOY.
SO IF I'M ENGAGED TO A BOY, IT WOULDN'T MAKE SENSE.
POIK
HMMMM. . .
WHAT?
SCOPE SCOPE SCOPE
UGLY!

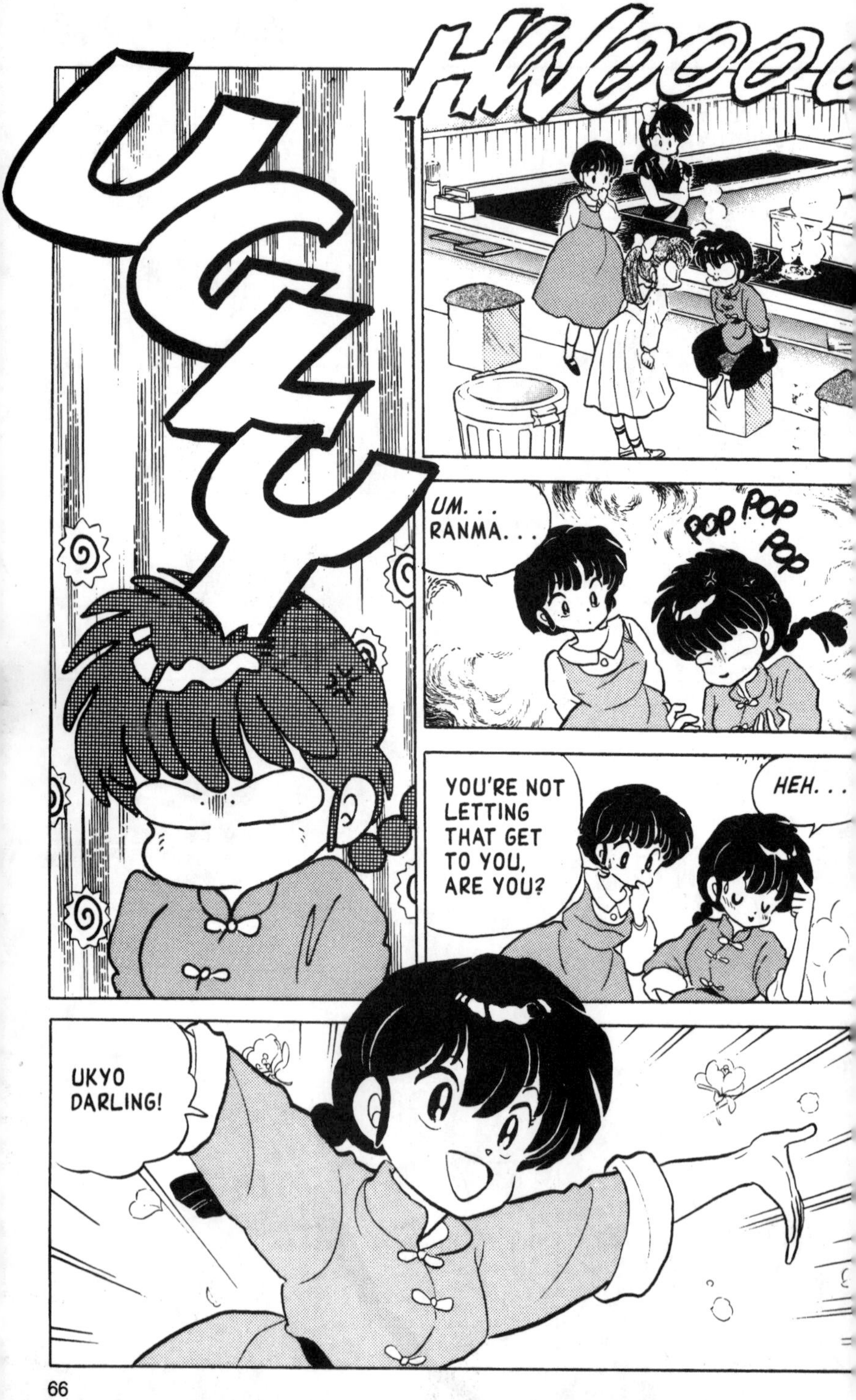
UGHH
HWOOO
UM... RANMA...
POP POP POP
YOU'RE NOT LETTING THAT GET TO YOU, ARE YOU?
HEH...
UKYO DARLING!

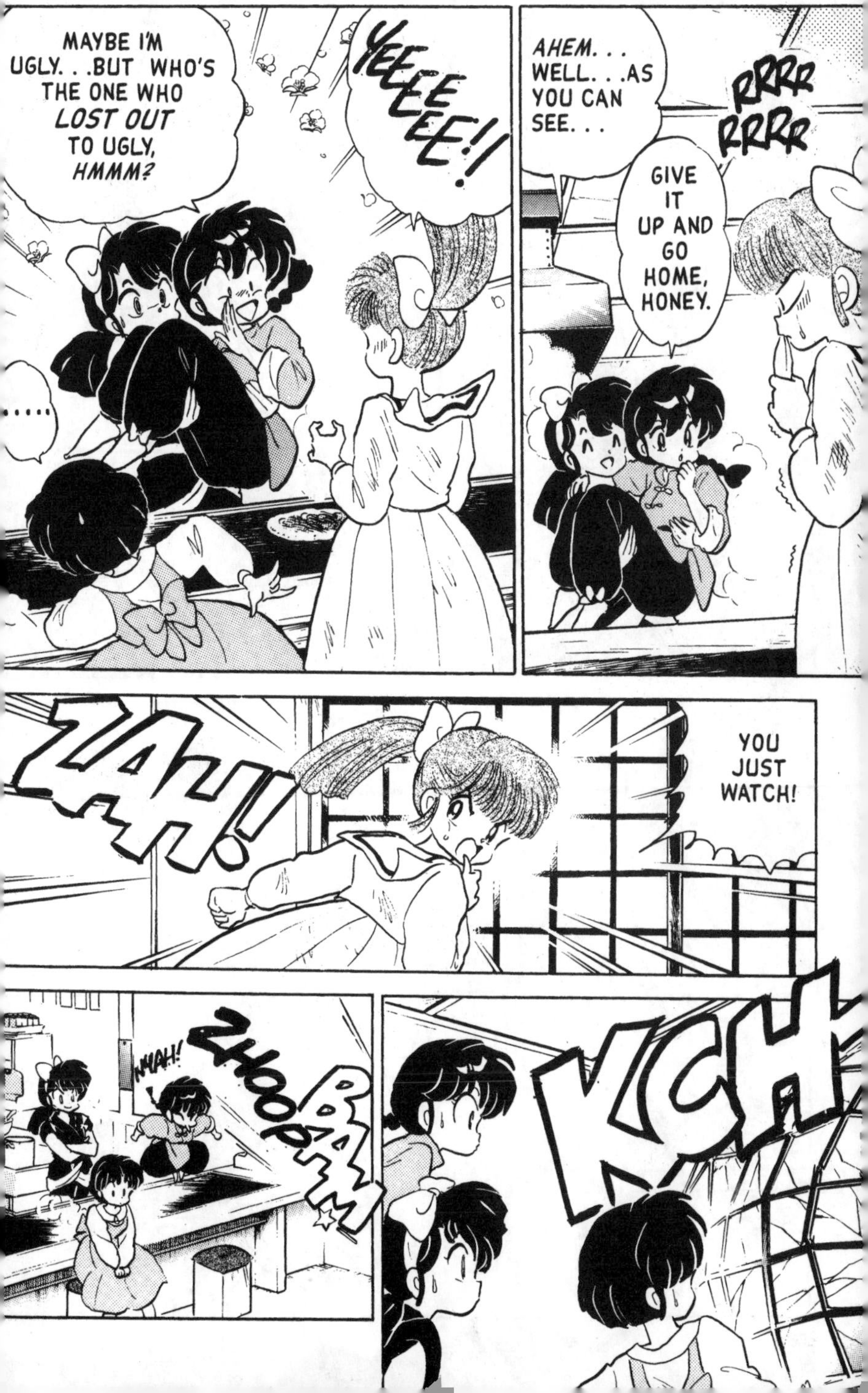

MAYBE I'M UGLY. . .BUT WHO'S THE ONE WHO LOST OUT TO UGLY, HMMM?
YEEEEEEE!!
.....
AHEM. . . WELL. . .AS YOU CAN SEE. . .
RRRR RRRR
GIVE IT UP AND GO HOME, HONEY.
ZAH!
YOU JUST WATCH!
WAAH!
ZHOOP
BAM
KCH

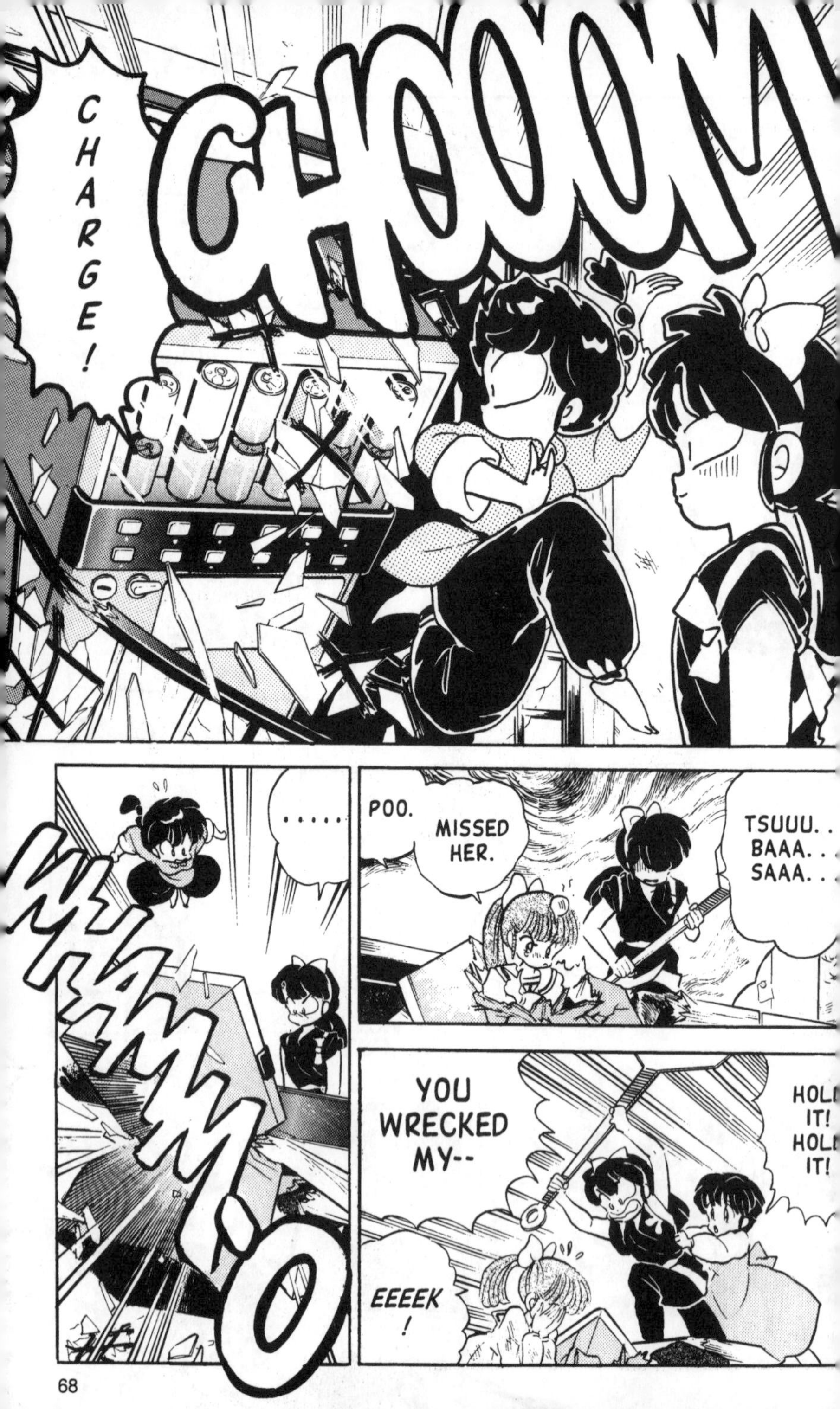

CHARGE!
CHOOOM
WHAMMO
.....
POO.
MISSED HER.
TSUUU... BAAA... SAAA...
YOU WRECKED MY--
HOL IT! HOL IT!
EEEEK!

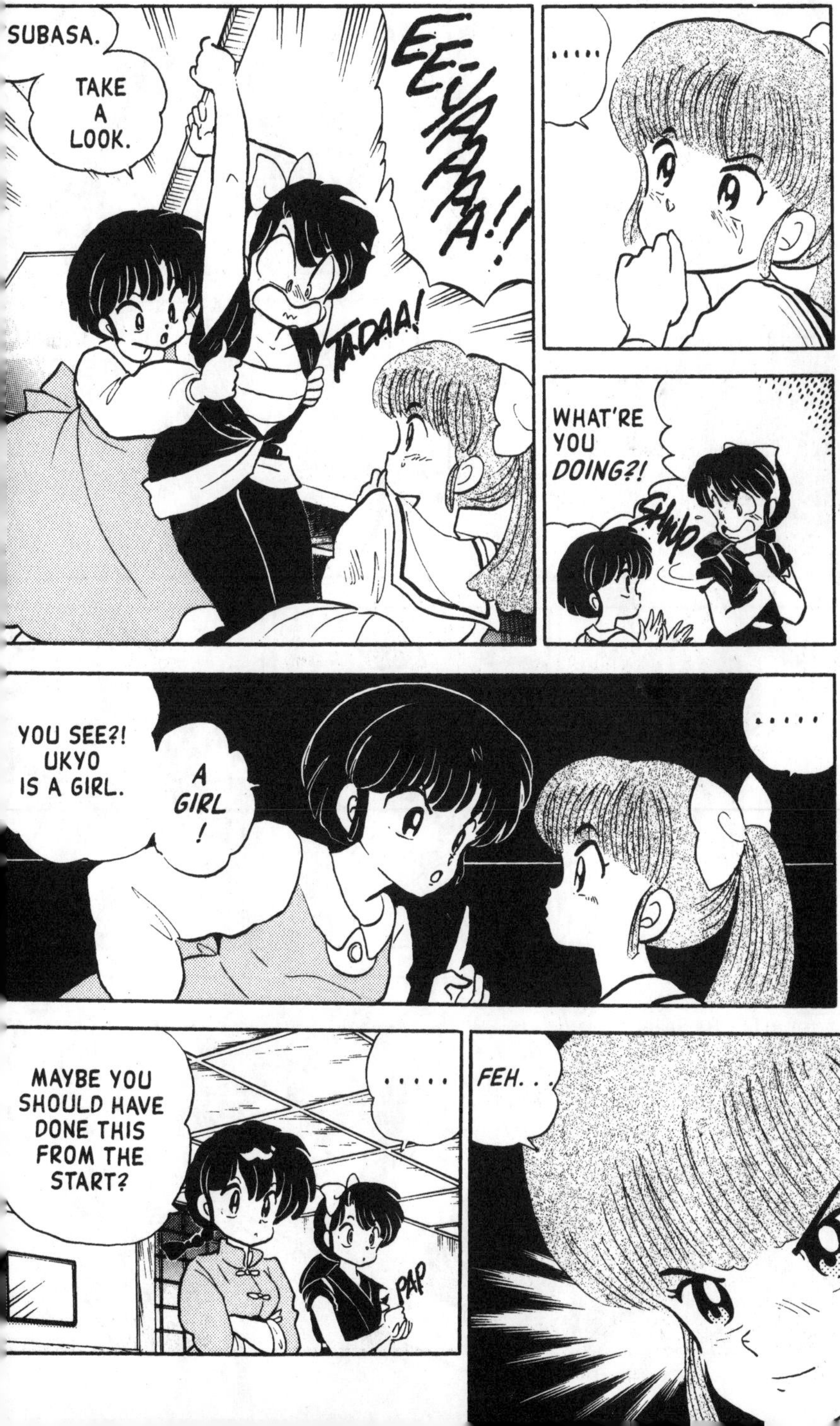
SUBASA.
TAKE A LOOK.
EEYAAAA!!
TADAA!
......
WHAT'RE YOU *DOING?!*
SHWP
YOU SEE?! UKYO IS A GIRL.
A GIRL!
......
MAYBE YOU SHOULD HAVE DONE THIS FROM THE START?
.....
PAP
FEH. . .

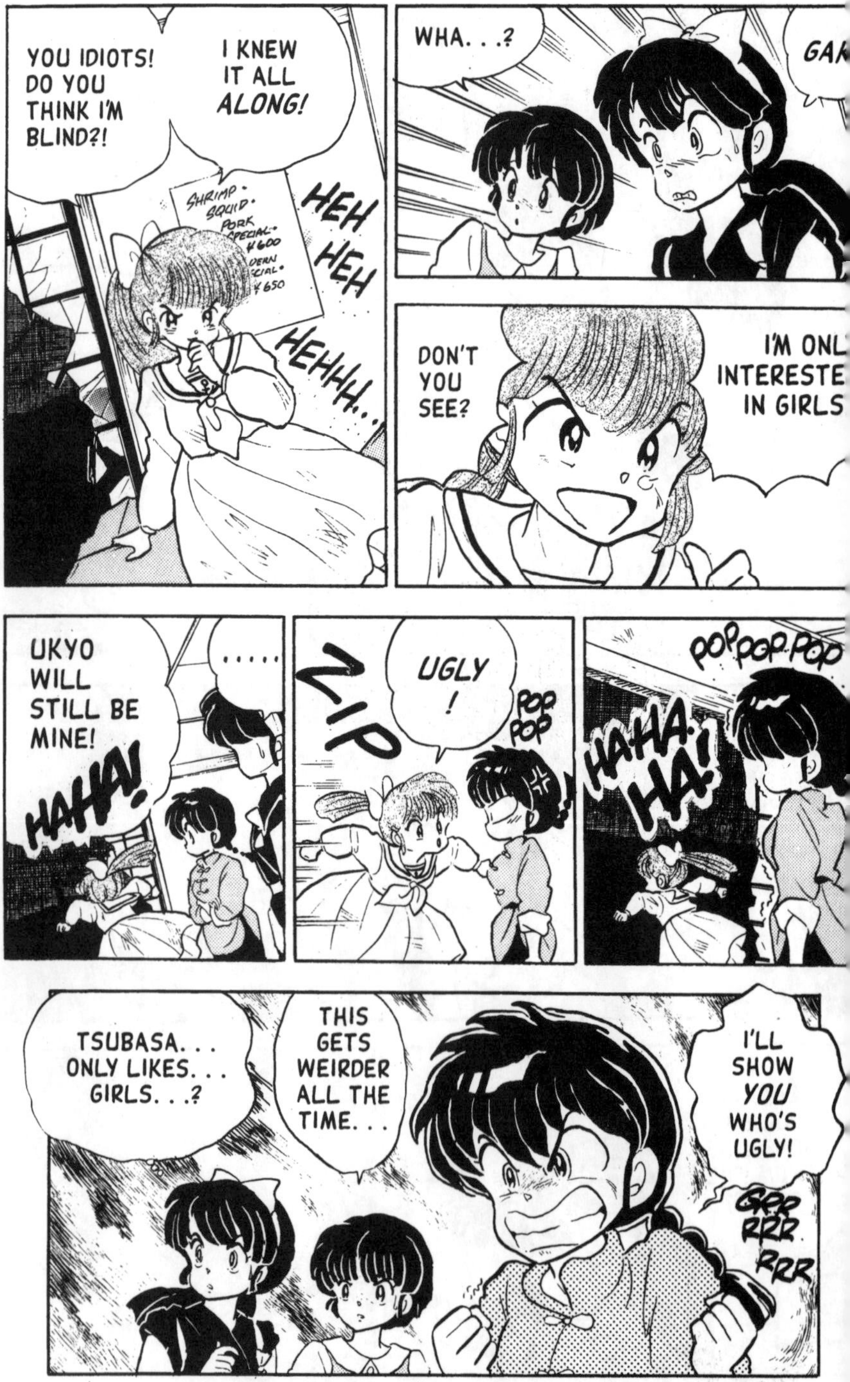
YOU IDIOTS! DO YOU THINK I'M BLIND?!
I KNEW IT ALL *ALONG!*
SHRIMP • SQUID • PORK SPECIAL • ¥600
¥650
HEH HEH HEHHH...
WHA. . .?
DON'T YOU SEE?
I'M ONL INTERESTE IN GIRLS
UKYO WILL STILL BE MINE!
HAHA!
. . . . .
ZIP
UGLY!
POP POP
POP POP POP
HAHA HA!
TSUBASA. . . ONLY LIKES. . . GIRLS. . .?
THIS GETS WEIRDER ALL THE TIME. . .
I'LL SHOW *YOU* WHO'S UGLY!
GRR RRR RRR

PART 5
LUNCHTIME LUNACY

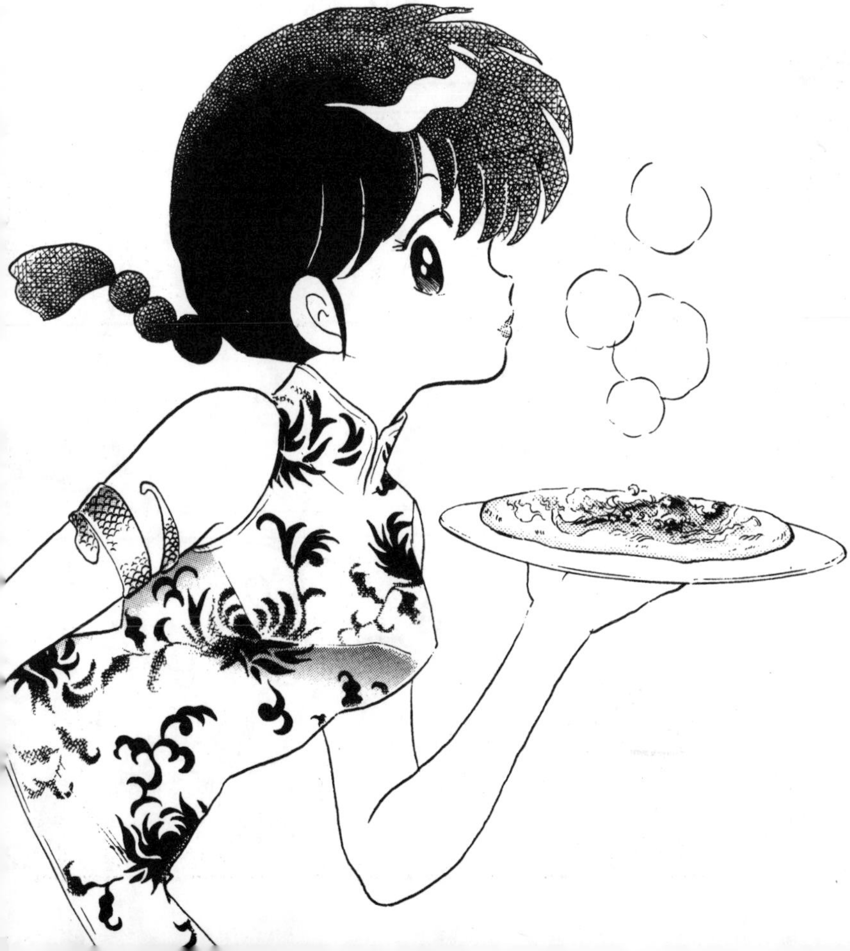

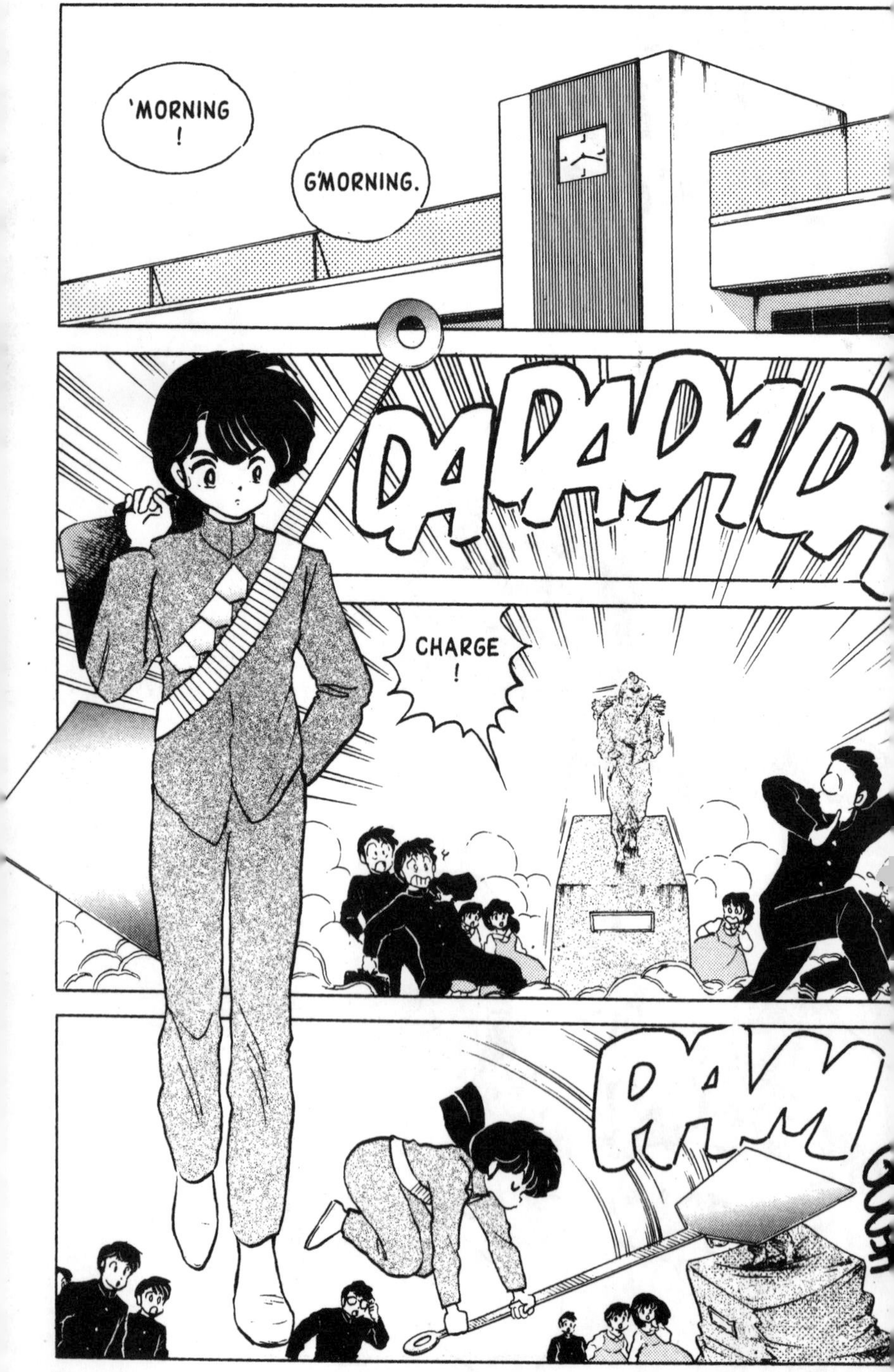
'MORNING !
G'MORNING.
DADADA
CHARGE !
PAM

HUH.

TSUBASA KURENAI...

OH. DEAREST UKYO, HOW COULD YOU?

WHOA! SHE'S CUTE!

TSUBASA-- I THOUGHT I TOLD YOU TO LEAVE ME ALONE.

DRIP

SNF SNF

DON'T YOU GET IT?

I'M ALREADY ENGAGED TO RAN-CHAN!

THAT... *UGLY* GIRL?!

YOU CAN'T BE ENGAGED TO *HER!*

I'VE BEEN TRYING TO TELL YOU, RANMA IS A B--

OHOHO-HOHO-HO, GOOD MORNING.

VUUUPP

OOO. OO. OO!

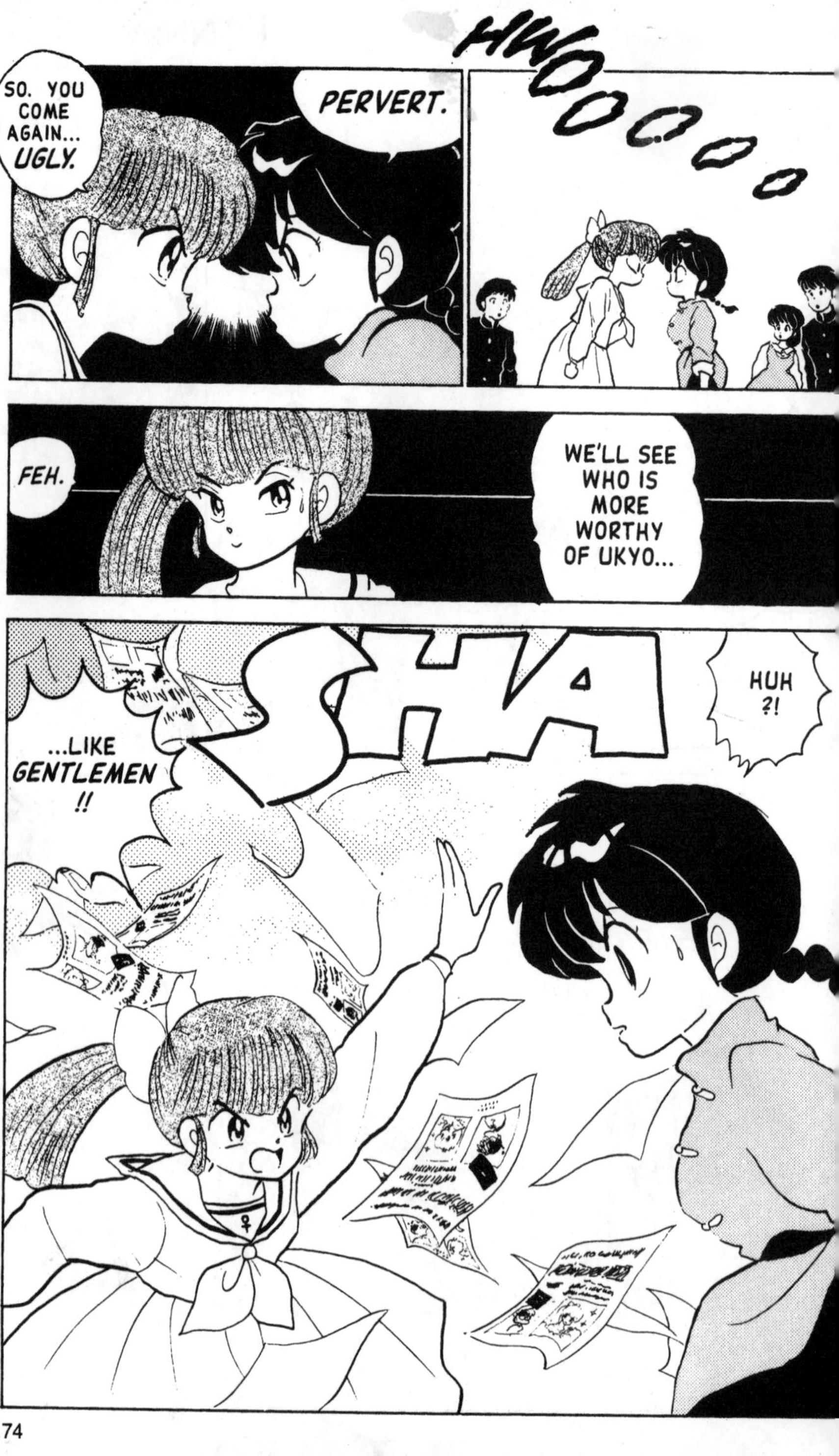
SO. YOU COME AGAIN... UGLY.
PERVERT.
HWOOOOOOO
FEH.
WE'LL SEE WHO IS MORE WORTHY OF UKYO...
...LIKE GENTLEMEN !!
SHA
HUH ?!

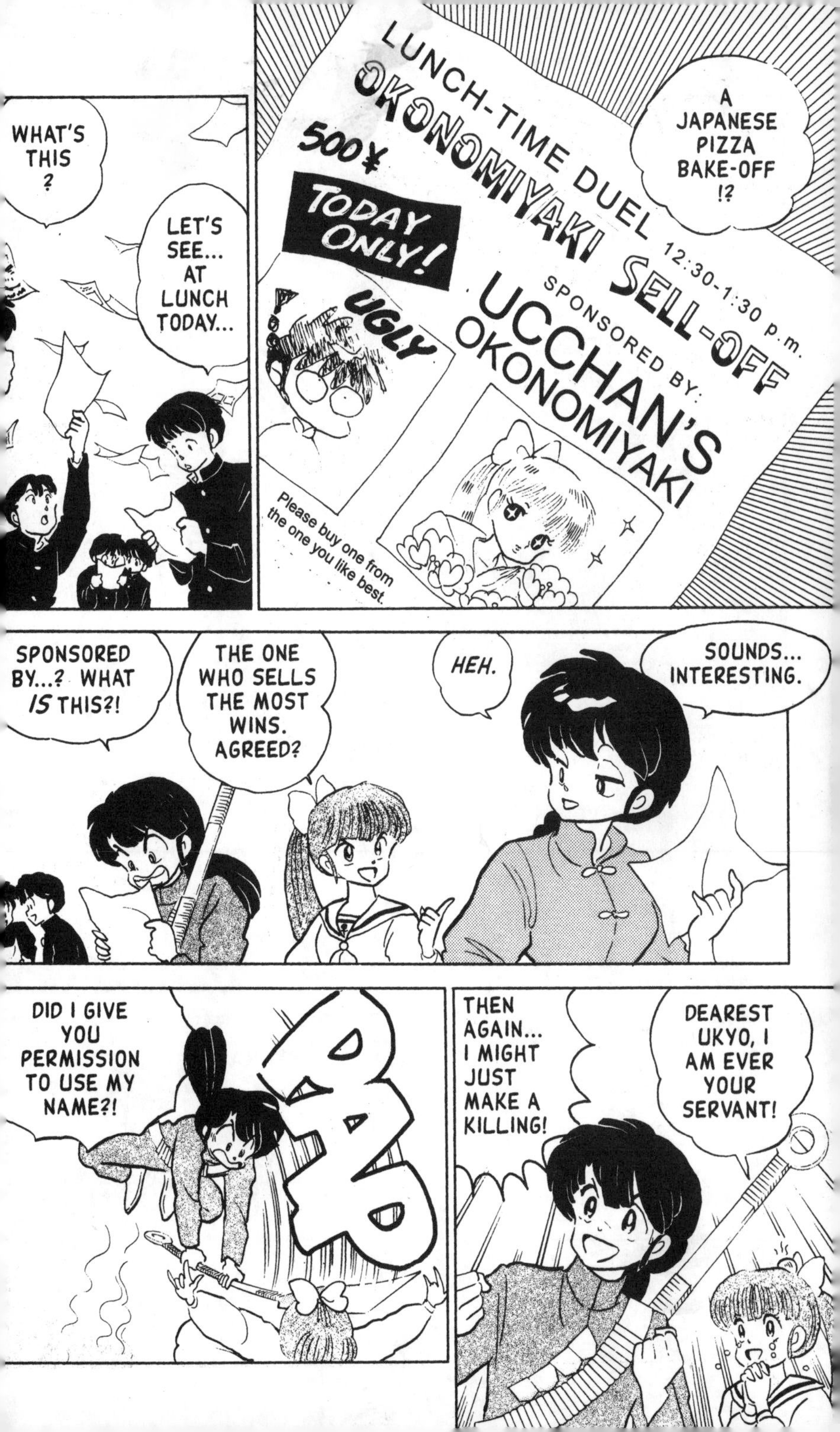
WHAT'S THIS?
LET'S SEE... AT LUNCH TODAY...
LUNCH-TIME DUEL
OKONOMIYAKI SELL-OFF
12:30-1:30 p.m.
500¥
TODAY ONLY!
UGLY
SPONSORED BY:
UCCHAN'S OKONOMIYAKI
Please buy one from the one you like best.
A JAPANESE PIZZA BAKE-OFF!?
SPONSORED BY...? WHAT *IS* THIS?!
THE ONE WHO SELLS THE MOST WINS. AGREED?
HEH.
SOUNDS... INTERESTING.
DID I GIVE YOU PERMISSION TO USE MY NAME?!
BAP
THEN AGAIN... I MIGHT JUST MAKE A KILLING!
DEAREST UKYO, I AM EVER YOUR SERVANT!

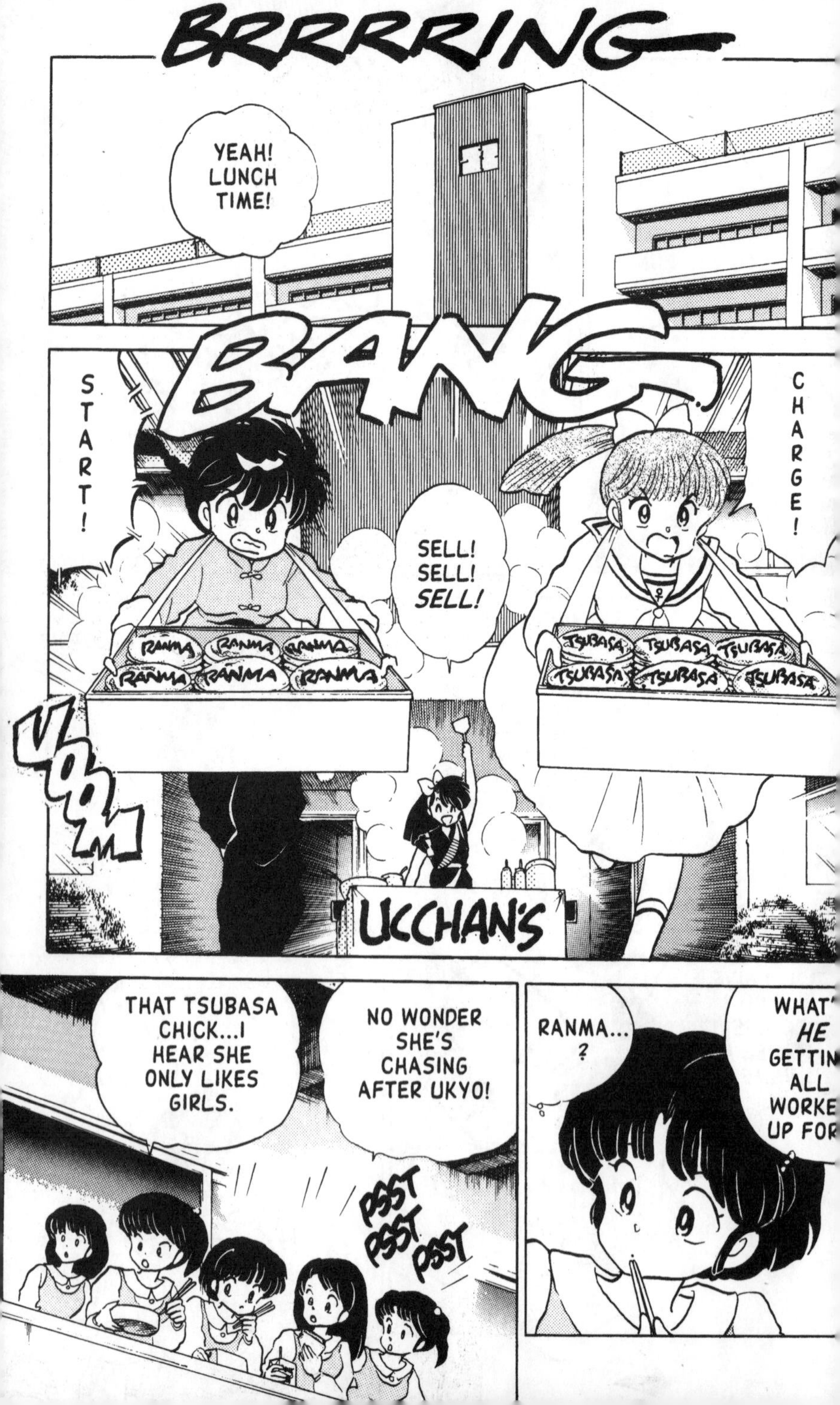
BRRRRING
YEAH! LUNCH TIME!
BANG
START!
SELL! SELL! SELL!
CHARGE!
RANMA RANMA RANMA RANMA RANMA RANMA
TSUBASA TSUBASA TSUBASA TSUBASA TSUBASA TSUBASA
VOOOM
UCCHAN'S
THAT TSUBASA CHICK...I HEAR SHE ONLY LIKES GIRLS.
NO WONDER SHE'S CHASING AFTER UKYO!
PSST PSST PSST
RANMA...?
WHAT' HE GETTIN ALL WORKE UP FOR

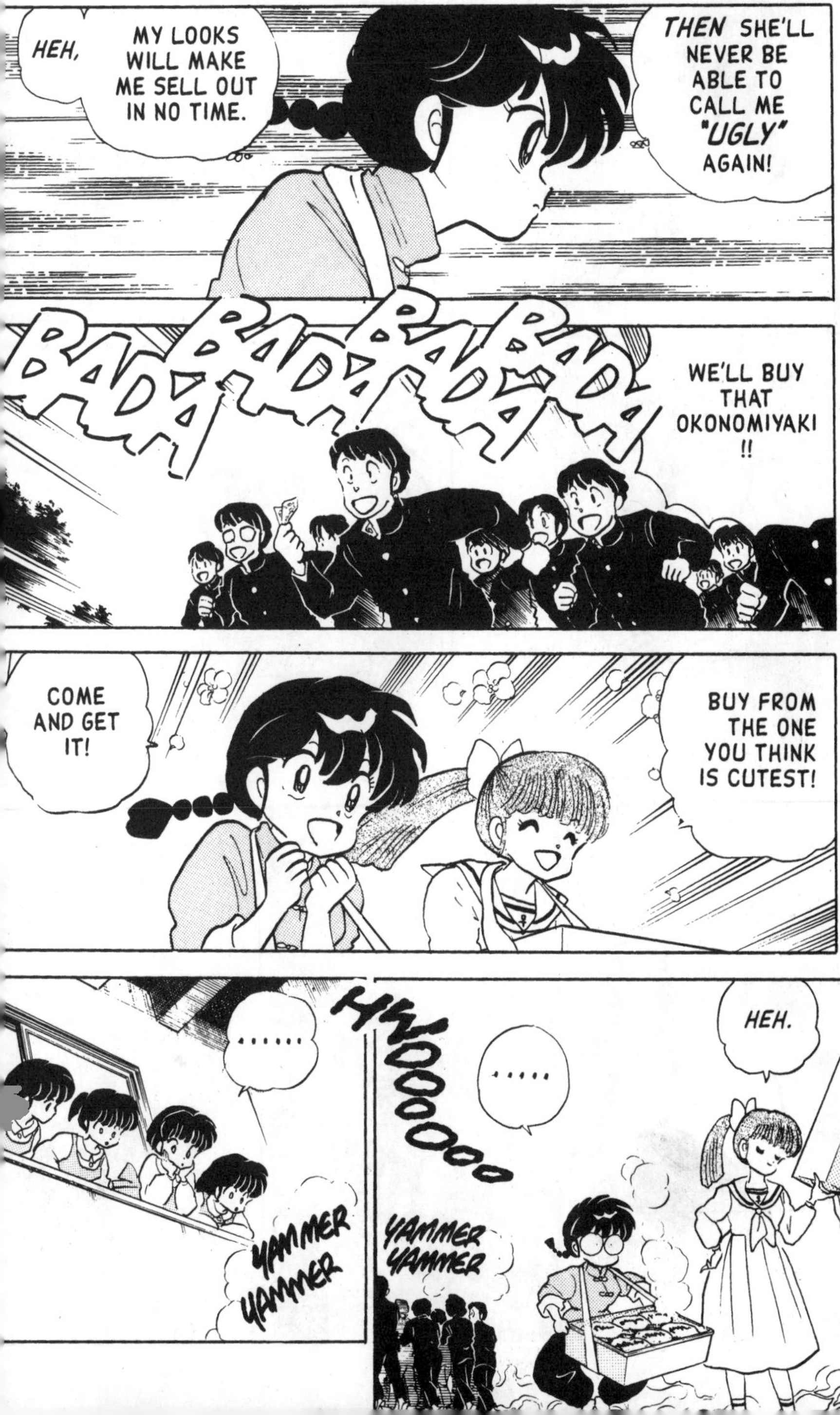
HEH,
MY LOOKS WILL MAKE ME SELL OUT IN NO TIME.
THEN SHE'LL NEVER BE ABLE TO CALL ME "UGLY" AGAIN!
BADA BADA BADA BADA
WE'LL BUY THAT OKONOMIYAKI !!
COME AND GET IT!
BUY FROM THE ONE YOU THINK IS CUTEST!
......
YAMMER YAMMER
HWOOOOOOOO
.....
HEH.
YAMMER YAMMER

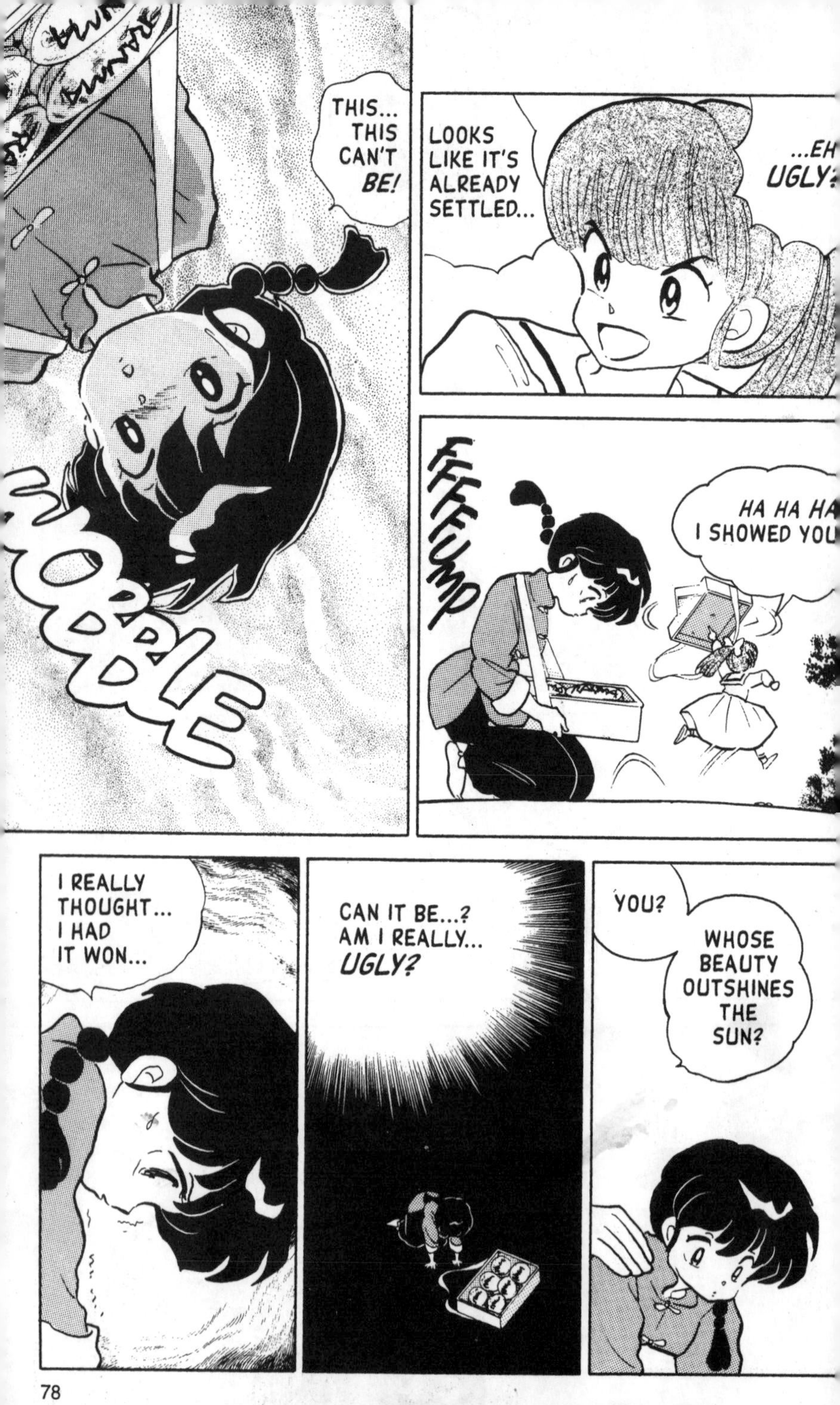

THIS... THIS CAN'T BE!
WOBBLE
LOOKS LIKE IT'S ALREADY SETTLED...
...EH UGLY?
FFFFUMP
HA HA HA I SHOWED YOU
I REALLY THOUGHT... I HAD IT WON...
CAN IT BE...? AM I REALLY... UGLY?
YOU?
WHOSE BEAUTY OUTSHINES THE SUN?

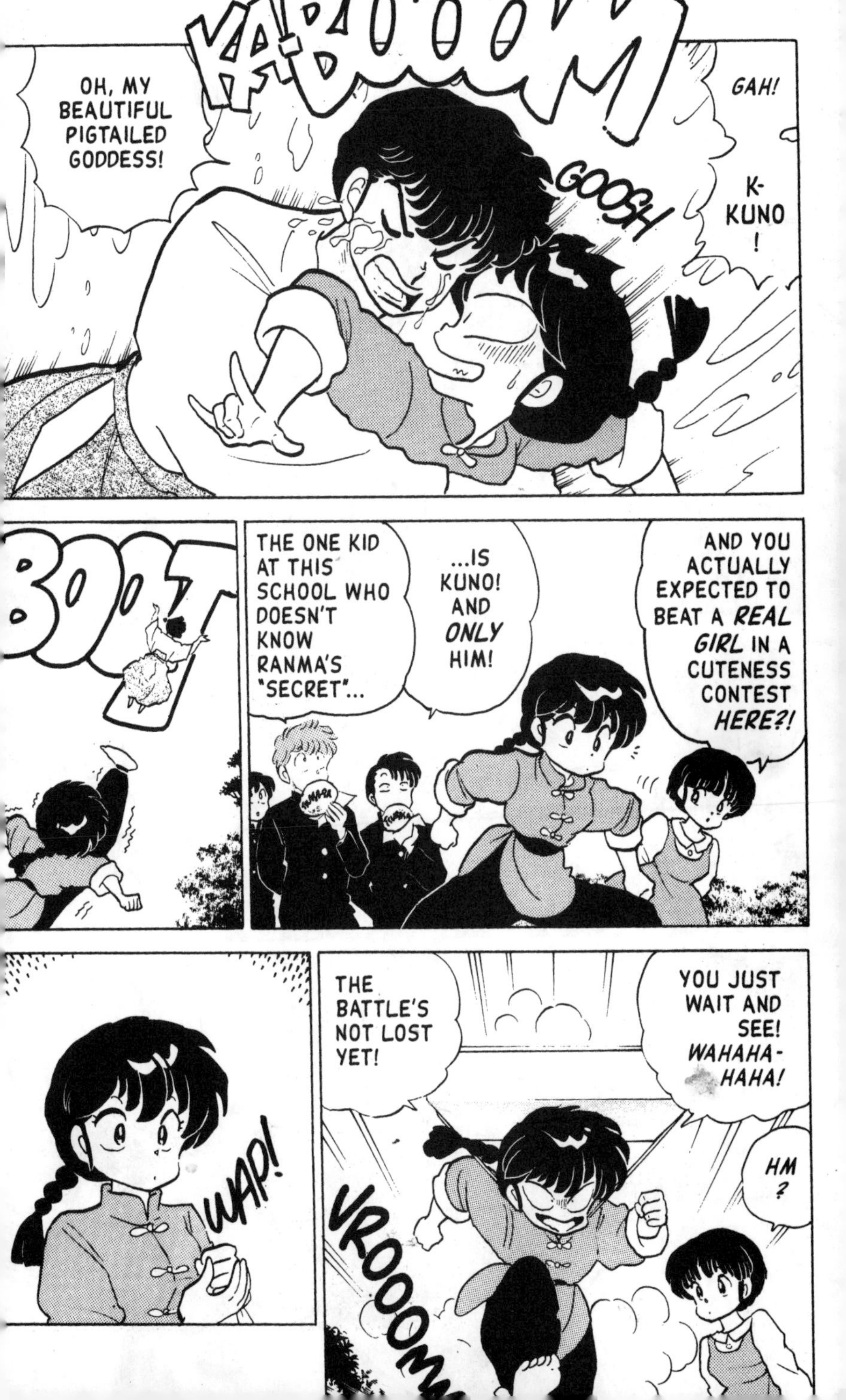
KA-BOOOM
OH, MY BEAUTIFUL PIGTAILED GODDESS!
GOOSH
GAH!
K-KUNO!
BOOT
THE ONE KID AT THIS SCHOOL WHO DOESN'T KNOW RANMA'S "SECRET"...
...IS KUNO! AND *ONLY* HIM!
AND YOU ACTUALLY EXPECTED TO BEAT A *REAL GIRL* IN A CUTENESS CONTEST *HERE?!*
WAP!
THE BATTLE'S NOT LOST YET!
YOU JUST WAIT AND SEE! *WAHAHA-HAHA!*
HM?
VROOOOM

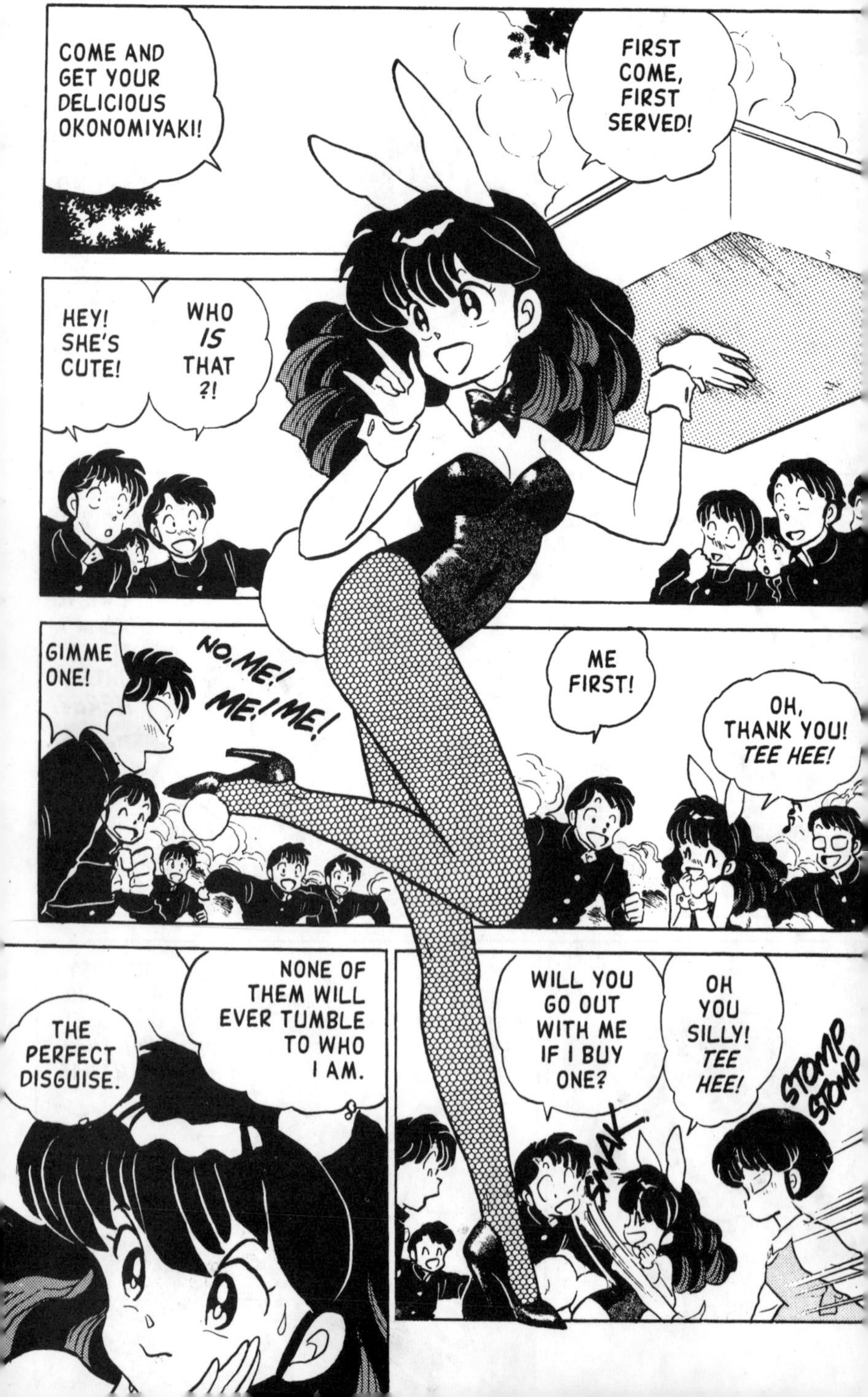
COME AND GET YOUR DELICIOUS OKONOMIYAKI!
FIRST COME, FIRST SERVED!
HEY! SHE'S CUTE!
WHO *IS* THAT ?!
GIMME ONE!
NO, ME! ME! ME!
ME FIRST!
OH, THANK YOU! *TEE HEE!*
THE PERFECT DISGUISE.
NONE OF THEM WILL EVER TUMBLE TO WHO I AM.
WILL YOU GO OUT WITH ME IF I BUY ONE?
SMAK
OH YOU SILLY! *TEE HEE!*
STOMP STOMP

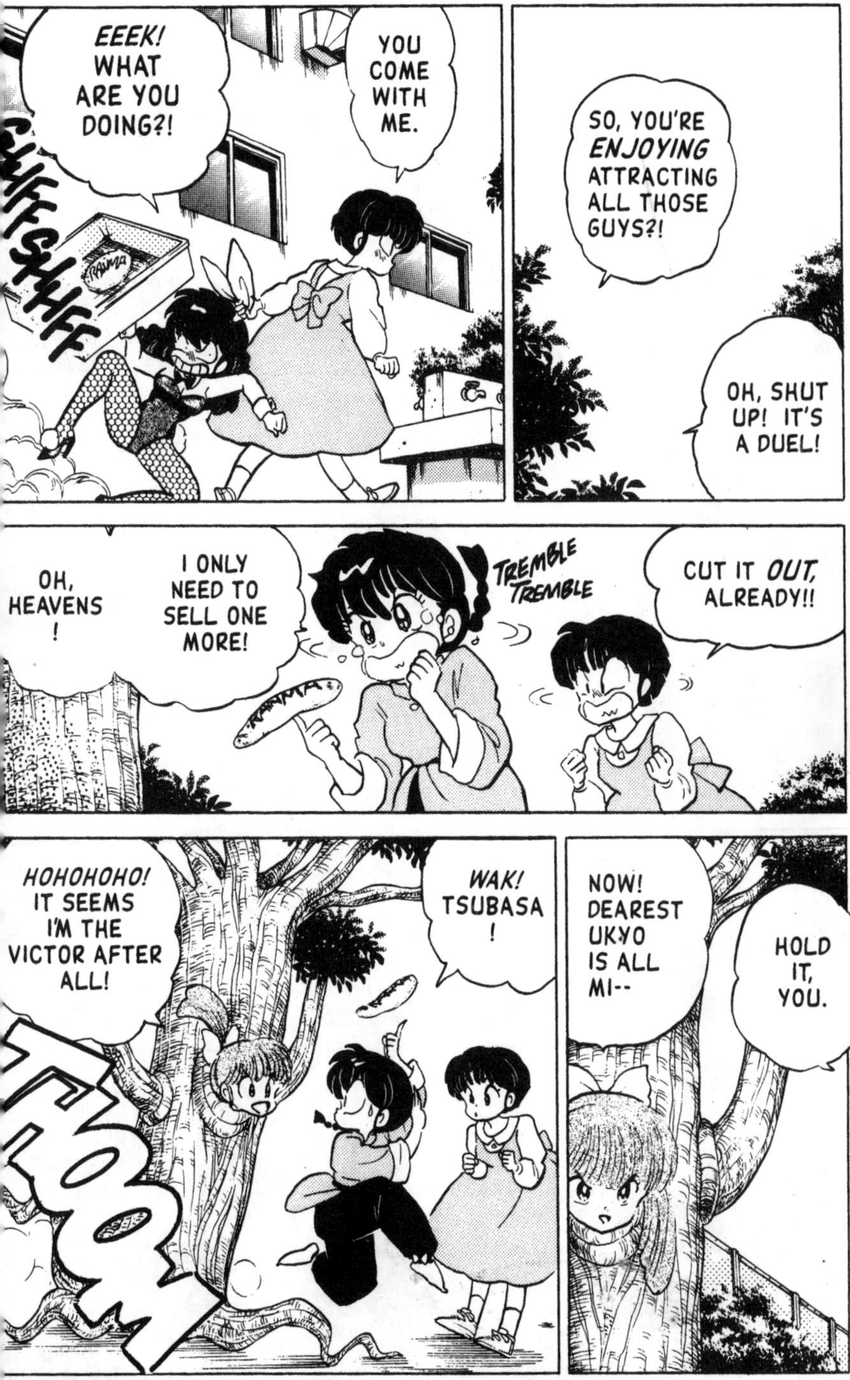
EEEK! WHAT ARE YOU DOING?!
YOU COME WITH ME.
SO, YOU'RE ENJOYING ATTRACTING ALL THOSE GUYS?!
OH, SHUT UP! IT'S A DUEL!
OH, HEAVENS!
I ONLY NEED TO SELL ONE MORE!
TREMBLE TREMBLE
CUT IT OUT, ALREADY!!
HOHOHOHO! IT SEEMS I'M THE VICTOR AFTER ALL!
WAK! TSUBASA!
NOW! DEAREST UKYO IS ALL MI--
HOLD IT, YOU.

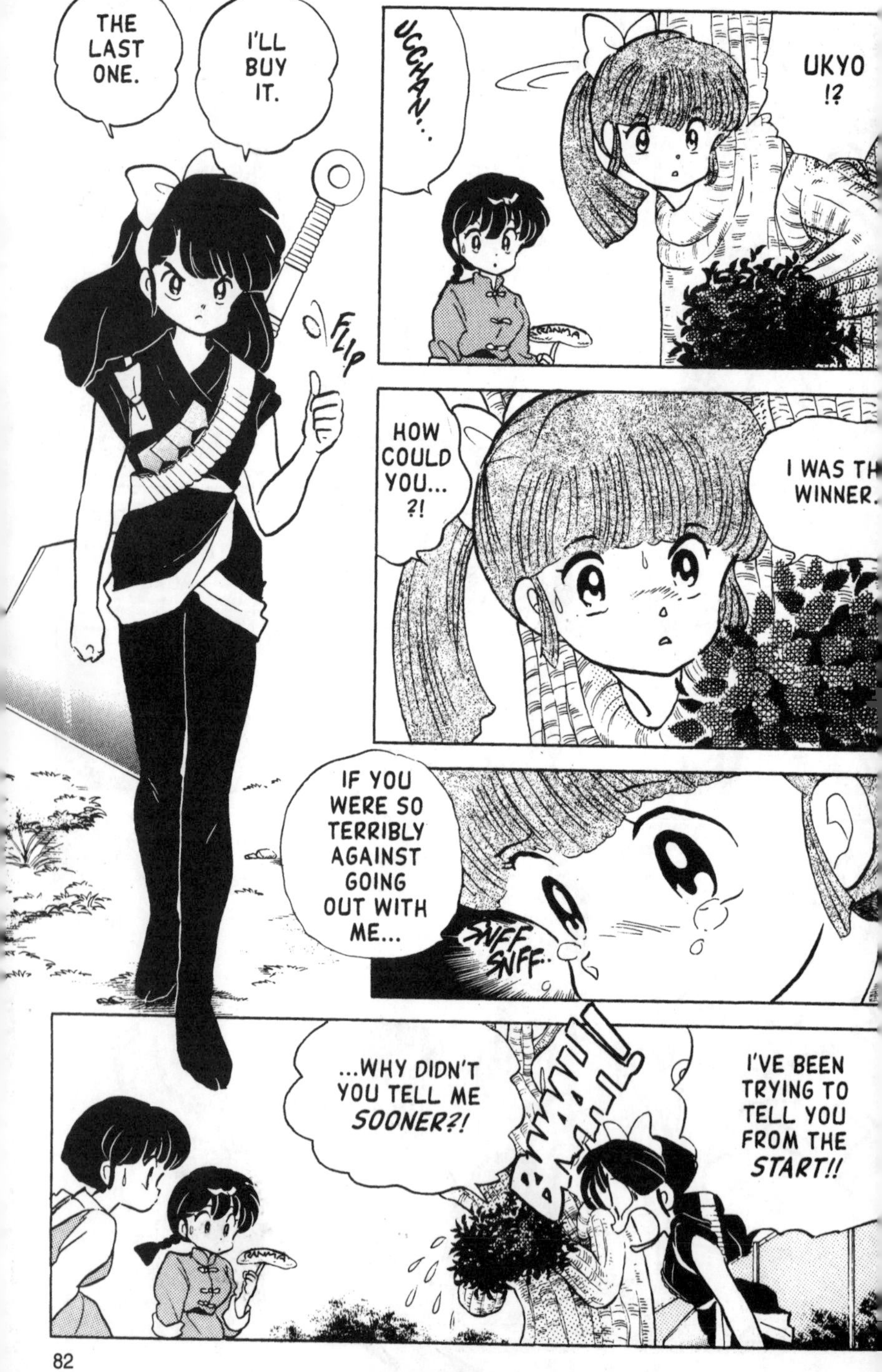
THE LAST ONE.
I'LL BUY IT.
FLIP
UCCHAN...
UKYO !?
RANMA
HOW COULD YOU... ?!
I WAS TH WINNER.
IF YOU WERE SO TERRIBLY AGAINST GOING OUT WITH ME...
SNIFF SNIFF
...WHY DIDN'T YOU TELL ME *SOONER?!*
I'VE BEEN TRYING TO TELL YOU FROM THE *START!!*
RANMA

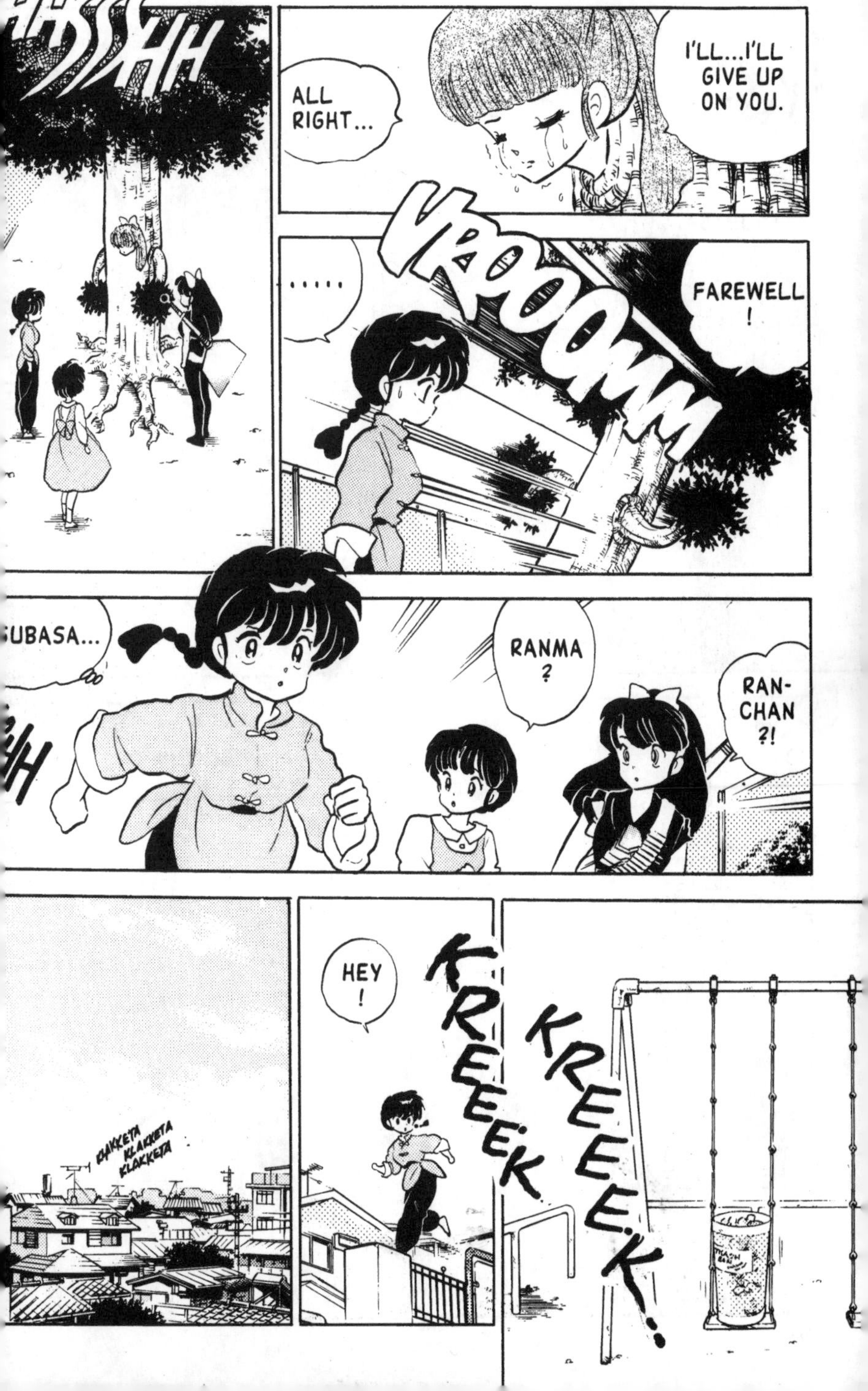
HHSSHH
ALL RIGHT...
I'LL...I'LL GIVE UP ON YOU.
.....
VROOOMM
FAREWELL!
UBASA...
RANMA?
RAN-CHAN?!
KLAKKETA KLAKKETA KLAKKETA
HEY!
KREEEEK...
KREEEEK...

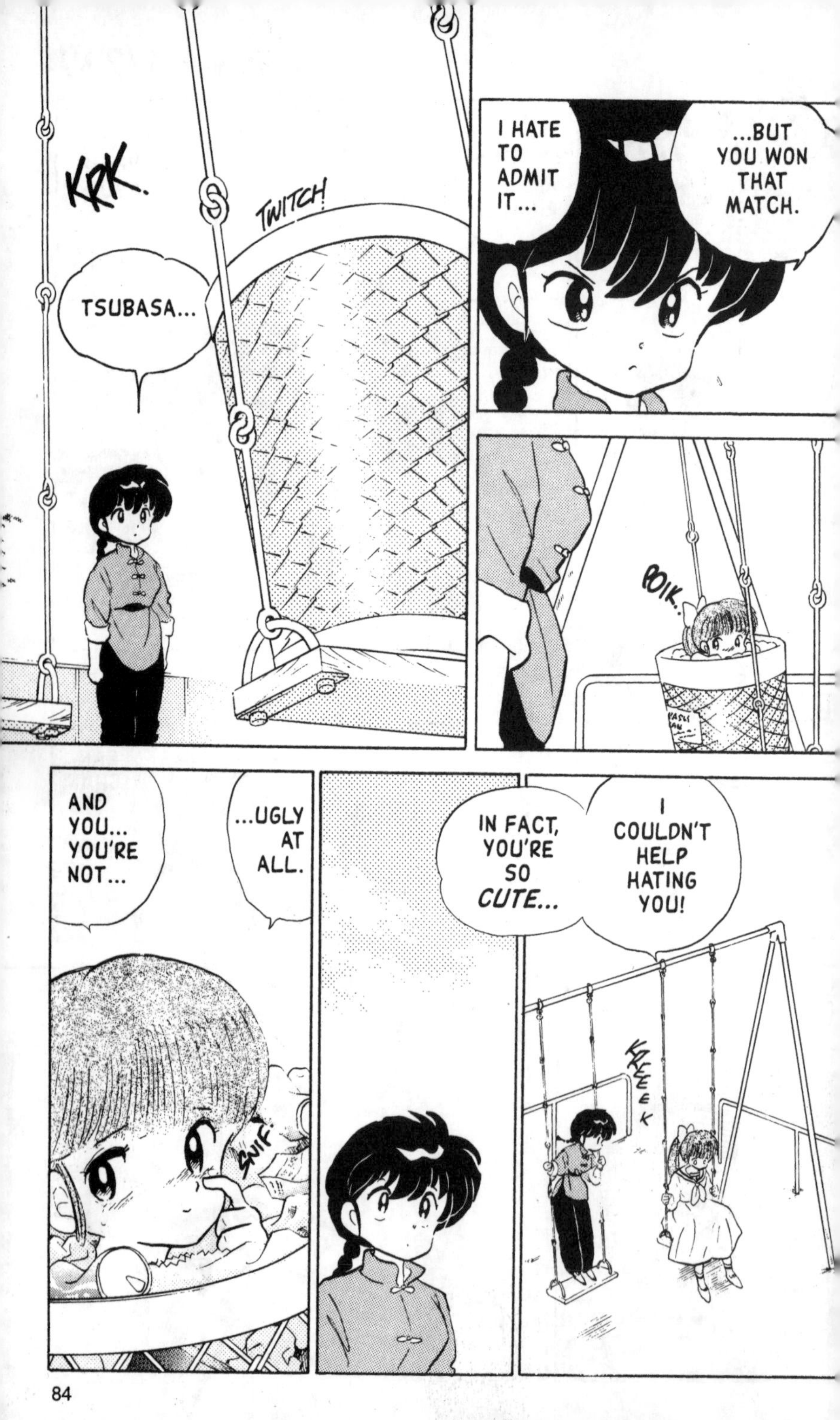
KRK.
TSUBASA...
TWITCH!
I HATE TO ADMIT IT...
...BUT YOU WON THAT MATCH.
BOIK...
AND YOU... YOU'RE NOT...
...UGLY AT ALL.
SNIF
IN FACT, YOU'RE SO CUTE...
I COULDN'T HELP HATING YOU!
KREEEK

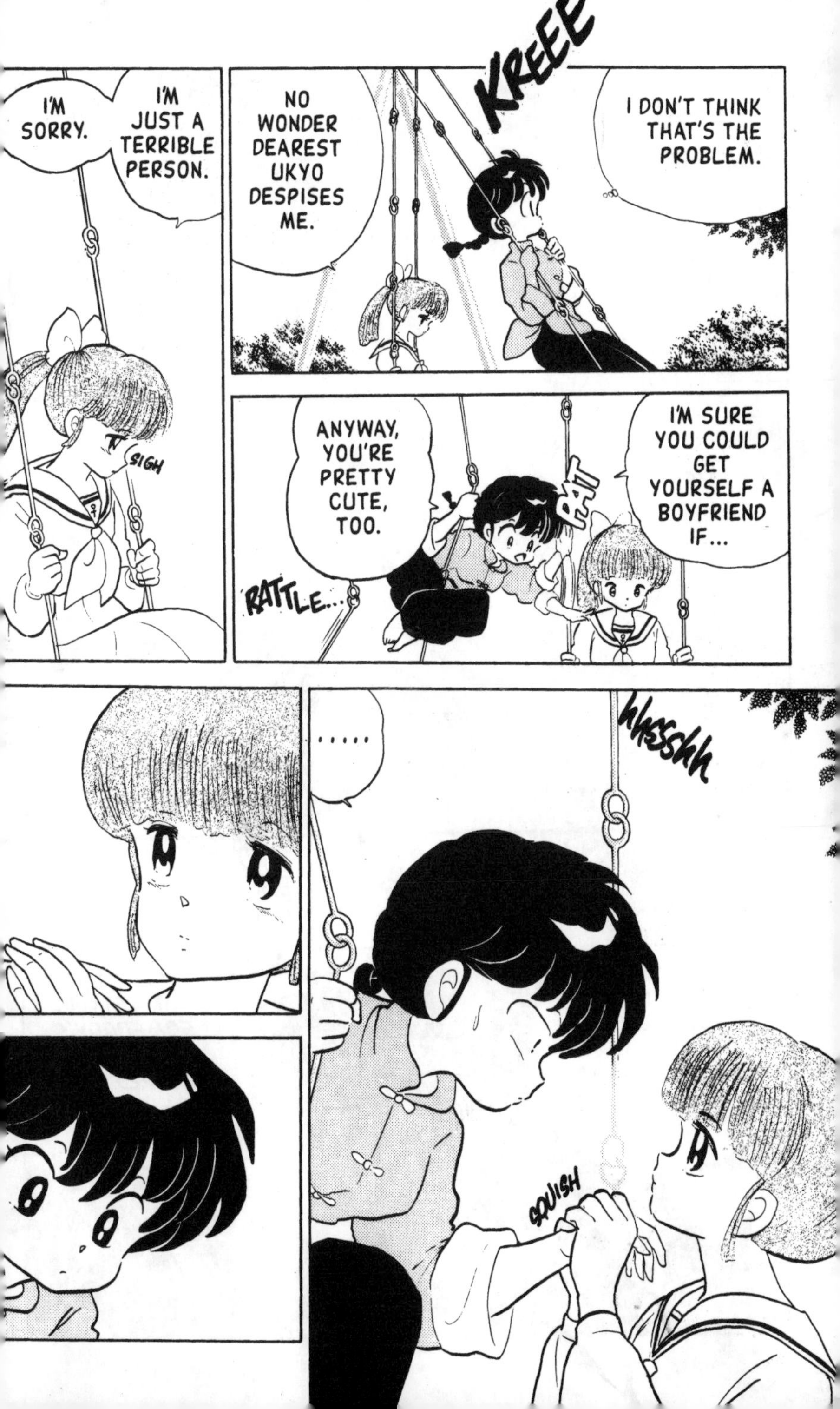
I'M SORRY.
I'M JUST A TERRIBLE PERSON.
SIGH
KREEE
NO WONDER DEAREST UKYO DESPISES ME.
I DON'T THINK THAT'S THE PROBLEM.
ANYWAY, YOU'RE PRETTY CUTE, TOO.
PAT
I'M SURE YOU COULD GET YOURSELF A BOYFRIEND IF...
RATTLE...
.....
WHSSSHH
SQUISH

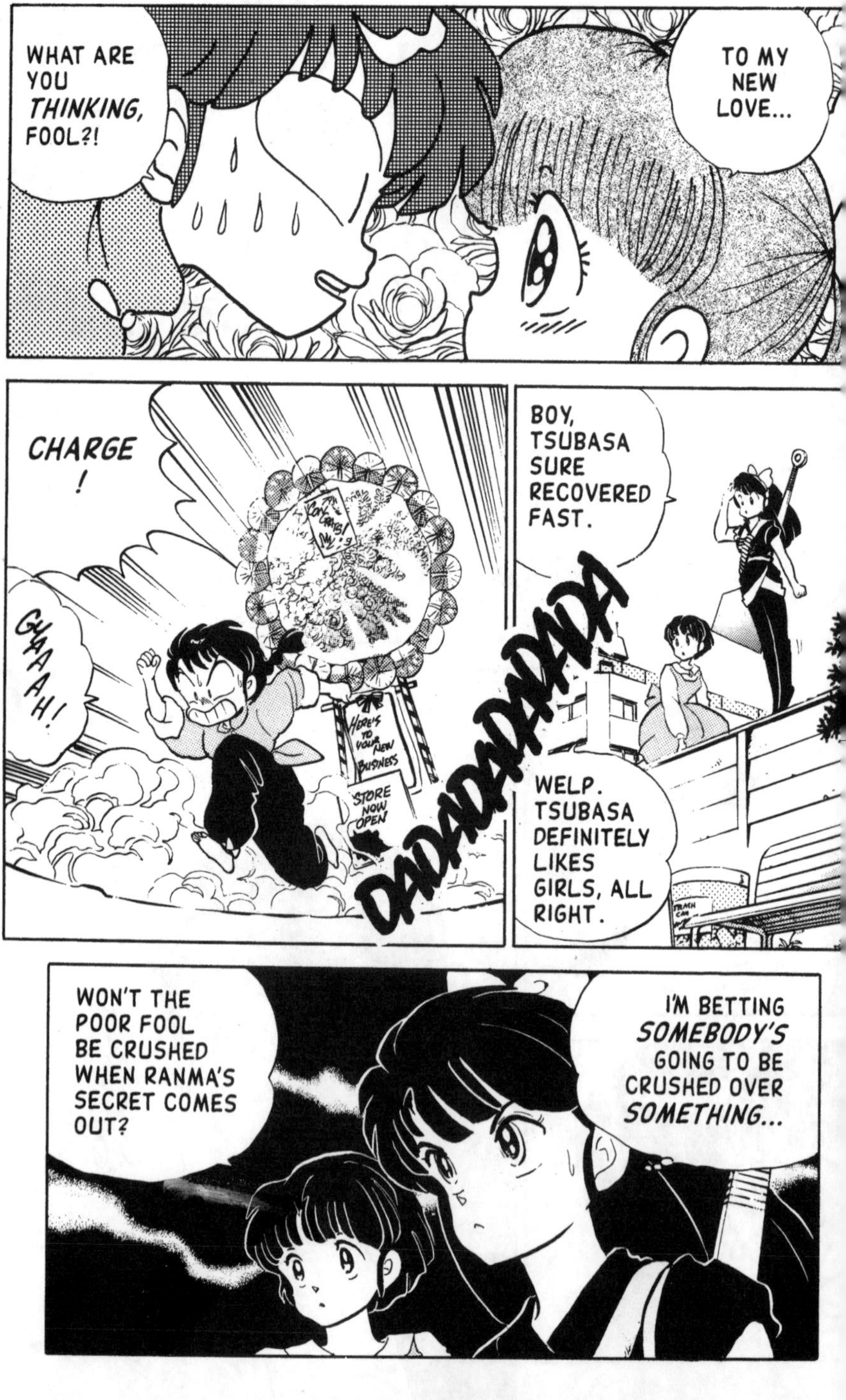
WHAT ARE YOU *THINKING,* FOOL?!
TO MY NEW LOVE...
CHARGE!
GYAAAAH!
HERE'S TO YOUR NEW BUSINESS
STORE NOW OPEN
DADADADADADA
BOY, TSUBASA SURE RECOVERED FAST.
WELP. TSUBASA DEFINITELY LIKES GIRLS, ALL RIGHT.
WON'T THE POOR FOOL BE CRUSHED WHEN RANMA'S SECRET COMES OUT?
I'M BETTING *SOMEBODY'S* GOING TO BE CRUSHED OVER *SOMETHING...*

PART 6
THE PERFECT MATCH

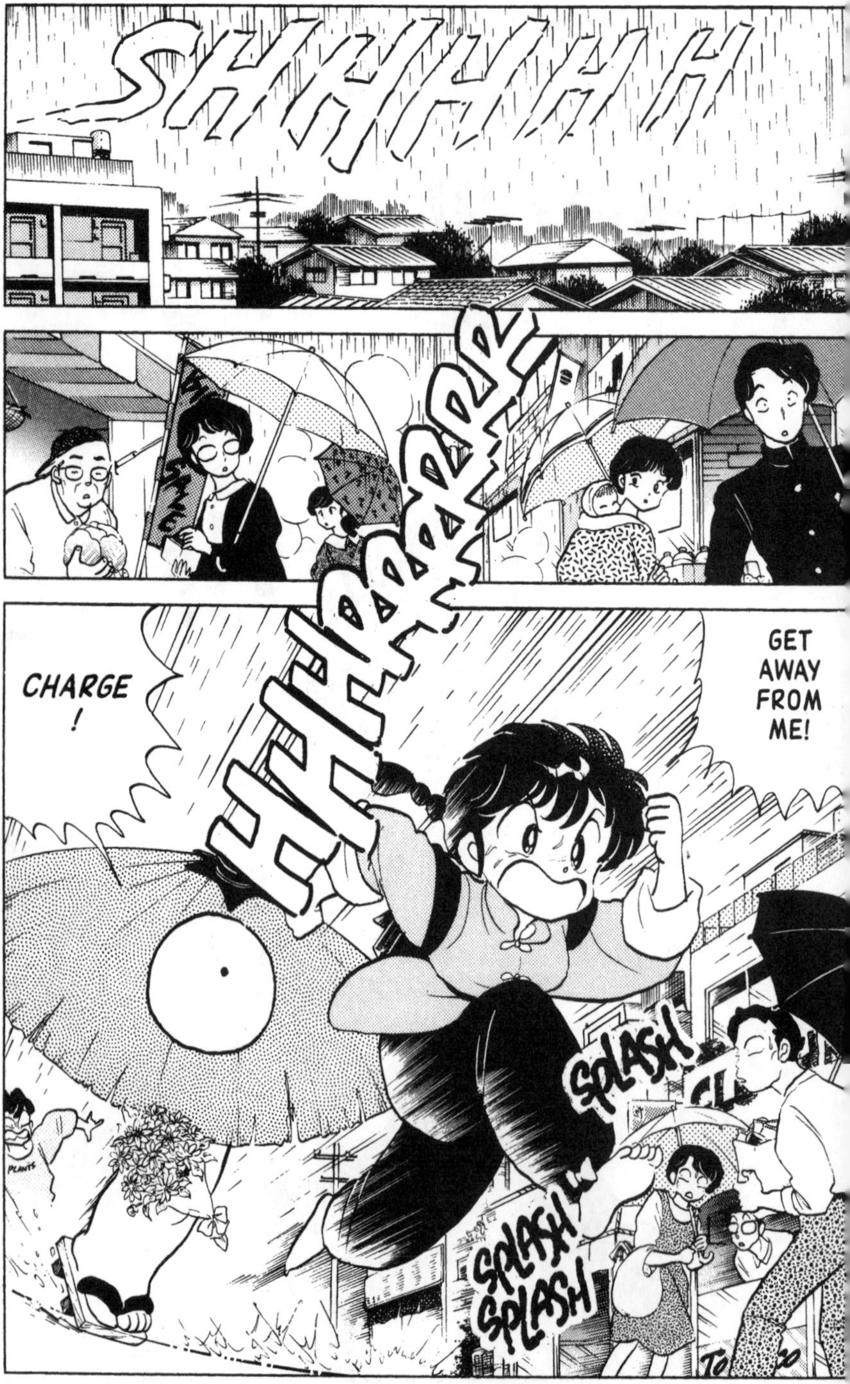
SHHHHHH!
CHARGE!
GET AWAY FROM ME!
SPLASH
SPLASH SPLASH

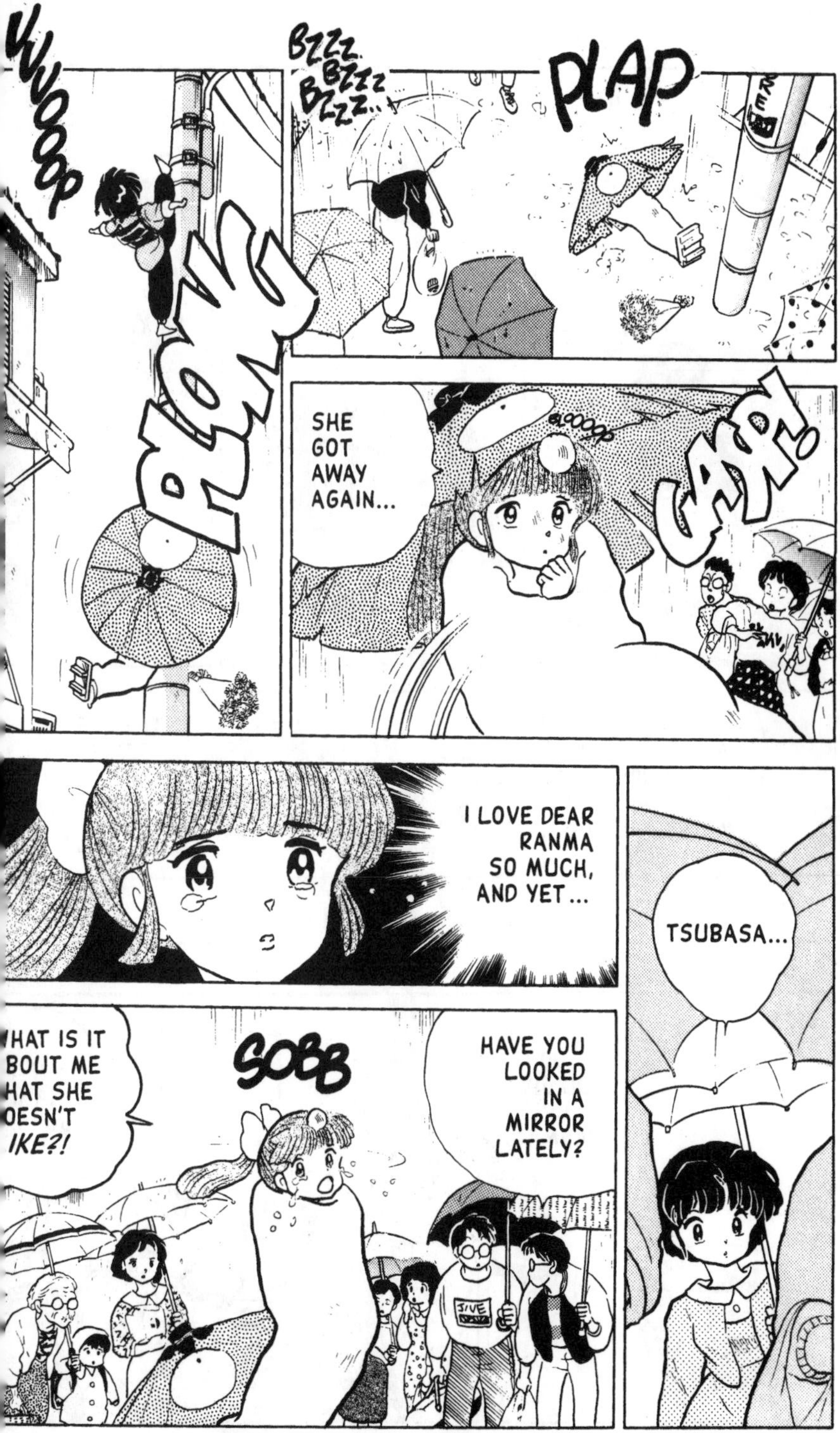

VVVOOOOP
PLOMP
BZZZ.. BZZZ BZZZ..
PLAP
SHE GOT AWAY AGAIN...
GLOOOP
GAP!
I LOVE DEAR RANMA SO MUCH, AND YET...
HAT IS IT BOUT ME HAT SHE OESN'T IKE?!
SOBB
HAVE YOU LOOKED IN A MIRROR LATELY?
TSUBASA...

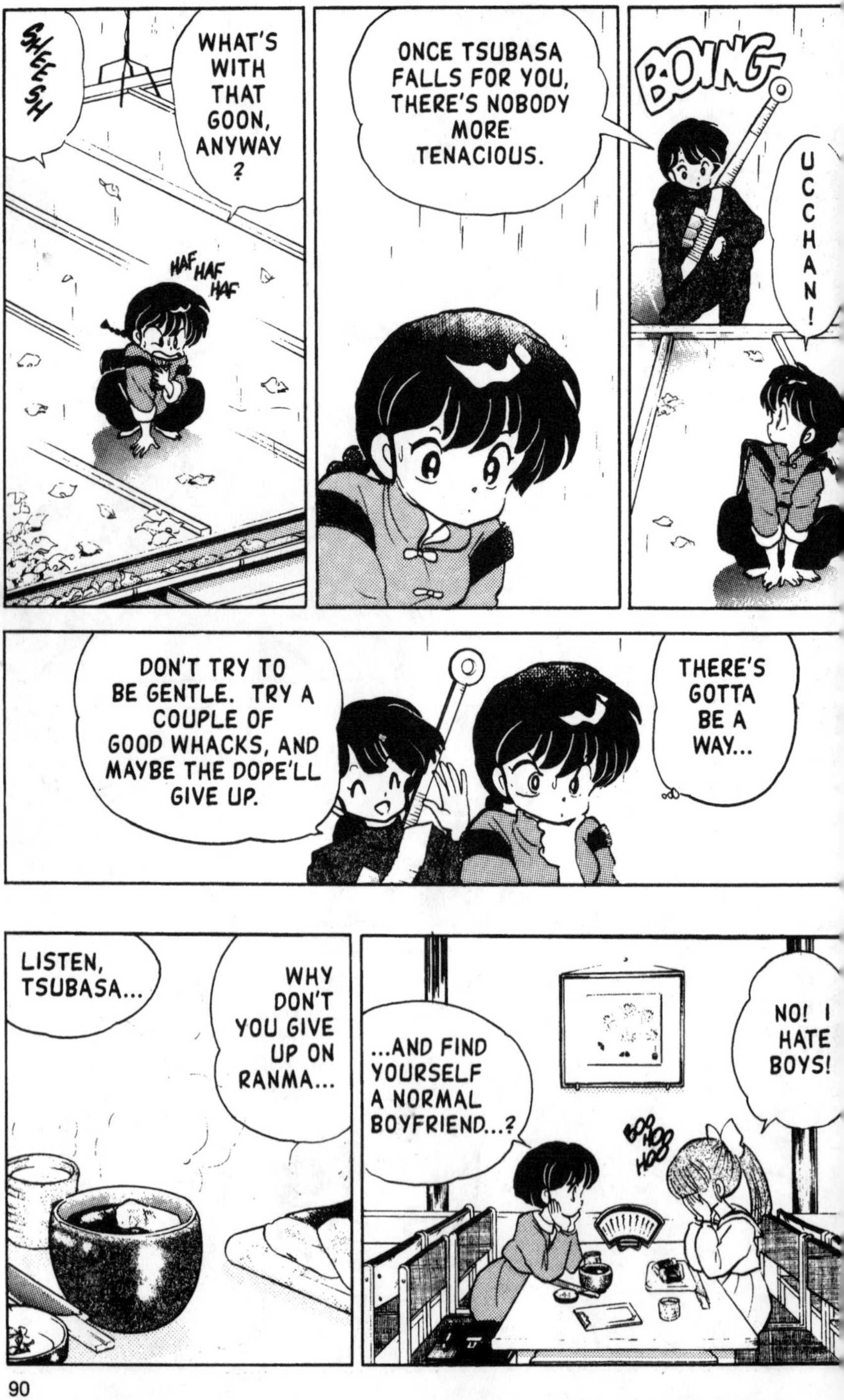
SHEESH
WHAT'S WITH THAT GOON, ANYWAY ?
ONCE TSUBASA FALLS FOR YOU, THERE'S NOBODY MORE TENACIOUS.
HAF HAF HAF
BOING
UCCHAN!
DON'T TRY TO BE GENTLE. TRY A COUPLE OF GOOD WHACKS, AND MAYBE THE DOPE'LL GIVE UP.
THERE'S GOTTA BE A WAY...
LISTEN, TSUBASA...
WHY DON'T YOU GIVE UP ON RANMA...
...AND FIND YOURSELF A NORMAL BOYFRIEND...?
BOO HOO HOO
NO! I HATE BOYS!

EAH, ELL...

...I DEFINITELY THINK YOU SHOULD GIVE UP ON RANMA.

WHY ?!

WHAT DO YOU MEAN, "WHY"?

C- CAN IT BE...

...THAT

...THAT YOU'RE IN LOVE WITH DEAREST RANMA AS WELL?!

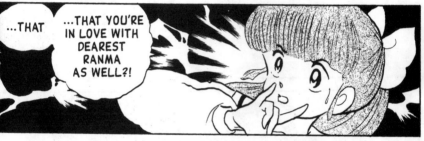

O-OF COURSE I'M NOT!

THANK GOODNESS! YOU HAD ME WORRIED FOR A SECOND!

IT'S JUST THAT...

...I DON'T WANT TO SEE YOU HURT.

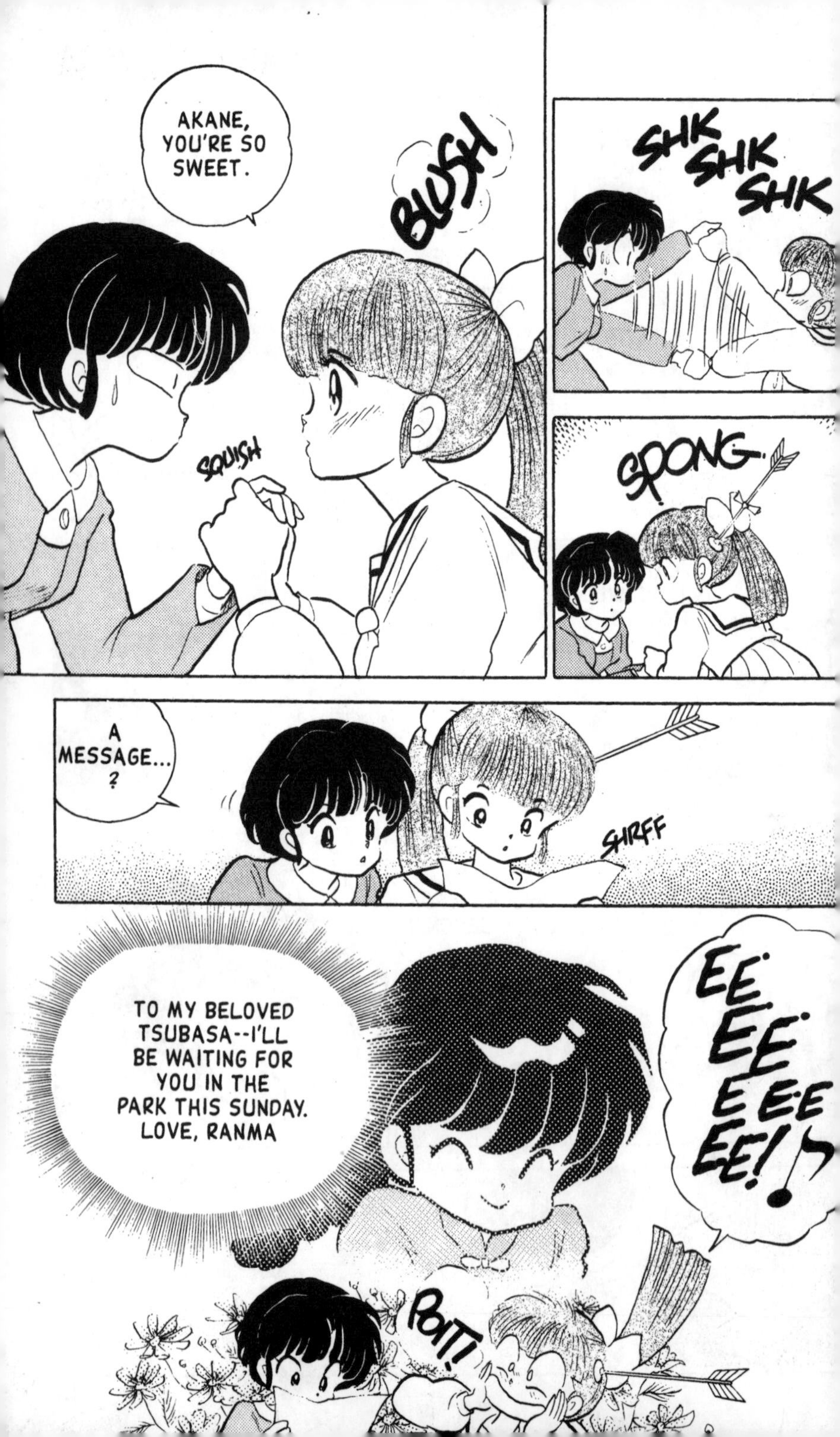
AKANE, YOU'RE SO SWEET.
BLUSH
SQUISH
SHK SHK SHK
SPONG
A MESSAGE...?
SHRFF
TO MY BELOVED TSUBASA--I'LL BE WAITING FOR YOU IN THE PARK THIS SUNDAY. LOVE, RANMA
EEEEEEEEE!?
POIT!

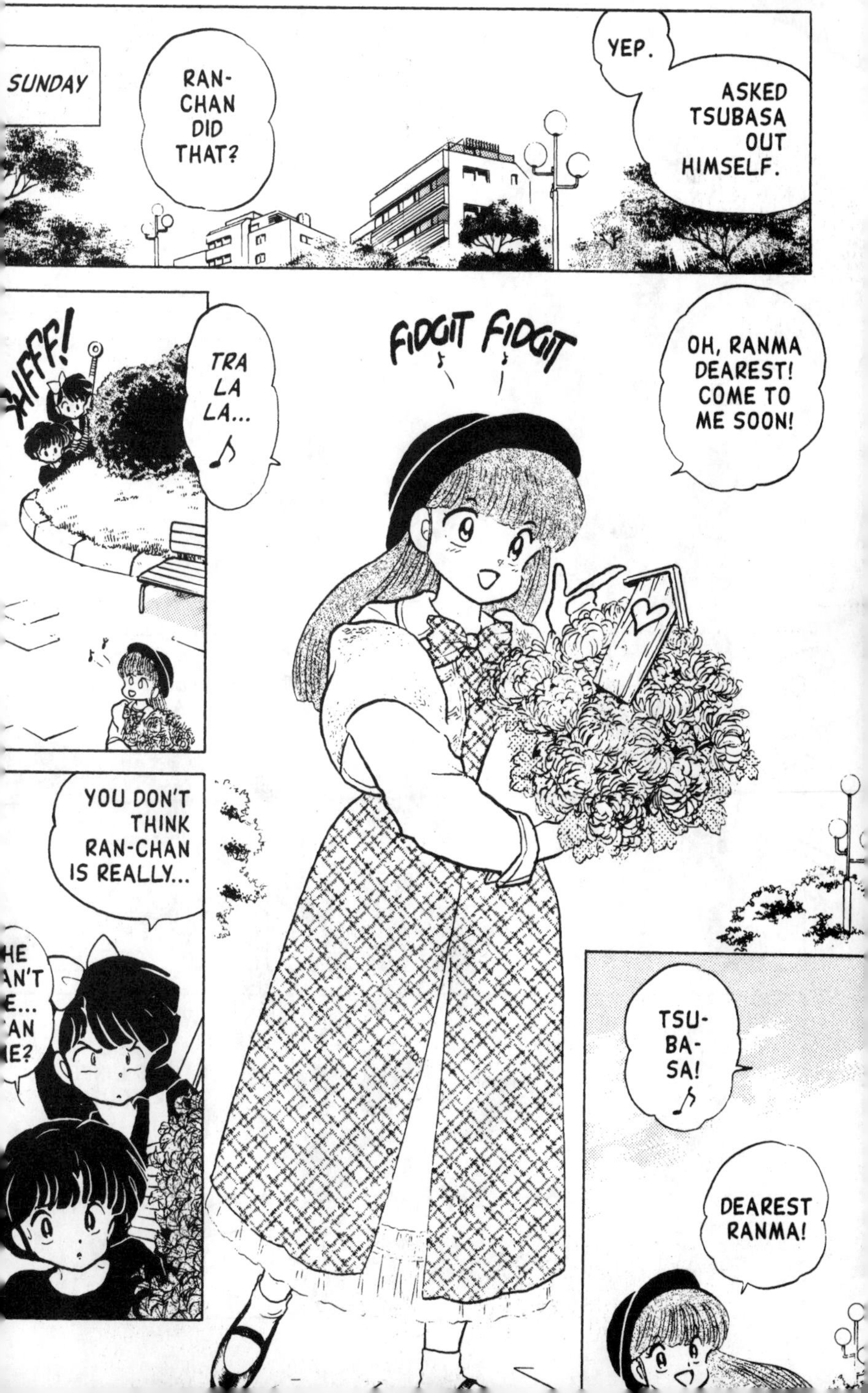
SUNDAY
RAN-CHAN DID THAT?
YEP.
ASKED TSUBASA OUT HIMSELF.
TRA LA LA...
FIDGIT FIDGIT
OH, RANMA DEAREST! COME TO ME SOON!
YOU DON'T THINK RAN-CHAN IS REALLY...
TSU-BA-SA!
DEAREST RANMA!

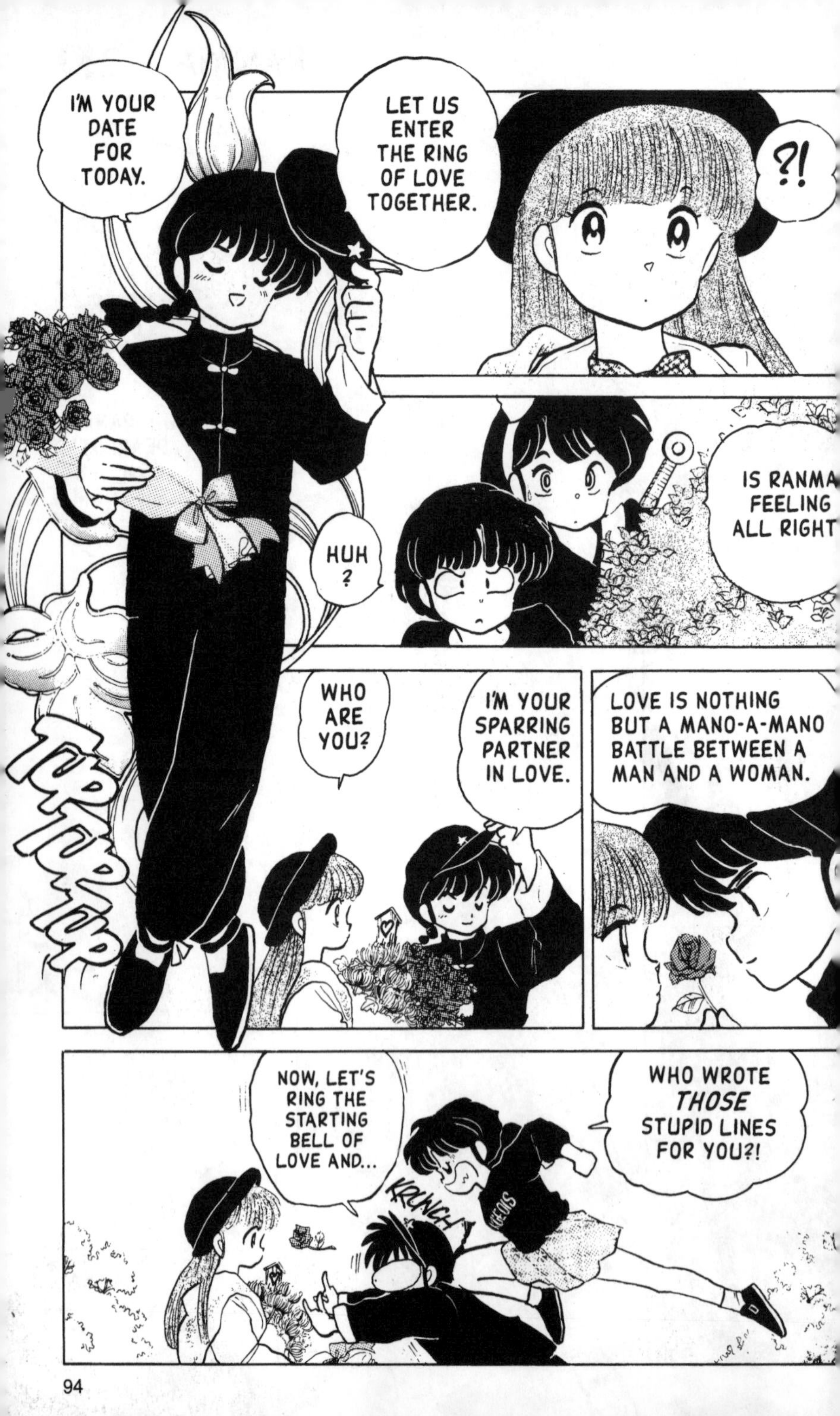
I'M YOUR DATE FOR TODAY.
LET US ENTER THE RING OF LOVE TOGETHER.
TIP TIP TIP
?!
HUH?
IS RANMA FEELING ALL RIGHT
WHO ARE YOU?
I'M YOUR SPARRING PARTNER IN LOVE.
LOVE IS NOTHING BUT A MANO-A-MANO BATTLE BETWEEN A MAN AND A WOMAN.
NOW, LET'S RING THE STARTING BELL OF LOVE AND...
KRUNCH
WHO WROTE *THOSE* STUPID LINES FOR YOU?!

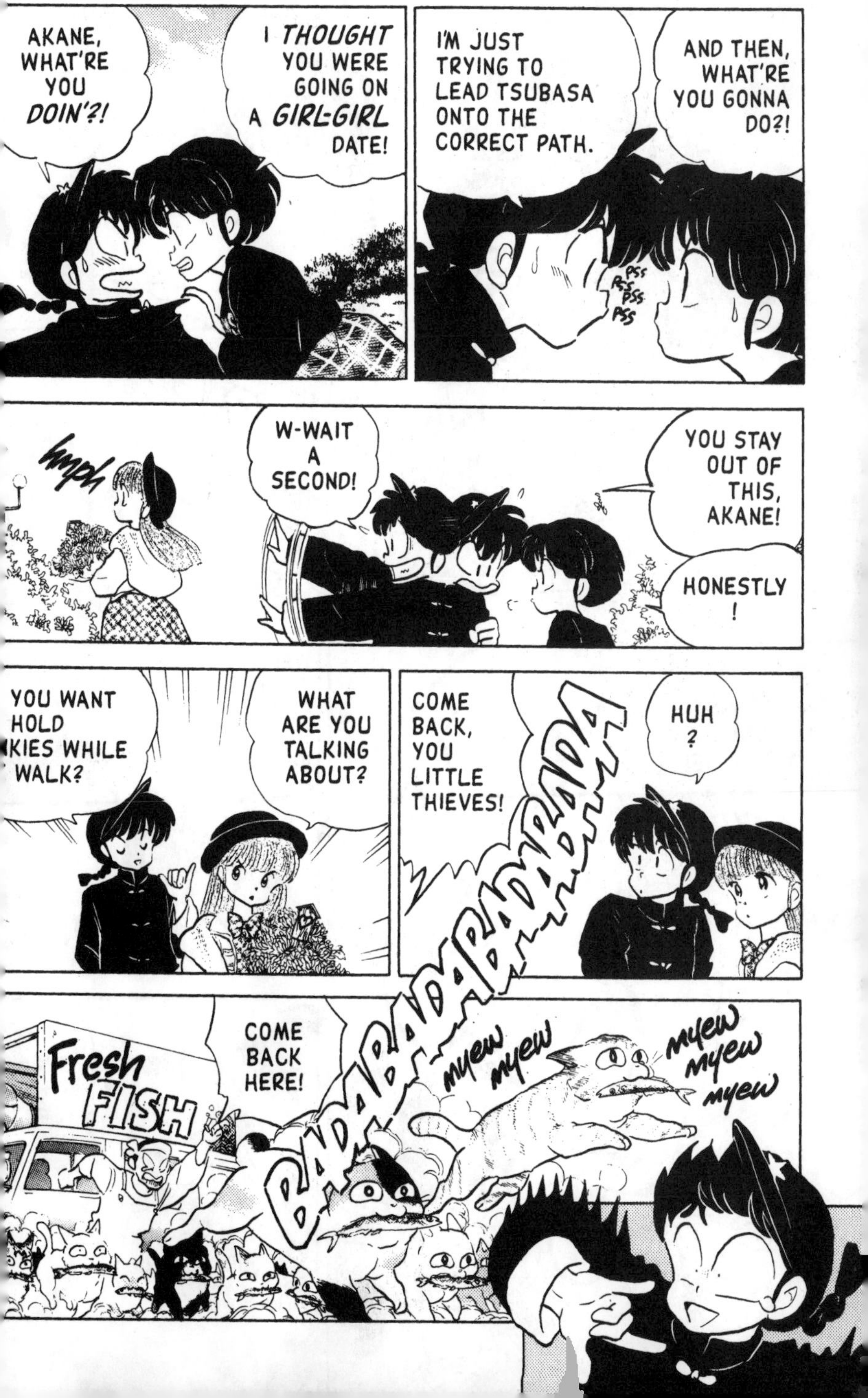
AKANE, WHAT'RE YOU DOIN'?!
I THOUGHT YOU WERE GOING ON A GIRL-GIRL DATE!
I'M JUST TRYING TO LEAD TSUBASA ONTO THE CORRECT PATH.
AND THEN, WHAT'RE YOU GONNA DO?!
PSS PSS PSS PSS
humph
W-WAIT A SECOND!
YOU STAY OUT OF THIS, AKANE!
HONESTLY!
YOU WANT HOLD KIES WHILE WALK?
WHAT ARE YOU TALKING ABOUT?
COME BACK, YOU LITTLE THIEVES!
HUH?
BADABADABADABADA
Fresh FISH
COME BACK HERE!
myew myew
myew myew myew

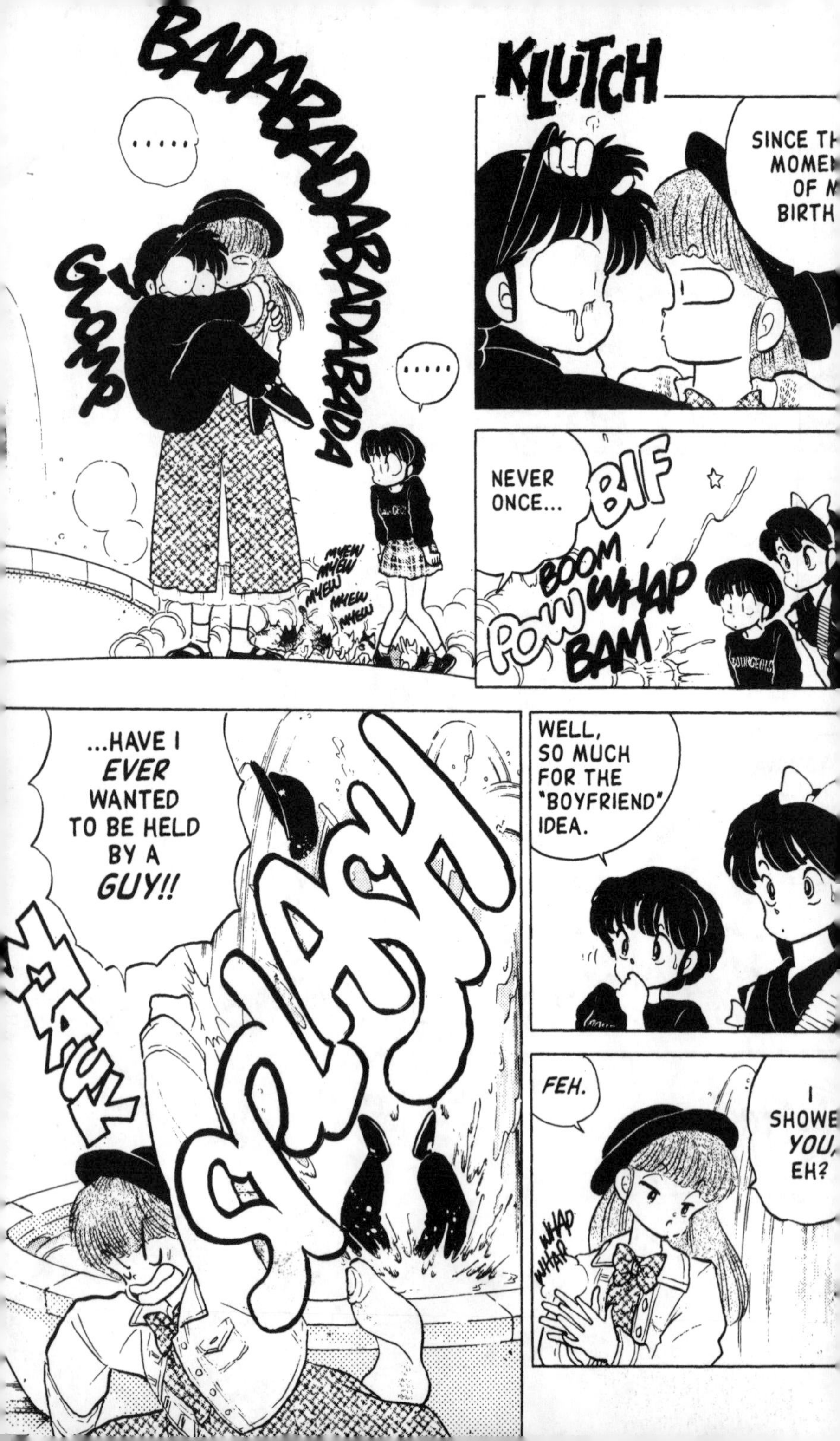
BADABADABADABADABADA
......
GLOMP
......
MYEW MYEW MYEW MYEW MYEW
KLUTCH
SINCE TH MOMEN OF M BIRTH
NEVER ONCE...
BIF
BOOM
POW
WHAP
BAM
...HAVE I EVER WANTED TO BE HELD BY A GUY!!
SPLASH
WELL, SO MUCH FOR THE "BOYFRIEND" IDEA.
FEH.
I SHOWE YOU, EH?
WHAP WHAP

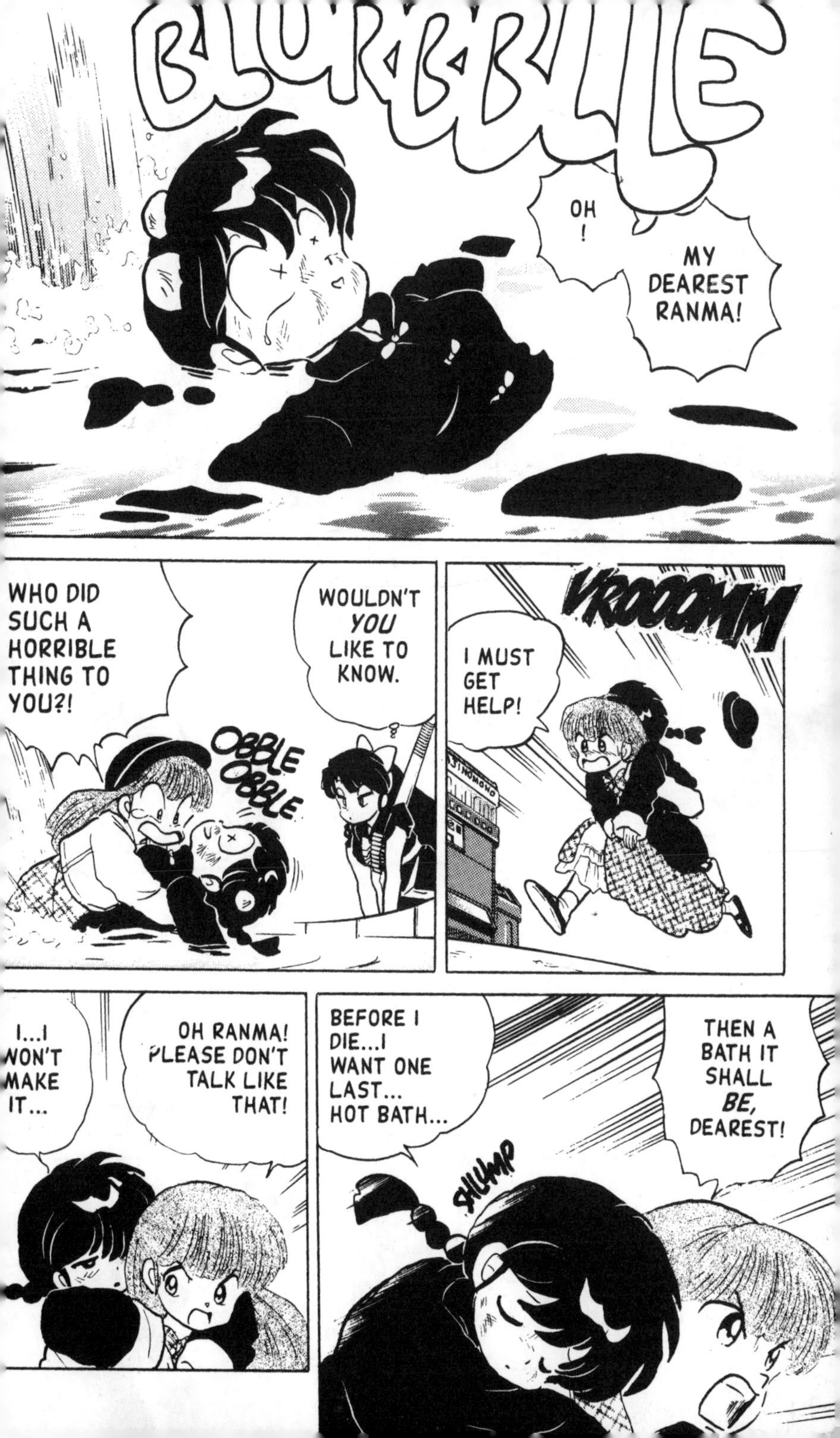
BLUBBBBLLE
OH!
MY DEAREST RANMA!
WHO DID SUCH A HORRIBLE THING TO YOU?!
OBBLE OBBLE
WOULDN'T YOU LIKE TO KNOW.
VROOOMM
I MUST GET HELP!
I...I WON'T MAKE IT...
OH RANMA! PLEASE DON'T TALK LIKE THAT!
BEFORE I DIE...I WANT ONE LAST... HOT BATH...
SHUMP
THEN A BATH IT SHALL BE, DEAREST!

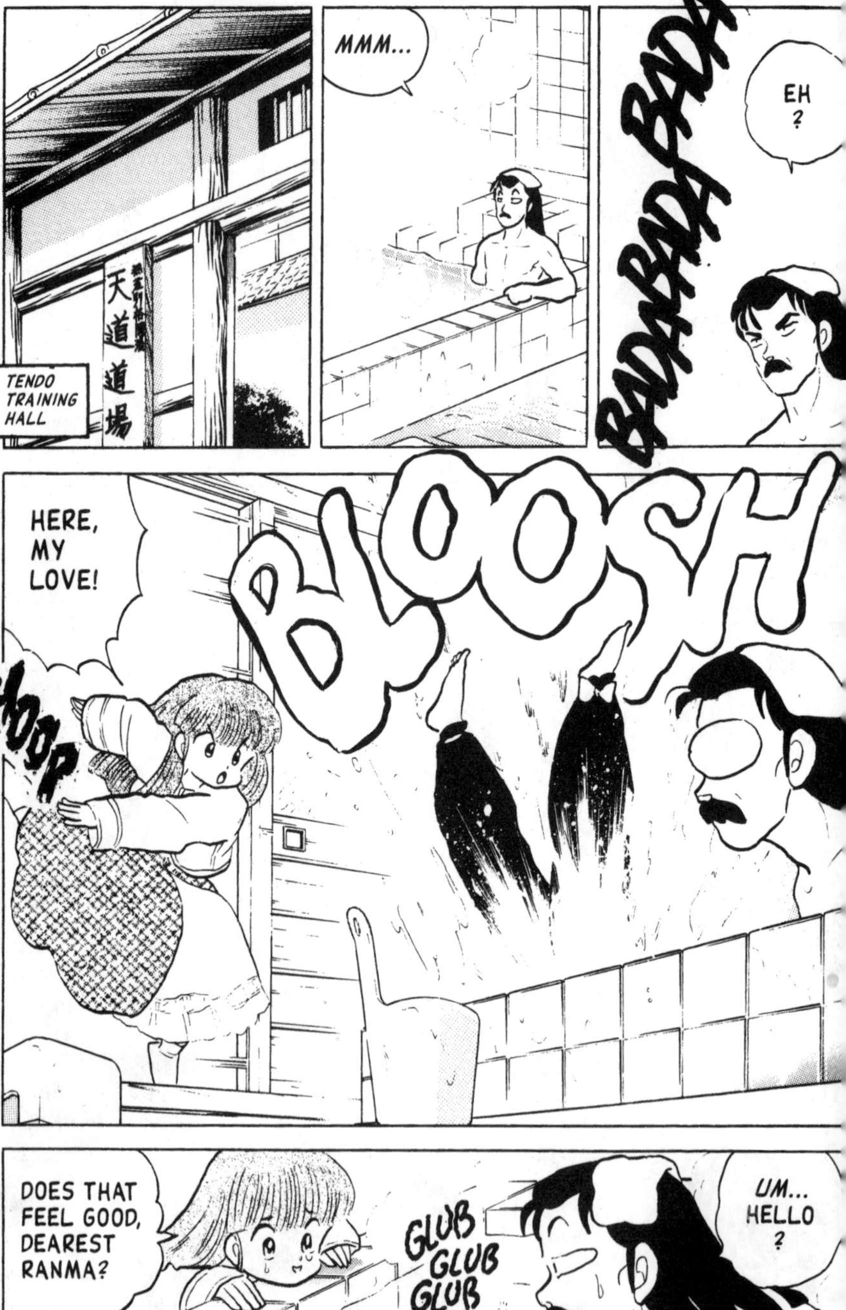
TENDO TRAINING HALL
天道道場
MMM...
BADABADABADA
EH ?
HERE, MY LOVE!
ZHOOOP
BLOOSH
DOES THAT FEEL GOOD, DEAREST RANMA?
GLUB GLUB GLUB
UM... HELLO ?

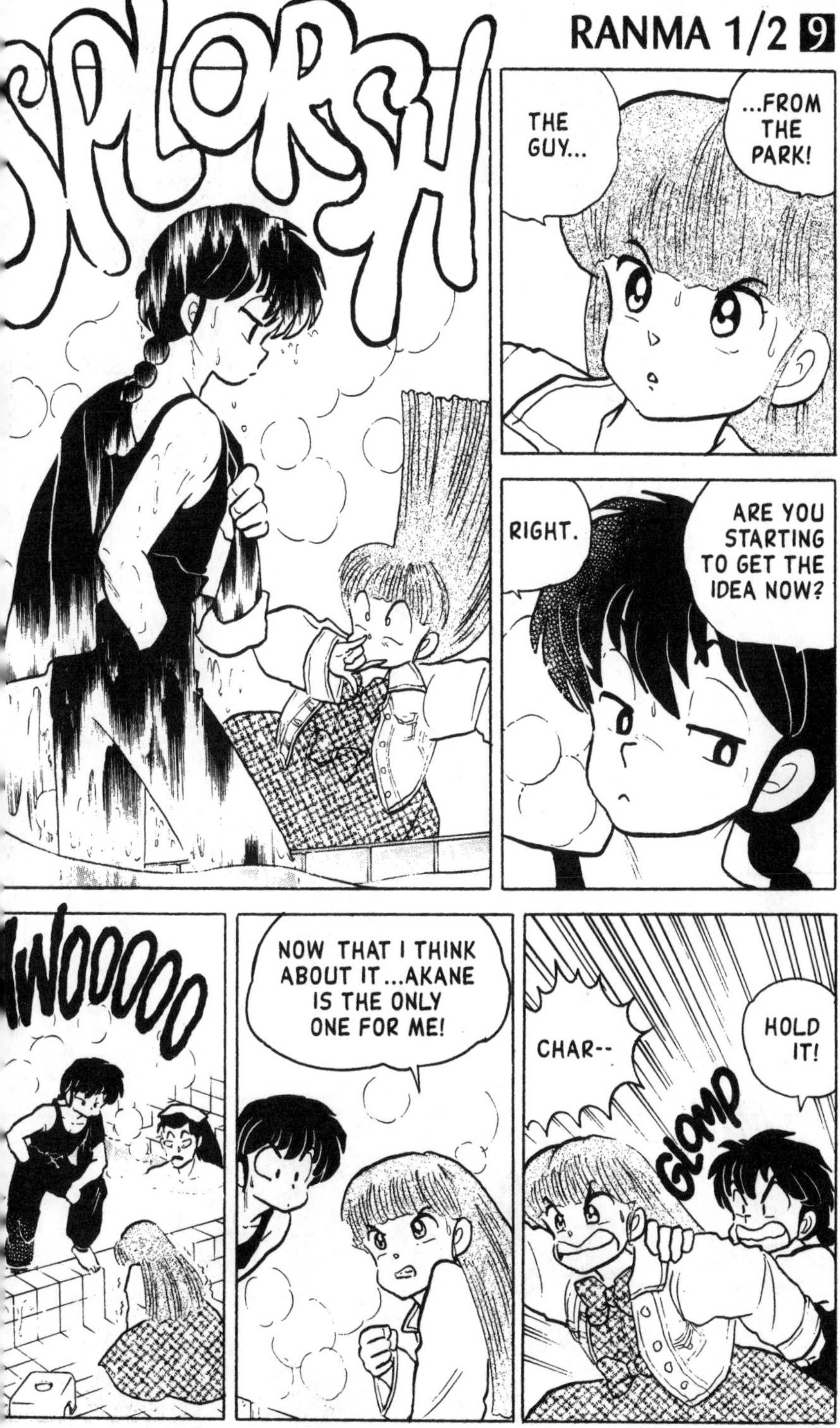
SPLORSH!
THE GUY...
...FROM THE PARK!
RIGHT.
ARE YOU STARTING TO GET THE IDEA NOW?
WOOOOO
NOW THAT I THINK ABOUT IT...AKANE IS THE ONLY ONE FOR ME!
CHAR--
GLOMP
HOLD IT!

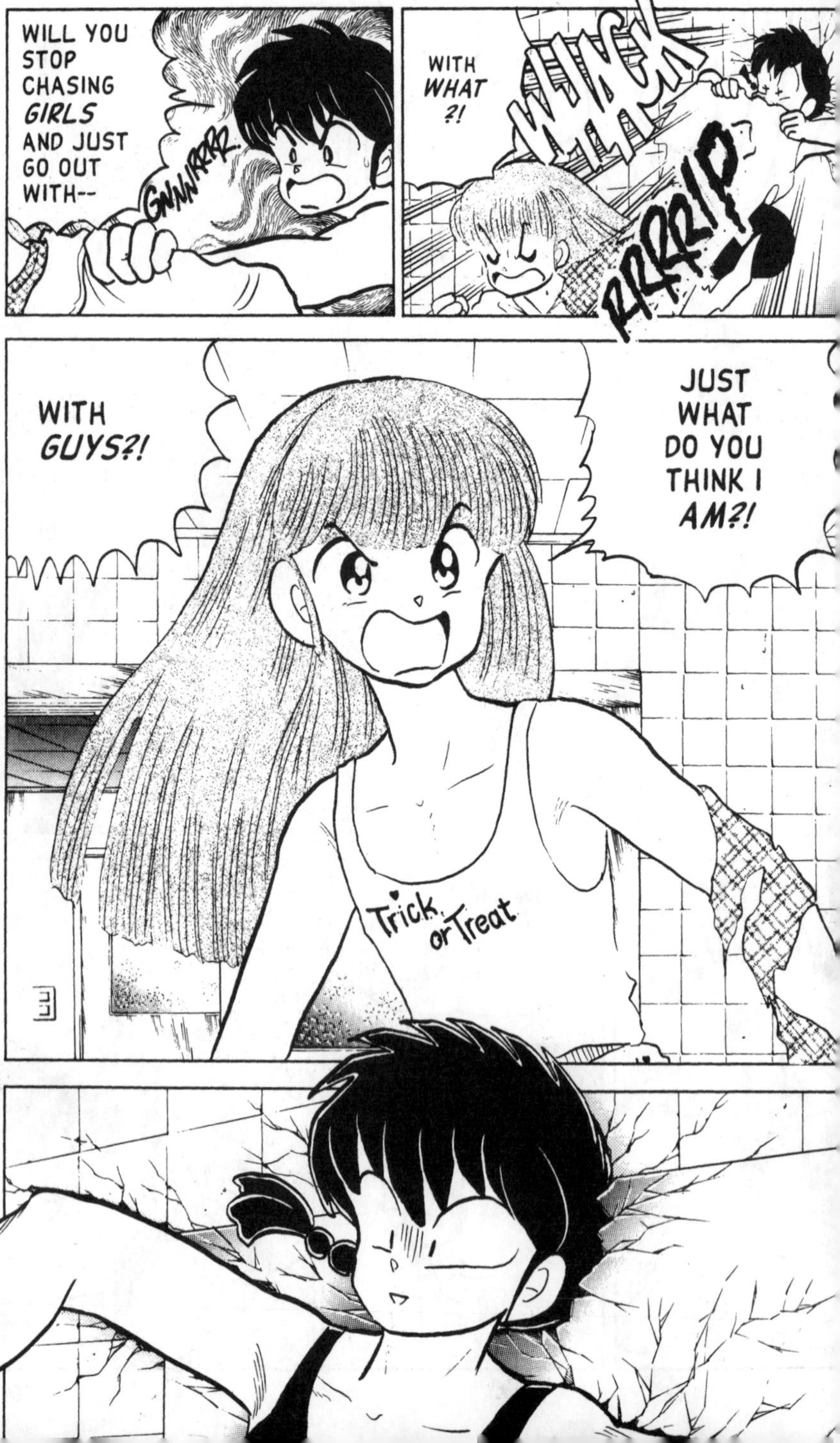
WILL YOU STOP CHASING GIRLS AND JUST GO OUT WITH--
GNNNRRRR
WITH WHAT ?!
WHACK
RRRRIP
WITH GUYS?!
JUST WHAT DO YOU THINK I AM?!
Trick or Treat

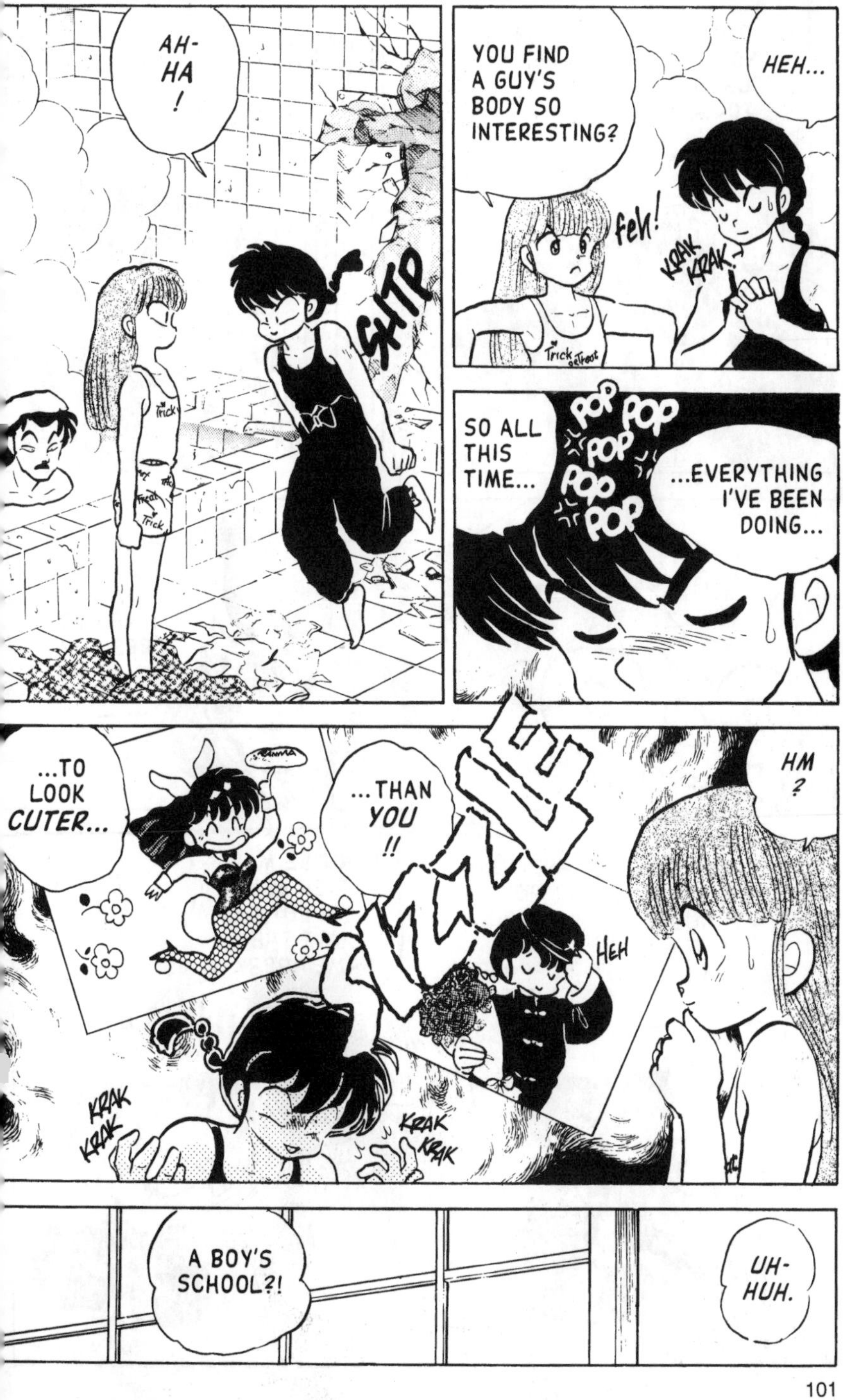
AH-HA!
SHTP
YOU FIND A GUY'S BODY SO INTERESTING?
HEH...
feh!
KRAK KRAK
SO ALL THIS TIME...
POP POP POP POP POP
...EVERYTHING I'VE BEEN DOING...
...TO LOOK CUTER...
...THAN YOU!!
HEH
KRAK KRAK
KRAK KRAK
HM?
A BOY'S SCHOOL?!
UH-HUH.

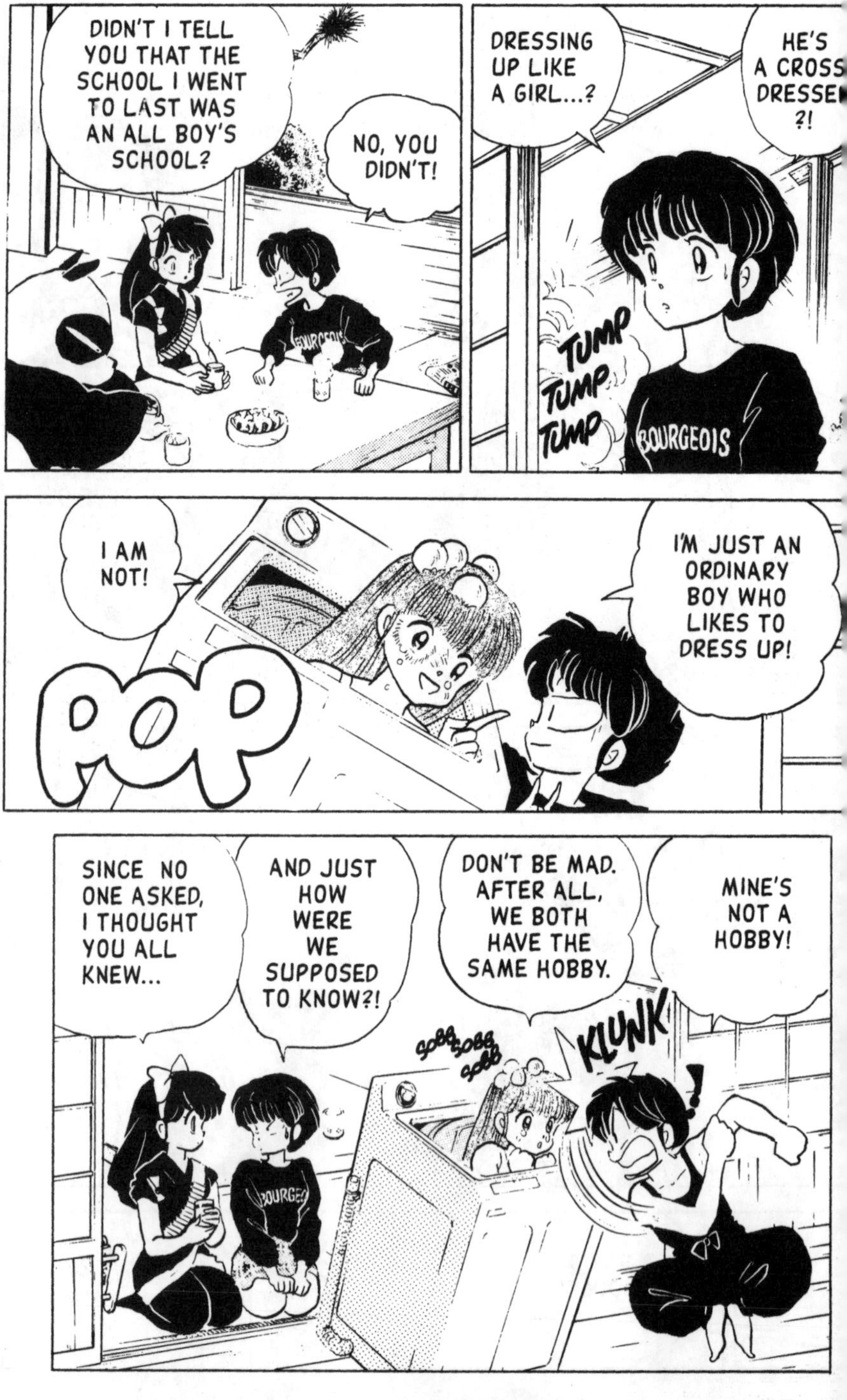

DIDN'T I TELL YOU THAT THE SCHOOL I WENT TO LAST WAS AN ALL BOY'S SCHOOL?
NO, YOU DIDN'T!
BOURGEOIS
DRESSING UP LIKE A GIRL...?
HE'S A CROSS DRESSE ?!
TUMP TUMP TUMP
BOURGEOIS
I AM NOT!
POP
I'M JUST AN ORDINARY BOY WHO LIKES TO DRESS UP!
SINCE NO ONE ASKED, I THOUGHT YOU ALL KNEW...
AND JUST HOW WERE WE SUPPOSED TO KNOW?!
DON'T BE MAD. AFTER ALL, WE BOTH HAVE THE SAME HOBBY.
MINE'S NOT A HOBBY!
SOBB SOBB SOBB
KLUNK

PART 7
RYOGA, COME HOME

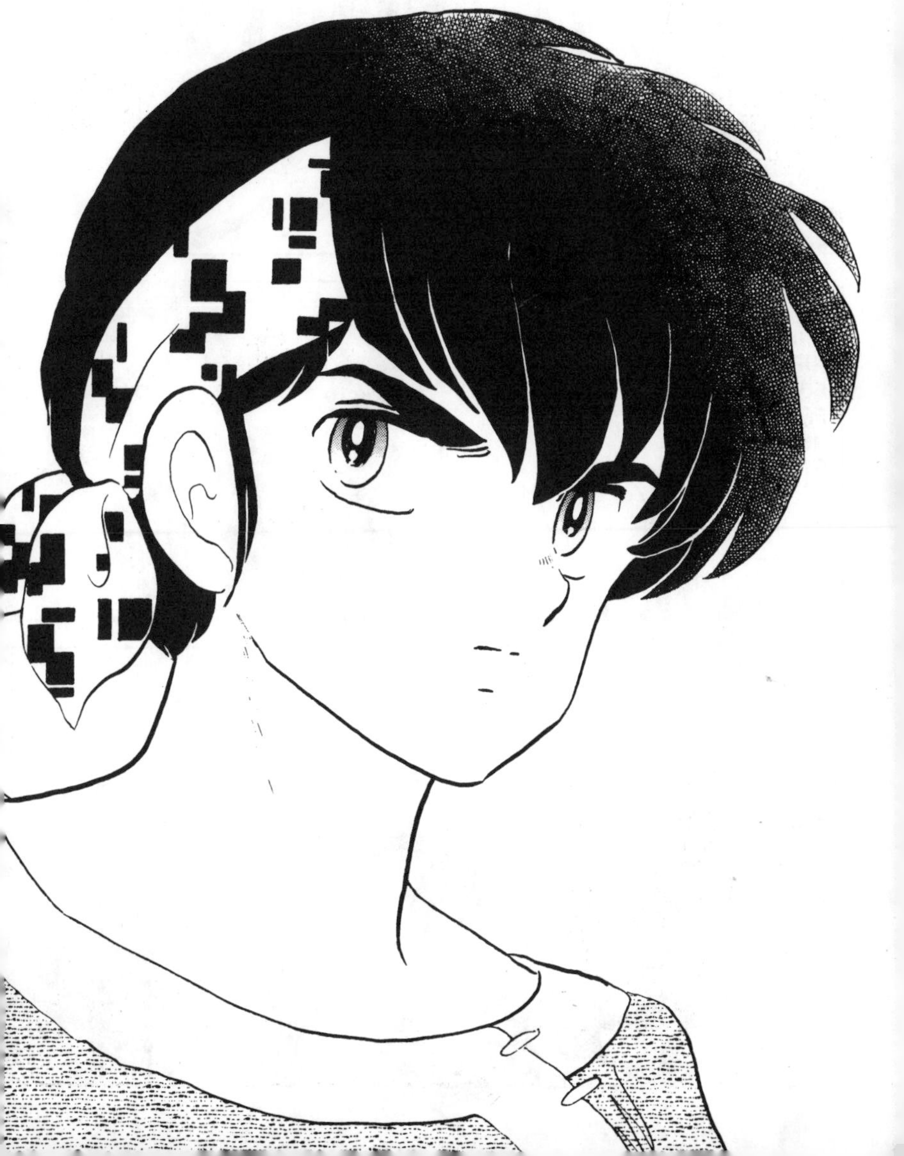

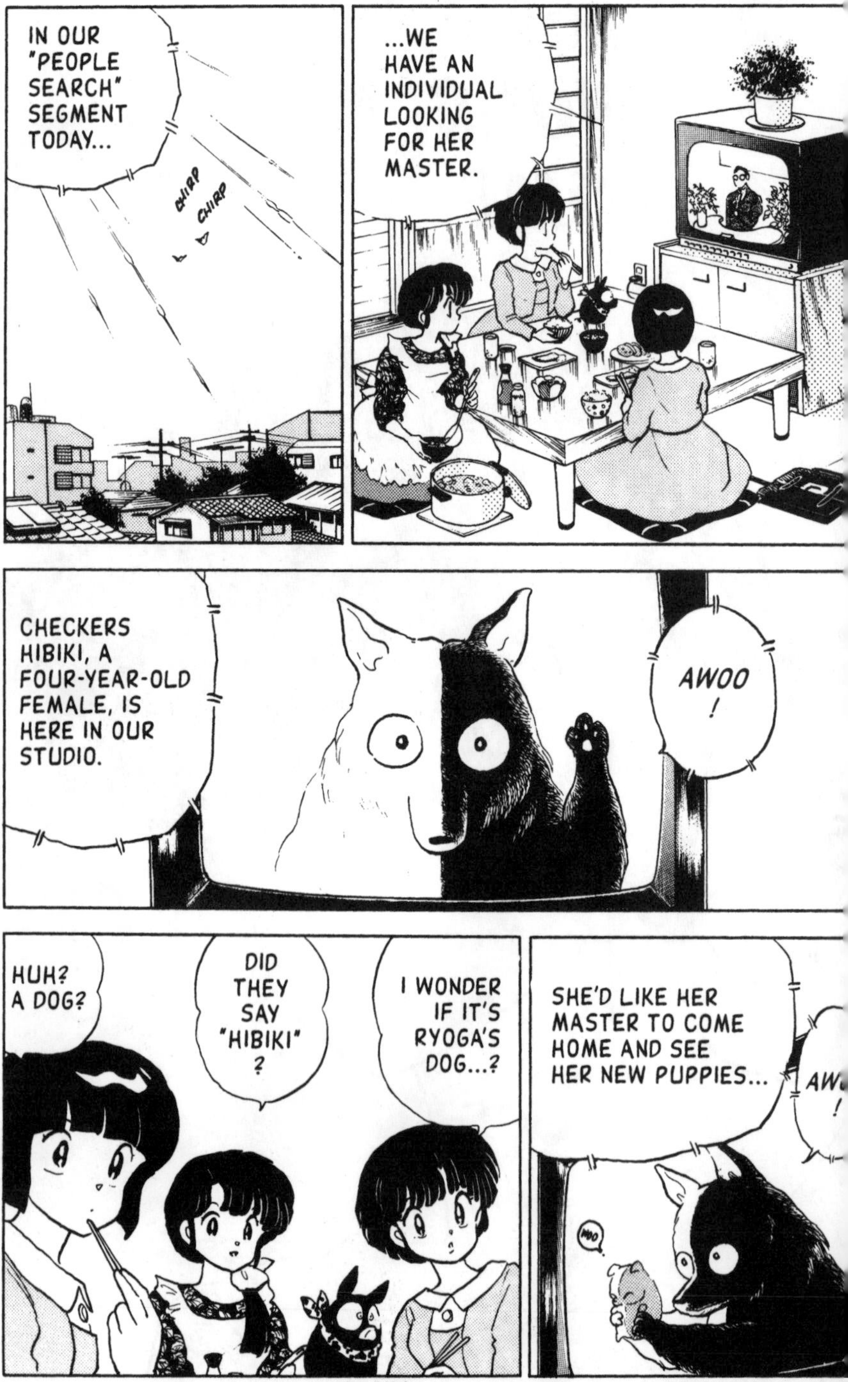
IN OUR "PEOPLE SEARCH" SEGMENT TODAY...
CHIRP
CHIRP
...WE HAVE AN INDIVIDUAL LOOKING FOR HER MASTER.
CHECKERS HIBIKI, A FOUR-YEAR-OLD FEMALE, IS HERE IN OUR STUDIO.
AWOO !
HUH? A DOG?
DID THEY SAY "HIBIKI" ?
I WONDER IF IT'S RYOGA'S DOG...?
SHE'D LIKE HER MASTER TO COME HOME AND SEE HER NEW PUPPIES...

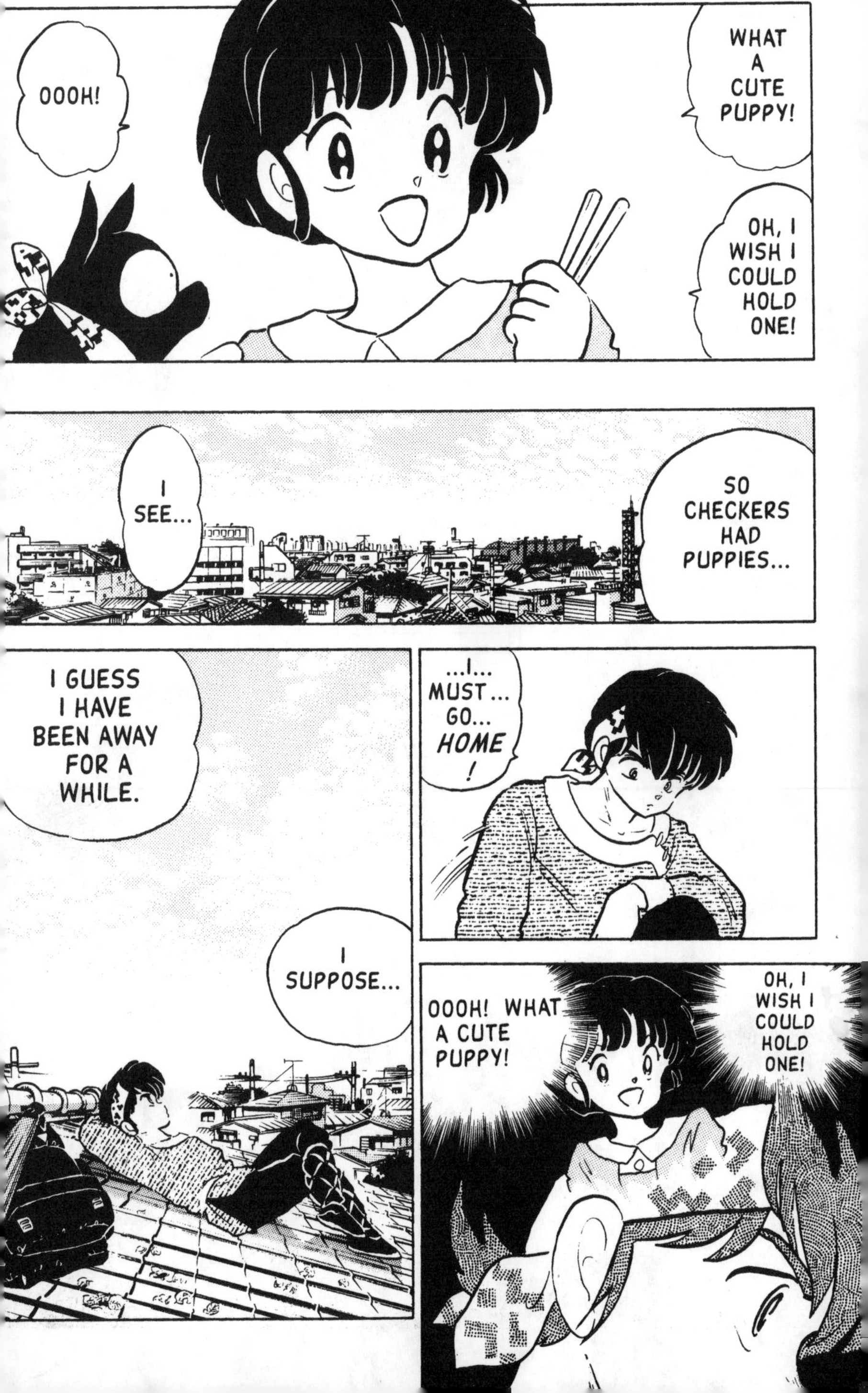
OOOH!
WHAT A CUTE PUPPY!
OH, I WISH I COULD HOLD ONE!
I SEE...
SO CHECKERS HAD PUPPIES...
I GUESS I HAVE BEEN AWAY FOR A WHILE.
I SUPPOSE...
...I... MUST... GO... HOME!
OOOH! WHAT A CUTE PUPPY!
OH, I WISH I COULD HOLD ONE!

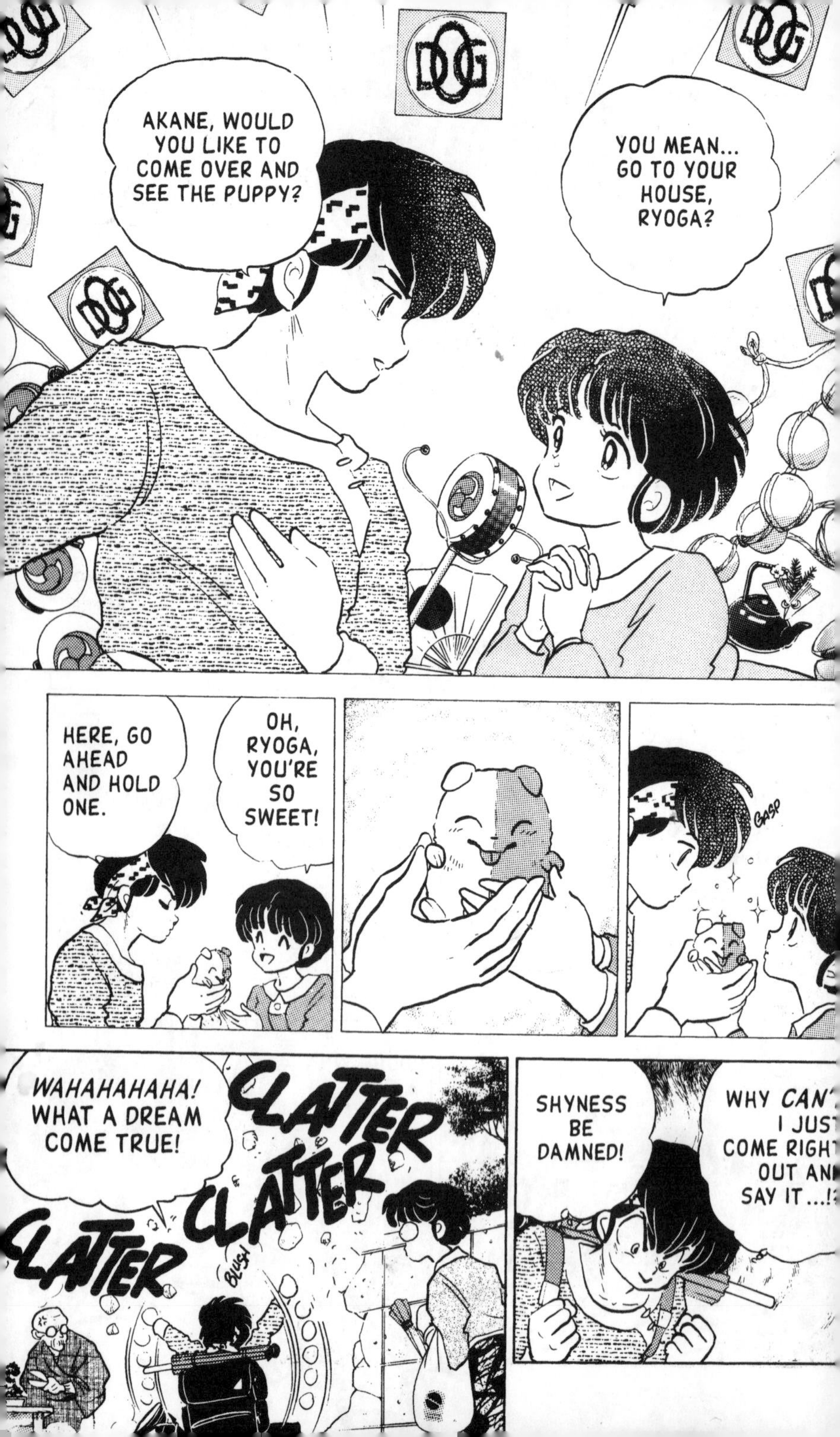
AKANE, WOULD YOU LIKE TO COME OVER AND SEE THE PUPPY?
YOU MEAN... GO TO YOUR HOUSE, RYOGA?
HERE, GO AHEAD AND HOLD ONE.
OH, RYOGA, YOU'RE SO SWEET!
GASP
WAHAHAHAHA! WHAT A DREAM COME TRUE!
CLATTER
CLATTER
CLATTER
BLUSH
SHYNESS BE DAMNED!
WHY CAN'T I JUST COME RIGHT OUT AND SAY IT...!?

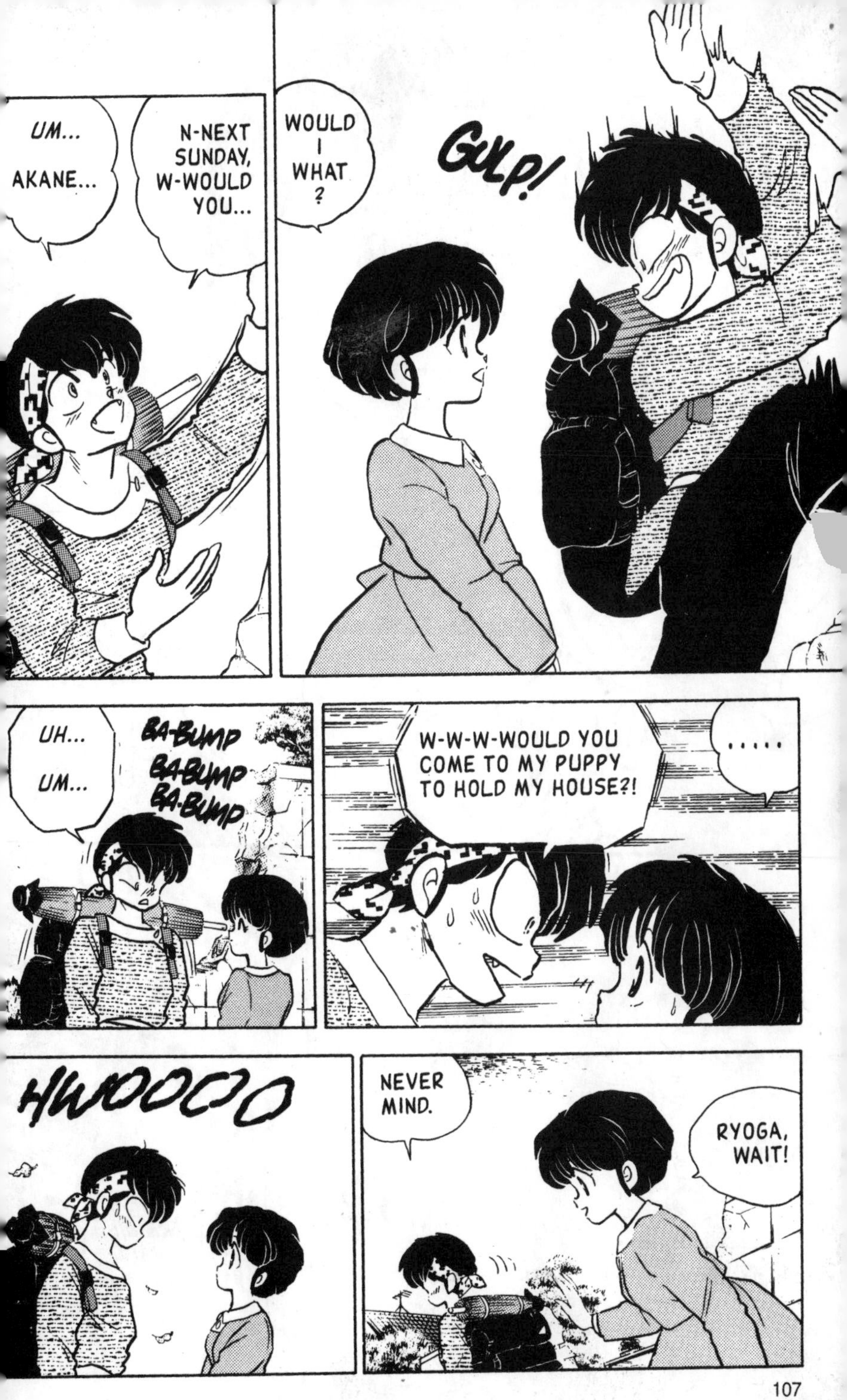
UM... AKANE...
N-NEXT SUNDAY, W-WOULD YOU...
WOULD I WHAT ?
GULP!
UH... UM...
BA-BUMP BA-BUMP BA-BUMP
W-W-W-WOULD YOU COME TO MY PUPPY TO HOLD MY HOUSE?!
.....
HWOOOO
NEVER MIND.
RYOGA, WAIT!

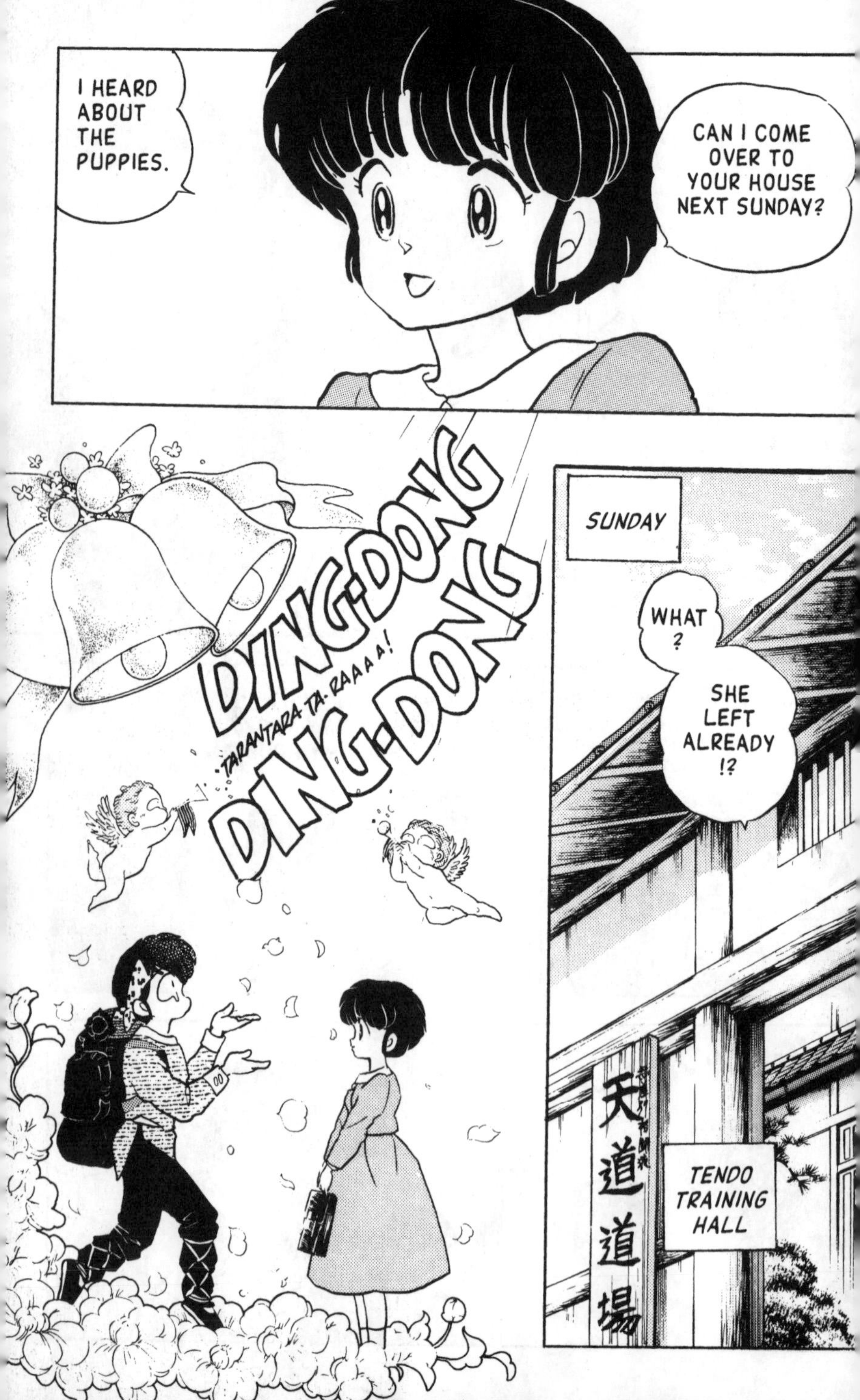
I HEARD ABOUT THE PUPPIES.
CAN I COME OVER TO YOUR HOUSE NEXT SUNDAY?
DING-DONG
TARANTARA TA-RAAAA!
DING-DONG
SUNDAY
WHAT?
SHE LEFT ALREADY!?
天道道場
TENDO TRAINING HALL

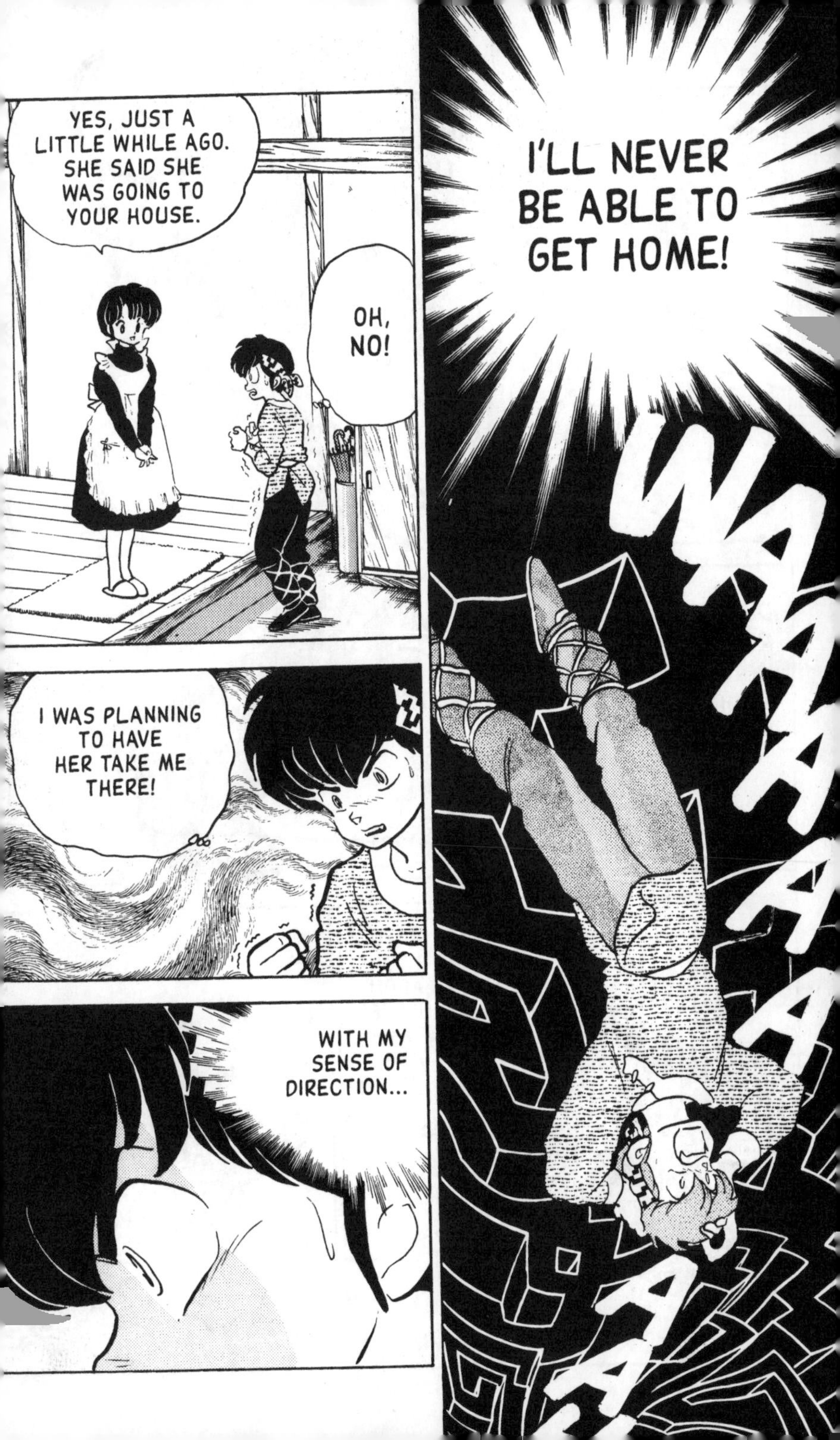
YES, JUST A LITTLE WHILE AGO. SHE SAID SHE WAS GOING TO YOUR HOUSE.
OH, NO!
I WAS PLANNING TO HAVE HER TAKE ME THERE!
WITH MY SENSE OF DIRECTION...
I'LL NEVER BE ABLE TO GET HOME!

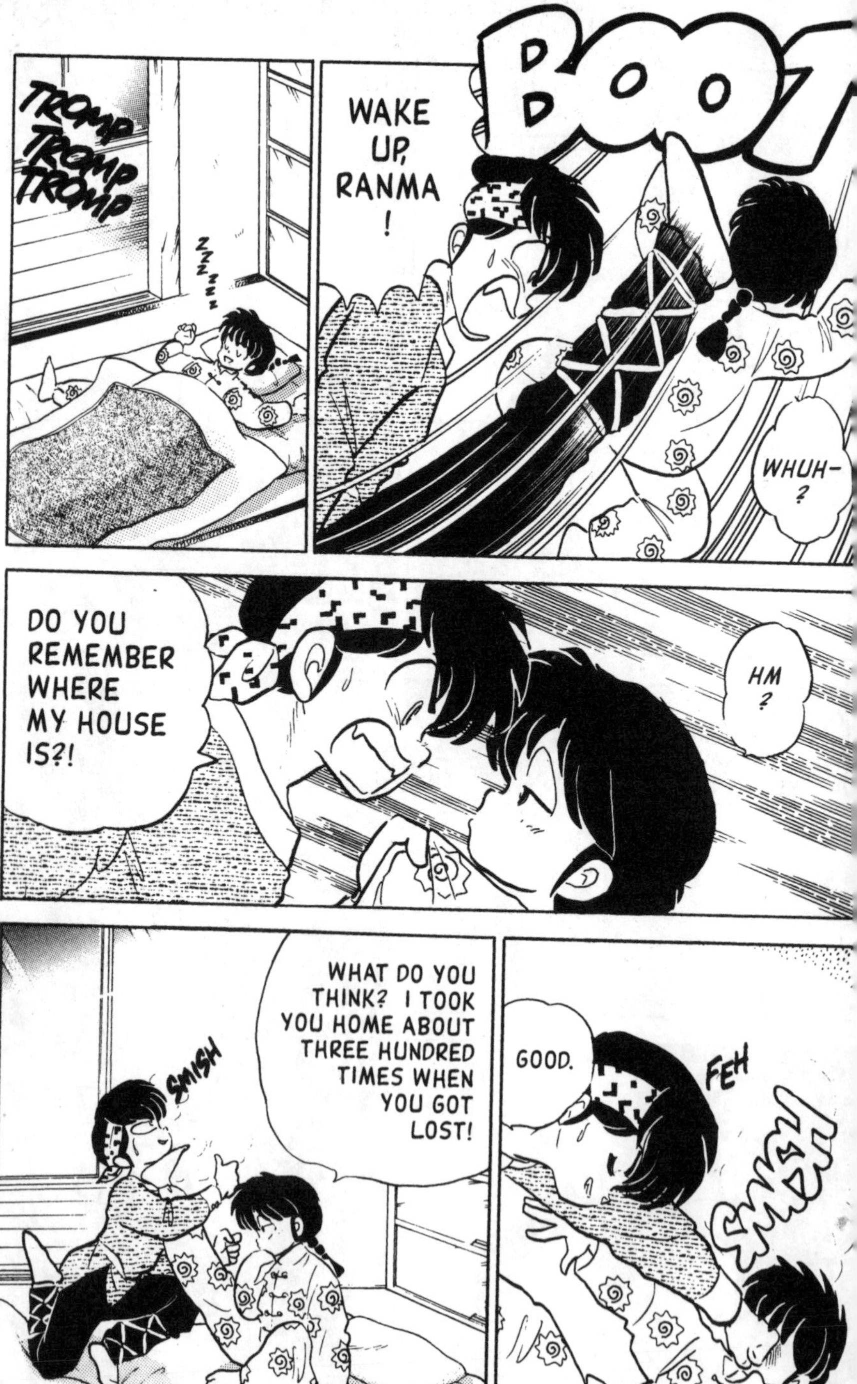
TROMP TROMP TROMP
ZZZZZZ
WAKE UP, RANMA!
BOOT
WHUH-?
DO YOU REMEMBER WHERE MY HOUSE IS?!
HM?
SMISH
WHAT DO YOU THINK? I TOOK YOU HOME ABOUT THREE HUNDRED TIMES WHEN YOU GOT LOST!
GOOD.
FEH
SMISH SMISH

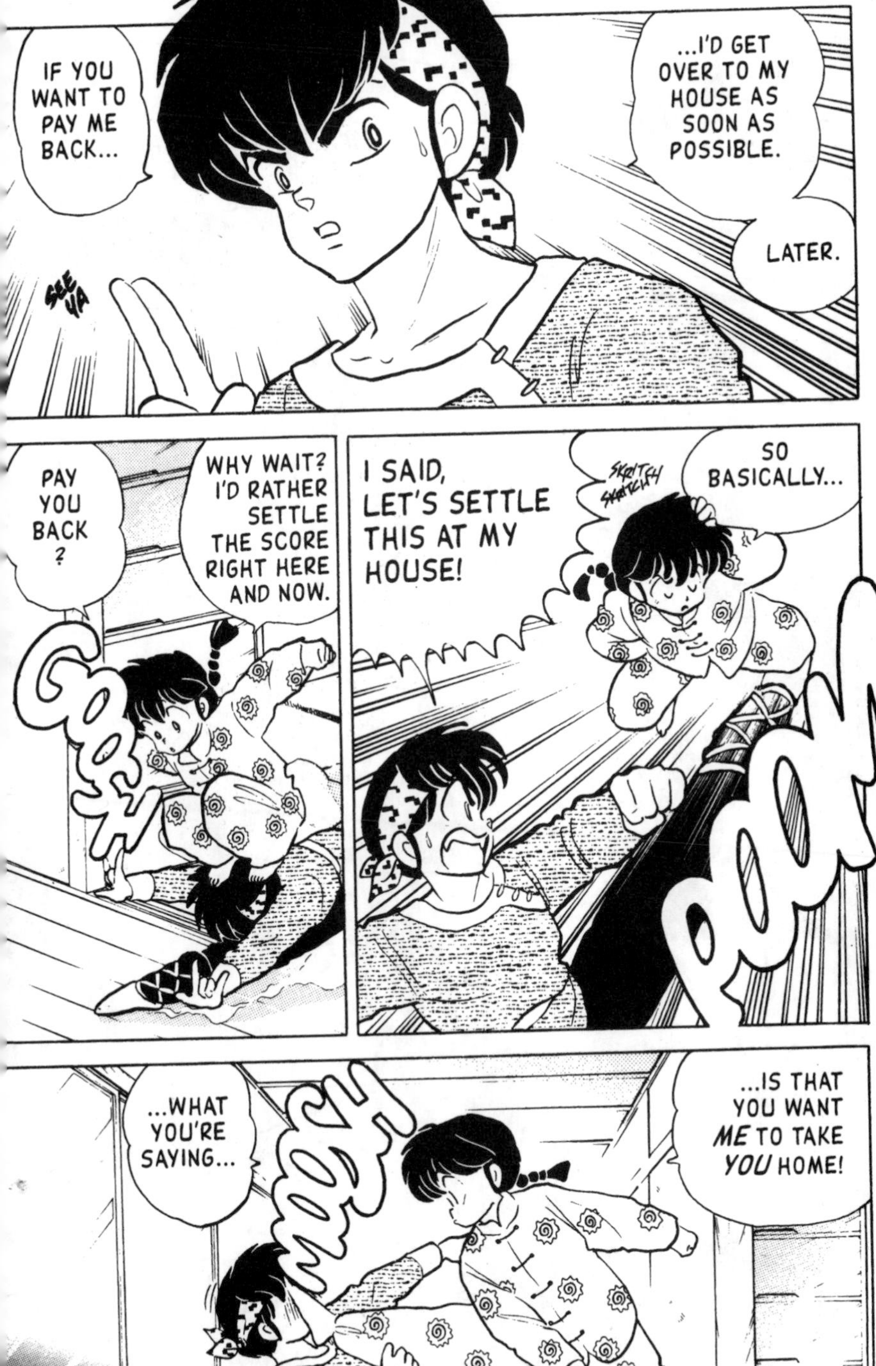
IF YOU WANT TO PAY ME BACK...
SEE YA
...I'D GET OVER TO MY HOUSE AS SOON AS POSSIBLE.
LATER.
PAY YOU BACK?
WHY WAIT? I'D RATHER SETTLE THE SCORE RIGHT HERE AND NOW.
I SAID, LET'S SETTLE THIS AT MY HOUSE!
SKRITCH SKRITCH
SO BASICALLY...
...WHAT YOU'RE SAYING...
...IS THAT YOU WANT *ME* TO TAKE *YOU* HOME!

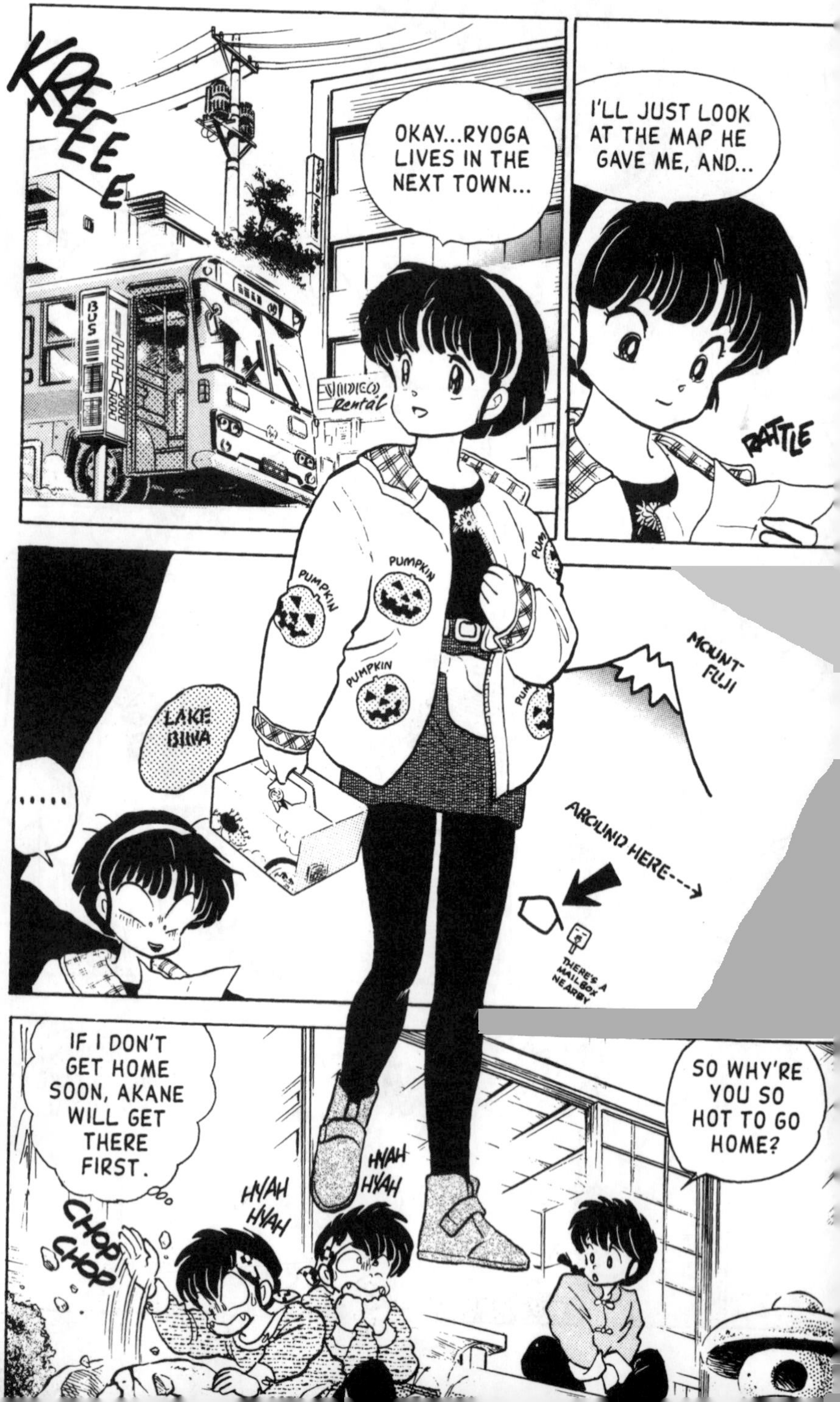
KREEEEE
OKAY...RYOGA LIVES IN THE NEXT TOWN...
I'LL JUST LOOK AT THE MAP HE GAVE ME, AND...
RATTLE
LAKE BIWA
.....
PUMPKIN
PUMPKIN
PUMPKIN
MOUNT FUJI
AROUND HERE--->
THERE'S A MAILBOX NEARBY
IF I DON'T GET HOME SOON, AKANE WILL GET THERE FIRST.
CHOP CHOP
HYAH HYAH
HYAH HYAH
SO WHY'RE YOU SO HOT TO GO HOME?

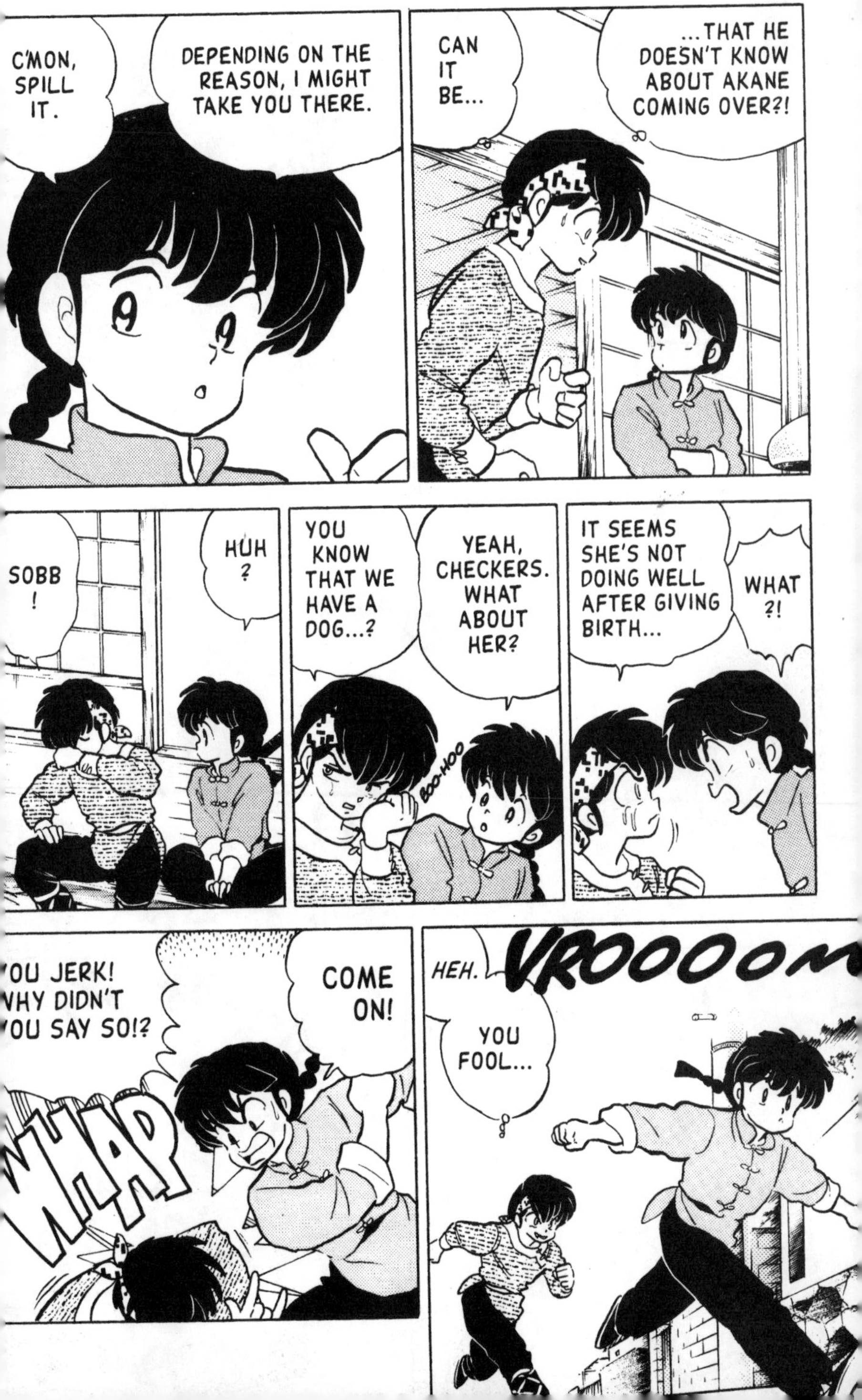
C'MON, SPILL IT.
DEPENDING ON THE REASON, I MIGHT TAKE YOU THERE.
CAN IT BE...
...THAT HE DOESN'T KNOW ABOUT AKANE COMING OVER?!
SOBB!
HUH?
YOU KNOW THAT WE HAVE A DOG...?
YEAH, CHECKERS. WHAT ABOUT HER?
BOO-HOO
IT SEEMS SHE'S NOT DOING WELL AFTER GIVING BIRTH...
WHAT?!
'OU JERK! VHY DIDN'T 'OU SAY SO!?
COME ON!
WHAP
HEH.
VROOOOOM
YOU FOOL...

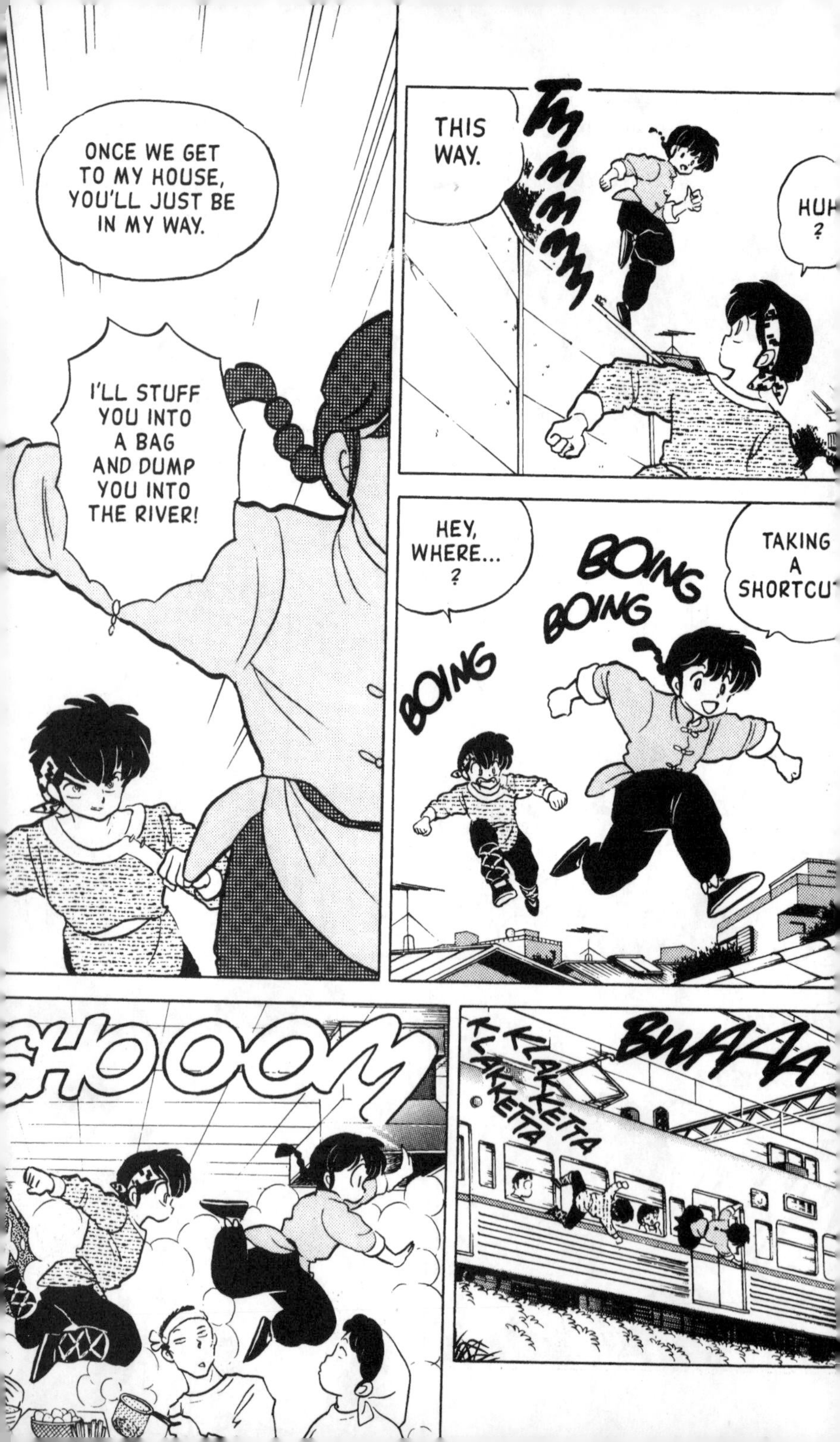
THIS WAY.
TMMMMMM
HUH ?
HEY, WHERE... ?
TAKING A SHORTCU
BOING
BOING
BOING
ONCE WE GET TO MY HOUSE, YOU'LL JUST BE IN MY WAY.
I'LL STUFF YOU INTO A BAG AND DUMP YOU INTO THE RIVER!
BWAAAA
KLAKKETTA KLAKKETTA
SHOOOM

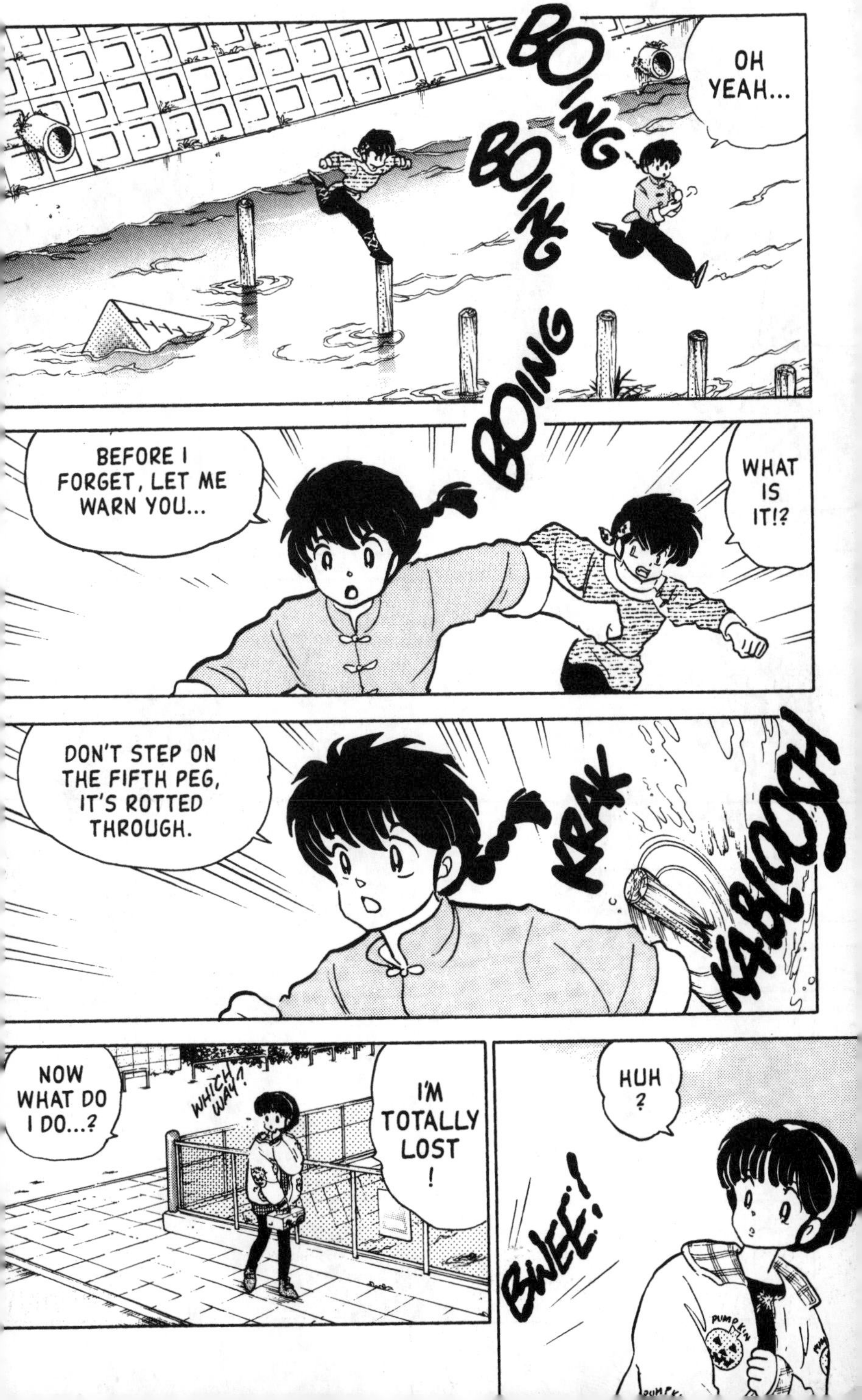
BOING
BOING
OH YEAH...
BEFORE I FORGET, LET ME WARN YOU...
BOING
WHAT IS IT!?
DON'T STEP ON THE FIFTH PEG, IT'S ROTTED THROUGH.
KRAK
KABLOOSH
NOW WHAT DO I DO...?
WHICH WAY?
I'M TOTALLY LOST!
HUH?
BWEE!

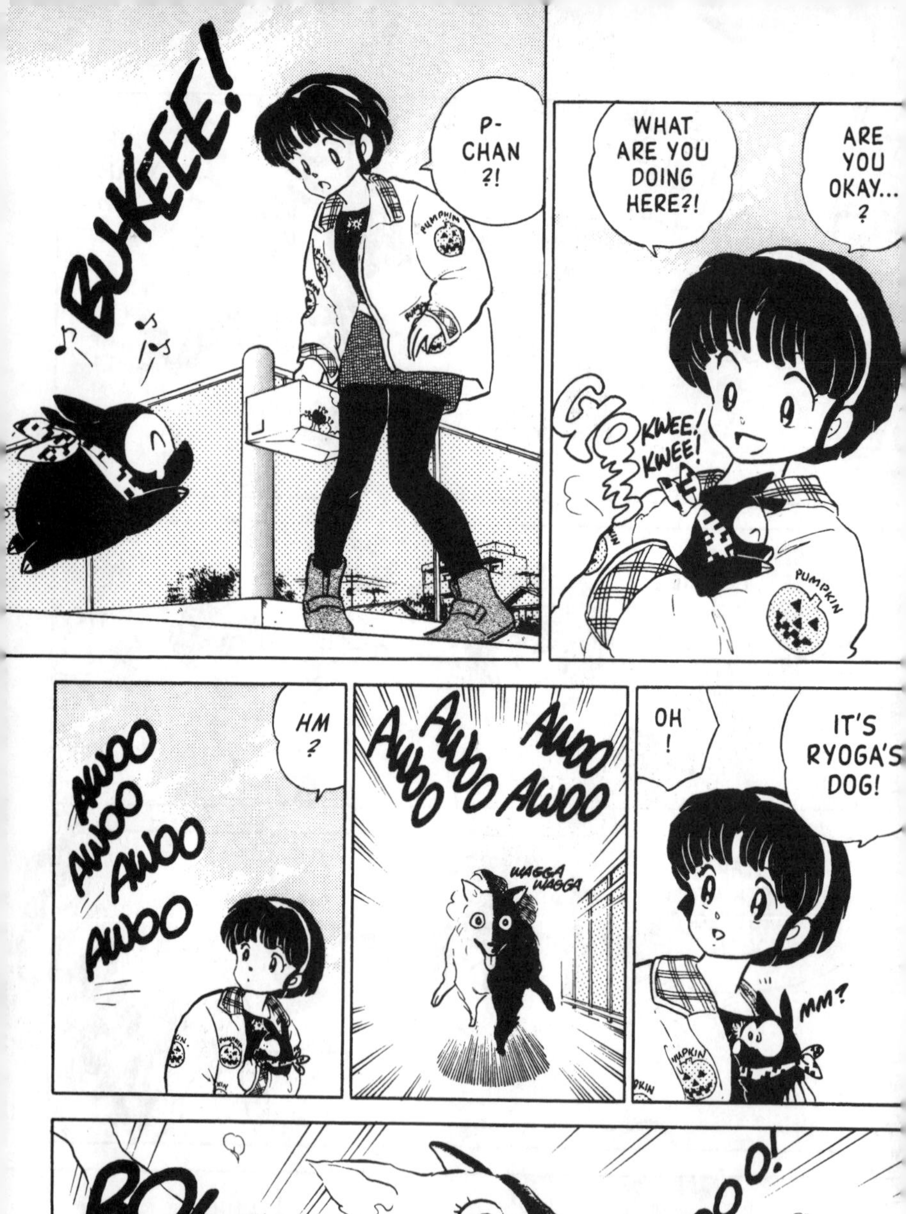
BUKEEE!
P-CHAN?!
WHAT ARE YOU DOING HERE?!
ARE YOU OKAY...?
GLOMP
KWEE! KWEE!
PUMPKIN
AWOO AWOO AWOO AWOO
HM?
AWOO AWOO AWOO AWOO AWOO AWOO
WAGGA WAGGA
OH!
IT'S RYOGA'S DOG!
MM?
BOING
AWOOOO!

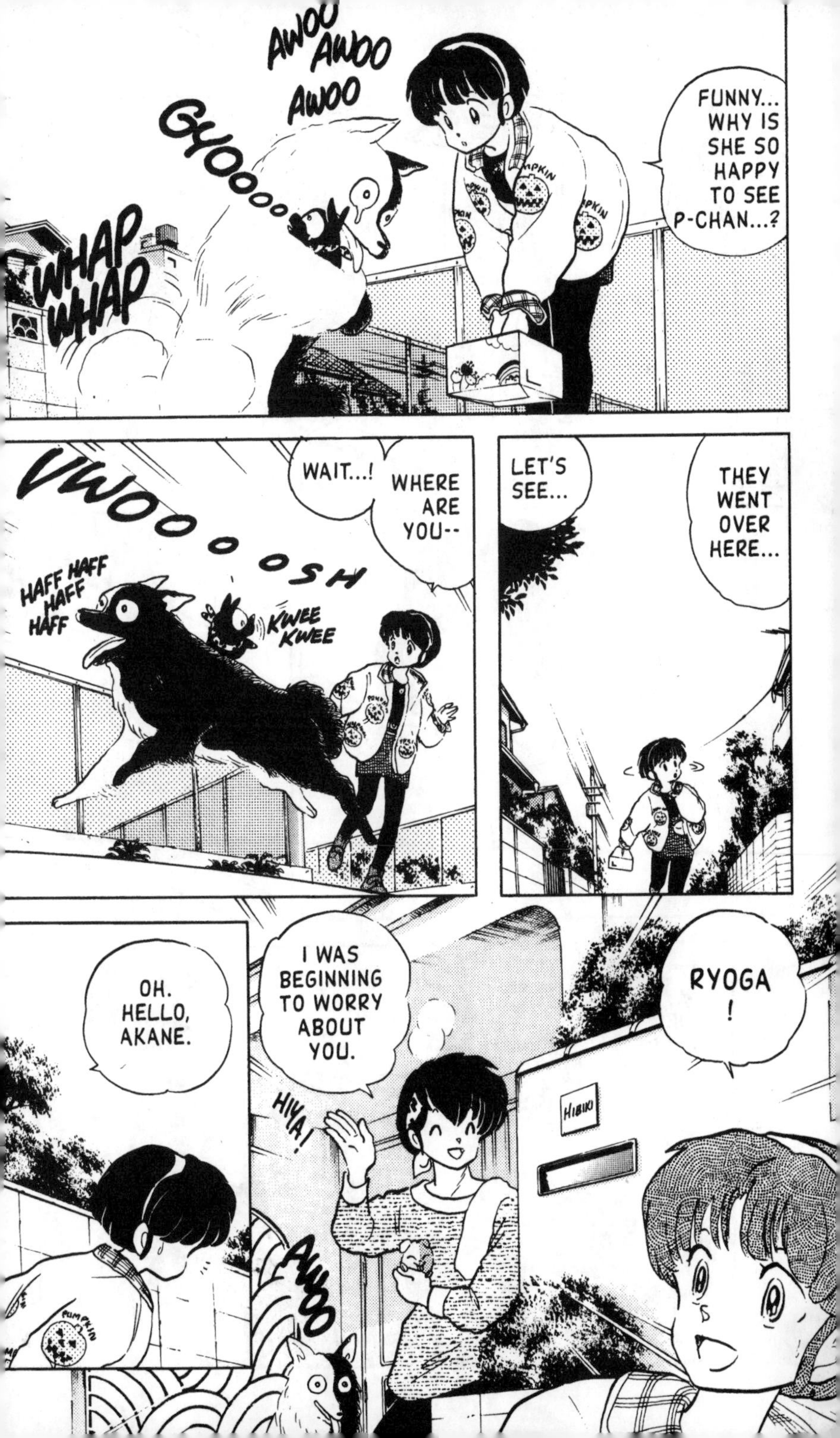
AWOO AWOO AWOO
GYOOOOO
WHAP WHAP
FUNNY... WHY IS SHE SO HAPPY TO SEE P-CHAN...?
VWOOOOOOSH
HAFF HAFF HAFF HAFF
KWEE KWEE
WAIT...!
WHERE ARE YOU--
LET'S SEE...
THEY WENT OVER HERE...
OH. HELLO, AKANE.
I WAS BEGINNING TO WORRY ABOUT YOU.
HIYA!
AWOO
RYOGA !
HIBIKI

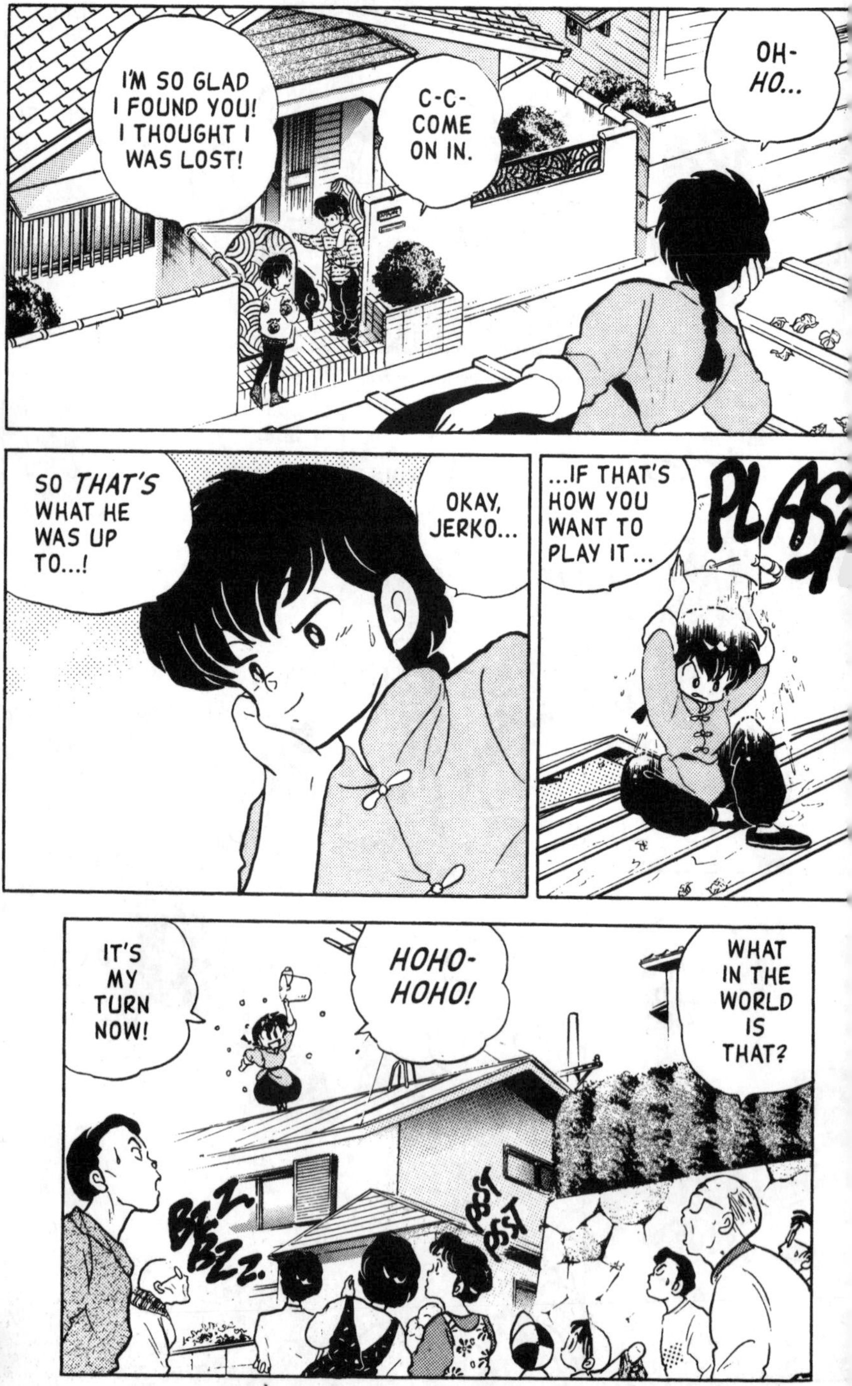
I'M SO GLAD I FOUND YOU! I THOUGHT I WAS LOST!
C-C-COME ON IN.
OH-HO...
SO THAT'S WHAT HE WAS UP TO...!
OKAY, JERKO...
...IF THAT'S HOW YOU WANT TO PLAY IT...
PLASH
IT'S MY TURN NOW!
HOHO-HOHO!
WHAT IN THE WORLD IS THAT?
BZZ BZZ.
PSST PSST

PART 8
OH, BROTHER!

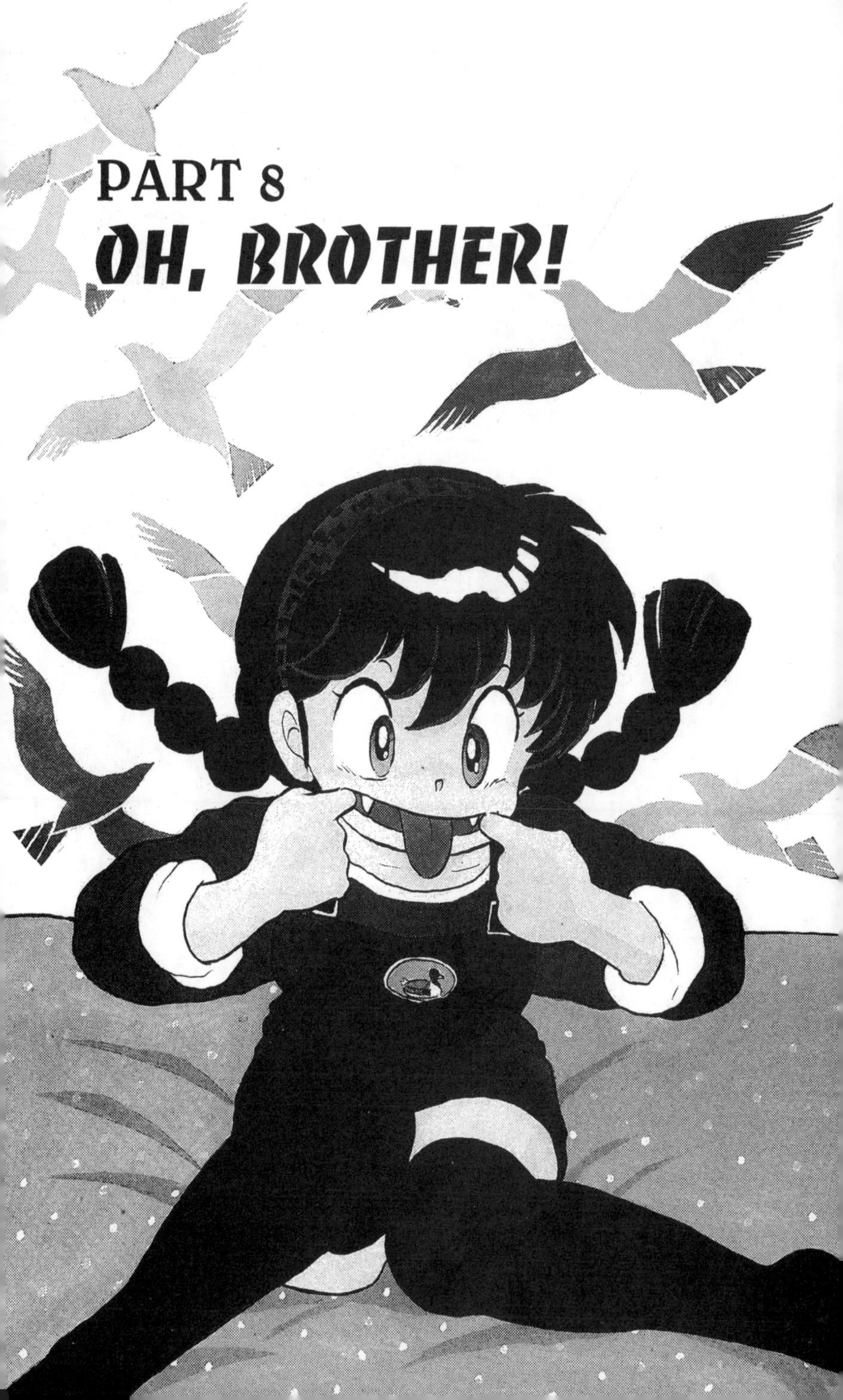

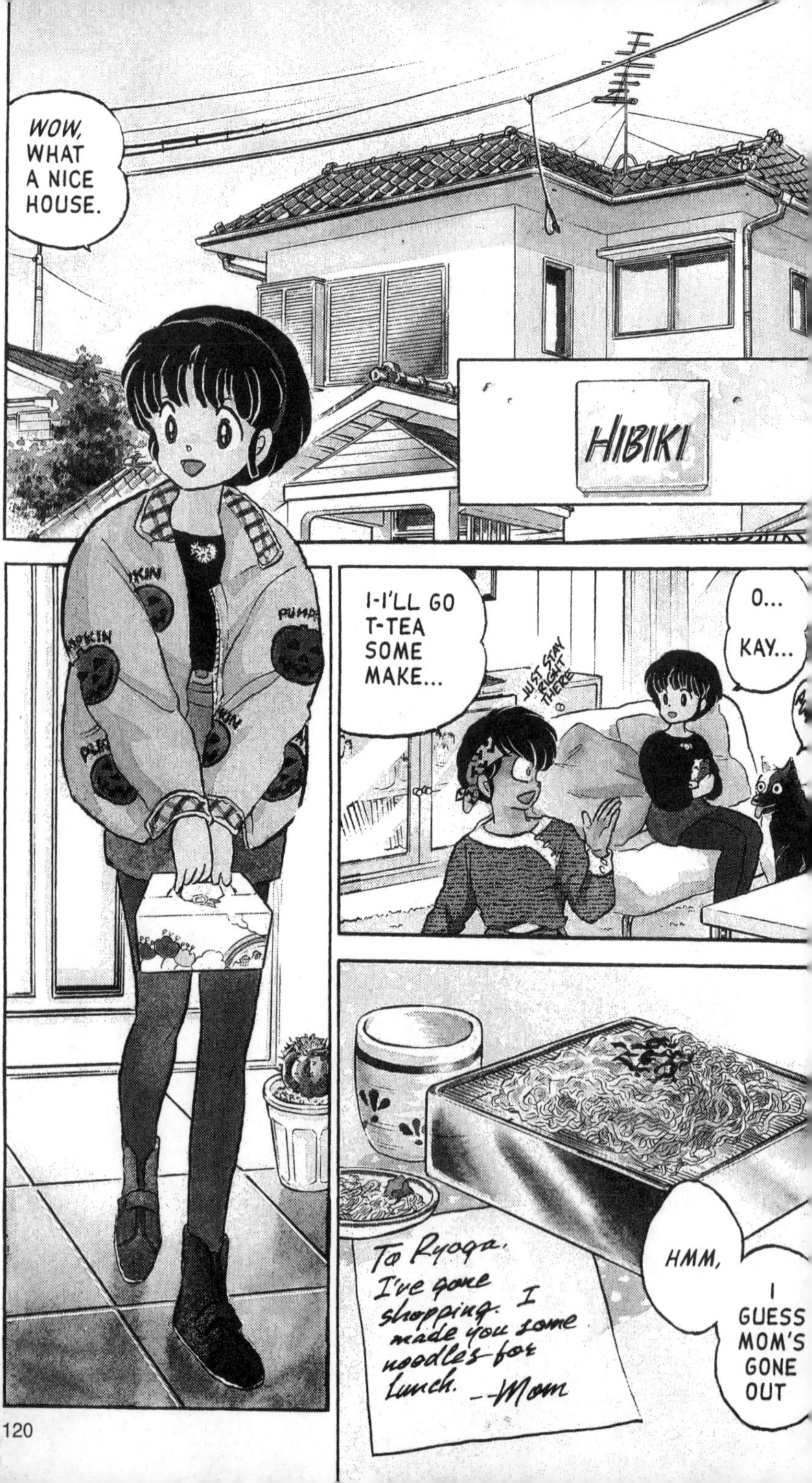
WOW, WHAT A NICE HOUSE.
HIBIKI
I-I'LL GO T-TEA SOME MAKE...
JUST STAY RIGHT THERE
O... KAY...
To Ryoga. I've gone shopping. I made you some noodles for lunch. --Mom
HMM,
I GUESS MOM'S GONE OUT

JUDGING FROM THE RIGIDITY OF THE NOODLES...

AND THE CRISPINESS OF THE WITHERED GREEN ONIONS...

I'D SAY IT'S BEEN AT LEAST 10 DAYS.

TCH,

SHE MUST BE LOST AGAIN.

AND DAD'S IN HOKKAIDO.

I've gone to Hokkaido on business. Be back in the summer.
--Dad

THAT MEANS...

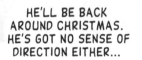

HE'LL BE BACK AROUND CHRISTMAS. HE'S GOT NO SENSE OF DIRECTION EITHER...

H!

WHICH WOULD MEAN...

NOBODY'S HOME BUT US !!

YOU MEAN WE HAVE THE HOUSE ALL TO OURSELVES?

BLUSH

OH, YESSSS !

SSSSSS

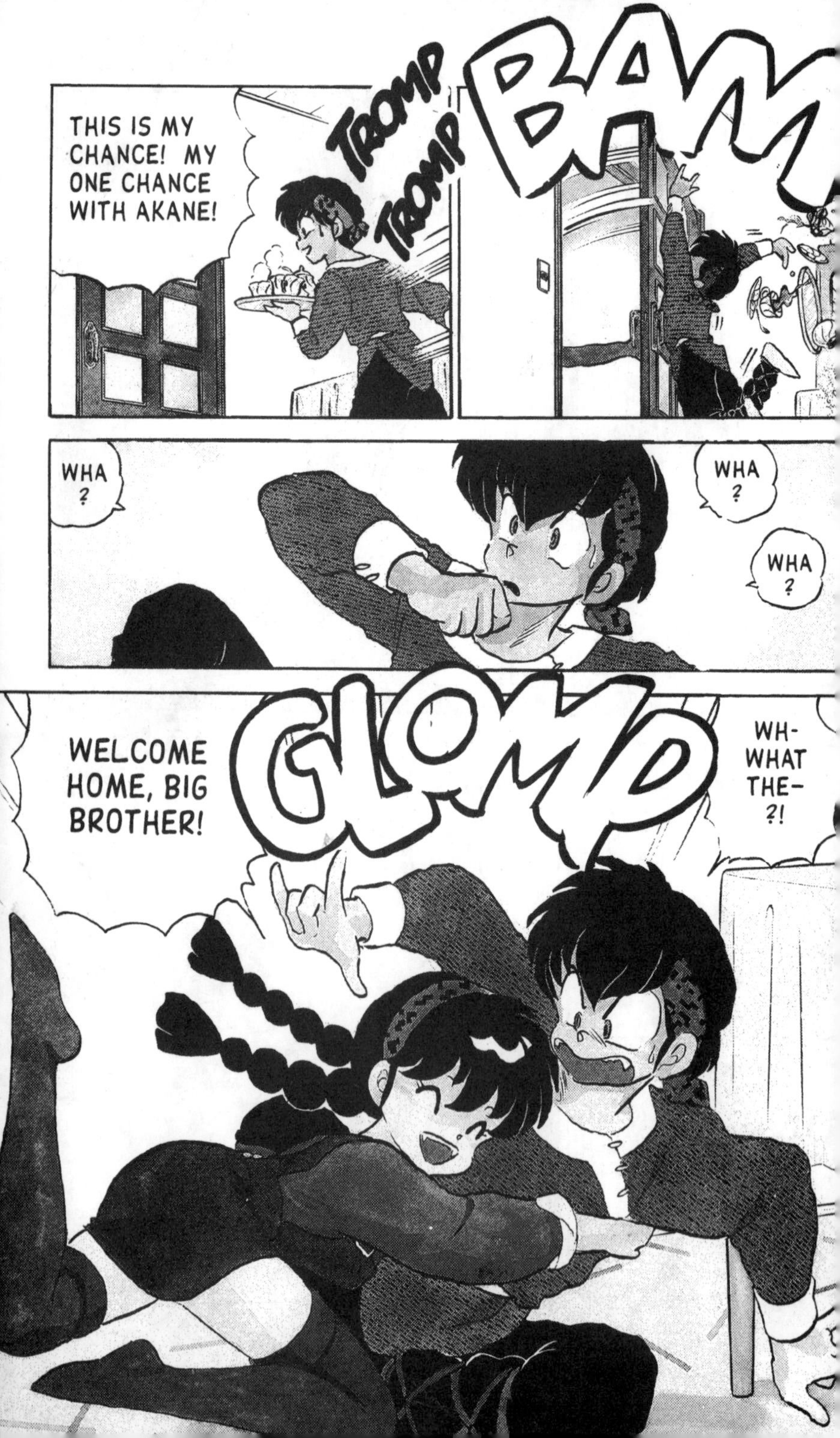
THIS IS MY CHANCE! MY ONE CHANCE WITH AKANE!
TROMP TROMP
BAM
WHA ?
WHA ?
WHA ?
WELCOME HOME, BIG BROTHER!
GLOMP
WH-WHAT THE-?!

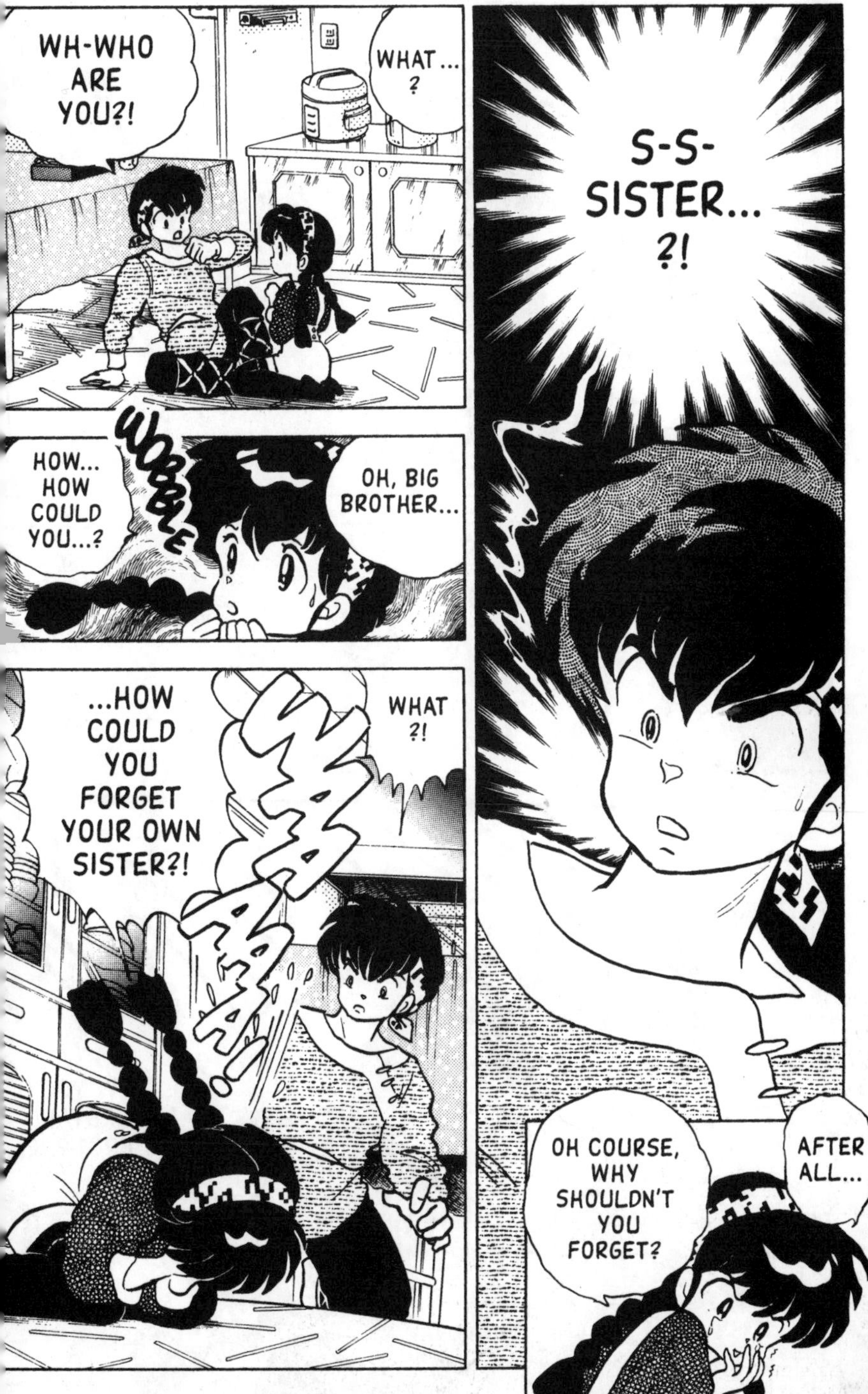
WH-WHO ARE YOU?!
WHAT...?
HOW... HOW COULD YOU...?
WOBBLE
OH, BIG BROTHER...
...HOW COULD YOU FORGET YOUR OWN SISTER?!
WHAT?!
S-S-SISTER...?!
OH COURSE, WHY SHOULDN'T YOU FORGET?
AFTER ALL...

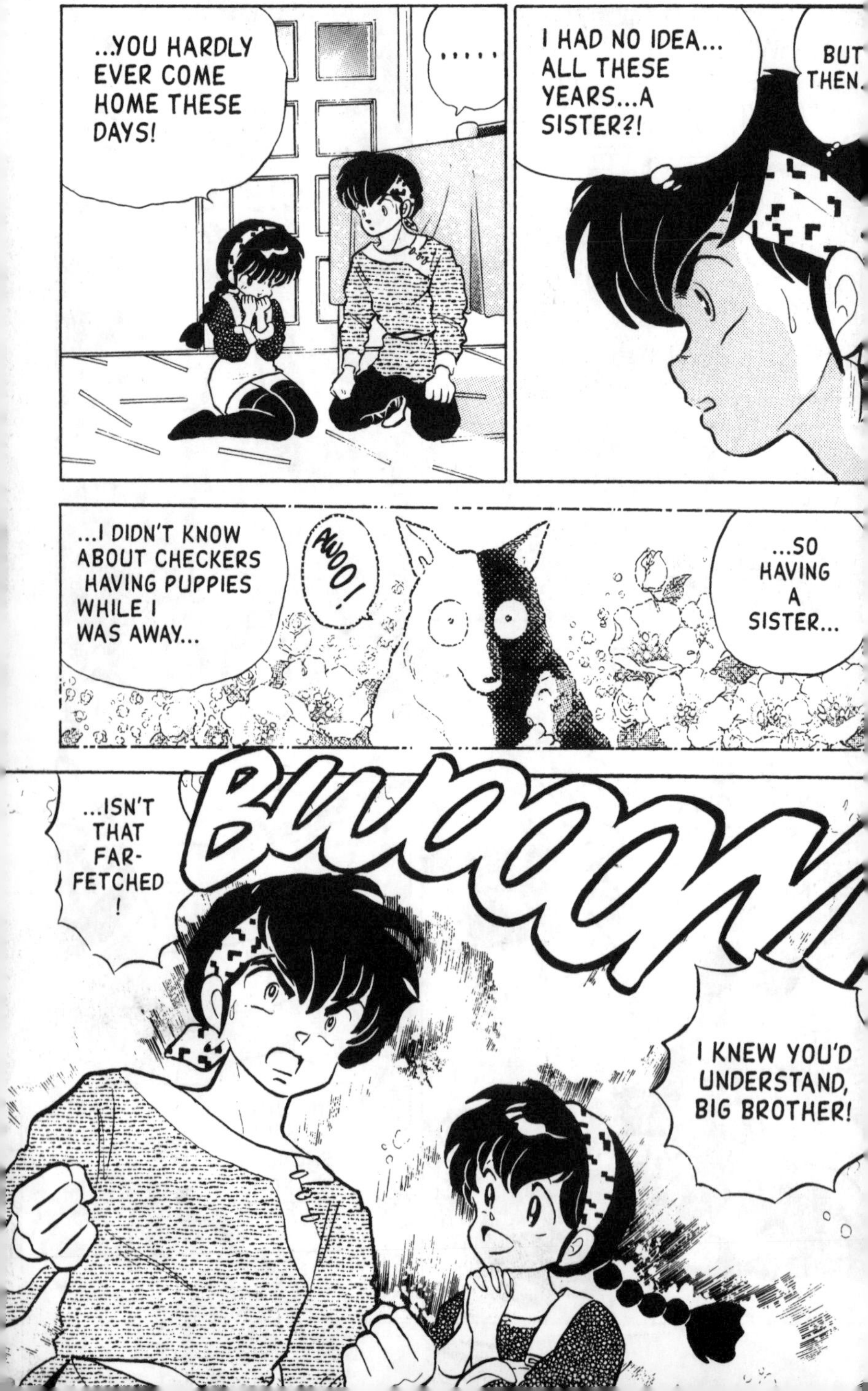
...YOU HARDLY EVER COME HOME THESE DAYS!
.....
I HAD NO IDEA... ALL THESE YEARS...A SISTER?!
BUT THEN.
...I DIDN'T KNOW ABOUT CHECKERS HAVING PUPPIES WHILE I WAS AWAY...
AWOO!
...SO HAVING A SISTER...
...ISN'T THAT FAR-FETCHED!
I KNEW YOU'D UNDERSTAND, BIG BROTHER!

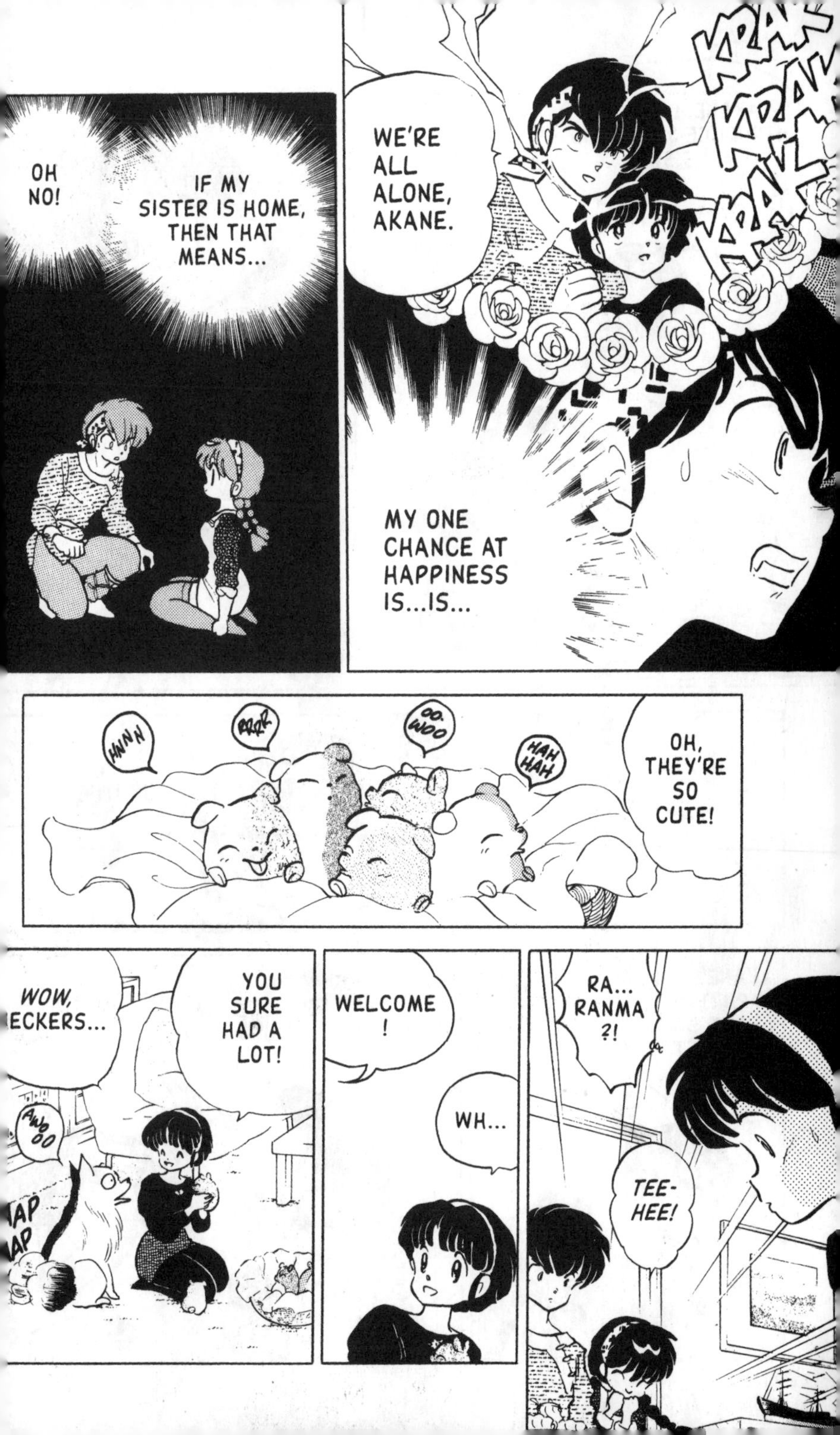
OH NO!
IF MY SISTER IS HOME, THEN THAT MEANS...
WE'RE ALL ALONE, AKANE.
KRAK KRAK KRAK
MY ONE CHANCE AT HAPPINESS IS...IS...
HNNN
RRRR
OO-WOO
HAH HAH
OH, THEY'RE SO CUTE!
WOW, ECKERS...
YOU SURE HAD A LOT!
AWOOO
AP AP
WELCOME!
WH...
RA... RANMA?!
TEE-HEE!

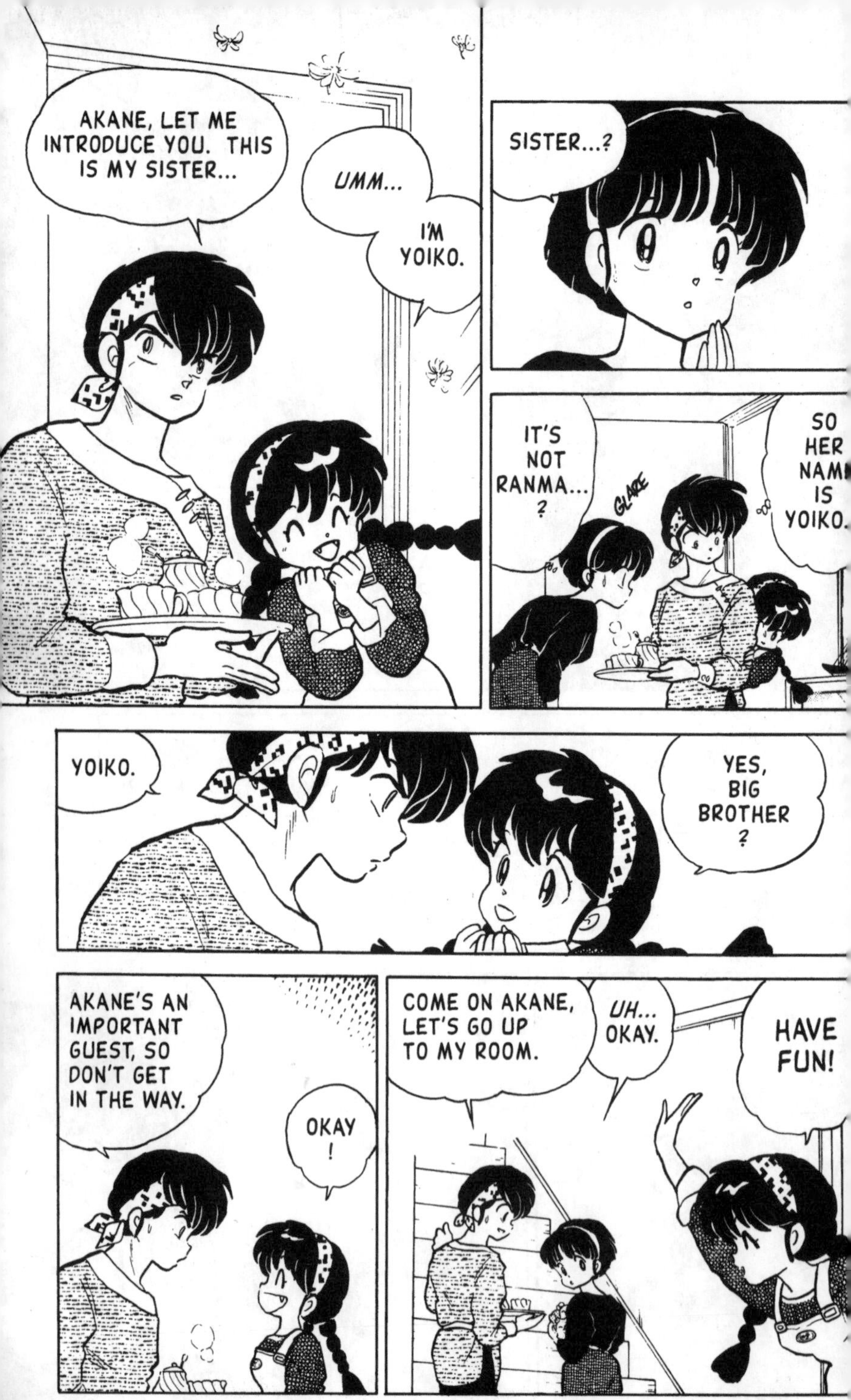
AKANE, LET ME INTRODUCE YOU. THIS IS MY SISTER...
UMM...
I'M YOIKO.
SISTER...?
IT'S NOT RANMA...?
GLARE
SO HER NAM IS YOIKO.
YOIKO.
YES, BIG BROTHER?
AKANE'S AN IMPORTANT GUEST, SO DON'T GET IN THE WAY.
OKAY!
COME ON AKANE, LET'S GO UP TO MY ROOM.
UH... OKAY.
HAVE FUN!

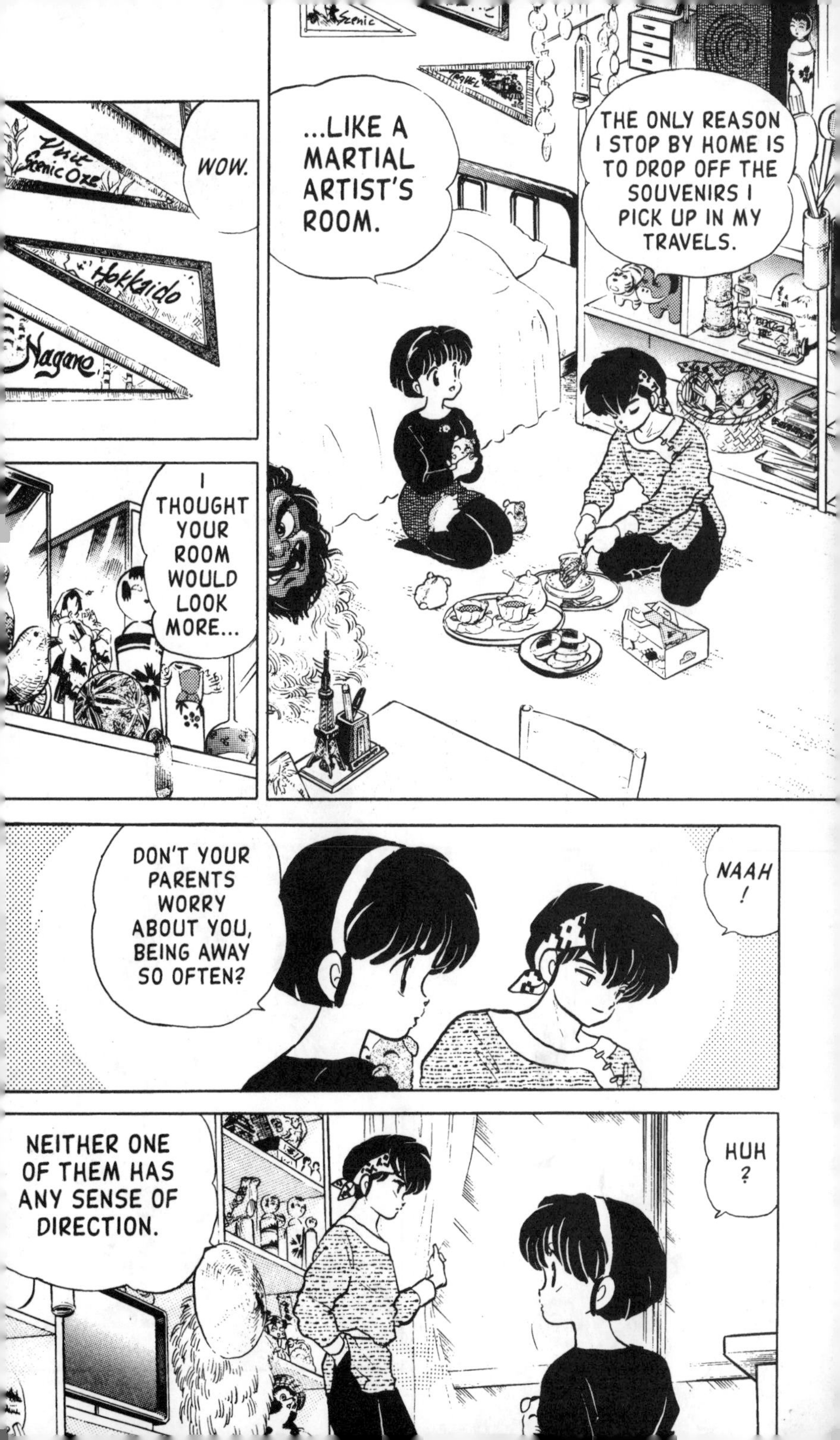
Visit Scenic Oze
Hokkaido
Nagano
WOW.
I THOUGHT YOUR ROOM WOULD LOOK MORE...
Scenic
...LIKE A MARTIAL ARTIST'S ROOM.
THE ONLY REASON I STOP BY HOME IS TO DROP OFF THE SOUVENIRS I PICK UP IN MY TRAVELS.
DON'T YOUR PARENTS WORRY ABOUT YOU, BEING AWAY SO OFTEN?
NAAH!
NEITHER ONE OF THEM HAS ANY SENSE OF DIRECTION.
HUH?

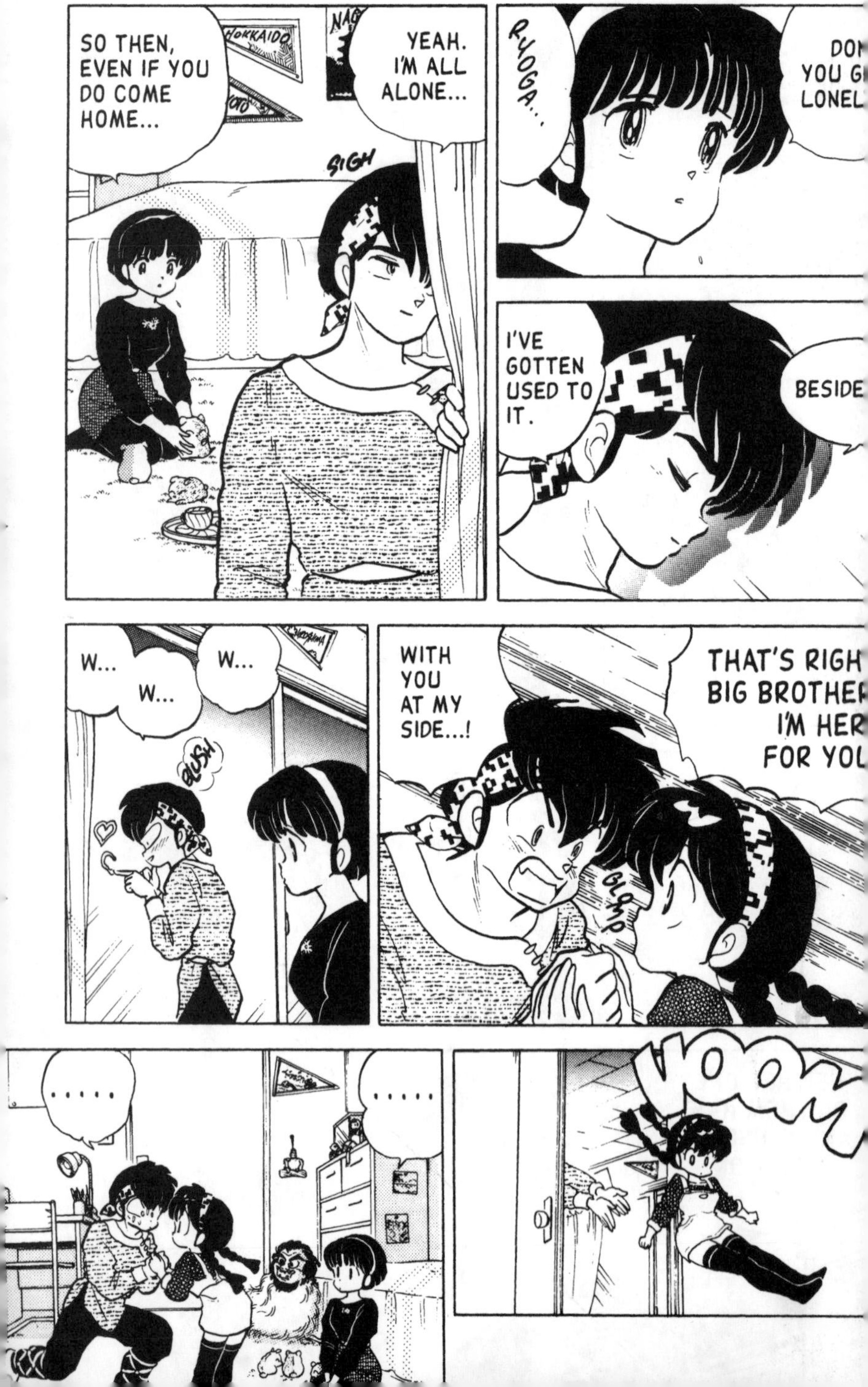

SO THEN, EVEN IF YOU DO COME HOME...
YEAH. I'M ALL ALONE...
SIGH
RYOGA...
DON YOU G LONEL
I'VE GOTTEN USED TO IT.
BESIDE
W...
W...
W...
BLUSH
WITH YOU AT MY SIDE...!
THAT'S RIGH BIG BROTHER I'M HER FOR YOU
GLOMP
.....
.....
VOOM

SORRY ABOUT MY SISTER...

IT'S OKAY.

YOUR SISTER...

...DOESN'T LOOK MUCH LIKE YOU, DOES SHE?

I DO TOO!

POP

THESE FANGS ARE PROOF THAT WE'RE RELATED!

BOOT

HEH

.....

DO YOU WANT TO SEE A VIDEO OF CHECKERS AS A PUPPY?

OH, YES!

I'D LOVE TO!

HMPH.

THE MOOD ISN'T QUITE RIGHT... YET...

AWOO

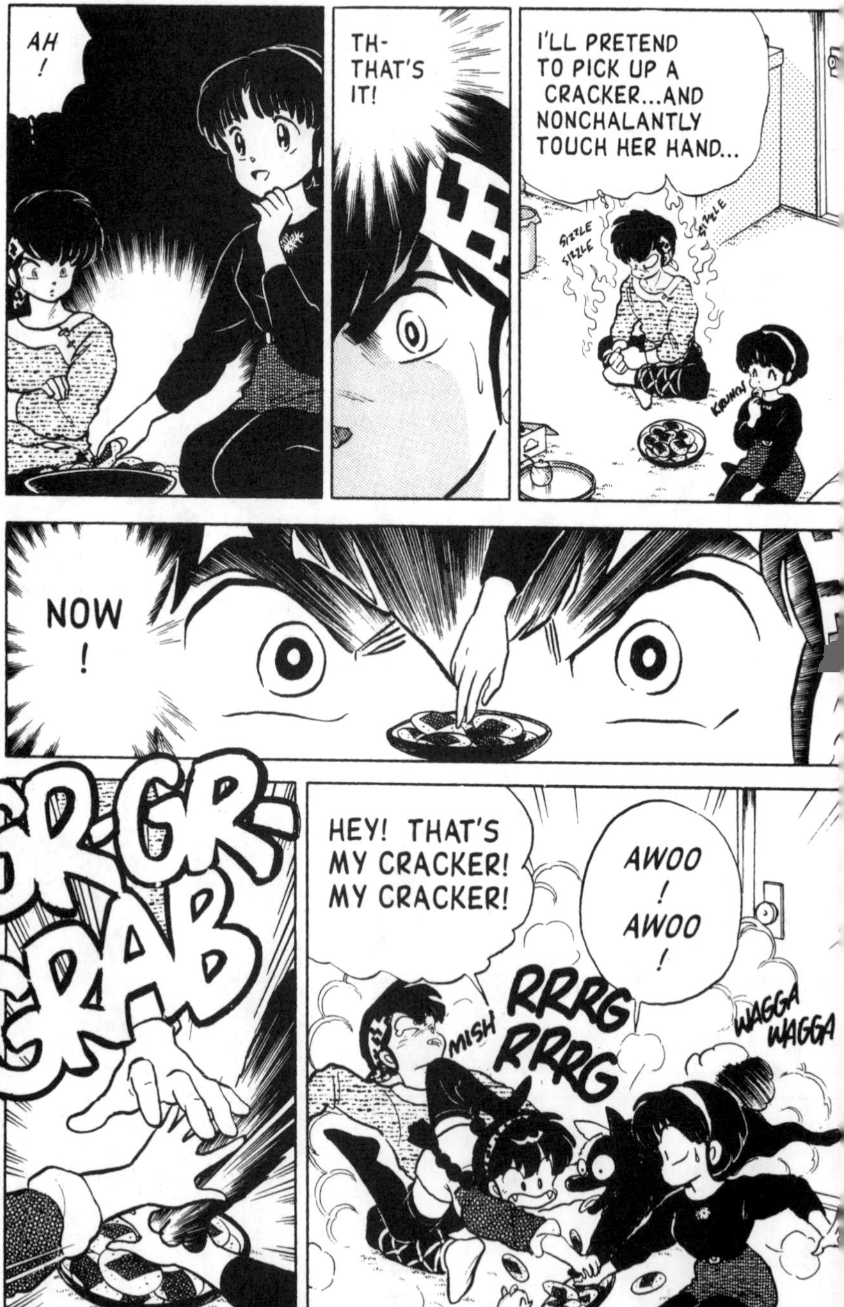
AH!
TH- THAT'S IT!
I'LL PRETEND TO PICK UP A CRACKER...AND NONCHALANTLY TOUCH HER HAND...
SIZZLE SIZZLE
SIZZLE
KRUNCH
NOW!
GR-GR-GRAB
HEY! THAT'S MY CRACKER! MY CRACKER!
AWOO! AWOO!
MISH
RRRG RRRG
WAGGA WAGGA

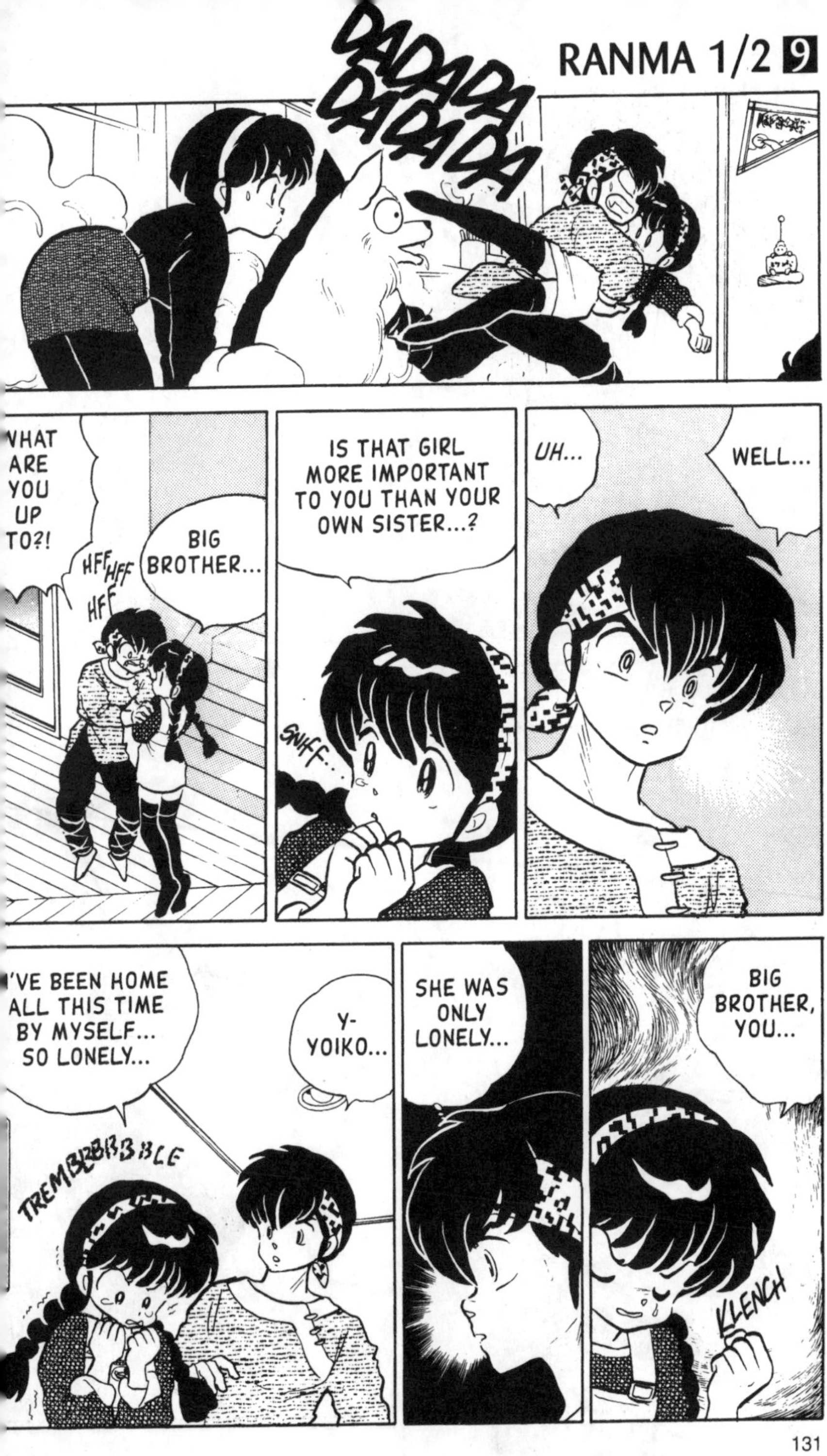
DADADA DADADA
WHAT ARE YOU UP TO?!
HFF HFF HFF
BIG BROTHER...
IS THAT GIRL MORE IMPORTANT TO YOU THAN YOUR OWN SISTER...?
SNIFF...
UH...
WELL...
I'VE BEEN HOME ALL THIS TIME BY MYSELF... SO LONELY...
TREMBLBLBLBLE
Y- YOIKO...
SHE WAS ONLY LONELY...
BIG BROTHER, YOU...
KLENCH

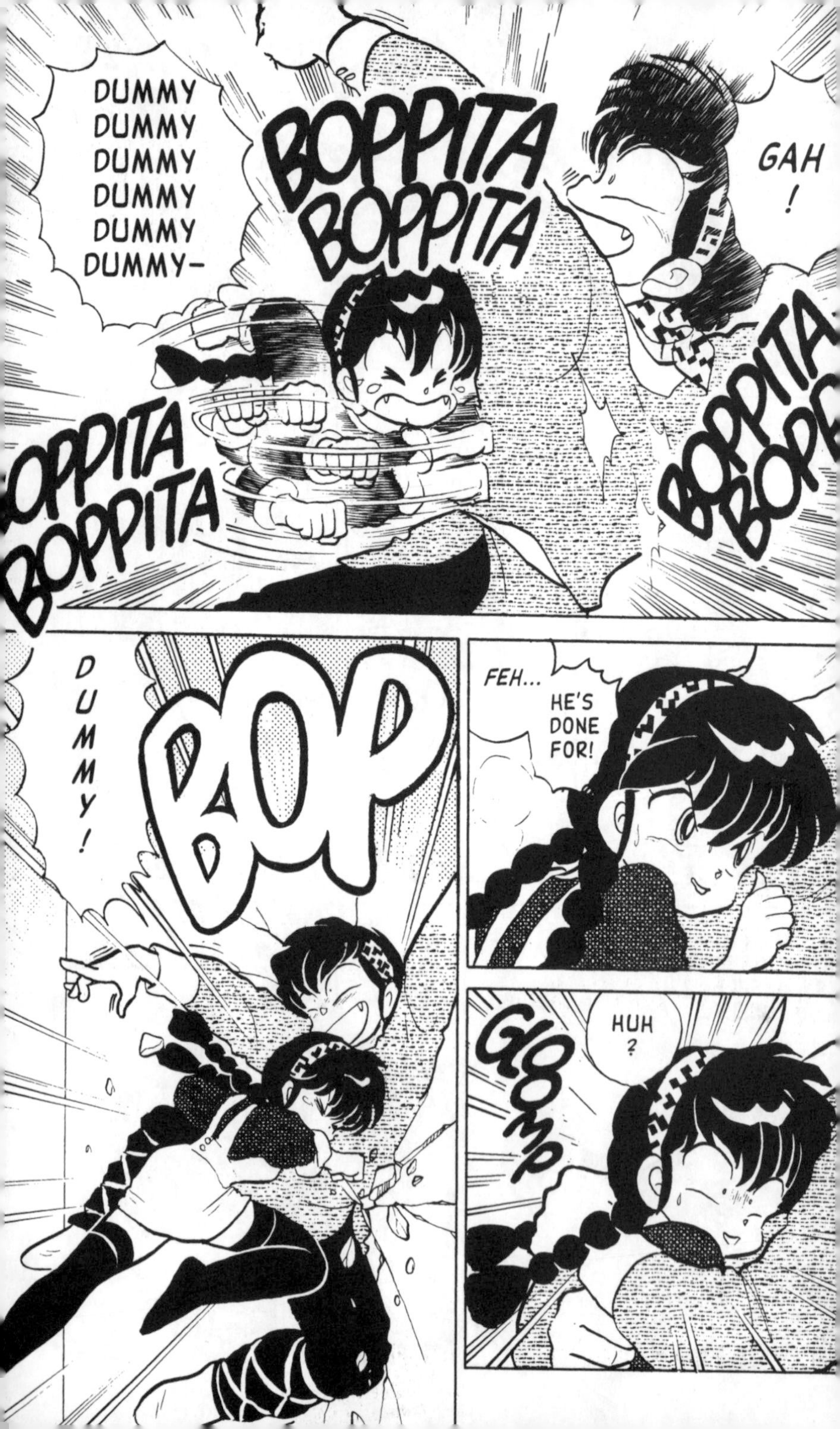
DUMMY DUMMY DUMMY DUMMY DUMMY DUMMY DUMMY-
BOPPITA BOPPITA
GAH !
BOPPITA BOPPITA
BOPPITA BOPP
DUMMY!
BOP
FEH...
HE'S DONE FOR!
HUH ?
GLOMP

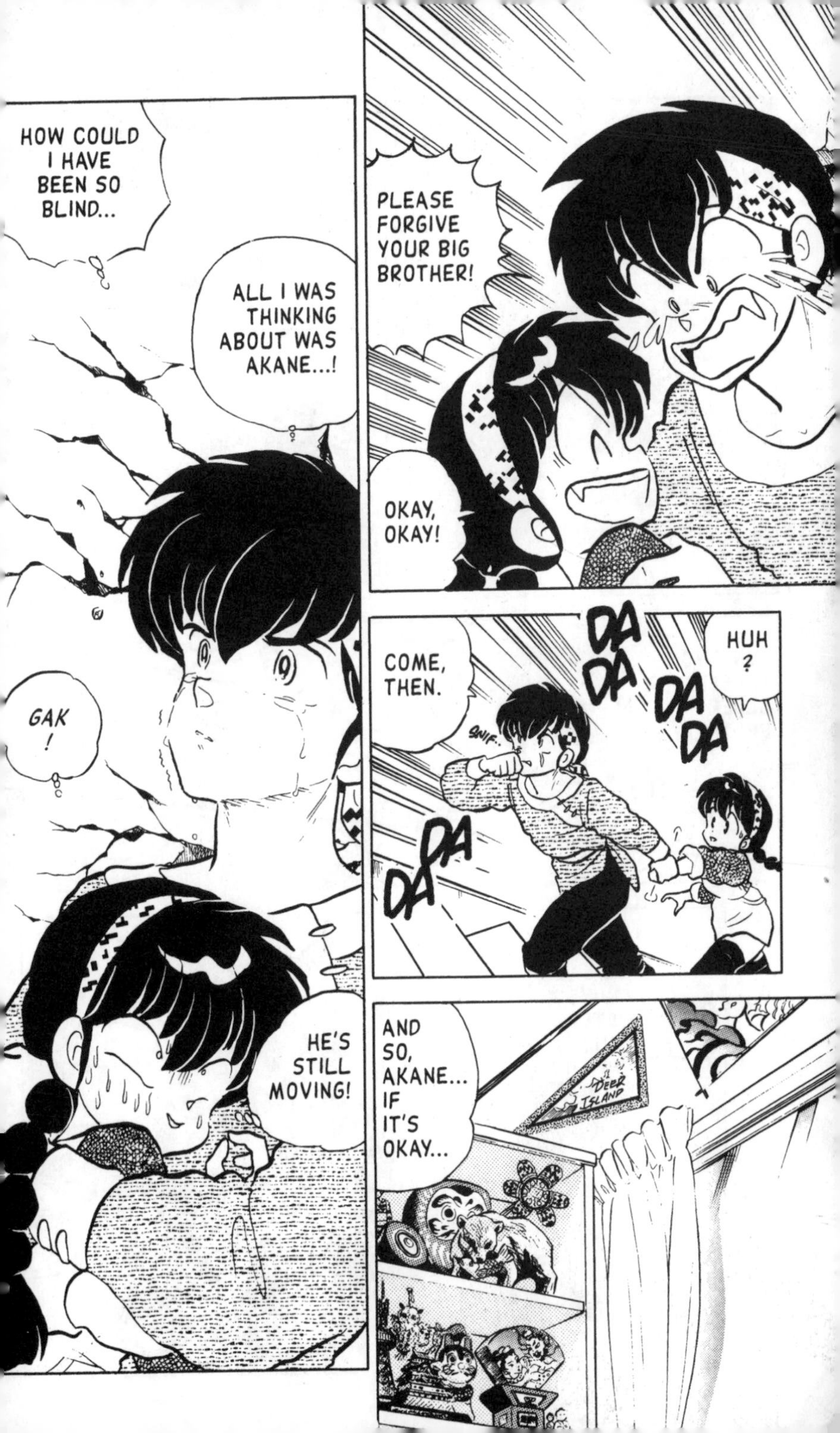
HOW COULD I HAVE BEEN SO BLIND...
ALL I WAS THINKING ABOUT WAS AKANE...!
GAK!
HE'S STILL MOVING!
PLEASE FORGIVE YOUR BIG BROTHER!
OKAY, OKAY!
COME, THEN.
SNIF..
DA DA
DA DA
HUH?
DA DA
AND SO, AKANE... IF IT'S OKAY...
DEER ISLAND

...WILL YOU ALLOW MY SISTER TO JOIN US?

UM...IT'S OKAY WITH ME, BUT...

WELL, IF I STILL GOT HIM HOOKED...

...I GUE I BETTE KEEP REELIN HIM IN

I'M SORRY, BIG BROTHER! YOU WERE FLIRTING WITH HER WEREN'T YOU:

TEE HEE

DON'T YOU TEASE YOUR OLDER BROTHER!

POKE

HEH... IT'S NOT SO BAD HAVING A SISTER... I GUESS.

OH, BIG BROTHER...

SHE SURE LOOKS A LOT LIKE RANMA.

BLUSH

SKRITCH SKRITCH

PART 9
GET LOST, YOIKO!

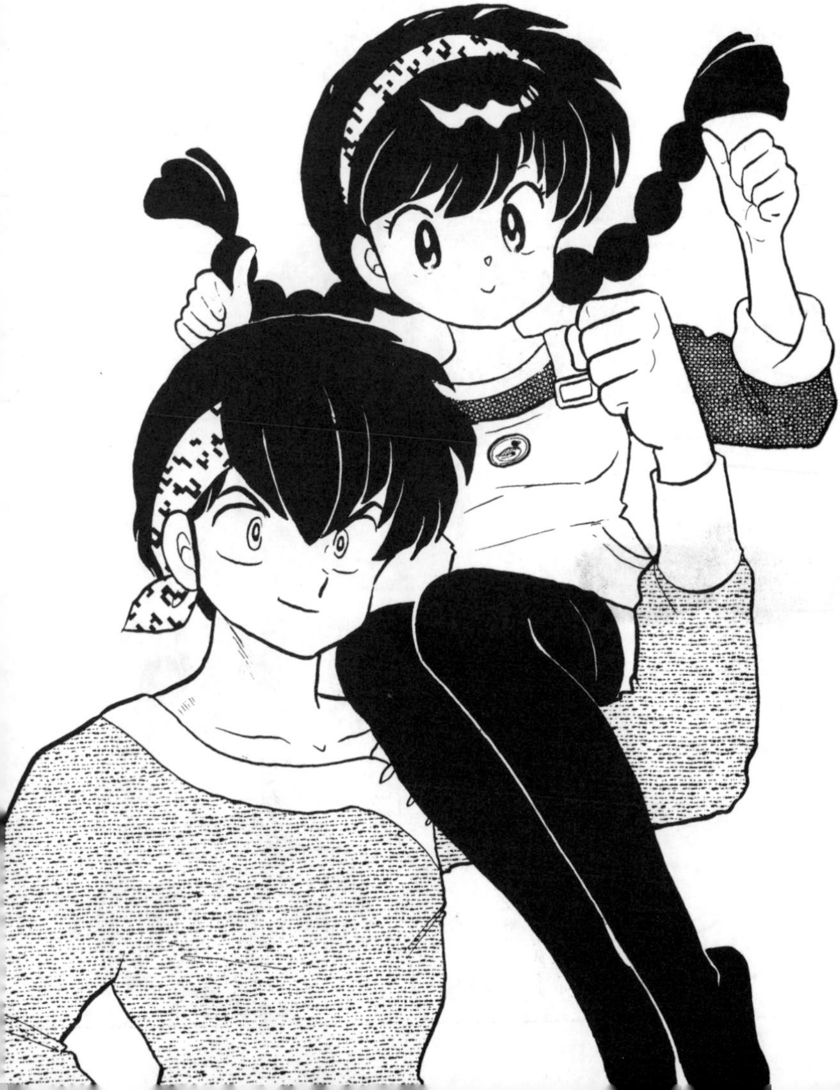

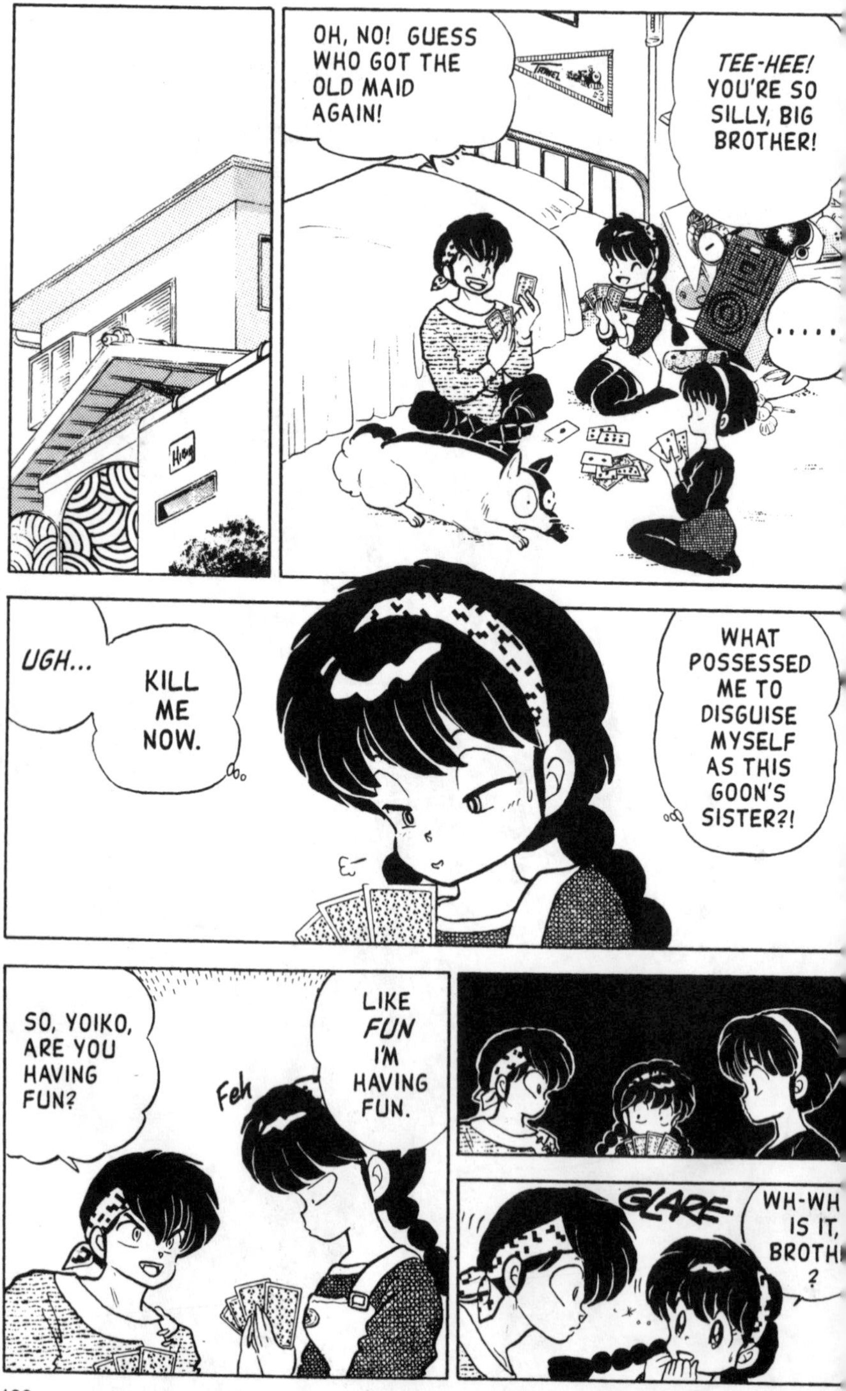
OH, NO! GUESS WHO GOT THE OLD MAID AGAIN!
TEE-HEE! YOU'RE SO SILLY, BIG BROTHER!
.....
UGH... KILL ME NOW.
WHAT POSSESSED ME TO DISGUISE MYSELF AS THIS GOON'S SISTER?!
SO, YOIKO, ARE YOU HAVING FUN?
Feh
LIKE FUN I'M HAVING FUN.
GLARE
WH-WH IS IT, BROTH ?

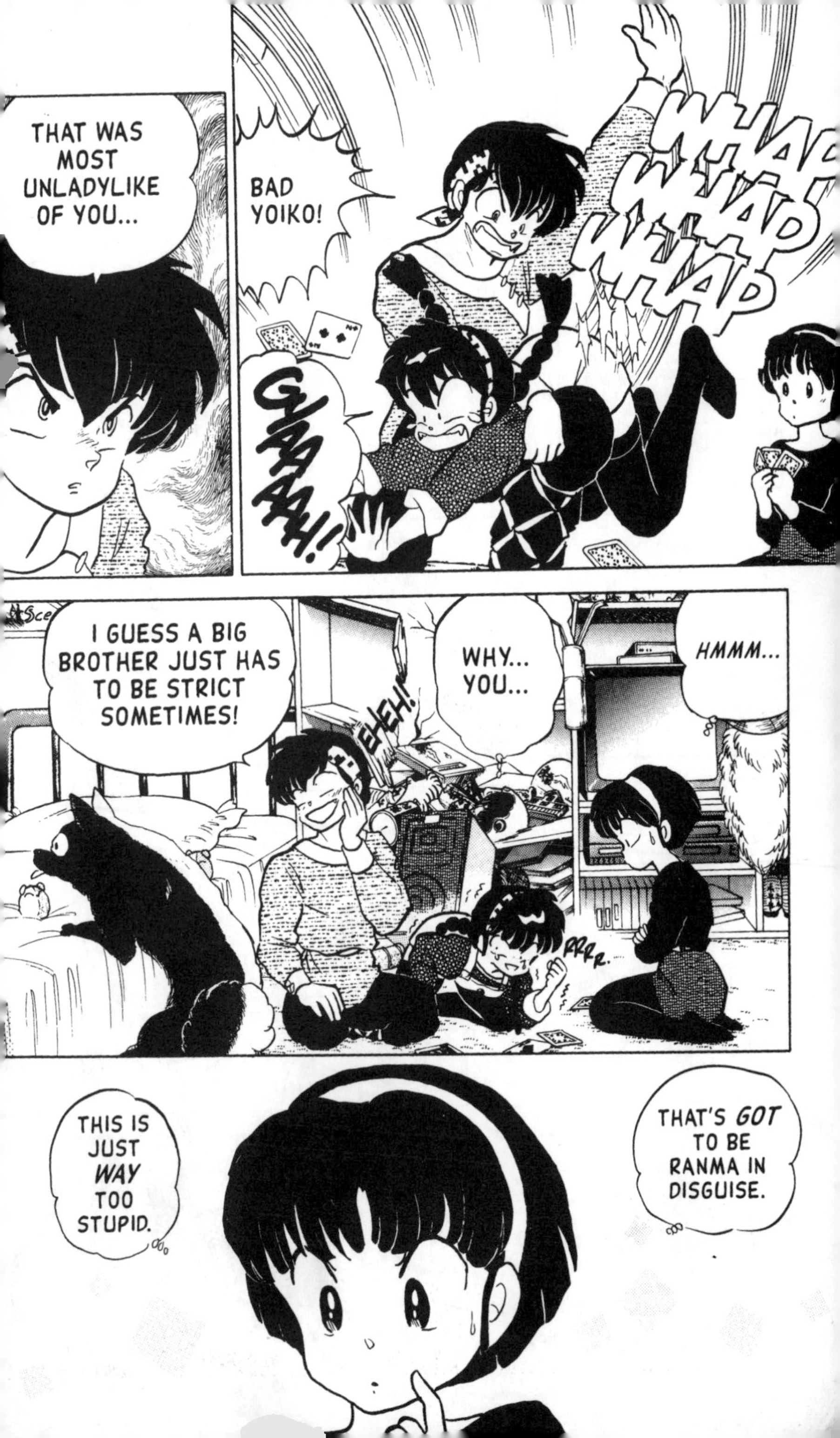
THAT WAS MOST UNLADYLIKE OF YOU...
BAD YOIKO!
WHAP WHAP WHAP WHAP
GWAAAAH!!
I GUESS A BIG BROTHER JUST HAS TO BE STRICT SOMETIMES!
EHEH!
WHY... YOU...
RRRR.
HMMM...
THIS IS JUST *WAY* TOO STUPID.
THAT'S *GOT* TO BE RANMA IN DISGUISE.

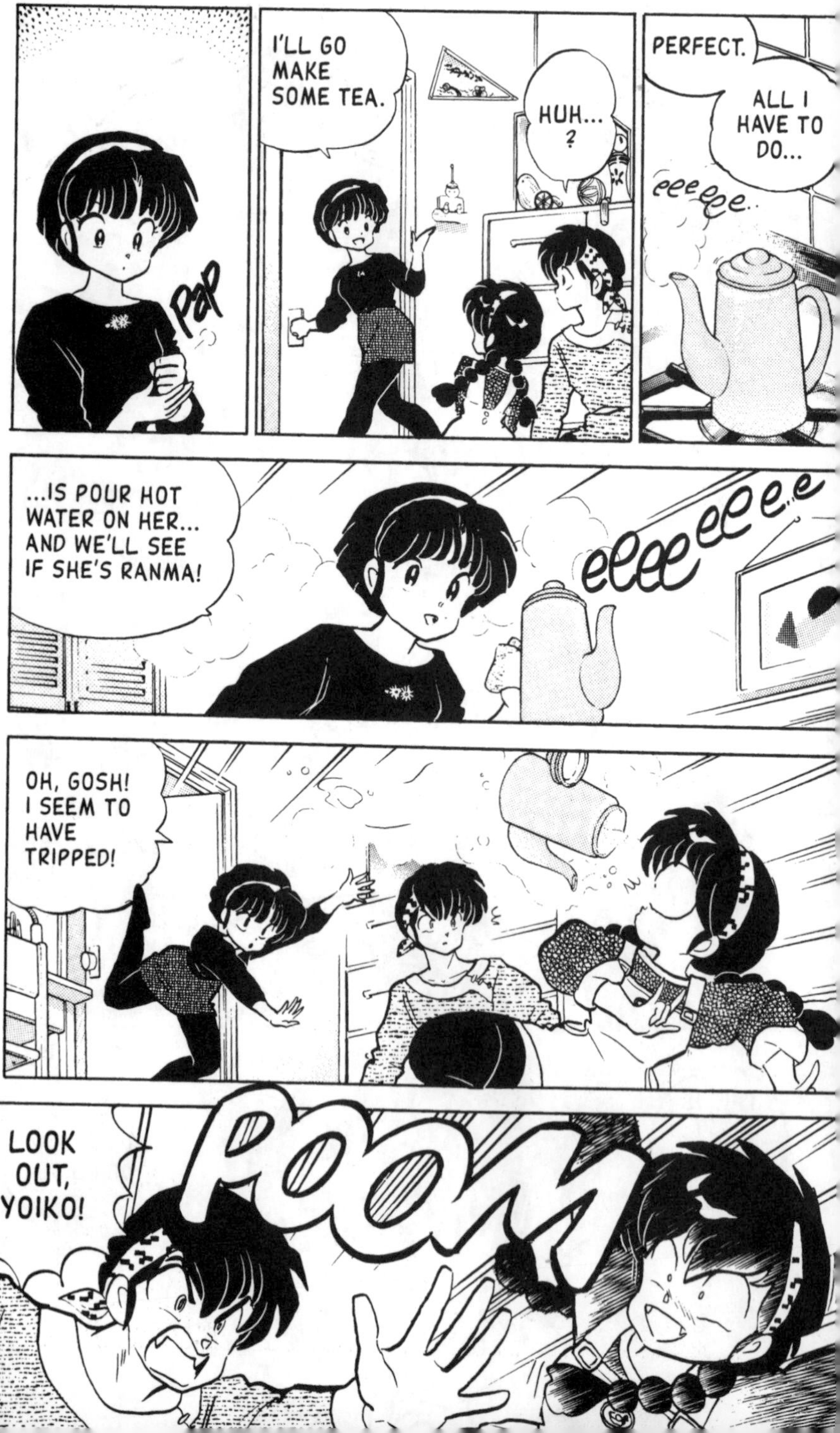
PAP
I'LL GO MAKE SOME TEA.
HUH...?
PERFECT.
ALL I HAVE TO DO...
eeeeee..
...IS POUR HOT WATER ON HER... AND WE'LL SEE IF SHE'S RANMA!
eeeeeeee
OH, GOSH! I SEEM TO HAVE TRIPPED!
LOOK OUT, YOIKO!
POOM

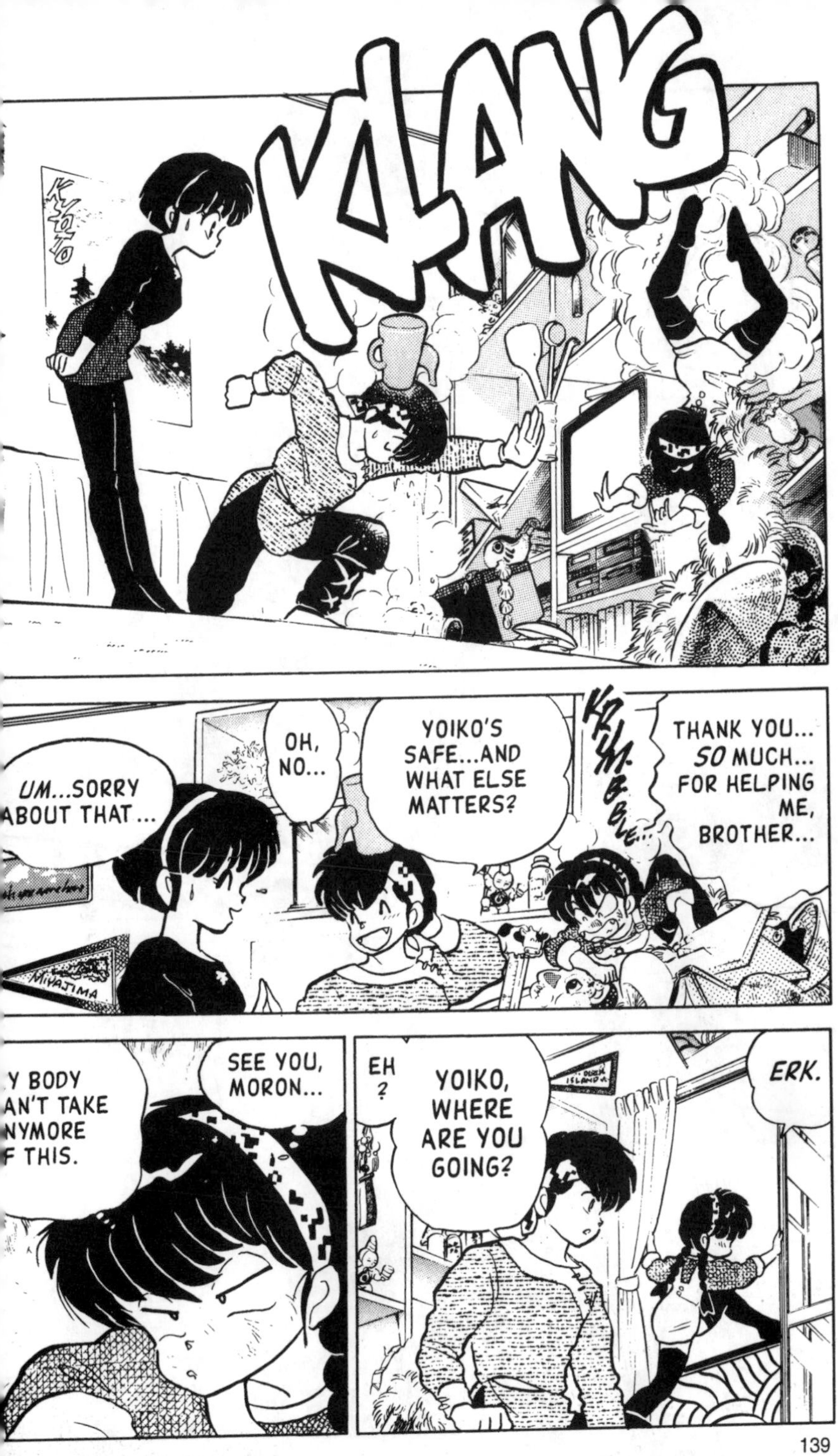
KLANG
KYOTO
UM...SORRY ABOUT THAT...
OH, NO...
YOIKO'S SAFE...AND WHAT ELSE MATTERS?
KRUMBBLE...
THANK YOU... SO MUCH... FOR HELPING ME, BROTHER...
MIYAJIMA
Y BODY AN'T TAKE NYMORE F THIS.
SEE YOU, MORON...
EH ?
YOIKO, WHERE ARE YOU GOING?
ERK.

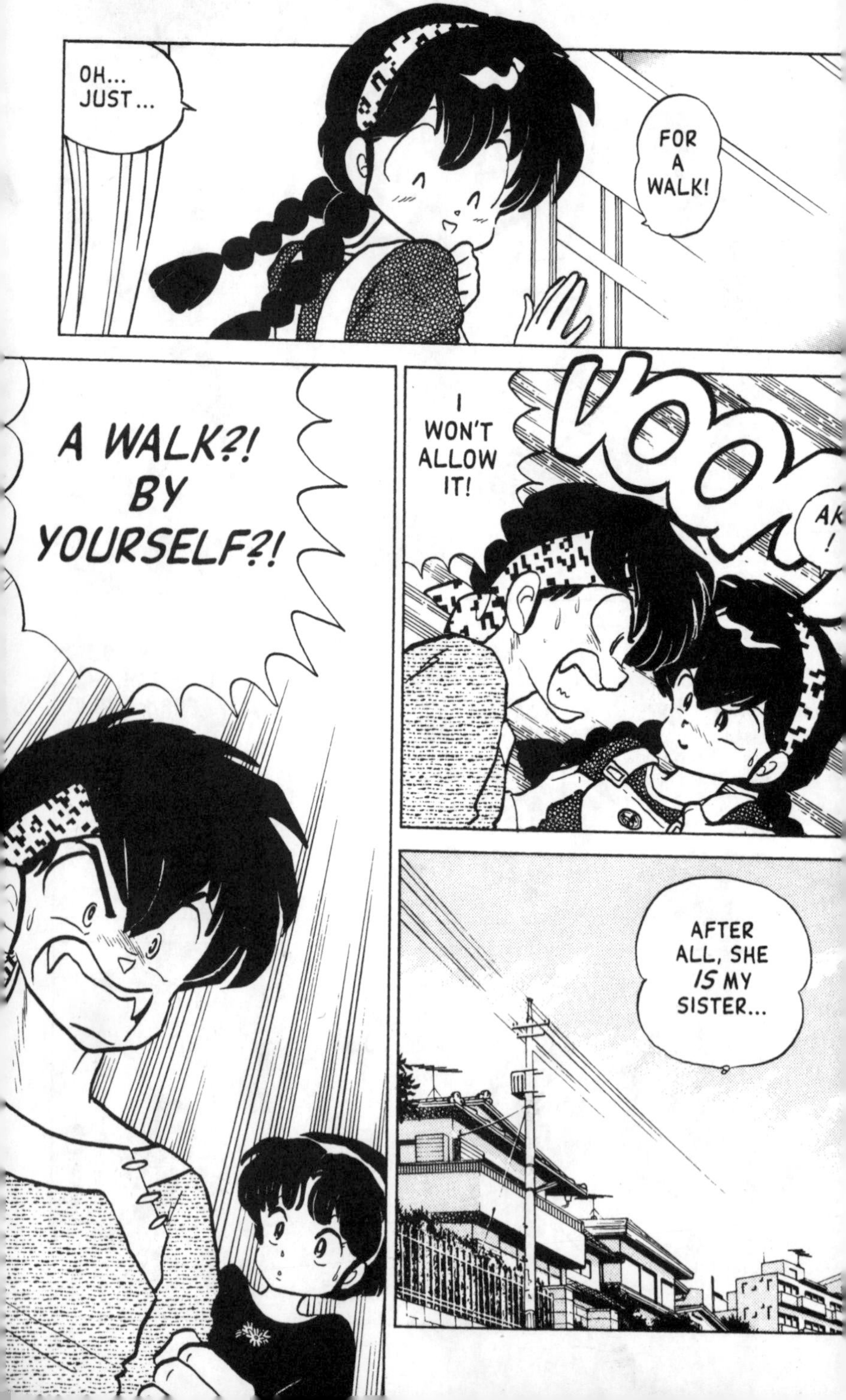
OH... JUST...
FOR A WALK!
A WALK?! BY YOURSELF?!
I WON'T ALLOW IT!
VOOO
AK!
AFTER ALL, SHE IS MY SISTER...

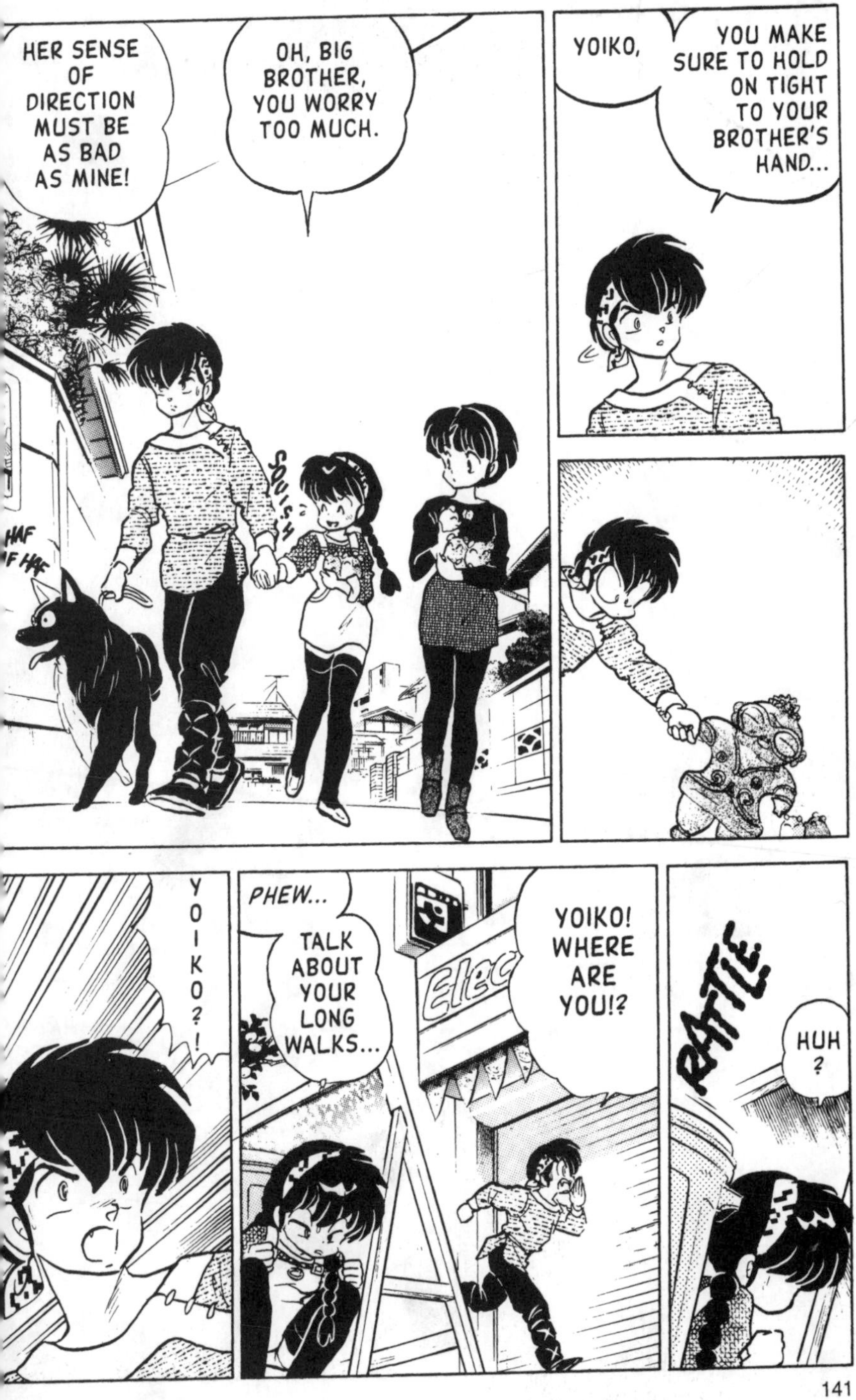
HER SENSE OF DIRECTION MUST BE AS BAD AS MINE!
OH, BIG BROTHER, YOU WORRY TOO MUCH.
SQUISH
HAF HAF
YOIKO,
YOU MAKE SURE TO HOLD ON TIGHT TO YOUR BROTHER'S HAND...
YOIKO?!
PHEW...
TALK ABOUT YOUR LONG WALKS...
Elec
YOIKO! WHERE ARE YOU!?
RATTLE
HUH?

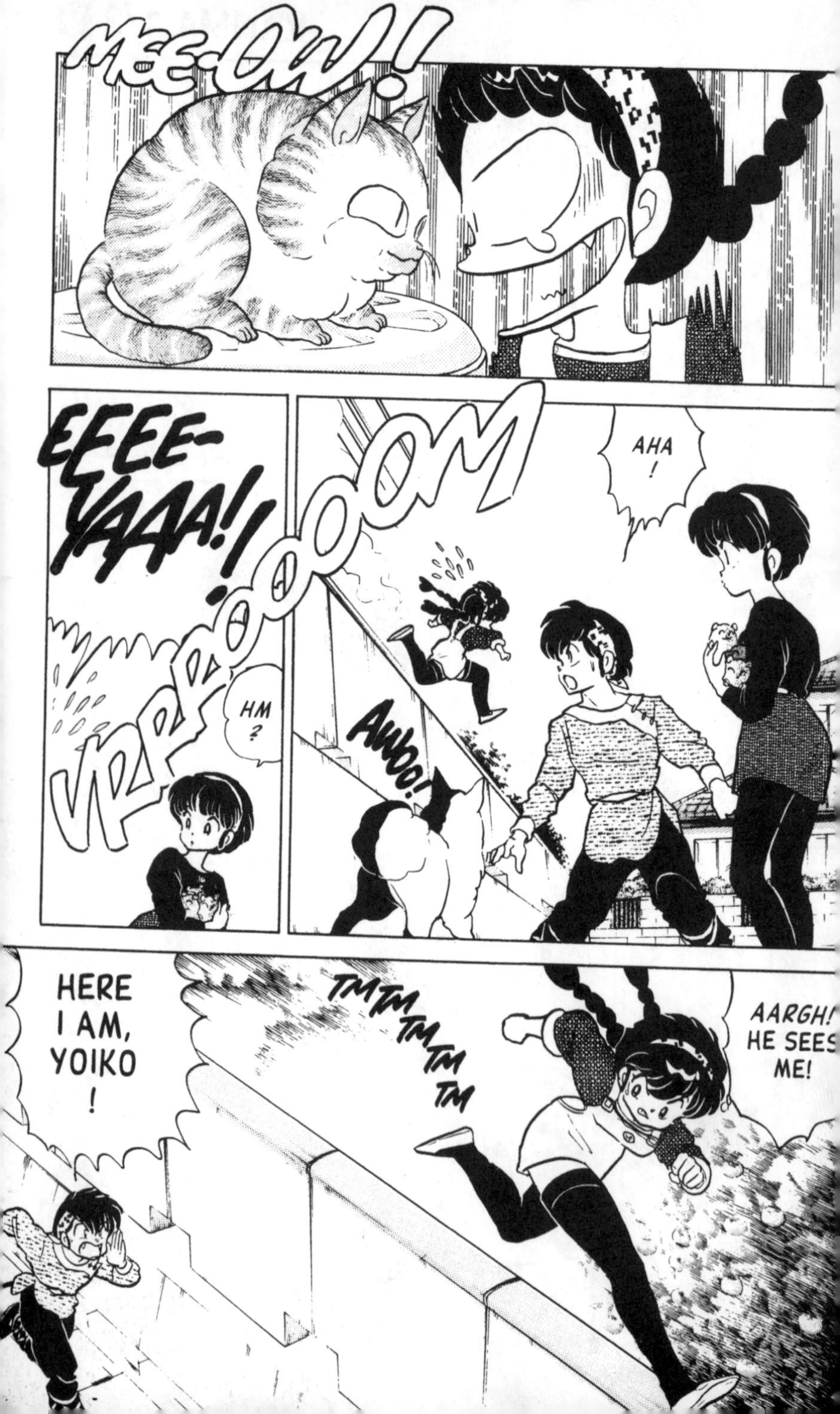
MEE-OW!
EEEE-YAAA!!
VRRROOOOOOM
HM?
AHA!
AWOO!
HERE I AM, YOIKO!
TM TM TM TM TM TM
AARGH! HE SEES ME!

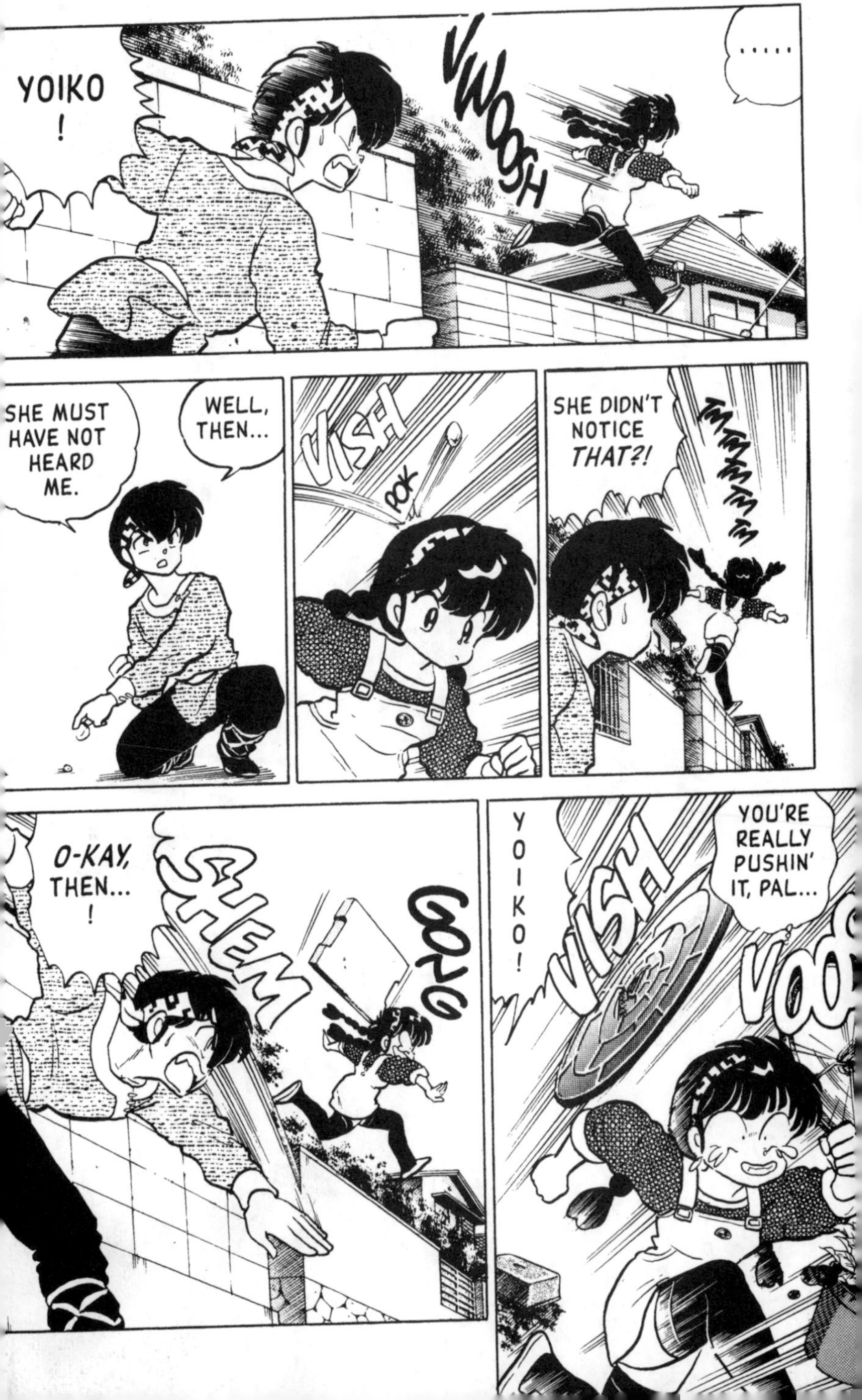
YOIKO
!
VWOOSH
.....
SHE MUST HAVE NOT HEARD ME.
WELL, THEN...
VISH
POK
SHE DIDN'T NOTICE *THAT?!*
TMTMTMTMTMTM
O-KAY, THEN...
!
SHEM
GONG
YOIKO!
VISH
YOU'RE REALLY PUSHIN' IT, PAL...
VOO

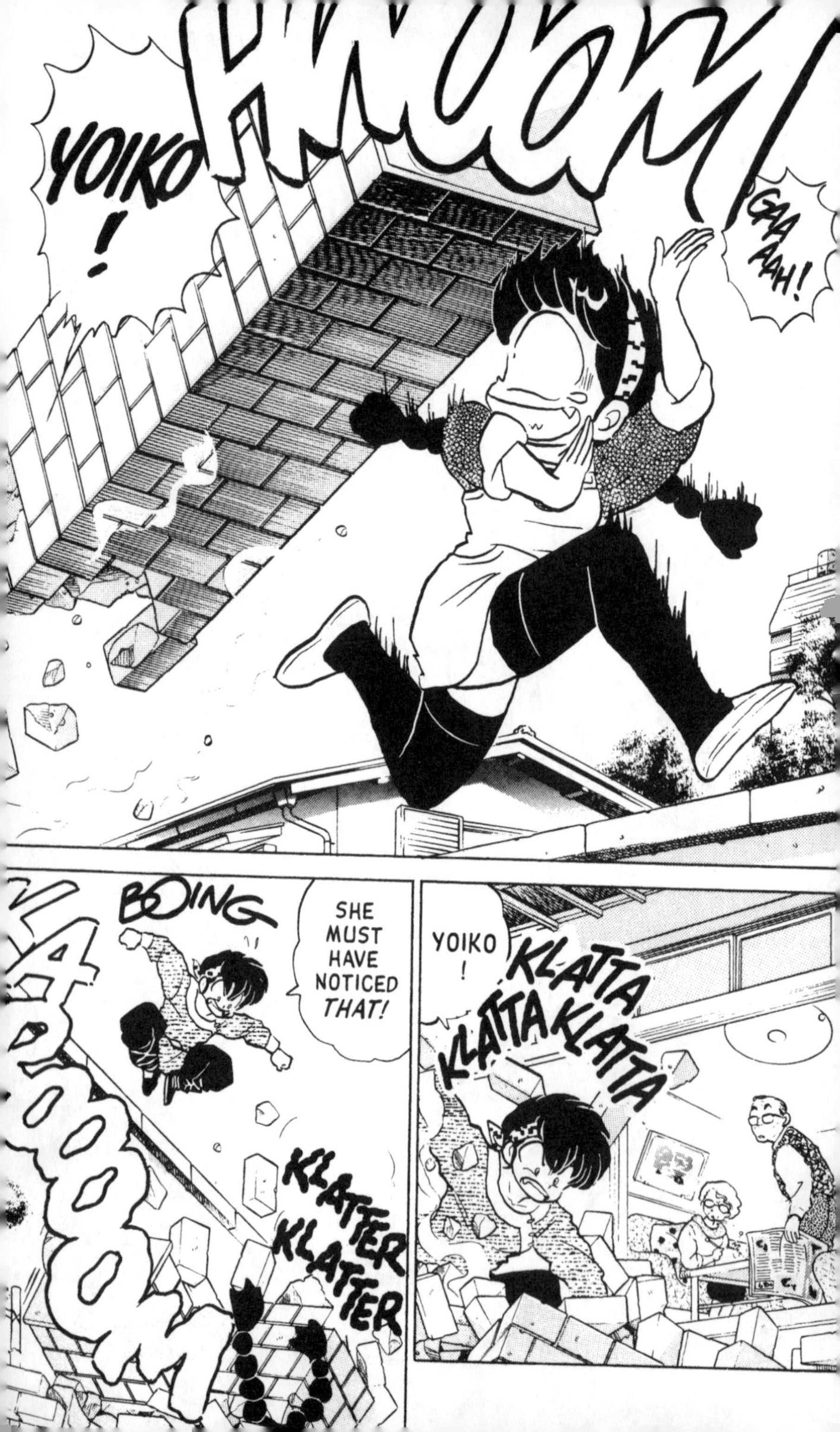
GAAAAH!
YOIKO!
YOIKO!
KLATTA KLATTA KLATTA KLATTA
BOING
SHE MUST HAVE NOTICED THAT!
KLATTER KLATTER

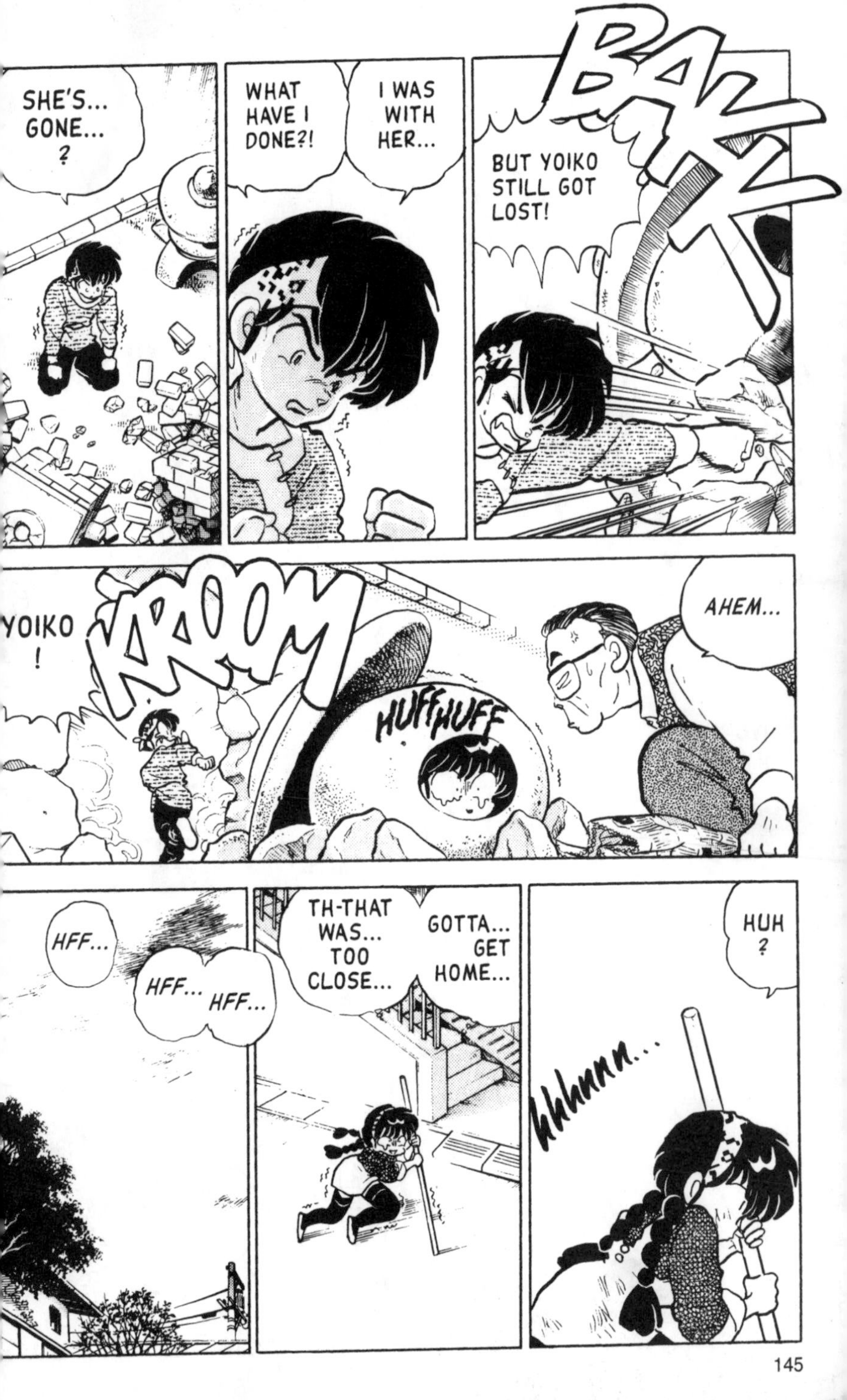

SHE'S... GONE... ?
WHAT HAVE I DONE?!
I WAS WITH HER...
BAKK
BUT YOIKO STILL GOT LOST!
YOIKO !
KROOM
HUFF HUFF
AHEM...
HFF...
HFF... HFF...
TH-THAT WAS... TOO CLOSE...
GOTTA... GET HOME...
HUH ?
hhhnnn...

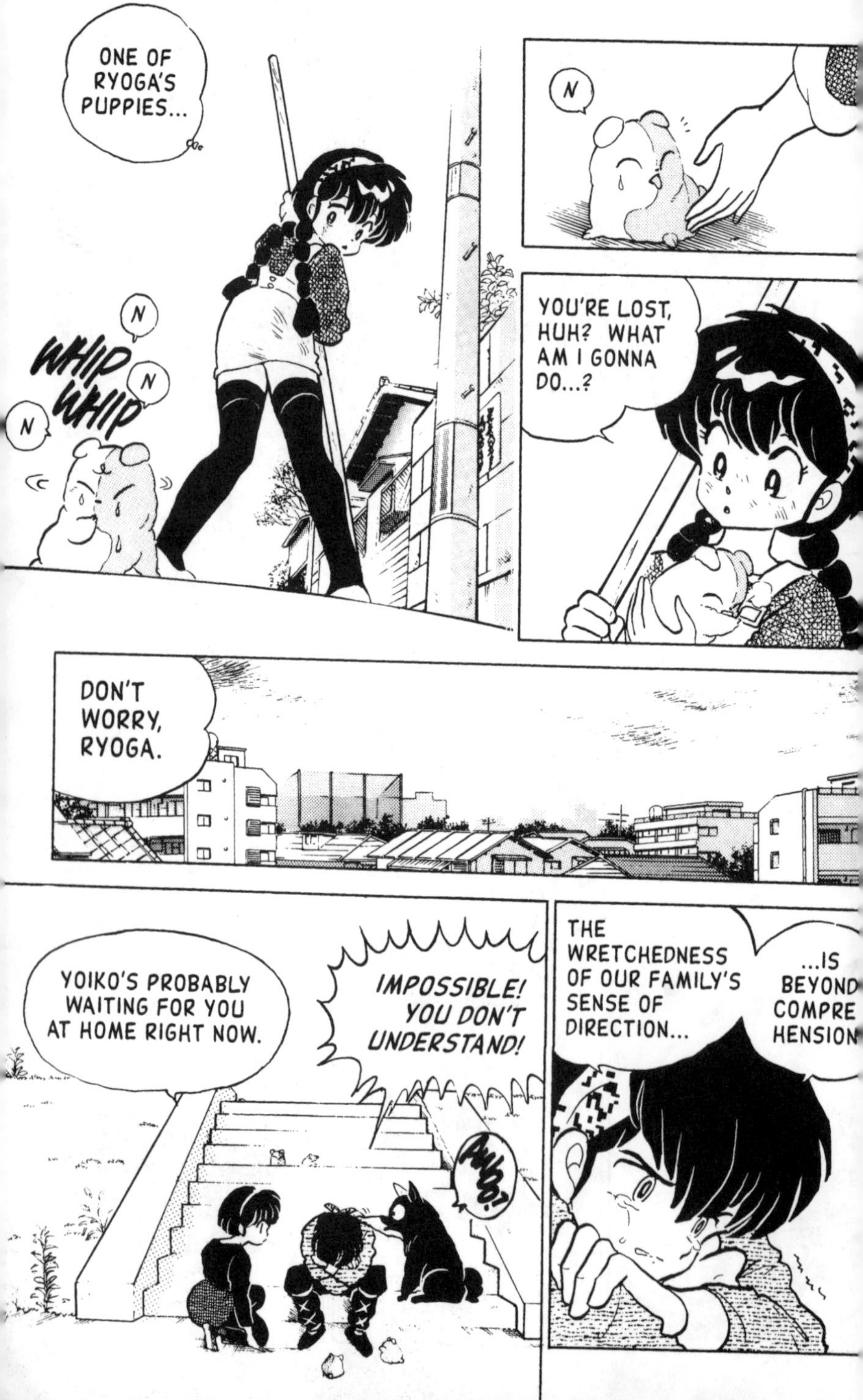
ONE OF RYOGA'S PUPPIES...
N
WHIP WHIP
N
N
N
YOU'RE LOST, HUH? WHAT AM I GONNA DO...?
DON'T WORRY, RYOGA.
YOIKO'S PROBABLY WAITING FOR YOU AT HOME RIGHT NOW.
IMPOSSIBLE! YOU DON'T UNDERSTAND!
AWOO?
THE WRETCHEDNESS OF OUR FAMILY'S SENSE OF DIRECTION...
...IS BEYOND COMPRE HENSION

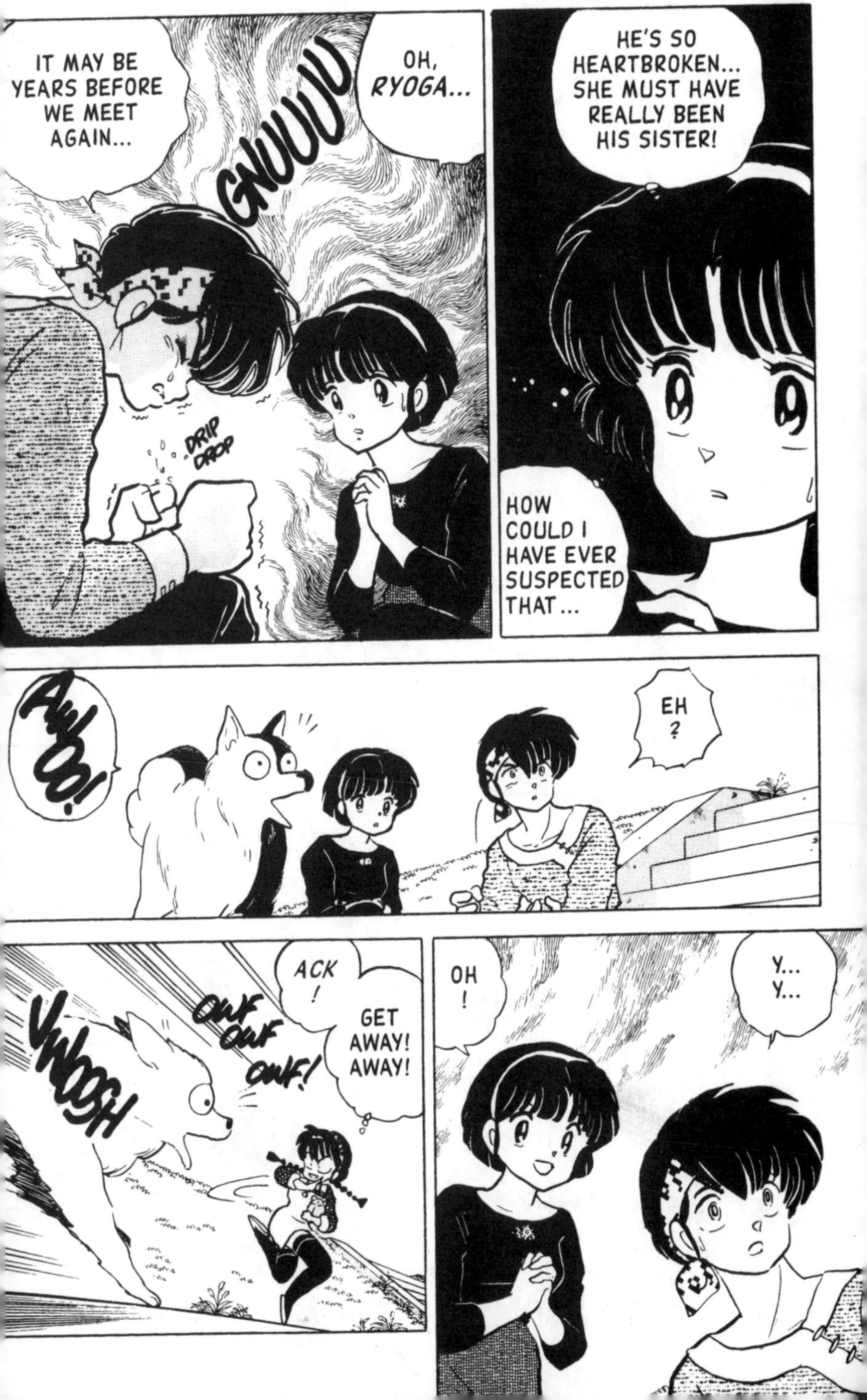
IT MAY BE YEARS BEFORE WE MEET AGAIN...
GNUUU
OH, RYOGA...
DRIP DROP
HE'S SO HEARTBROKEN... SHE MUST HAVE REALLY BEEN HIS SISTER!
HOW COULD I HAVE EVER SUSPECTED THAT...
AWOOO!
EH ?
VWOOSH
ACK !
OWF OWF OWF!
GET AWAY! AWAY!
OH !
Y... Y...

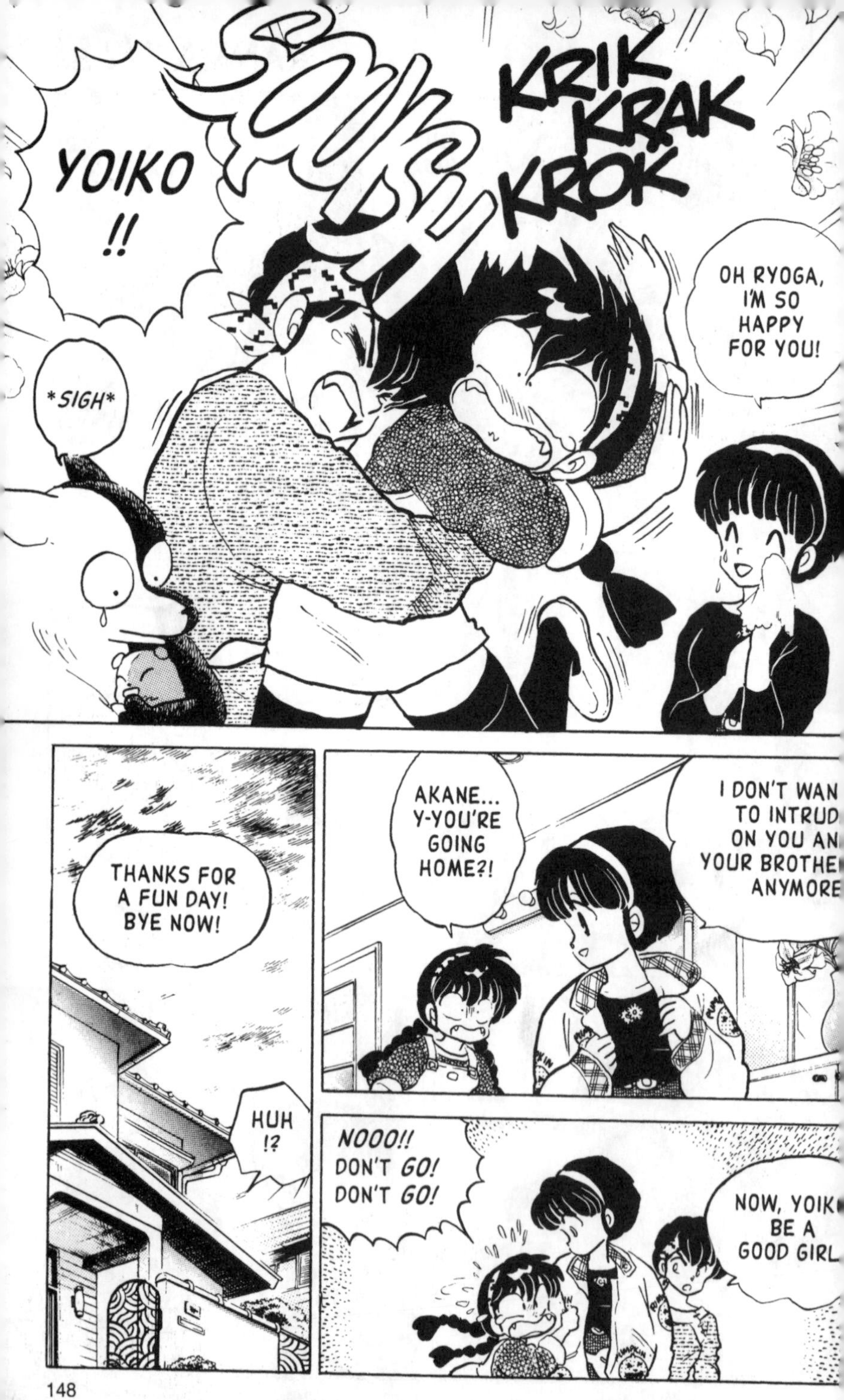
YOIKO !!
SQUISH
KRIK KRAK KROK
SIGH
OH RYOGA, I'M SO HAPPY FOR YOU!
THANKS FOR A FUN DAY! BYE NOW!
HUH !?
AKANE... Y-YOU'RE GOING HOME?!
I DON'T WAN TO INTRUD ON YOU AN YOUR BROTHE ANYMORE
NOOO!! DON'T GO! DON'T GO!
NOW, YOIK BE A GOOD GIRL

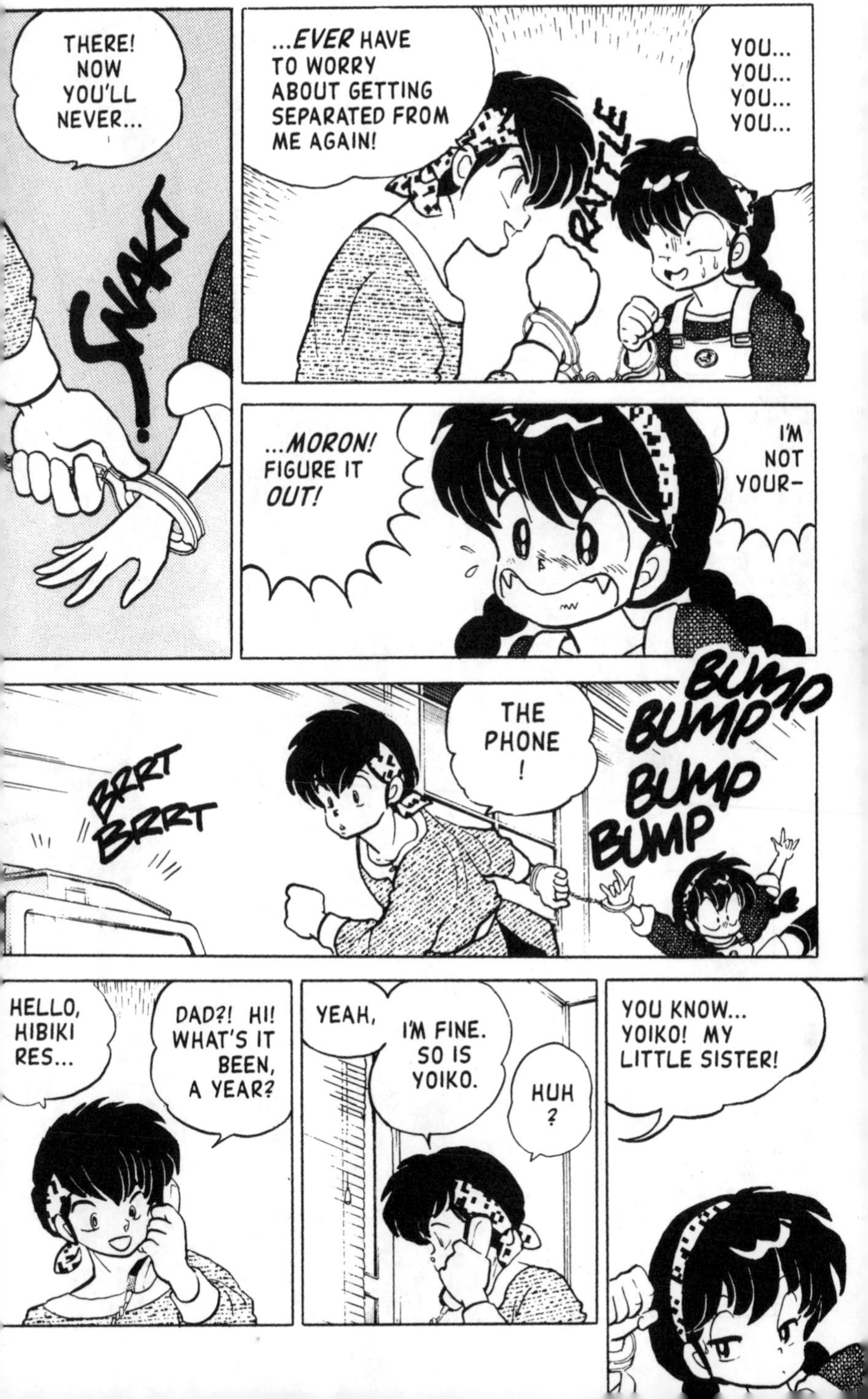
THERE! NOW YOU'LL NEVER...
SNAP!
...EVER HAVE TO WORRY ABOUT GETTING SEPARATED FROM ME AGAIN!
RATTLE
YOU... YOU... YOU... YOU...
I'M NOT YOUR–
...MORON! FIGURE IT OUT!
BRRT BRRT
THE PHONE!
BUMP BUMP BUMP BUMP
HELLO, HIBIKI RES...
DAD?! HI! WHAT'S IT BEEN, A YEAR?
YEAH,
I'M FINE. SO IS YOIKO.
HUH?
YOU KNOW... YOIKO! MY LITTLE SISTER!

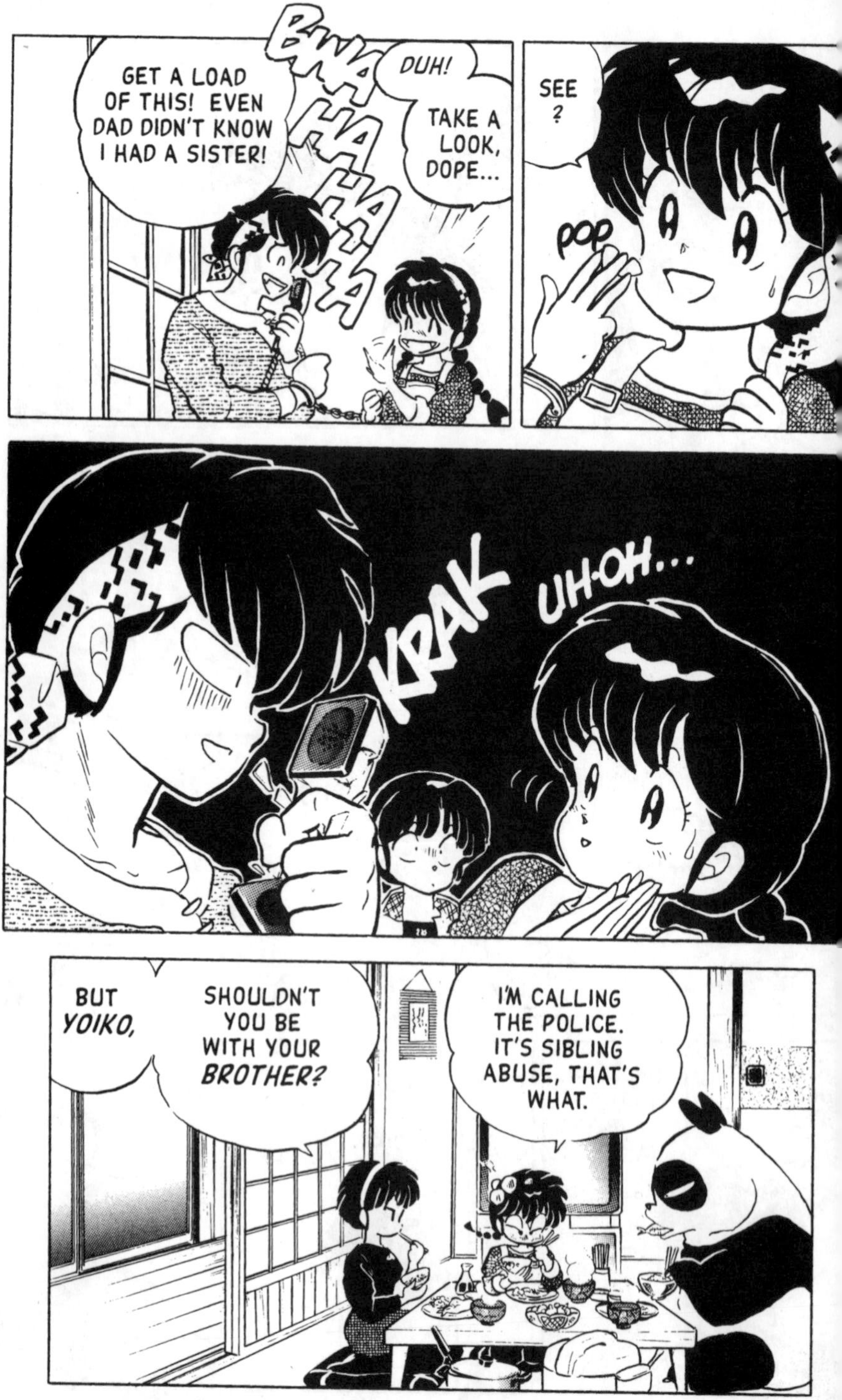
GET A LOAD OF THIS! EVEN DAD DIDN'T KNOW I HAD A SISTER!
BWAHAHAHAHA
DUH!
TAKE A LOOK, DOPE...
SEE?
POP
KRAK
UH-OH...
BUT YOIKO,
SHOULDN'T YOU BE WITH YOUR BROTHER?
I'M CALLING THE POLICE. IT'S SIBLING ABUSE, THAT'S WHAT.

PART 10
THE ULTIMATE TECHNIQUE

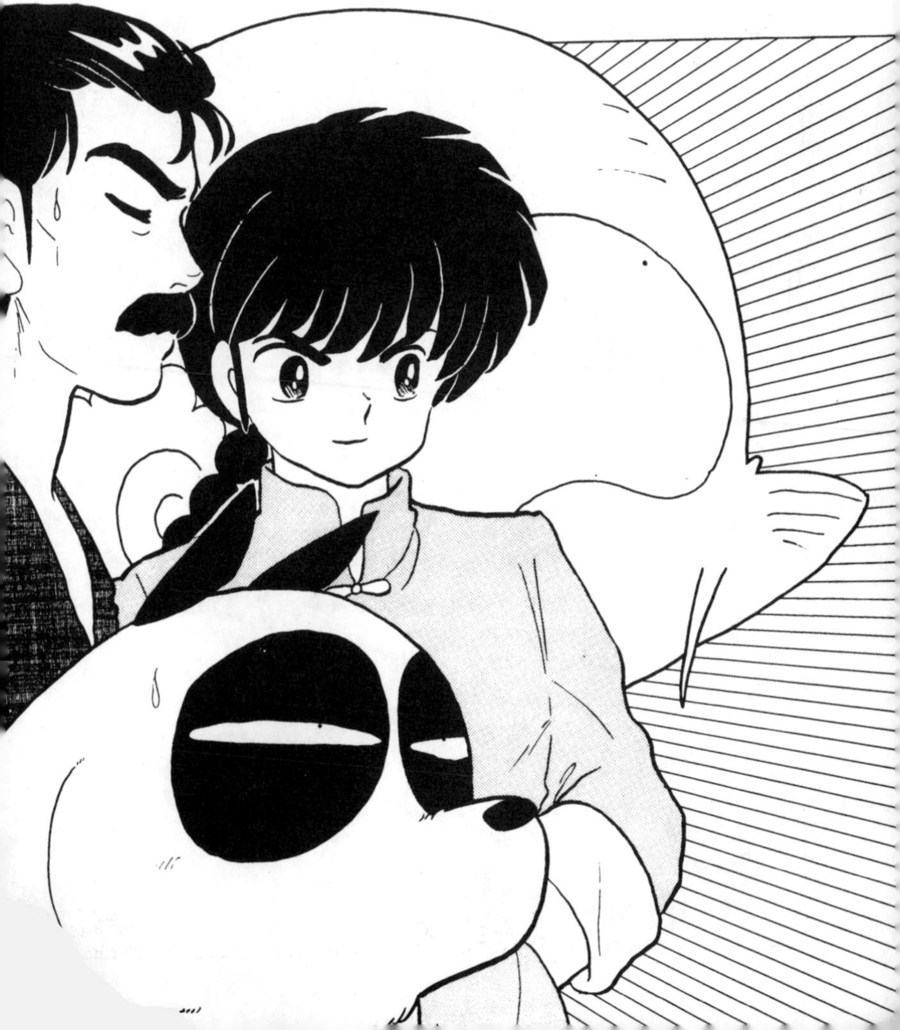

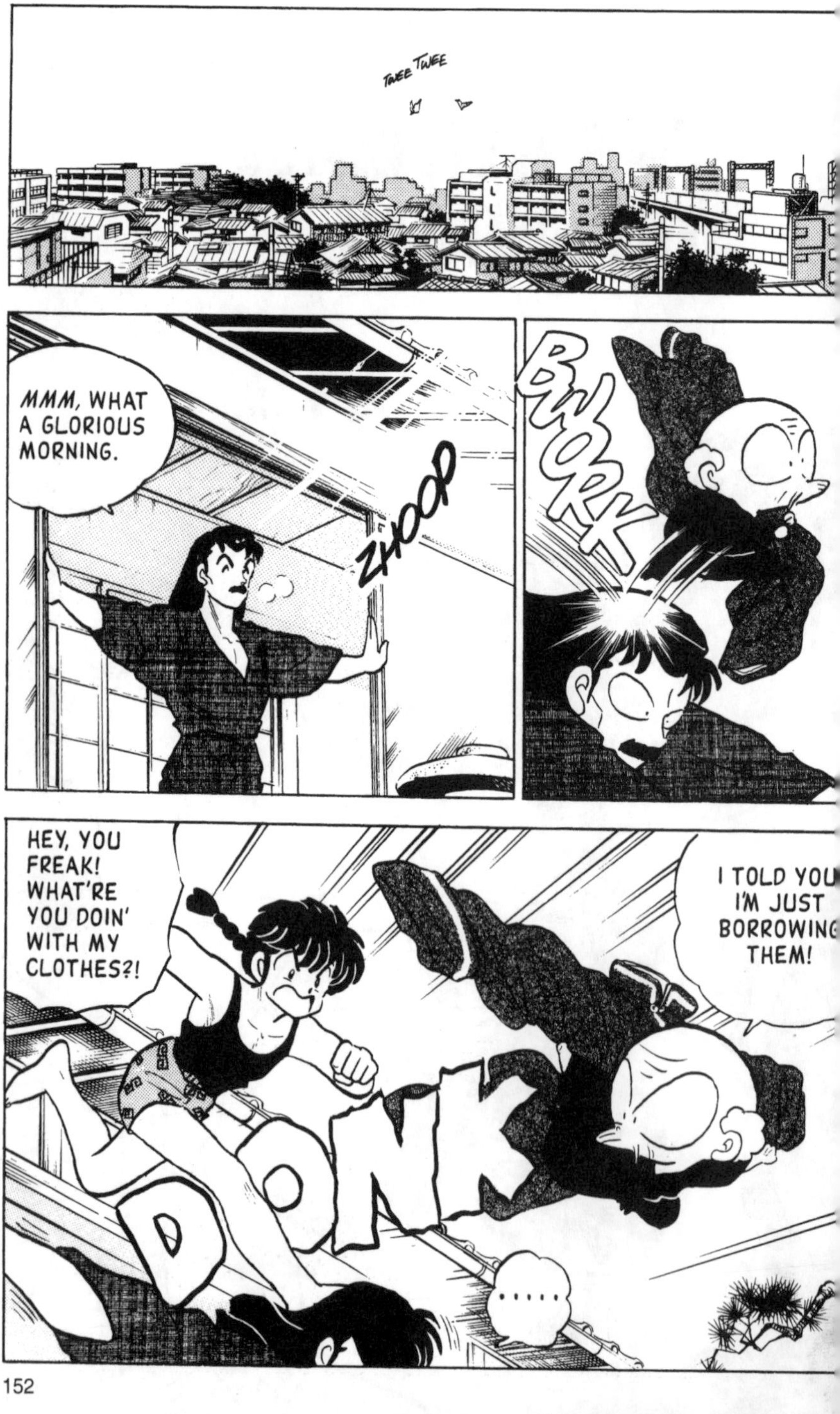
TWEE TWEE
MMM, WHAT A GLORIOUS MORNING.
ZHOOP
BWORK
HEY, YOU FREAK! WHAT'RE YOU DOIN' WITH MY CLOTHES?!
I TOLD YOU I'M JUST BORROWING THEM!
DONK
.....

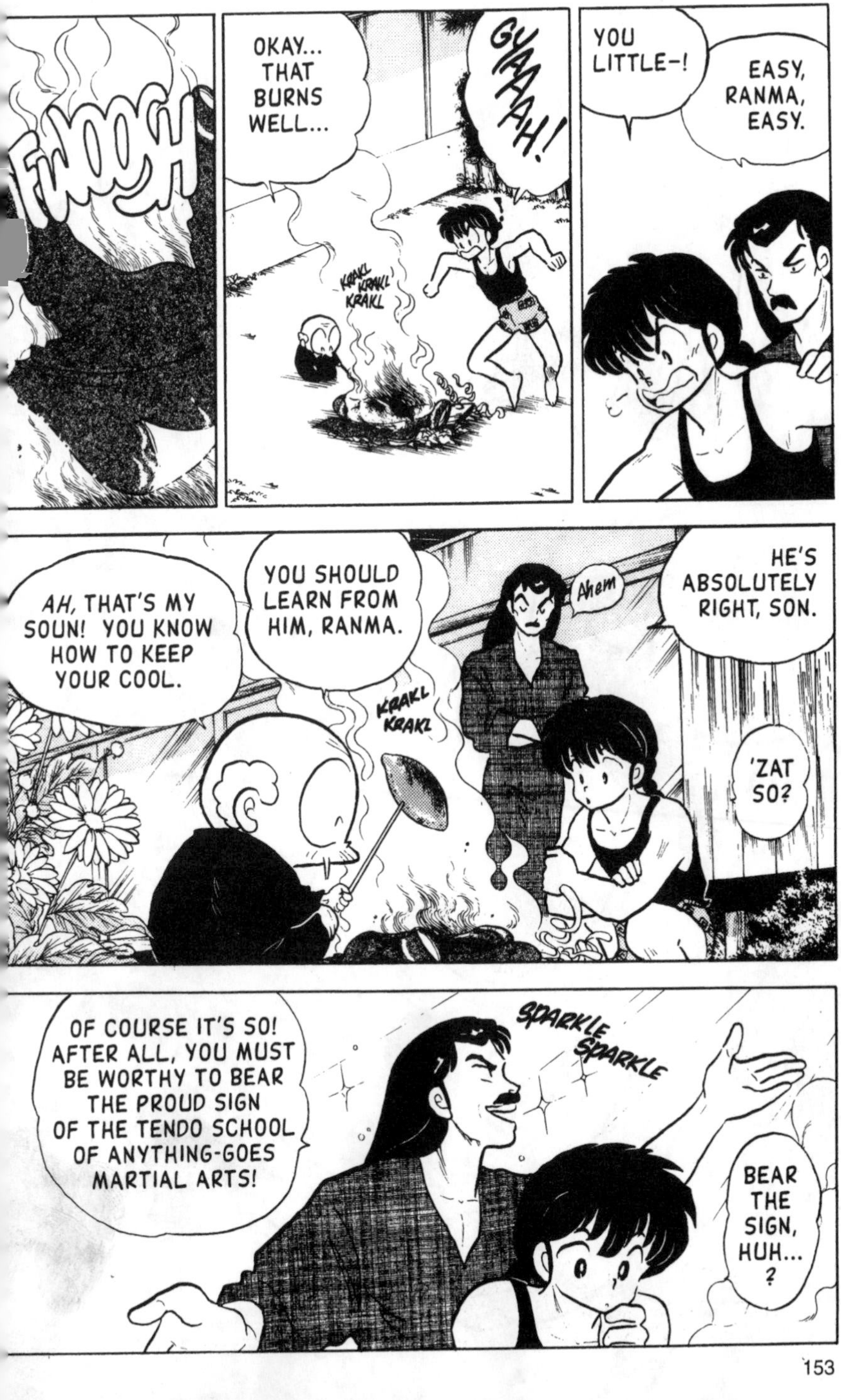
FWOOSH
OKAY... THAT BURNS WELL...
KRAKL KRAKL KRAKL
GYAAAAH!
YOU LITTLE-!
EASY, RANMA, EASY.
AH, THAT'S MY SOUN! YOU KNOW HOW TO KEEP YOUR COOL.
YOU SHOULD LEARN FROM HIM, RANMA.
KRAKL KRAKL
Ahem
HE'S ABSOLUTELY RIGHT, SON.
'ZAT SO?
OF COURSE IT'S SO! AFTER ALL, YOU MUST BE WORTHY TO BEAR THE PROUD SIGN OF THE TENDO SCHOOL OF ANYTHING-GOES MARTIAL ARTS!
SPARKLE SPARKLE
BEAR THE SIGN, HUH...?

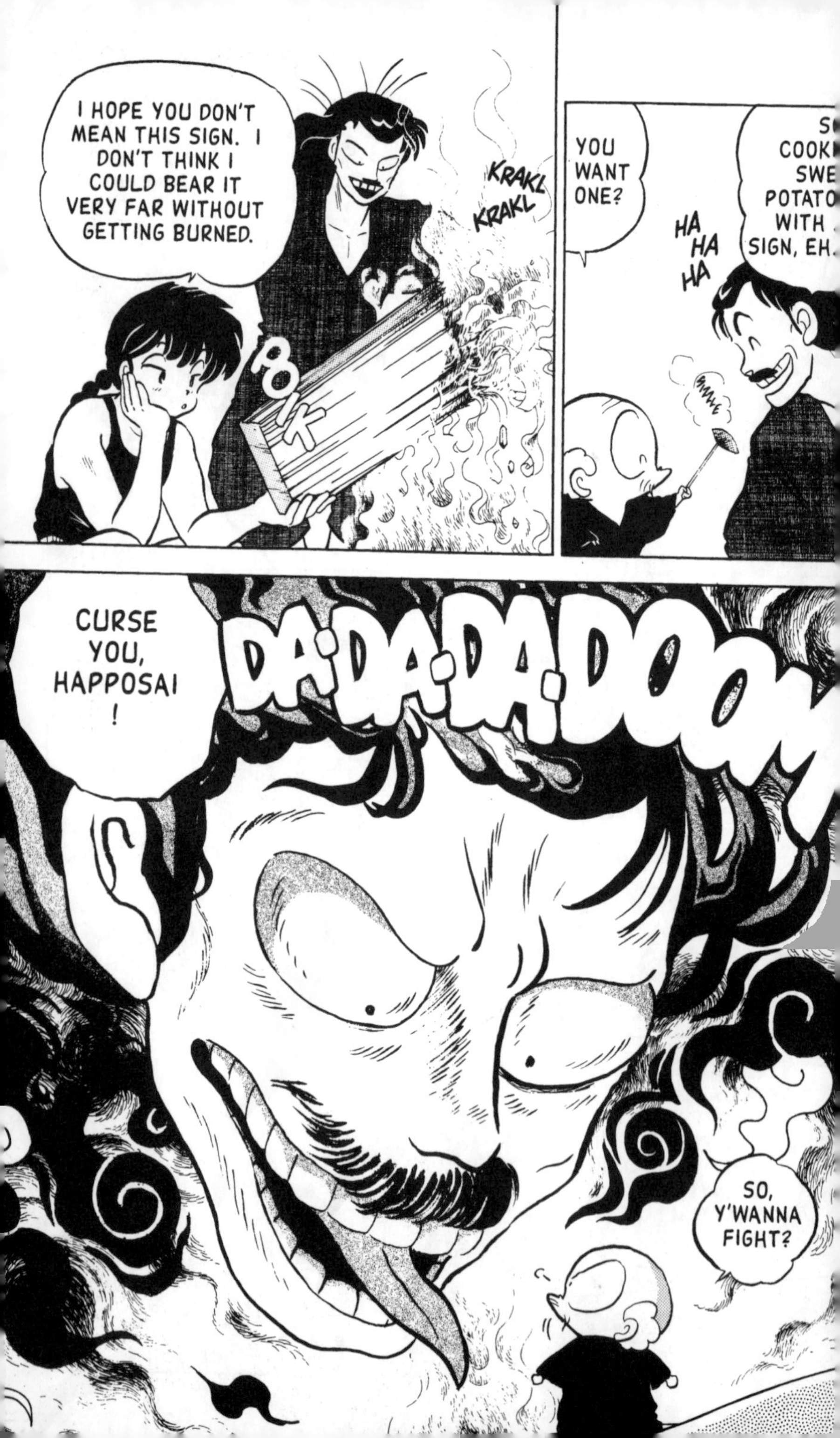
I HOPE YOU DON'T MEAN THIS SIGN. I DON'T THINK I COULD BEAR IT VERY FAR WITHOUT GETTING BURNED.
KRAKL KRAKL
POK
YOU WANT ONE?
HA HA HA
S COOKI SWE POTATO WITH SIGN, EH.
CURSE YOU, HAPPOSAI!
DA-DA-DA-DOO
SO, Y'WANNA FIGHT?

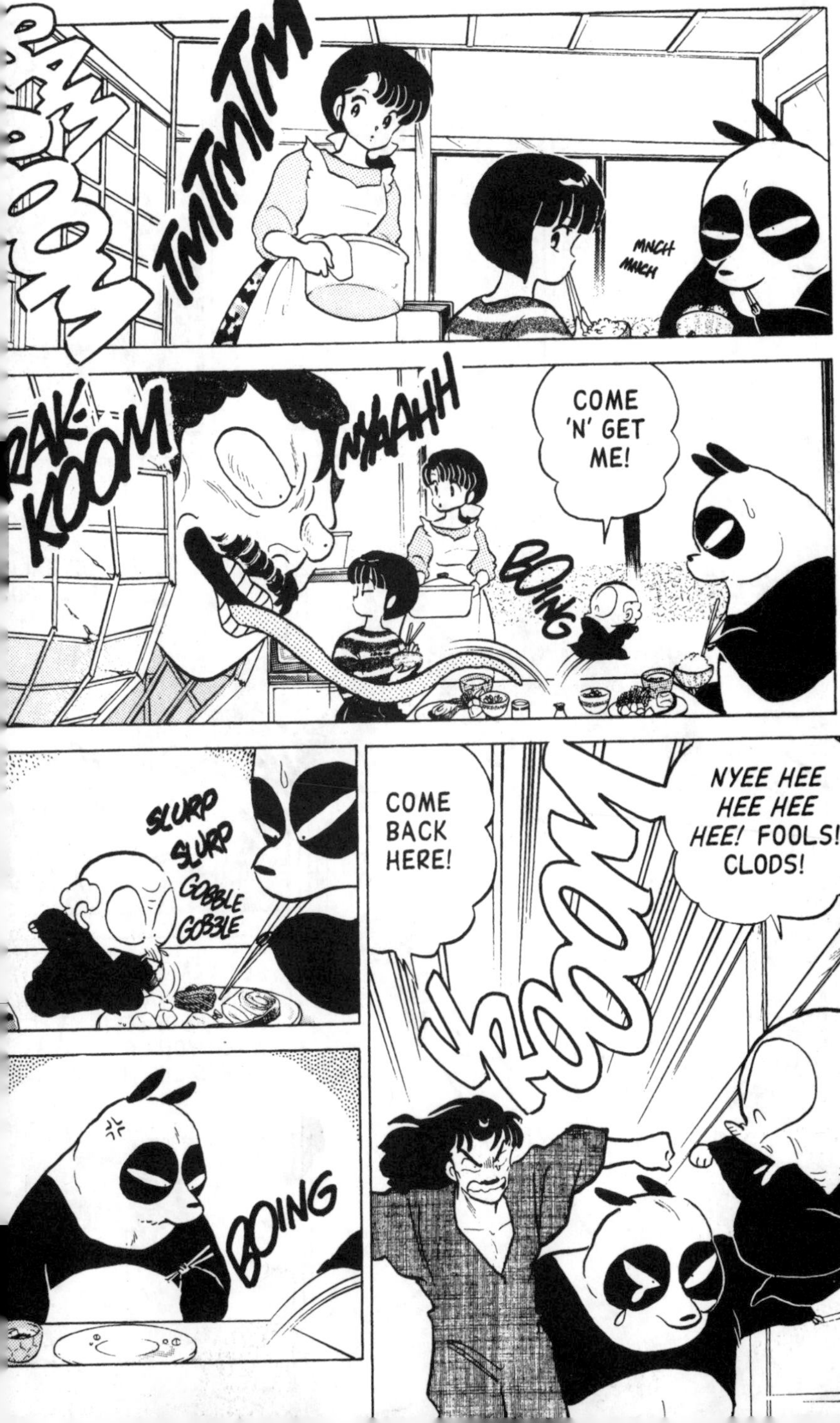
TMTMTMTM
MNCH MNCH
NYAAHH
COME 'N' GET ME!
BOING
SLURP SLURP GOBBLE GOBBLE
COME BACK HERE!
NYEE HEE HEE HEE HEE! FOOLS! CLODS!
BOING

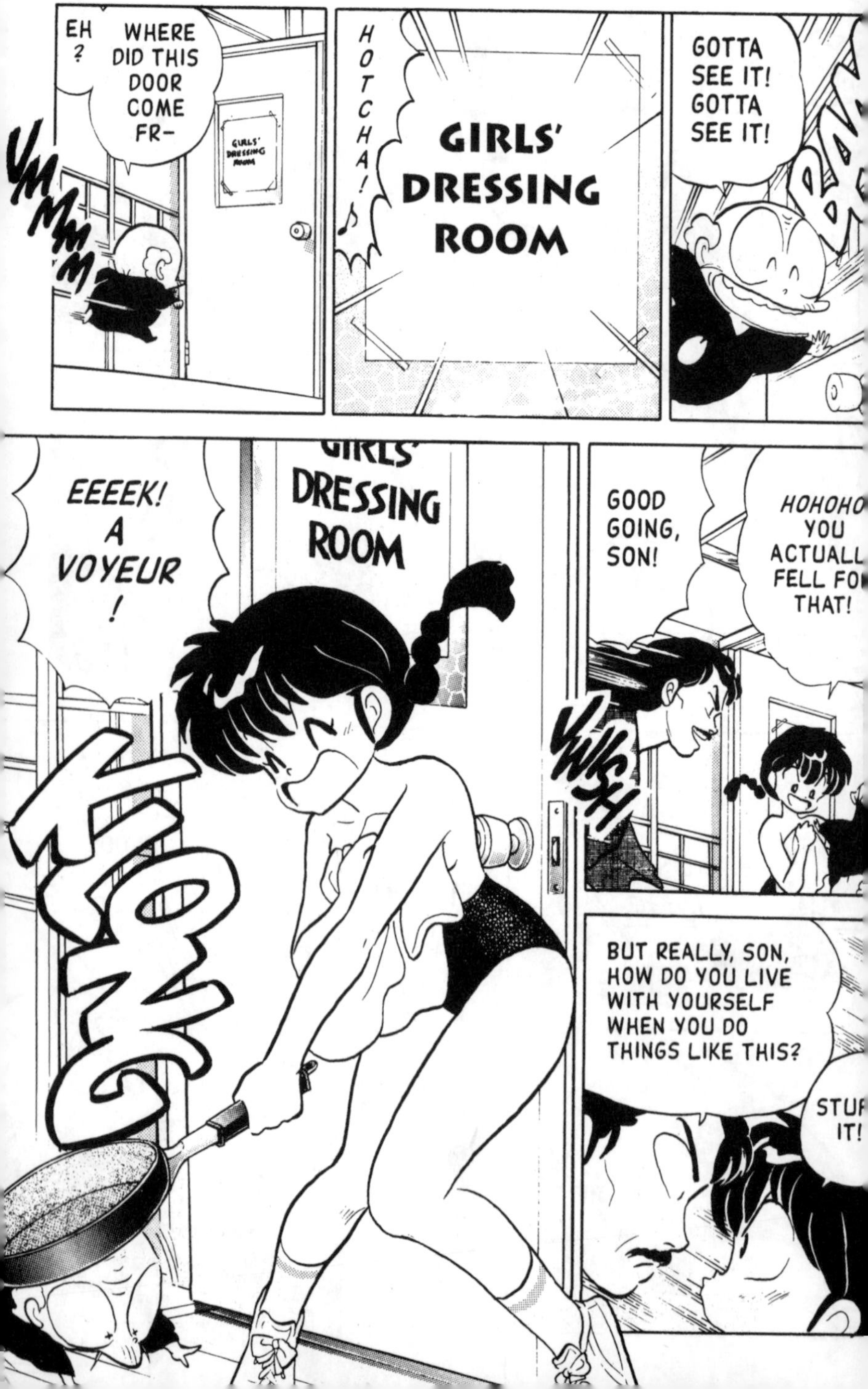
EH ?
WHERE DID THIS DOOR COME FR–
UMMMM
GIRLS' DRESSING ROOM
HOTCHA! ♪
GIRLS' DRESSING ROOM
GOTTA SEE IT! GOTTA SEE IT!
EEEEK! A VOYEUR !
GIRLS' DRESSING ROOM
KLONG
GOOD GOING, SON!
HOHOHO YOU ACTUALL FELL FO THAT!
VWISH
BUT REALLY, SON, HOW DO YOU LIVE WITH YOURSELF WHEN YOU DO THINGS LIKE THIS?
STUF IT!

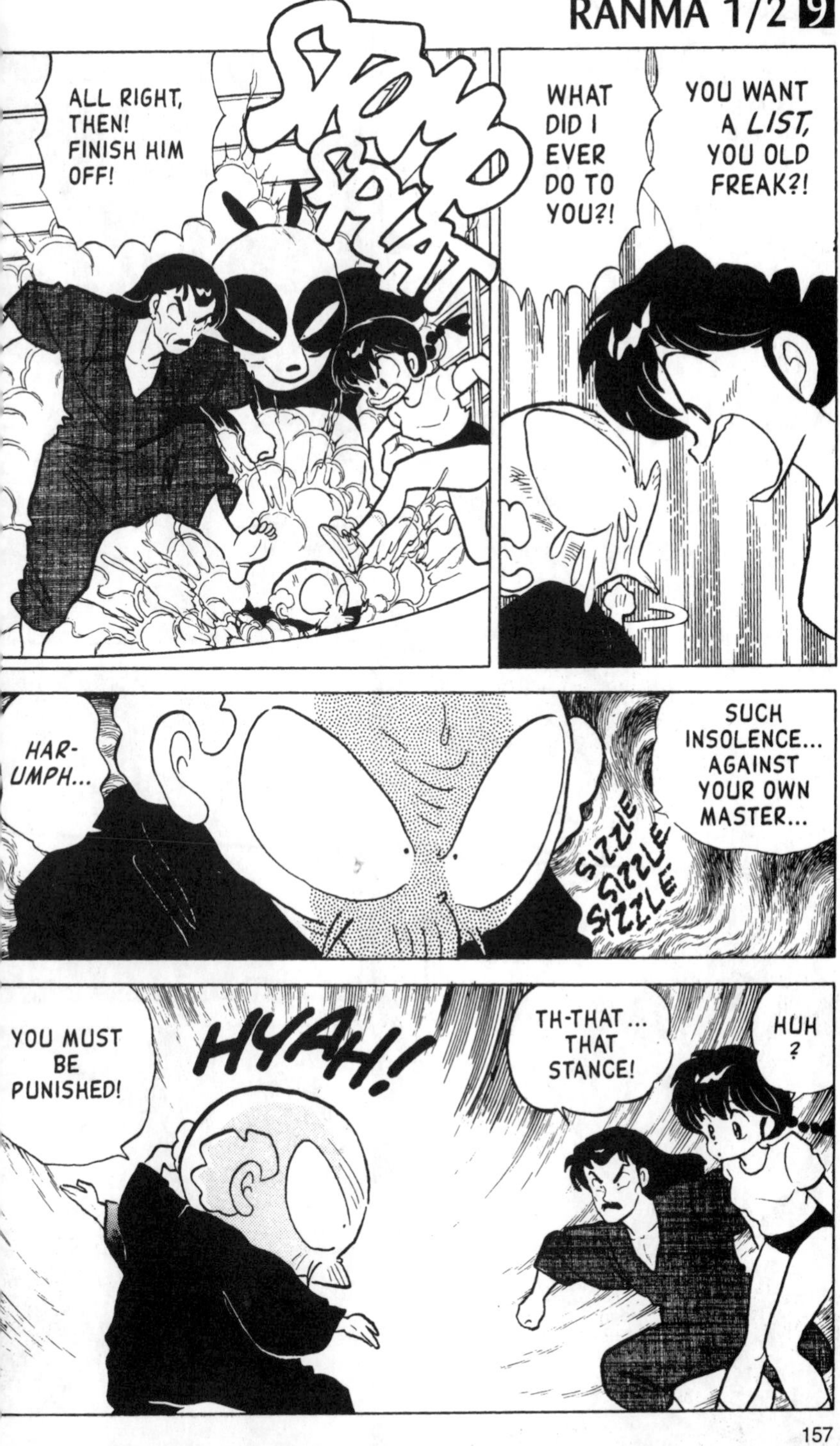
ALL RIGHT, THEN! FINISH HIM OFF!
STOMP SPLAT
WHAT DID I EVER DO TO YOU?!
YOU WANT A *LIST,* YOU OLD FREAK?!
HAR-UMPH...
SUCH INSOLENCE... AGAINST YOUR OWN MASTER...
SIZZLE SIZZLE SIZZLE
YOU MUST BE PUNISHED!
HYAH!
TH-THAT... THAT STANCE!
HUH?

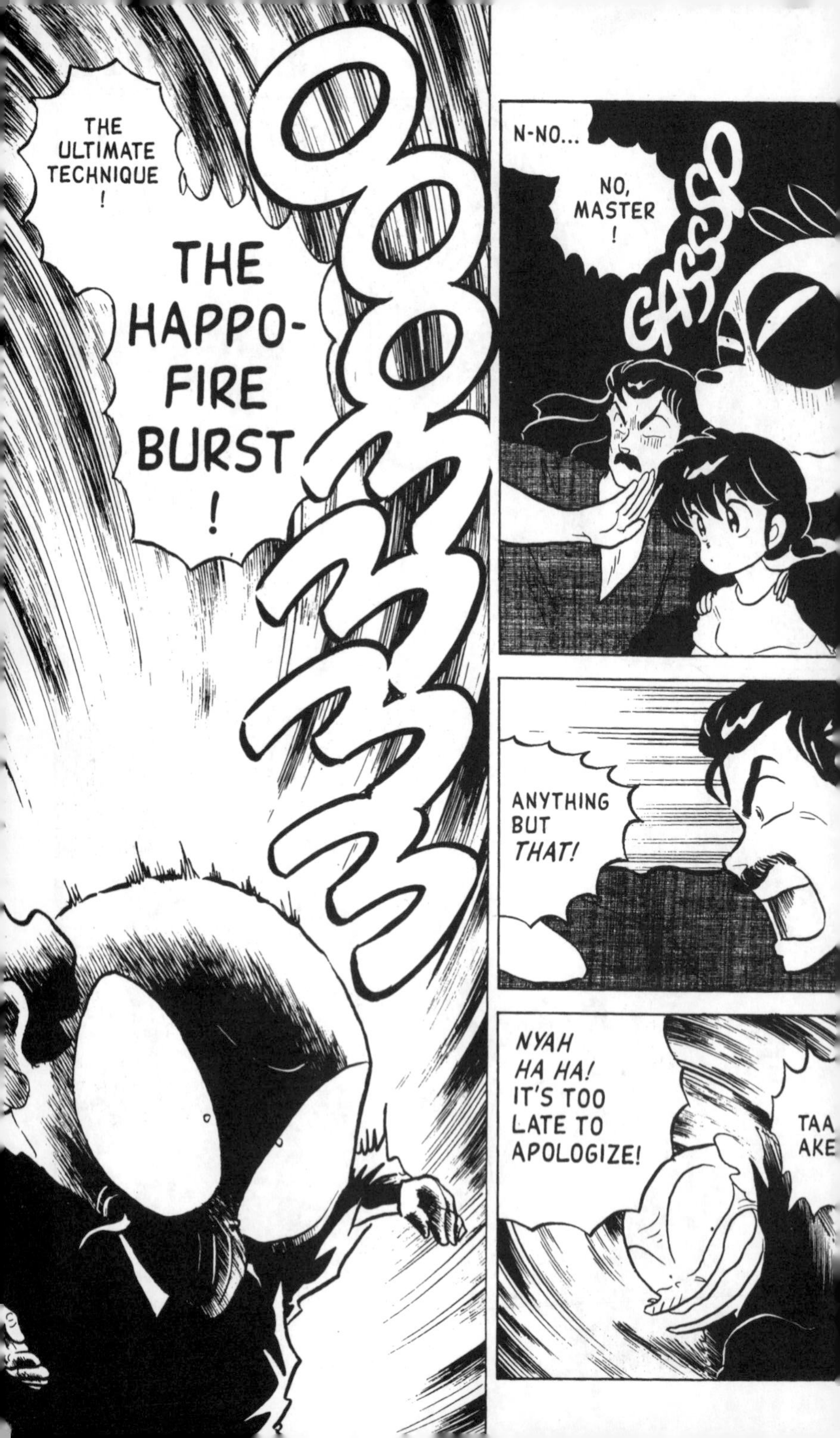
THE ULTIMATE TECHNIQUE!
THE HAPPO-FIRE BURST!
OOOMMMM
N-NO...
NO, MASTER!
GASSP
ANYTHING BUT *THAT!*
NYAH HA HA! IT'S TOO LATE TO APOLOGIZE!
TAA AKE

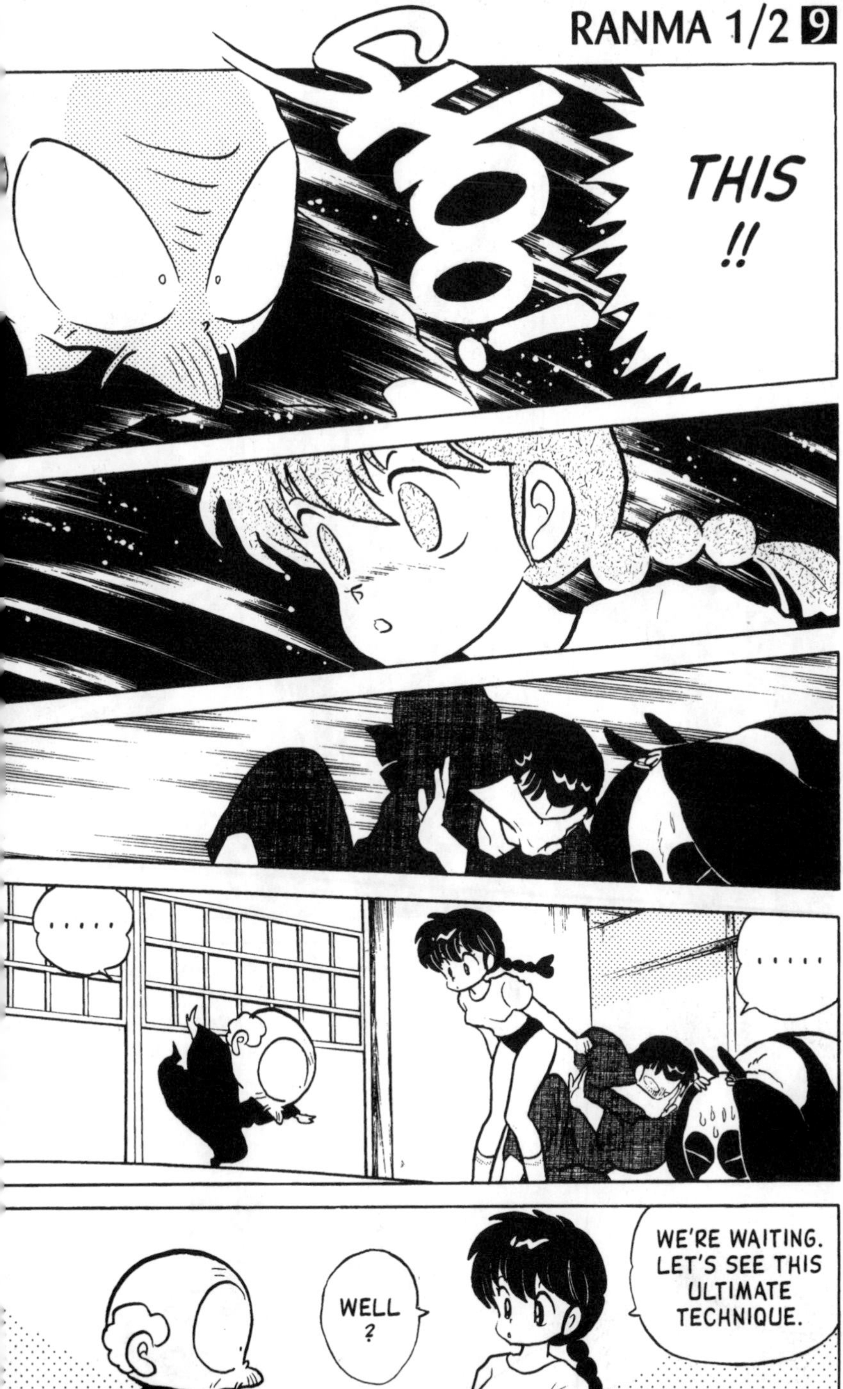
THIS !!
.....
.....
WELL ?
WE'RE WAITING. LET'S SEE THIS ULTIMATE TECHNIQUE.

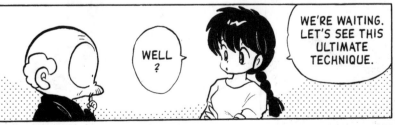

1

2

3

I FORGOT!

TOMP
TOMP
TOMP

POOM

THE ULTIMATE TECHNIQUE...

THE HAPPO-FIRE BURST...

JUST THINKING ABOUT IT MAKES MY HAIR STAND ON END.

YOU'VE ACTUALLY SEEN IT?

brr

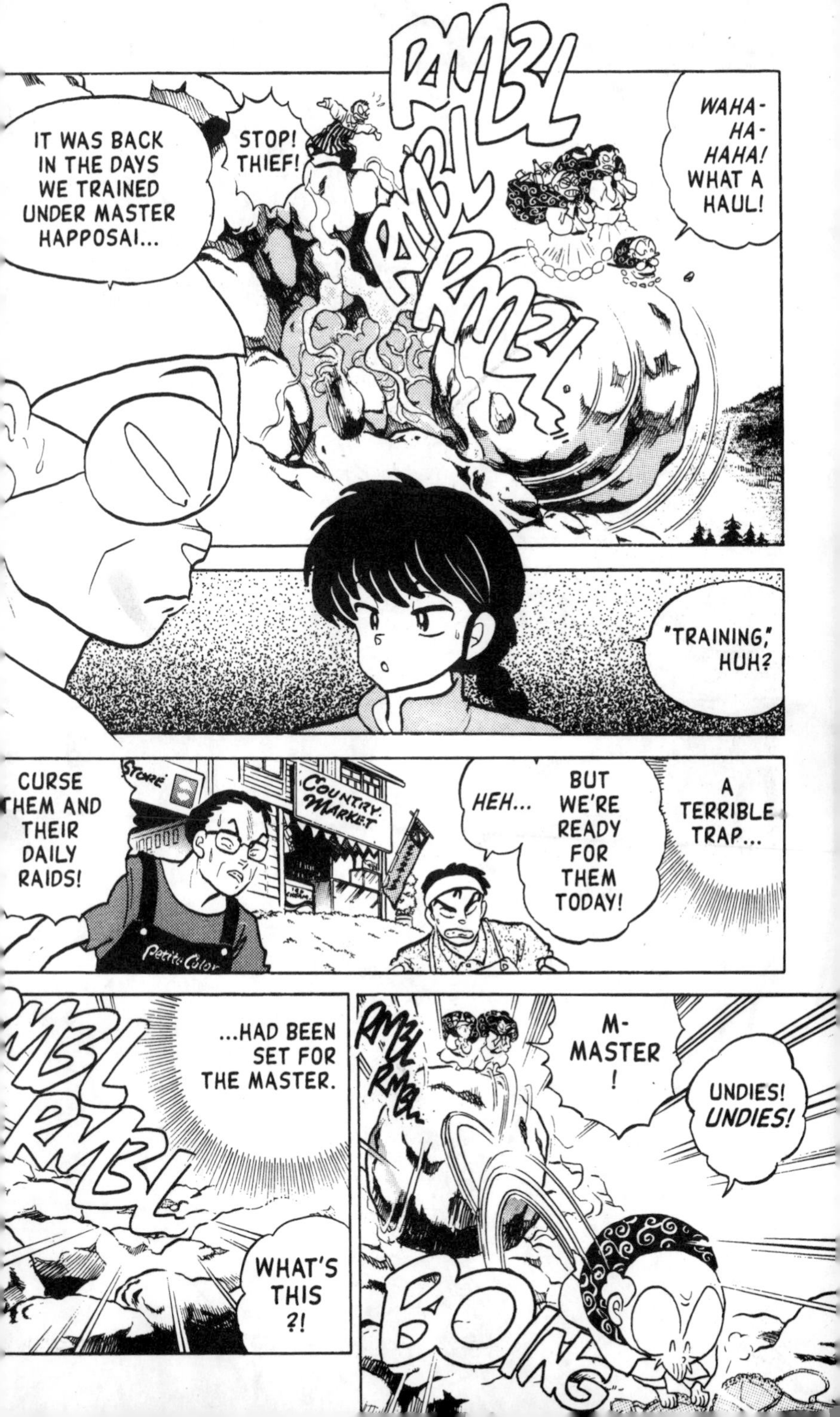
IT WAS BACK IN THE DAYS WE TRAINED UNDER MASTER HAPPOSAI...
STOP! THIEF!
RAMBL
RAMBL
RMBL
WAHA-HA-HAHA! WHAT A HAUL!
"TRAINING," HUH?
CURSE THEM AND THEIR DAILY RAIDS!
STORE
COUNTRY MARKET
Petite Color
HEH...
BUT WE'RE READY FOR THEM TODAY!
A TERRIBLE TRAP...
RMBL
RMBL
RMBL
...HAD BEEN SET FOR THE MASTER.
WHAT'S THIS?!
RMBL
RMBL
M-MASTER!
UNDIES! UNDIES!
BOING

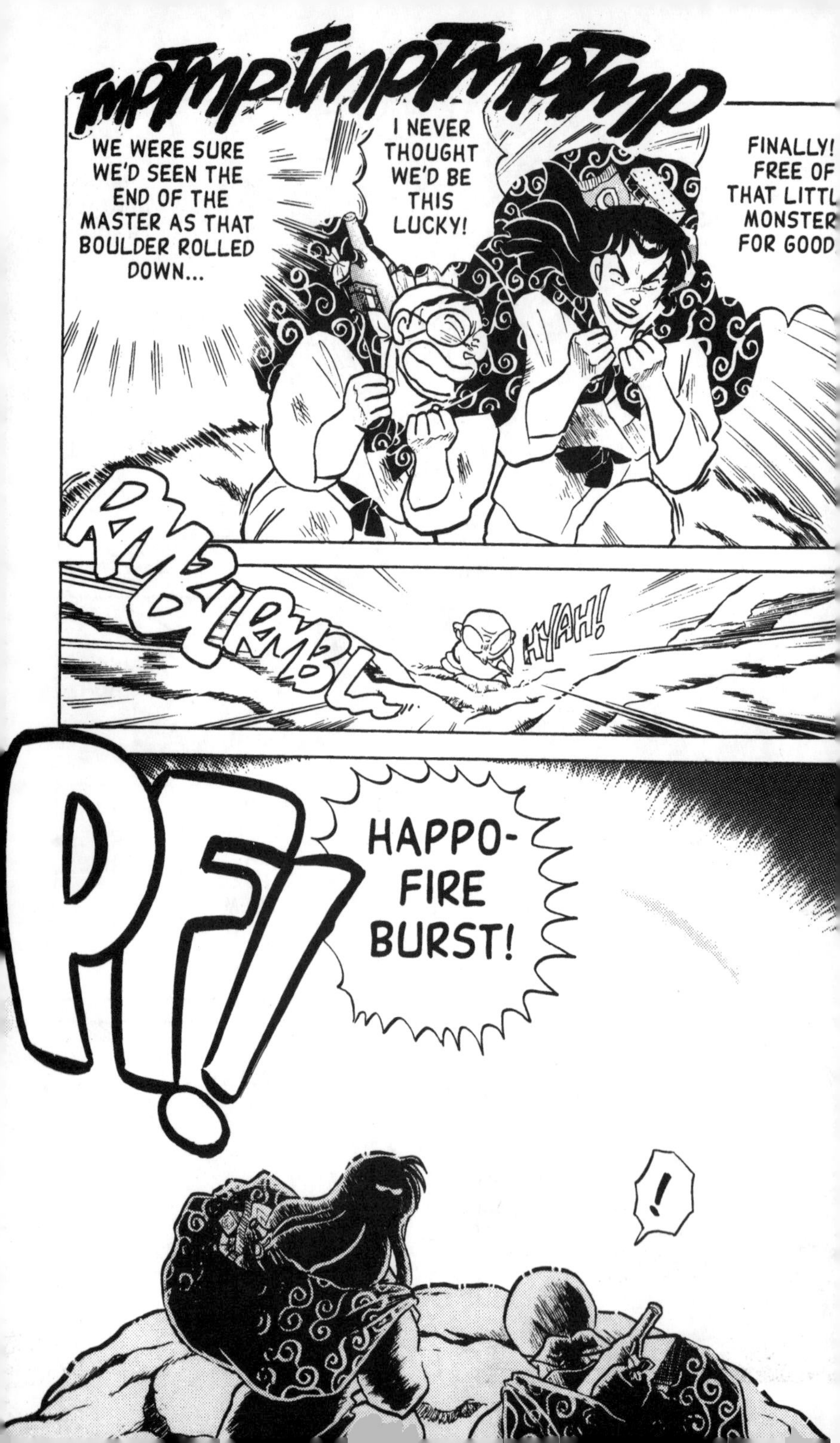

TMPTMPTMPTMPTMPTMP
WE WERE SURE WE'D SEEN THE END OF THE MASTER AS THAT BOULDER ROLLED DOWN...
I NEVER THOUGHT WE'D BE THIS LUCKY!
FINALLY! FREE OF THAT LITTL MONSTER FOR GOOD
RMBLRMBL
HYAH!
PF!!
HAPPO-FIRE BURST!
!

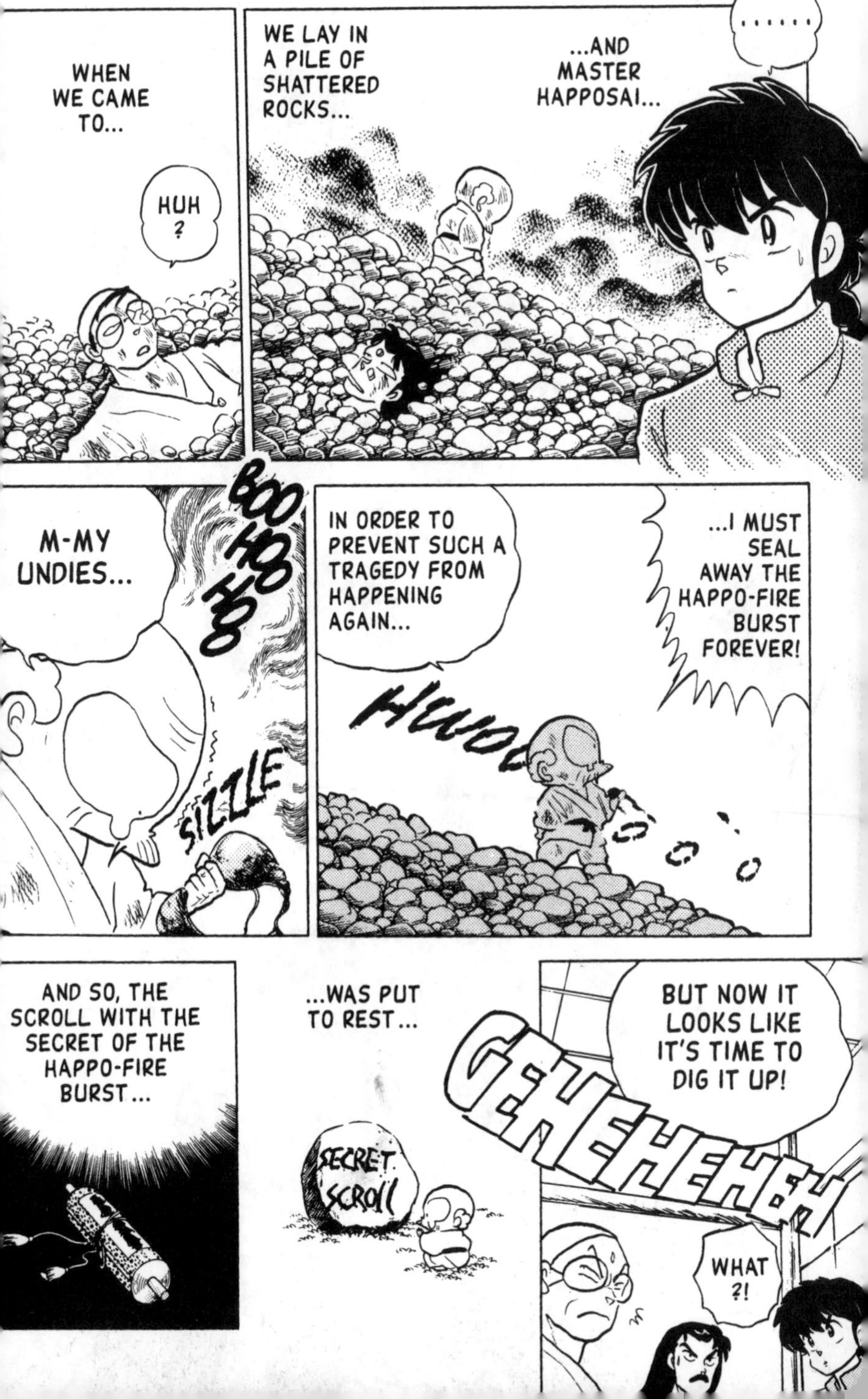

WHEN WE CAME TO...
HUH?
WE LAY IN A PILE OF SHATTERED ROCKS...
...AND MASTER HAPPOSAI...
......
M-MY UNDIES...
BOO HOO HOO
SIZZLE
IN ORDER TO PREVENT SUCH A TRAGEDY FROM HAPPENING AGAIN...
...I MUST SEAL AWAY THE HAPPO-FIRE BURST FOREVER!
HWOO
AND SO, THE SCROLL WITH THE SECRET OF THE HAPPO-FIRE BURST...
...WAS PUT TO REST...
SECRET SCROLL
BUT NOW IT LOOKS LIKE IT'S TIME TO DIG IT UP!
GEHEHEHEH
WHAT?!

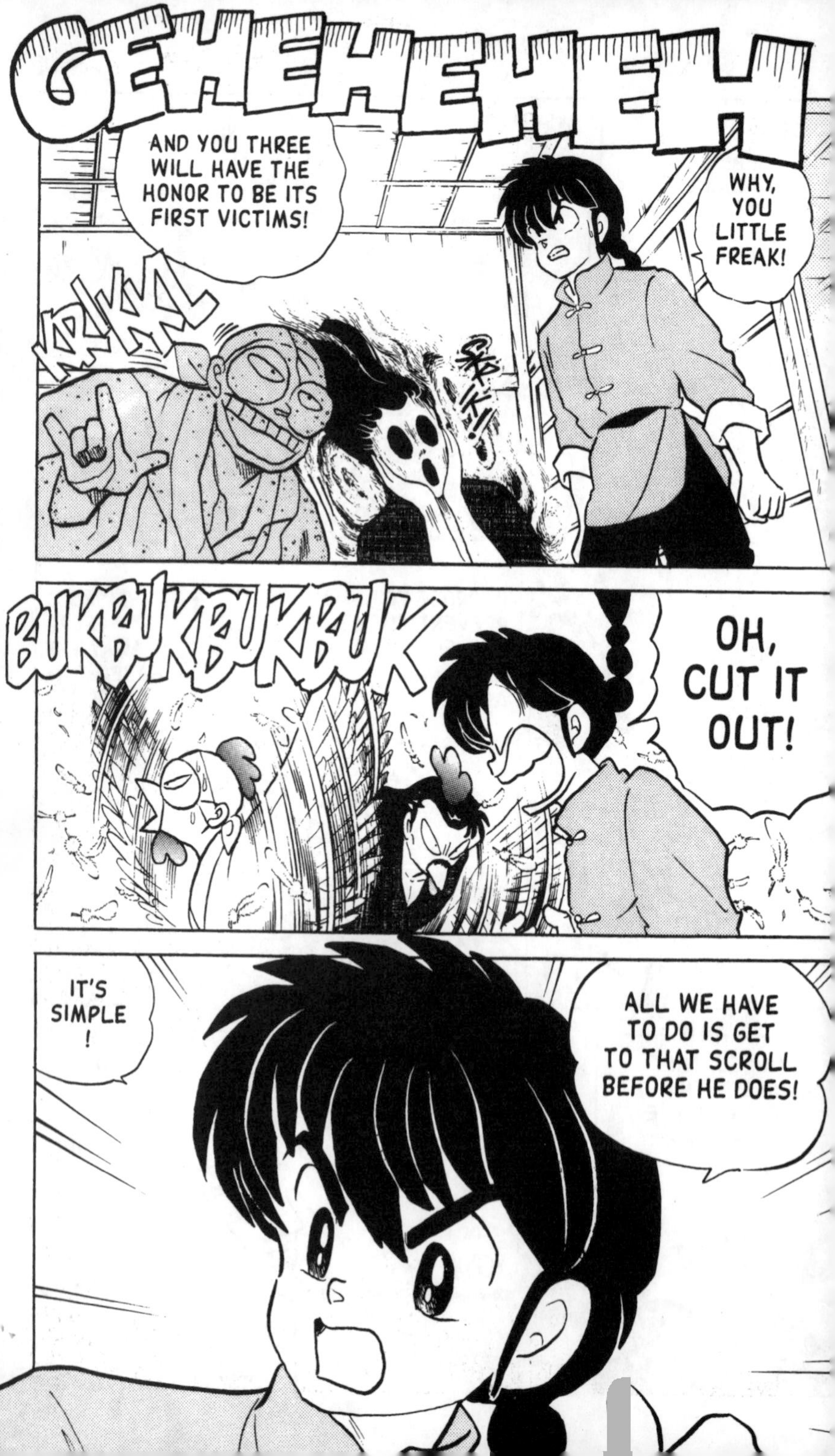
GEHEHEHEH
AND YOU THREE WILL HAVE THE HONOR TO BE ITS FIRST VICTIMS!
KRIKKL
WHY, YOU LITTLE FREAK!
BUKBUKBUKBUK
OH, CUT IT OUT!
IT'S SIMPLE!
ALL WE HAVE TO DO IS GET TO THAT SCROLL BEFORE HE DOES!

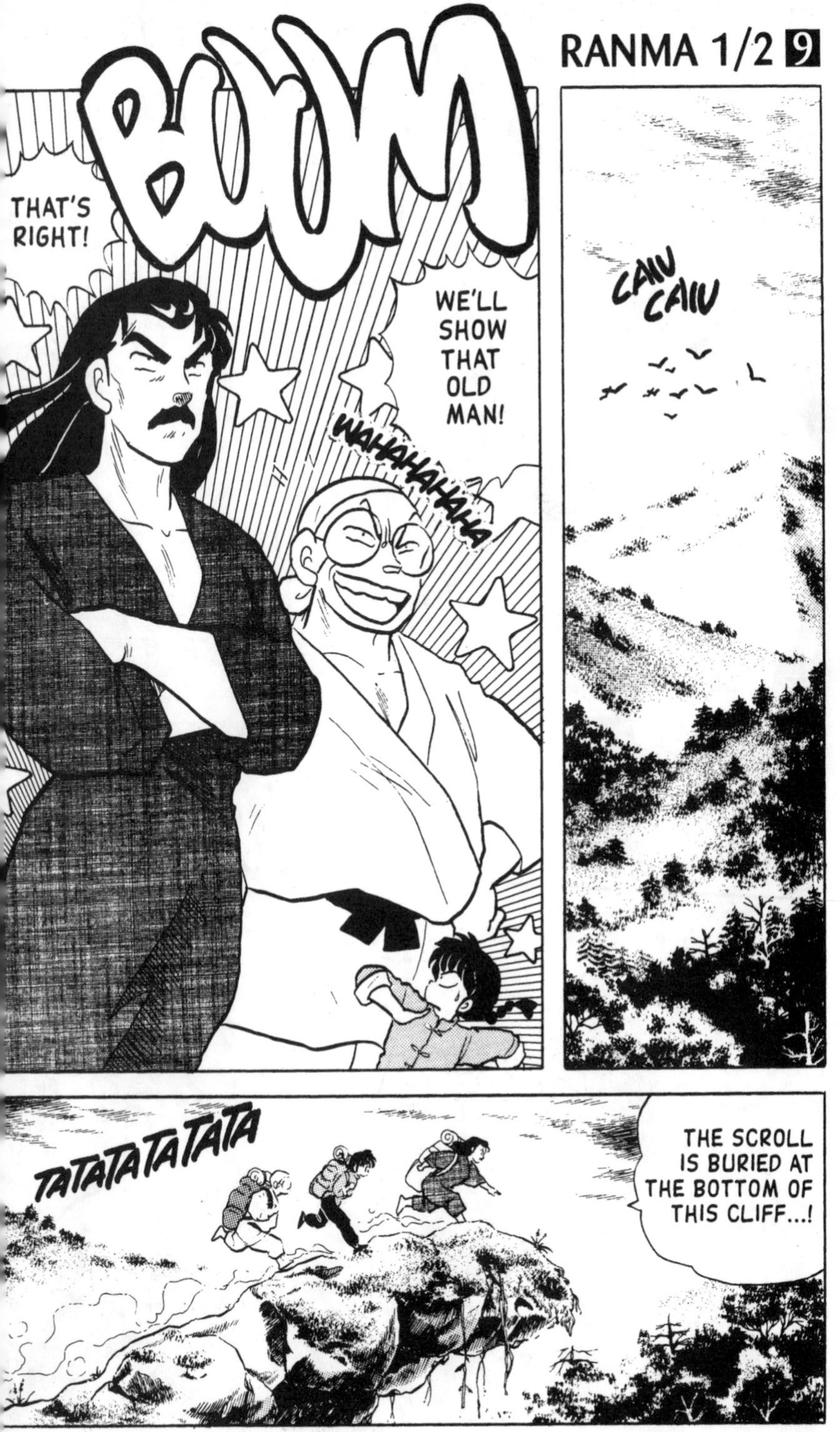
BOOM
THAT'S RIGHT!
WE'LL SHOW THAT OLD MAN!
WAHAHAHAHAHA
CAW CAW
TATATATATATA
THE SCROLL IS BURIED AT THE BOTTOM OF THIS CLIFF...!

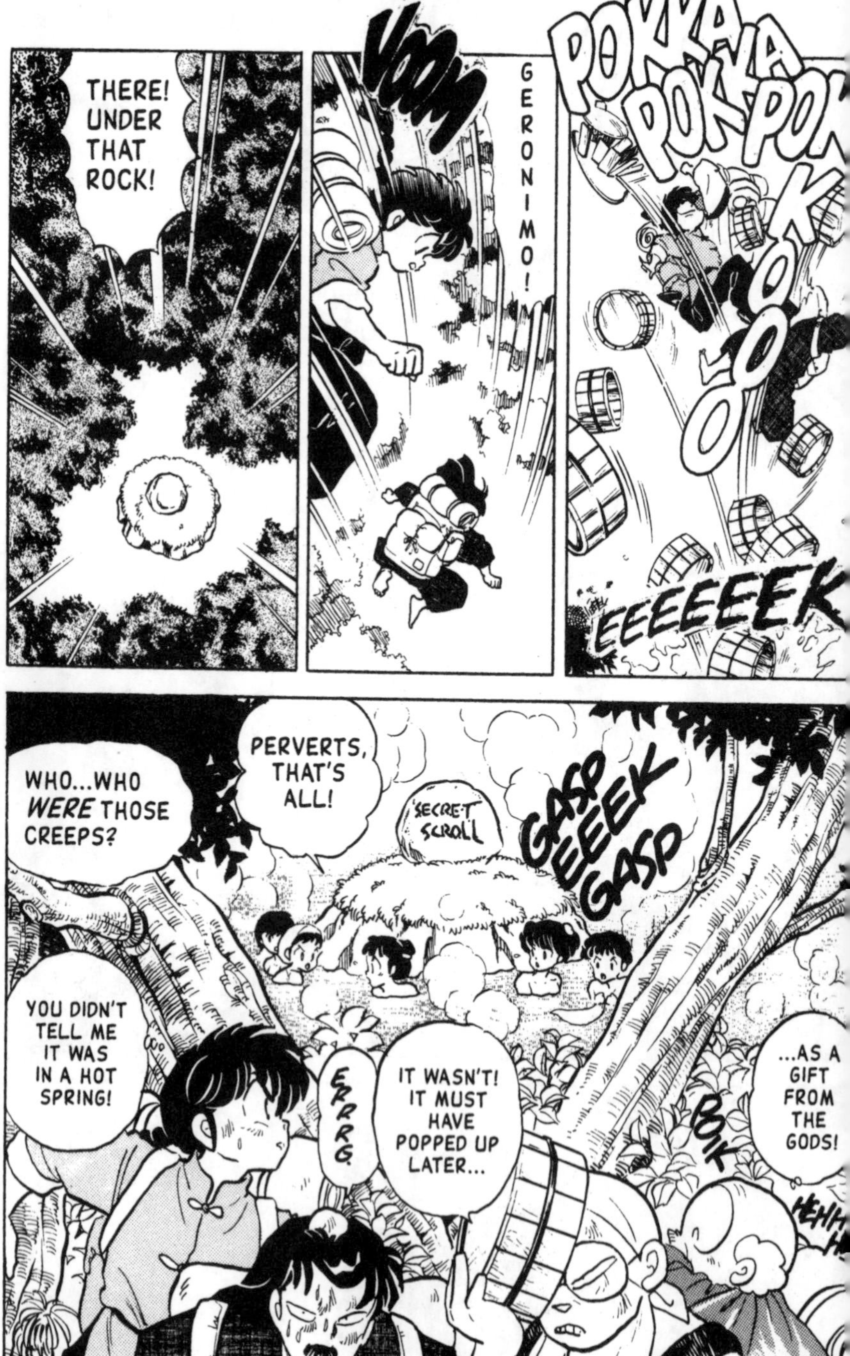
THERE! UNDER THAT ROCK!
VOOM
GERONIMO!
POKKA POKKA POK POK
KOOOO
EEEEEEEK
WHO...WHO *WERE* THOSE CREEPS?
PERVERTS, THAT'S ALL!
SECRET SCROLL
GASP EEEK GASP
YOU DIDN'T TELL ME IT WAS IN A HOT SPRING!
ERRRG
IT WASN'T! IT MUST HAVE POPPED UP LATER...
BOIK
...AS A GIFT FROM THE GODS!

PART 11
GET THE SECRET SCROLL!

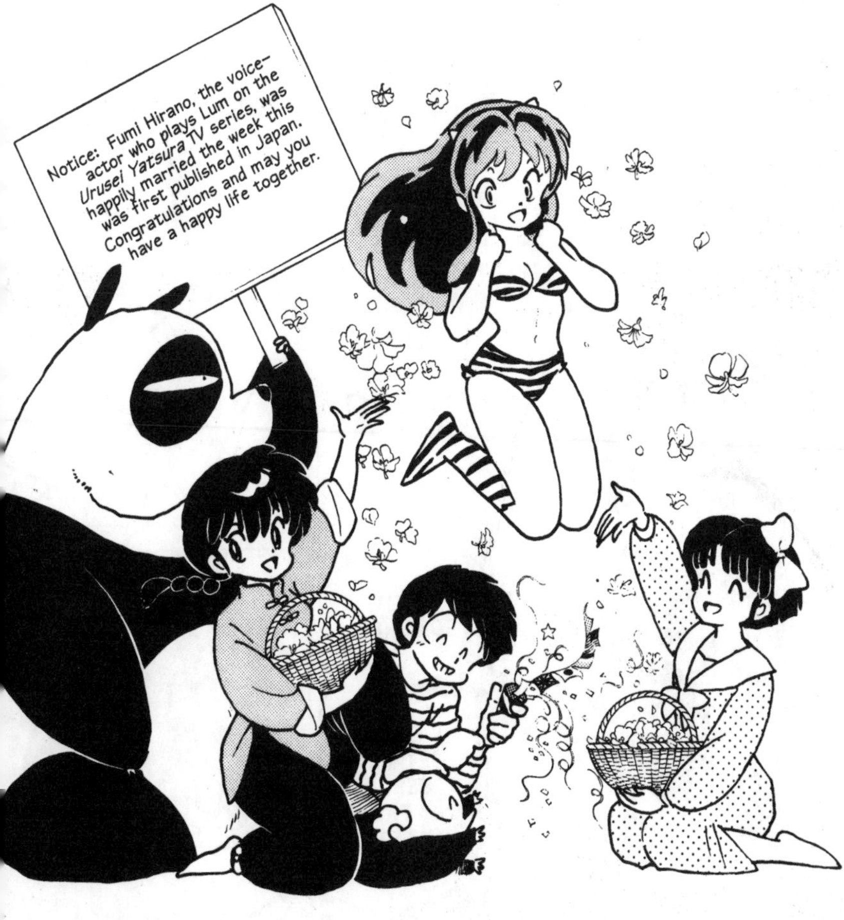
Notice: Fumi Hirano, the voice-actor who plays Lum on the *Urusei Yatsura* TV series, was happily married the week this was first published in Japan. Congratulations and may you have a happy life together.

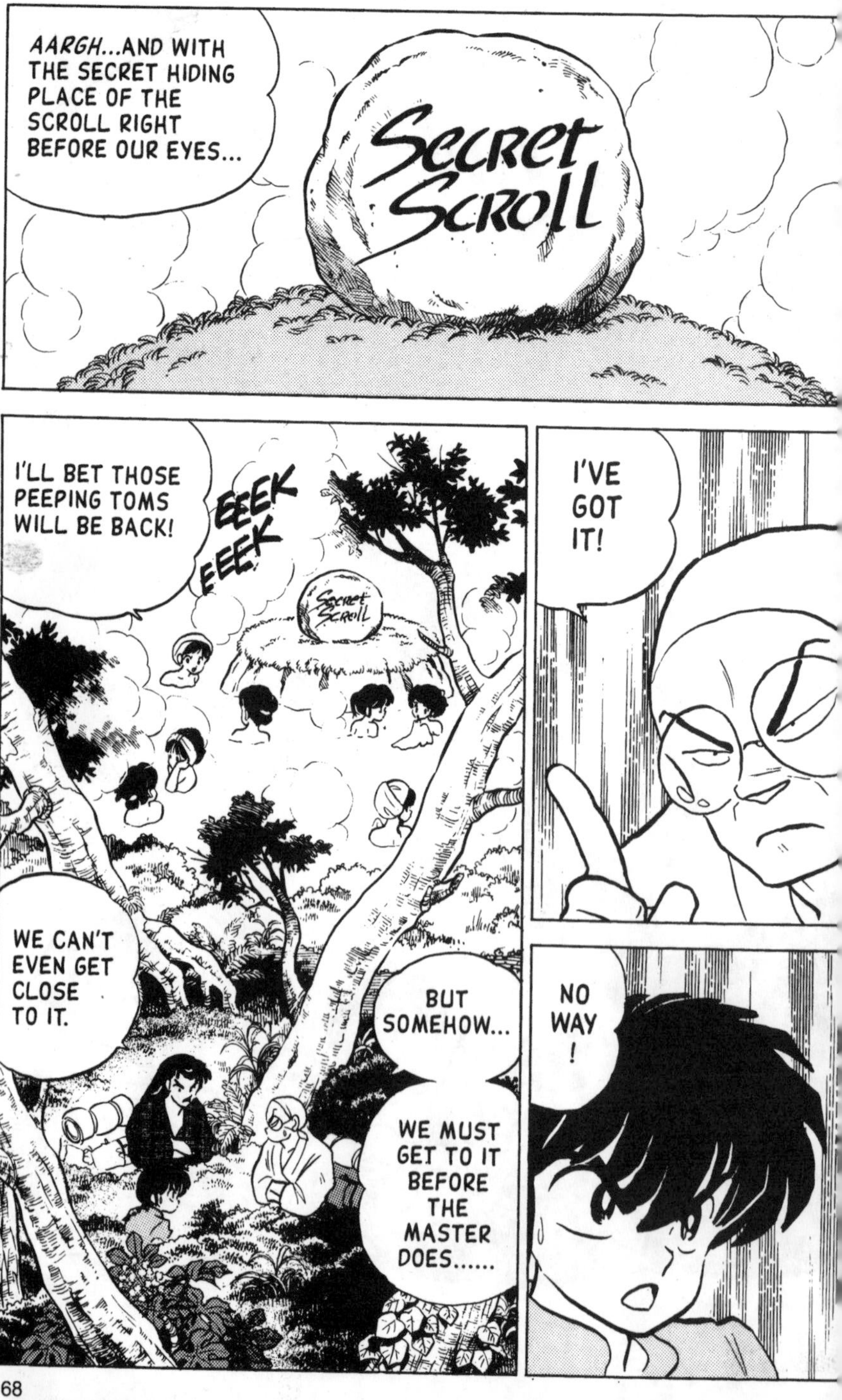
AARGH...AND WITH THE SECRET HIDING PLACE OF THE SCROLL RIGHT BEFORE OUR EYES...
Secret Scroll
I'LL BET THOSE PEEPING TOMS WILL BE BACK!
EEEK
EEEK
Secret Scroll
WE CAN'T EVEN GET CLOSE TO IT.
BUT SOMEHOW...
WE MUST GET TO IT BEFORE THE MASTER DOES......
I'VE GOT IT!
NO WAY !

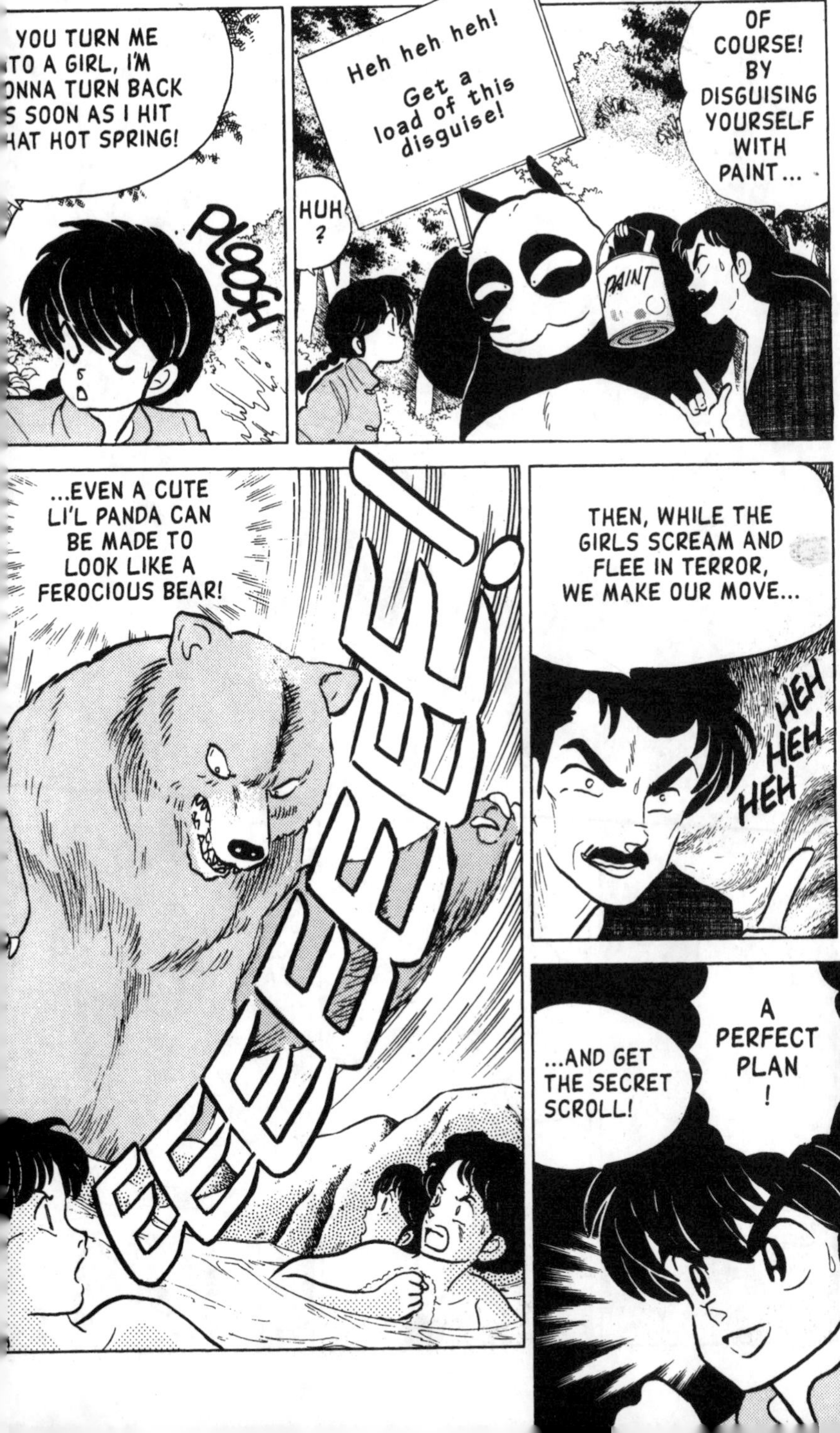

YOU TURN ME TO A GIRL, I'M GONNA TURN BACK AS SOON AS I HIT THAT HOT SPRING!
PLOOSH
Heh heh heh! Get a load of this disguise!
HUH?
OF COURSE! BY DISGUISING YOURSELF WITH PAINT...
PAINT
...EVEN A CUTE LI'L PANDA CAN BE MADE TO LOOK LIKE A FEROCIOUS BEAR!
EEEEEEEE!
THEN, WHILE THE GIRLS SCREAM AND FLEE IN TERROR, WE MAKE OUR MOVE...
HEH HEH HEH
...AND GET THE SECRET SCROLL!
A PERFECT PLAN!

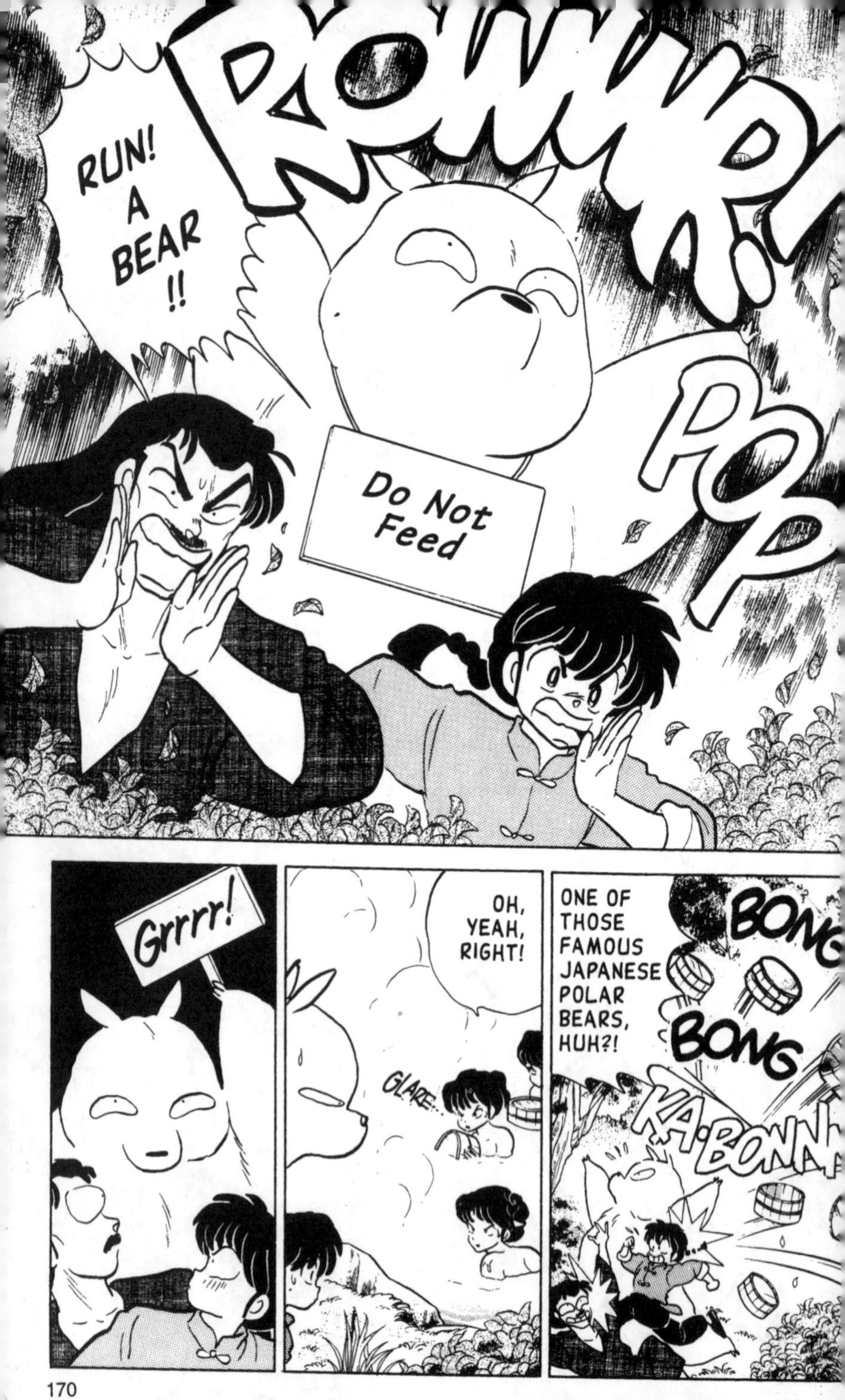
RUN! A BEAR!!
ROWWR!
Do Not Feed
POP
Grrrr!
OH, YEAH, RIGHT!
GLARE
ONE OF THOSE FAMOUS JAPANESE POLAR BEARS, HUH?!
BONG
BONG
KA-BONN

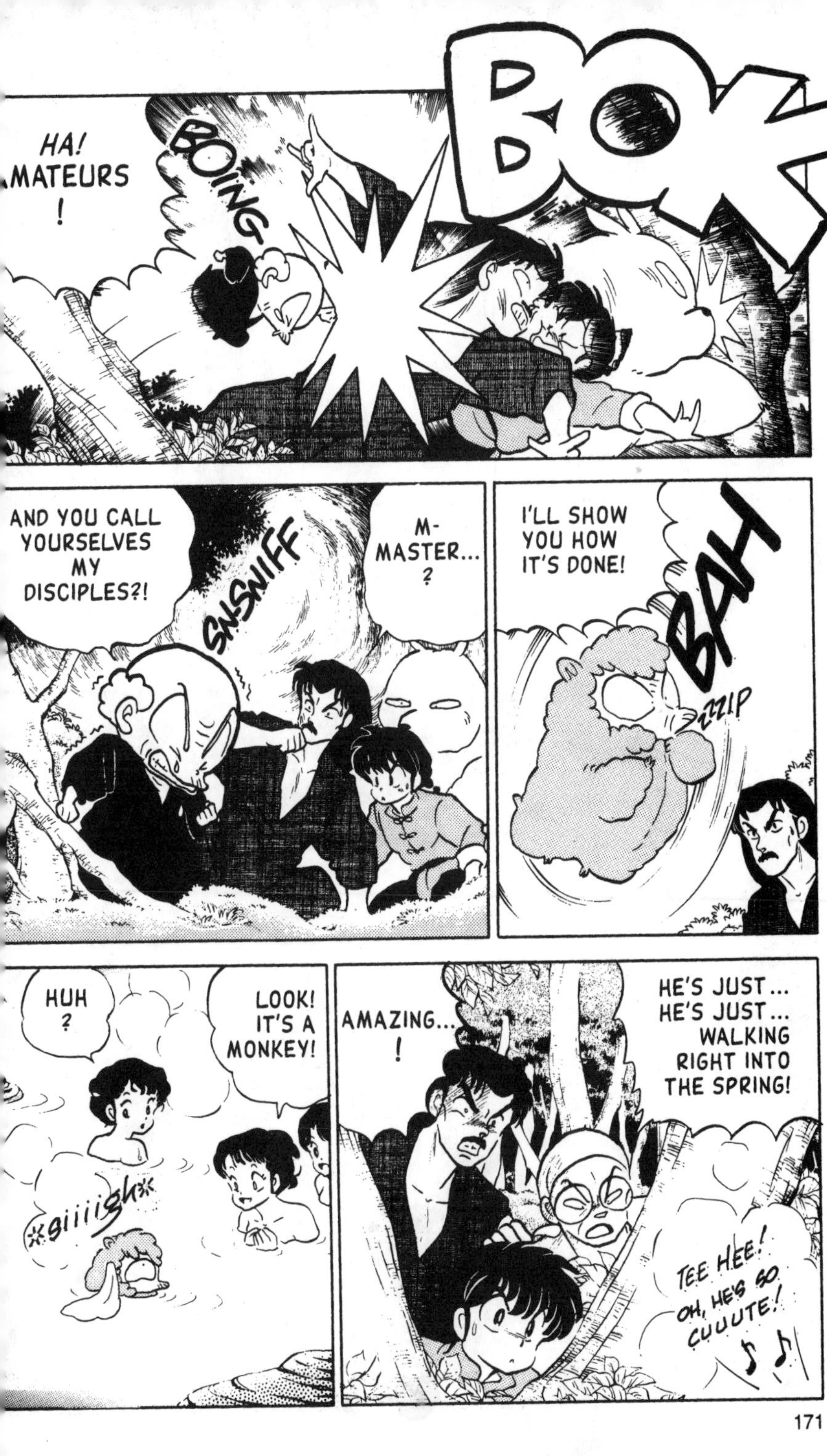
BOK
HA! AMATEURS!
BOING
AND YOU CALL YOURSELVES MY DISCIPLES?!
SNSNIFF
M-MASTER...?
I'LL SHOW YOU HOW IT'S DONE!
BAH
ZZZIP
HUH?
LOOK! IT'S A MONKEY!
※giiiigh※
AMAZING...!
HE'S JUST... HE'S JUST... WALKING RIGHT INTO THE SPRING!
TEE HEE! OH, HE'S SO CUUUTE!

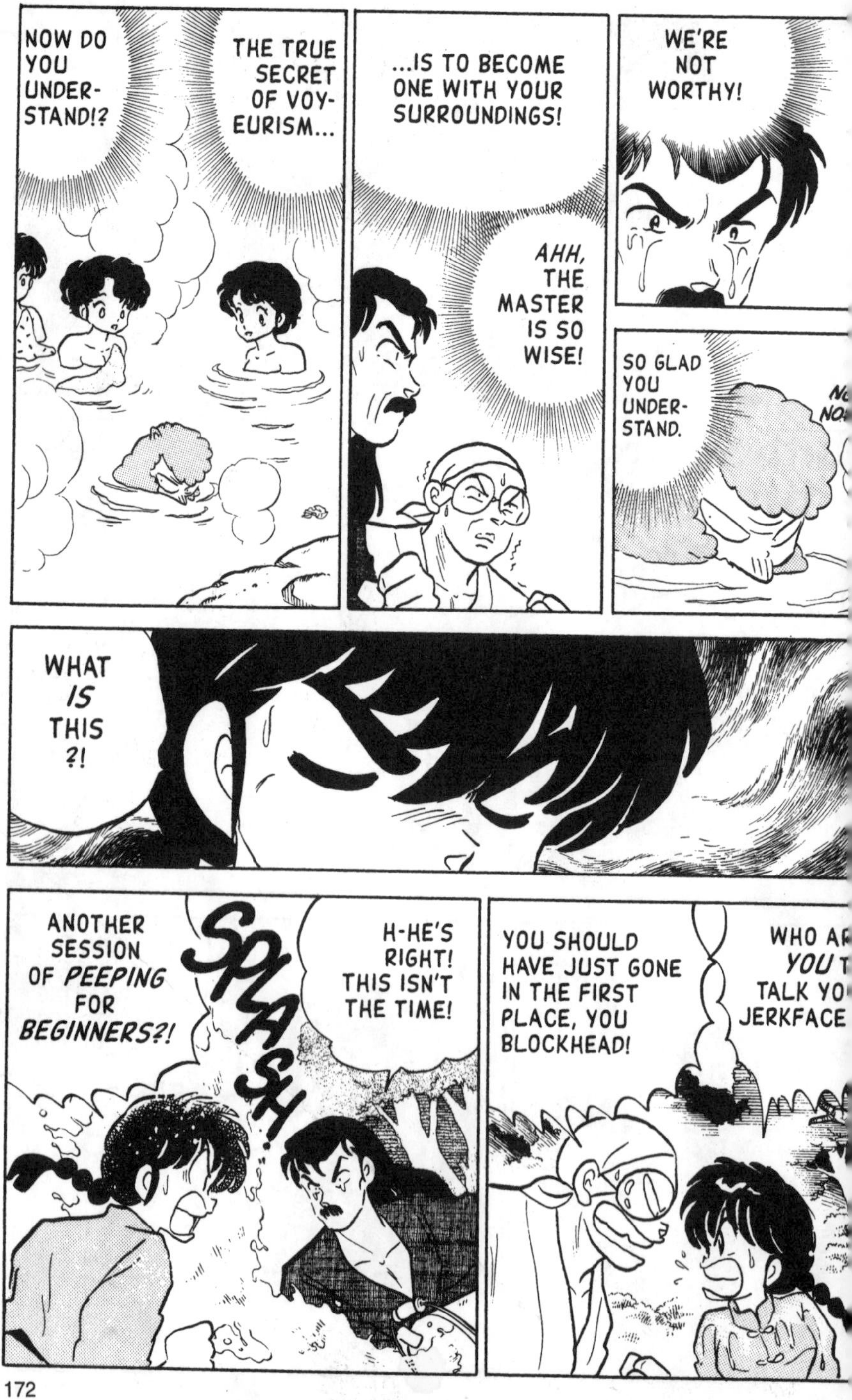
NOW DO YOU UNDER-STAND!?
THE TRUE SECRET OF VOY-EURISM...
...IS TO BECOME ONE WITH YOUR SURROUNDINGS!
AHH, THE MASTER IS SO WISE!
WE'RE NOT WORTHY!
SO GLAD YOU UNDER-STAND.
WHAT *IS* THIS ?!
ANOTHER SESSION OF *PEEPING* FOR *BEGINNERS?!*
SPLASH!
H-HE'S RIGHT! THIS ISN'T THE TIME!
YOU SHOULD HAVE JUST GONE IN THE FIRST PLACE, YOU BLOCKHEAD!
WHO AR
YOU T
TALK YO
JERKFACE

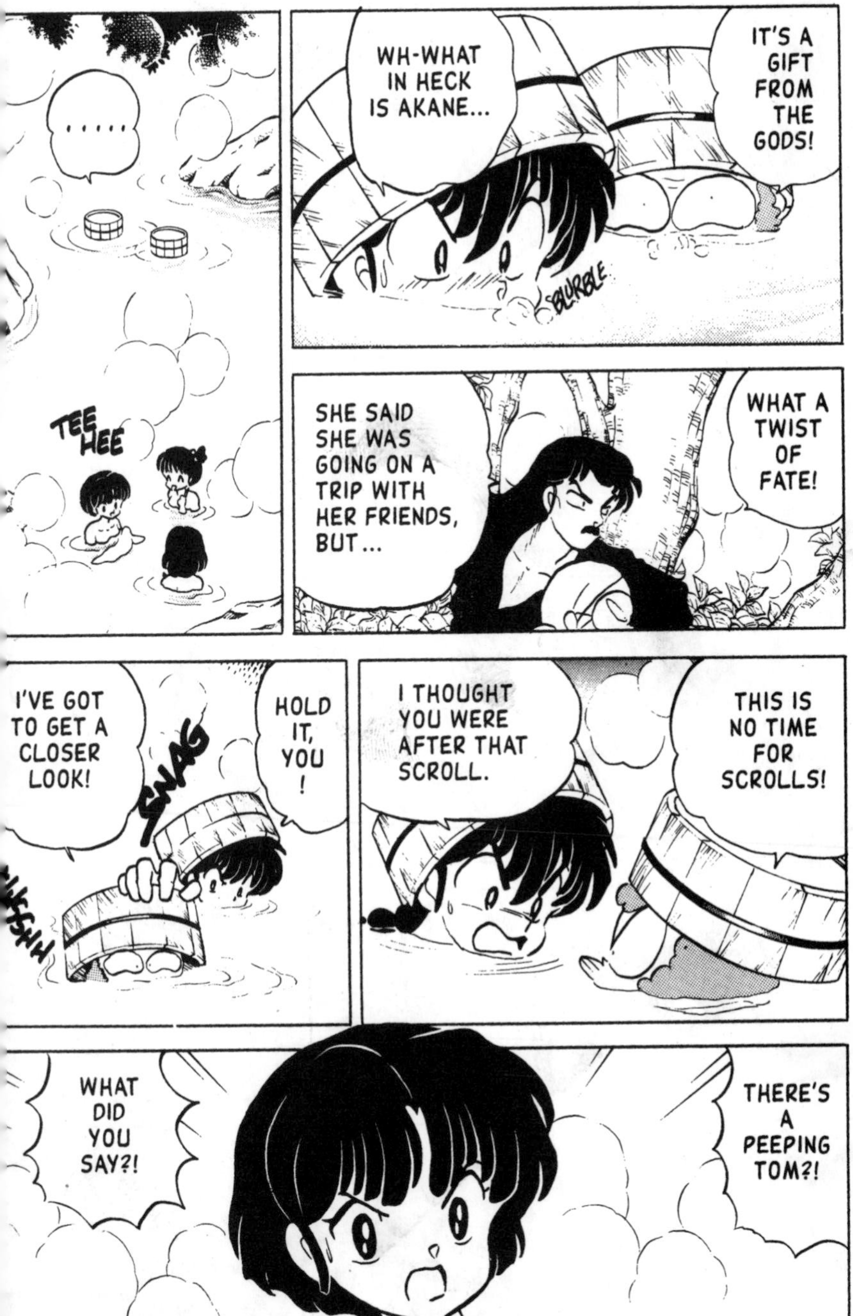
.....
TEE HEE
WH-WHAT IN HECK IS AKANE...
IT'S A GIFT FROM THE GODS!
BLURBLE
SHE SAID SHE WAS GOING ON A TRIP WITH HER FRIENDS, BUT...
WHAT A TWIST OF FATE!
I'VE GOT TO GET A CLOSER LOOK!
SNAG
HOLD IT, YOU!
I THOUGHT YOU WERE AFTER THAT SCROLL.
THIS IS NO TIME FOR SCROLLS!
WHAT DID YOU SAY?!
THERE'S A PEEPING TOM?!

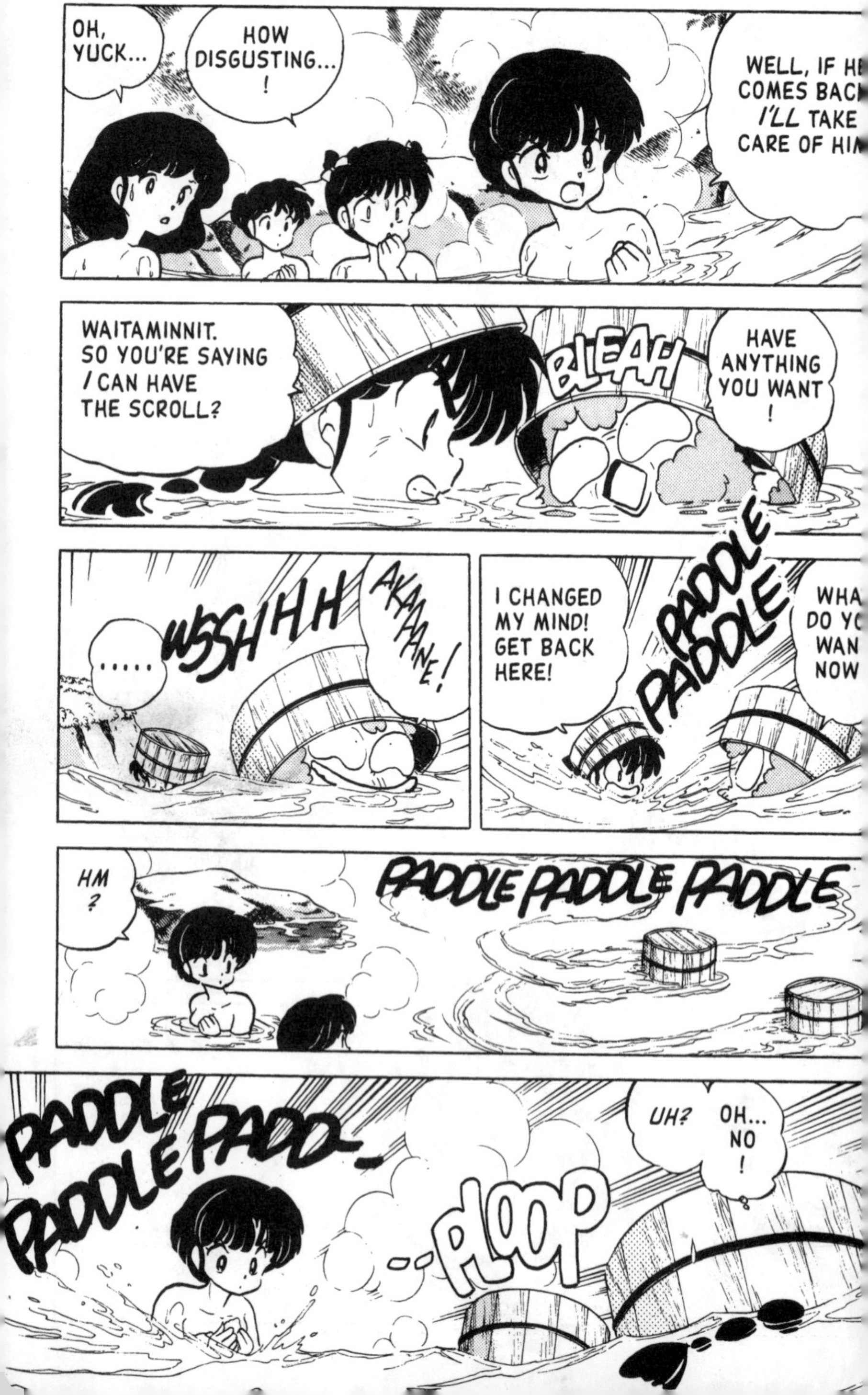
OH, YUCK...
HOW DISGUSTING... !
WELL, IF HE COMES BACK I'LL TAKE CARE OF HIM
WAITAMINNIT. SO YOU'RE SAYING I CAN HAVE THE SCROLL?
BLEAAH
HAVE ANYTHING YOU WANT !
.....
WSSHHH
AKAAAANE!
I CHANGED MY MIND! GET BACK HERE!
PADDLE PADDLE PADDLE
WHA DO YO WAN NOW
HM ?
PADDLE PADDLE PADDLE
PADDLE PADDLE PADD—
—PLOOP
UH?
OH... NO !

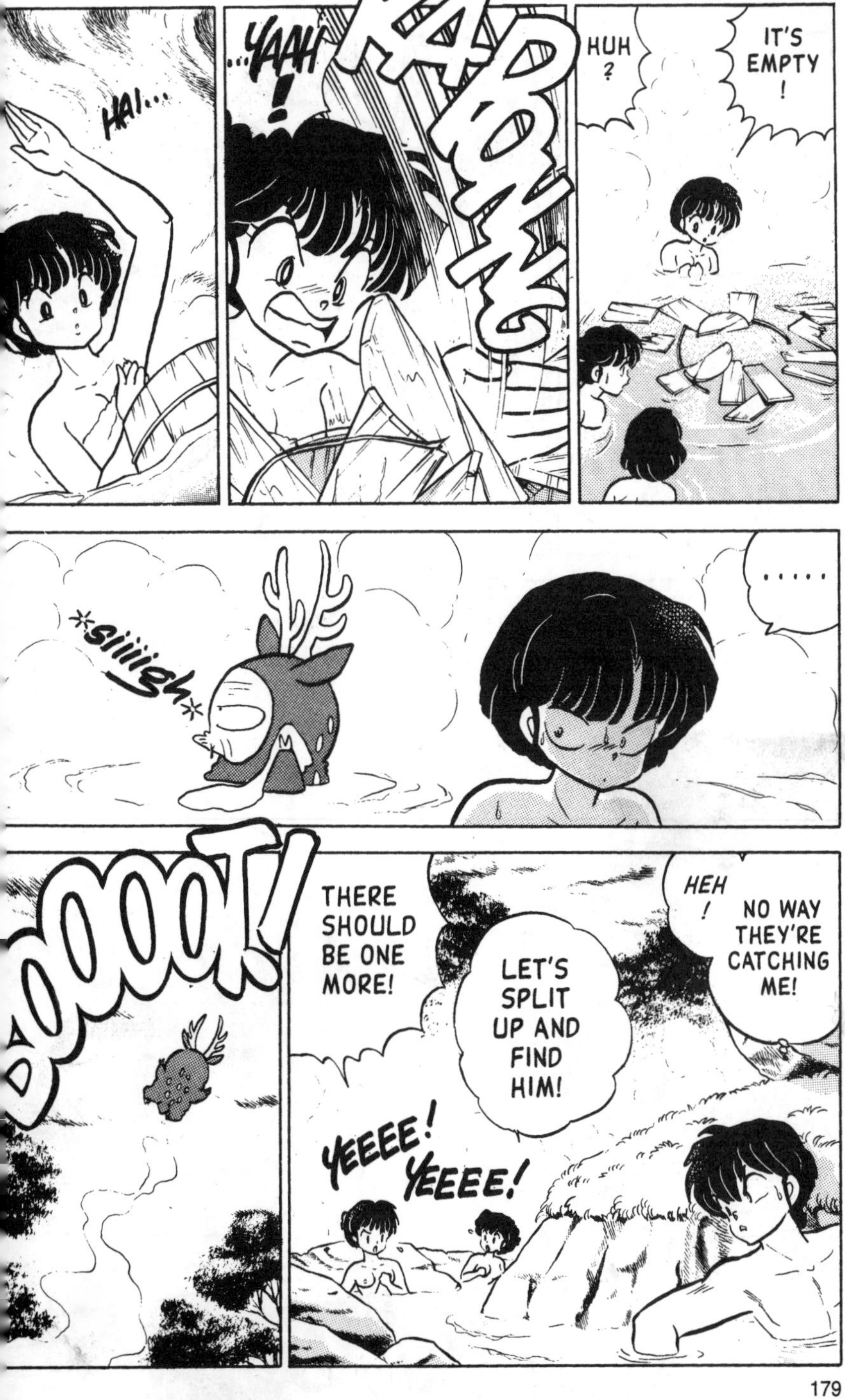
HAI...
...YAAH!
KA-BOWNG
HUH?
IT'S EMPTY!
siiiigh
.....
BOOOOOT!
THERE SHOULD BE ONE MORE!
LET'S SPLIT UP AND FIND HIM!
YEEEE! YEEEE!
HEH!
NO WAY THEY'RE CATCHING ME!

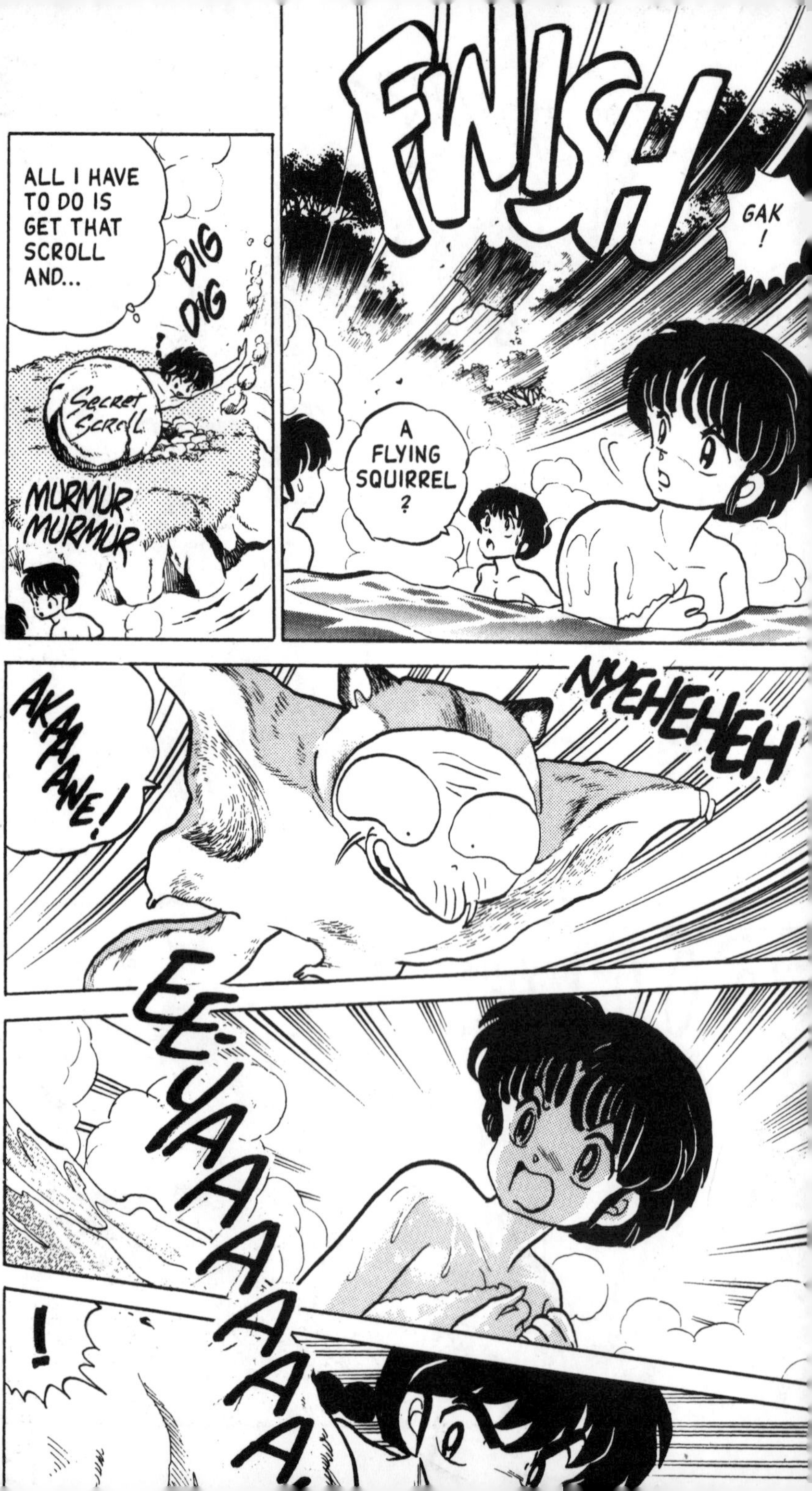

ALL I HAVE TO DO IS GET THAT SCROLL AND...
DIG DIG
Secret Scroll
MURMUR MURMUR
FWISH
GAK!
A FLYING SQUIRREL?
AKAAANE!
NYEHEHEH
EEEYAAAAAAAA
!

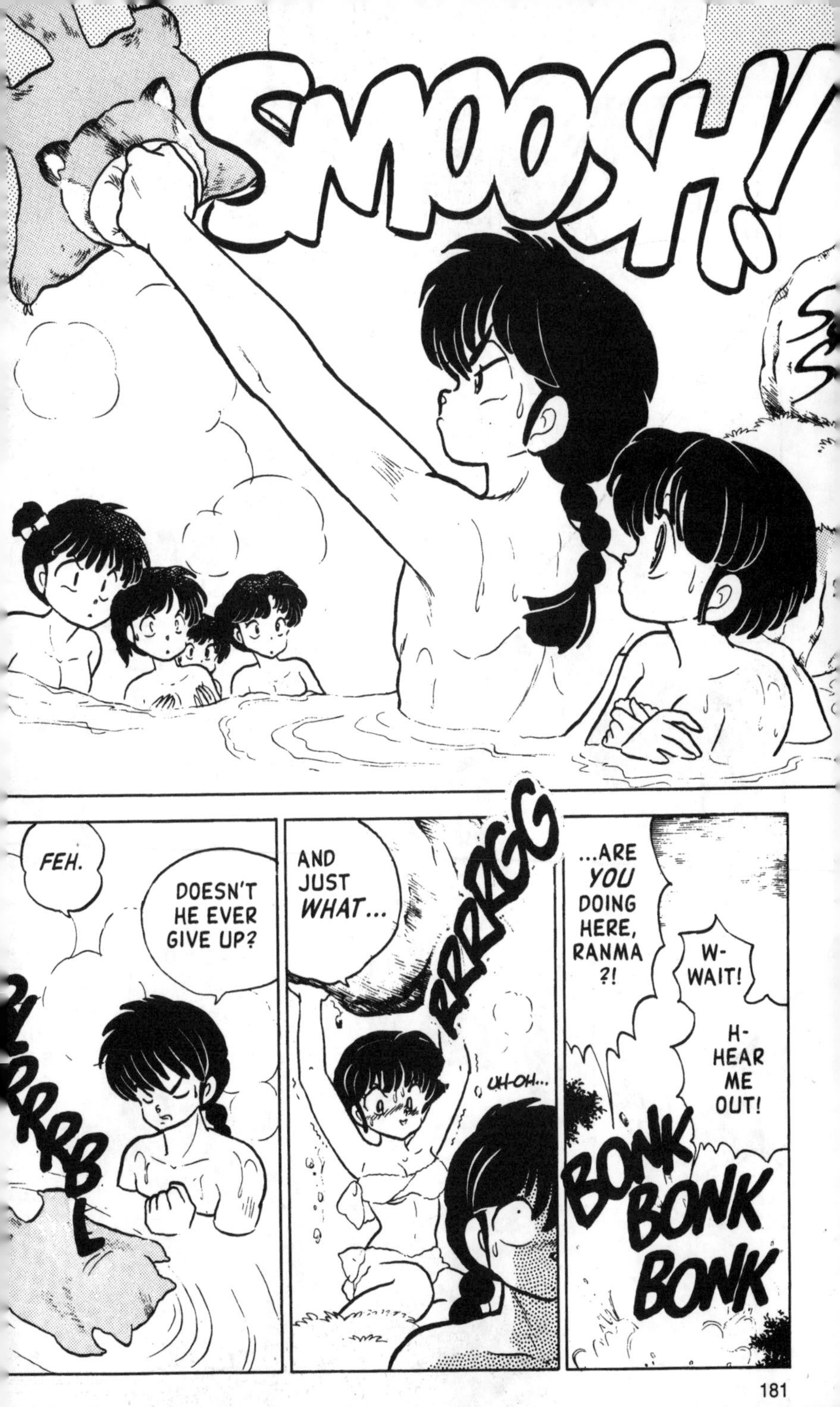
SMOOCH!
FEH.
DOESN'T HE EVER GIVE UP?
AND JUST WHAT...
UH-OH...
...ARE YOU DOING HERE, RANMA?!
W-WAIT!
H-HEAR ME OUT!
BONK
BONK
BONK

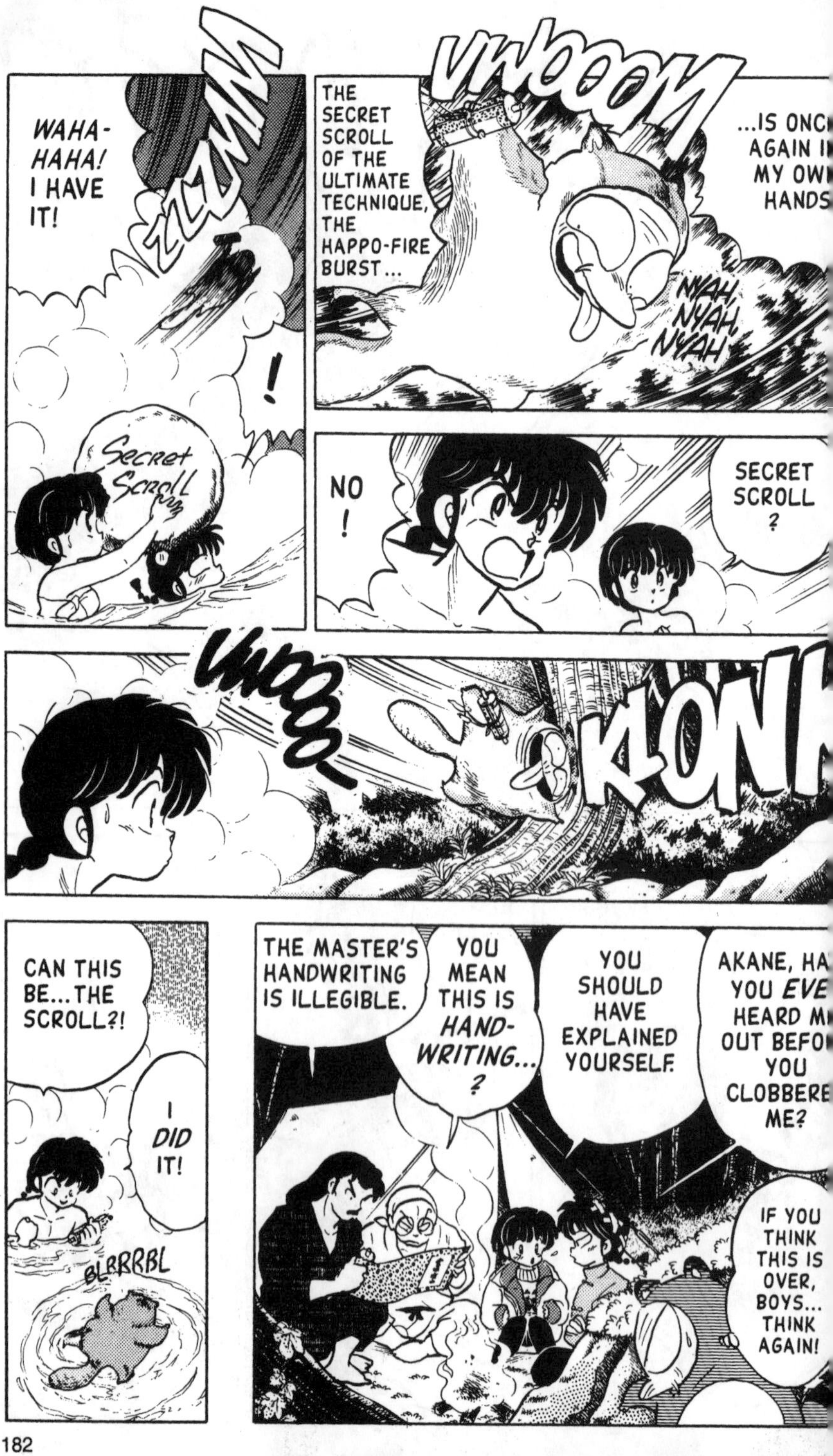
WAHA-HAHA! I HAVE IT!
ZZZWM
!
Secret Scroll
THE SECRET SCROLL OF THE ULTIMATE TECHNIQUE, THE HAPPO-FIRE BURST...
VWOOOM
...IS ONC AGAIN I MY OW HANDS
NYAH, NYAH, NYAH
NO!
SECRET SCROLL?
VWOOOO
KLONK
CAN THIS BE...THE SCROLL?!
I DID IT!
BLRRRBL
THE MASTER'S HANDWRITING IS ILLEGIBLE.
YOU MEAN THIS IS *HAND-WRITING*...?
YOU SHOULD HAVE EXPLAINED YOURSELF.
AKANE, HA YOU *EVE* HEARD M OUT BEFO YOU CLOBBERE ME?
IF YOU THINK THIS IS OVER, BOYS... THINK AGAIN!

PART 12
THE FIRE-BURST OF TERROR!

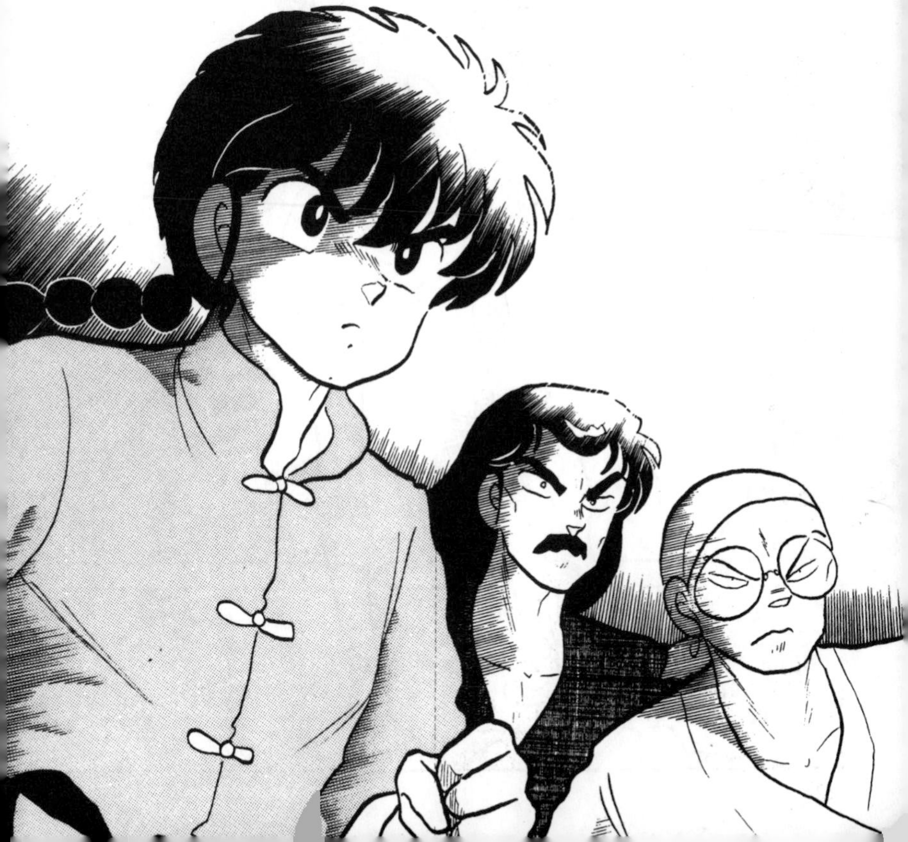

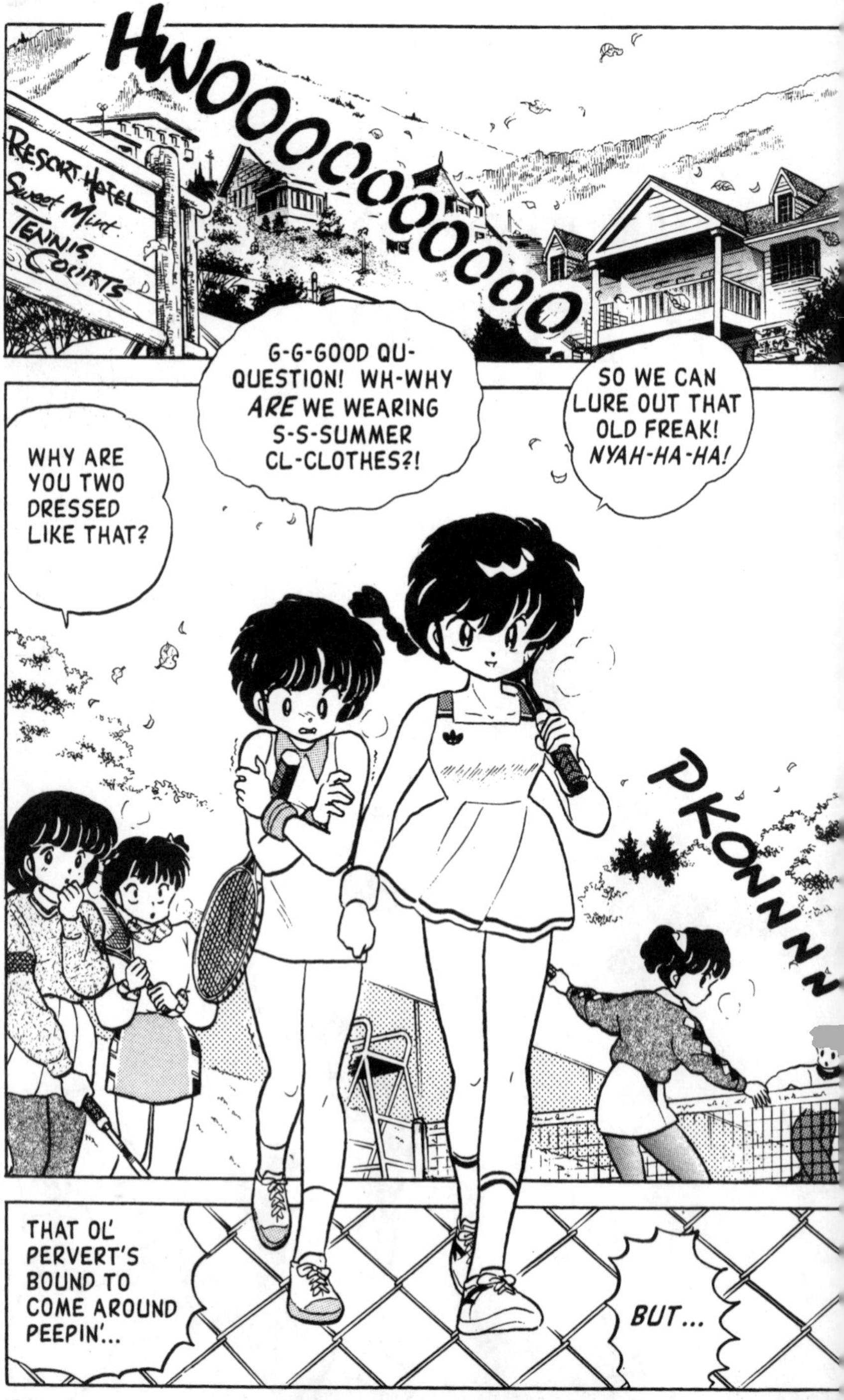
HWOOOOOOOOOOOOOOO
RESORT HOTEL Sweet Mint TENNIS COURTS
WHY ARE YOU TWO DRESSED LIKE THAT?
G-G-GOOD QU-QUESTION! WH-WHY *ARE* WE WEARING S-S-SUMMER CL-CLOTHES?!
SO WE CAN LURE OUT THAT OLD FREAK! *NYAH-HA-HA!*
PKONNNN
THAT OL' PERVERT'S BOUND TO COME AROUND PEEPIN'...
BUT...

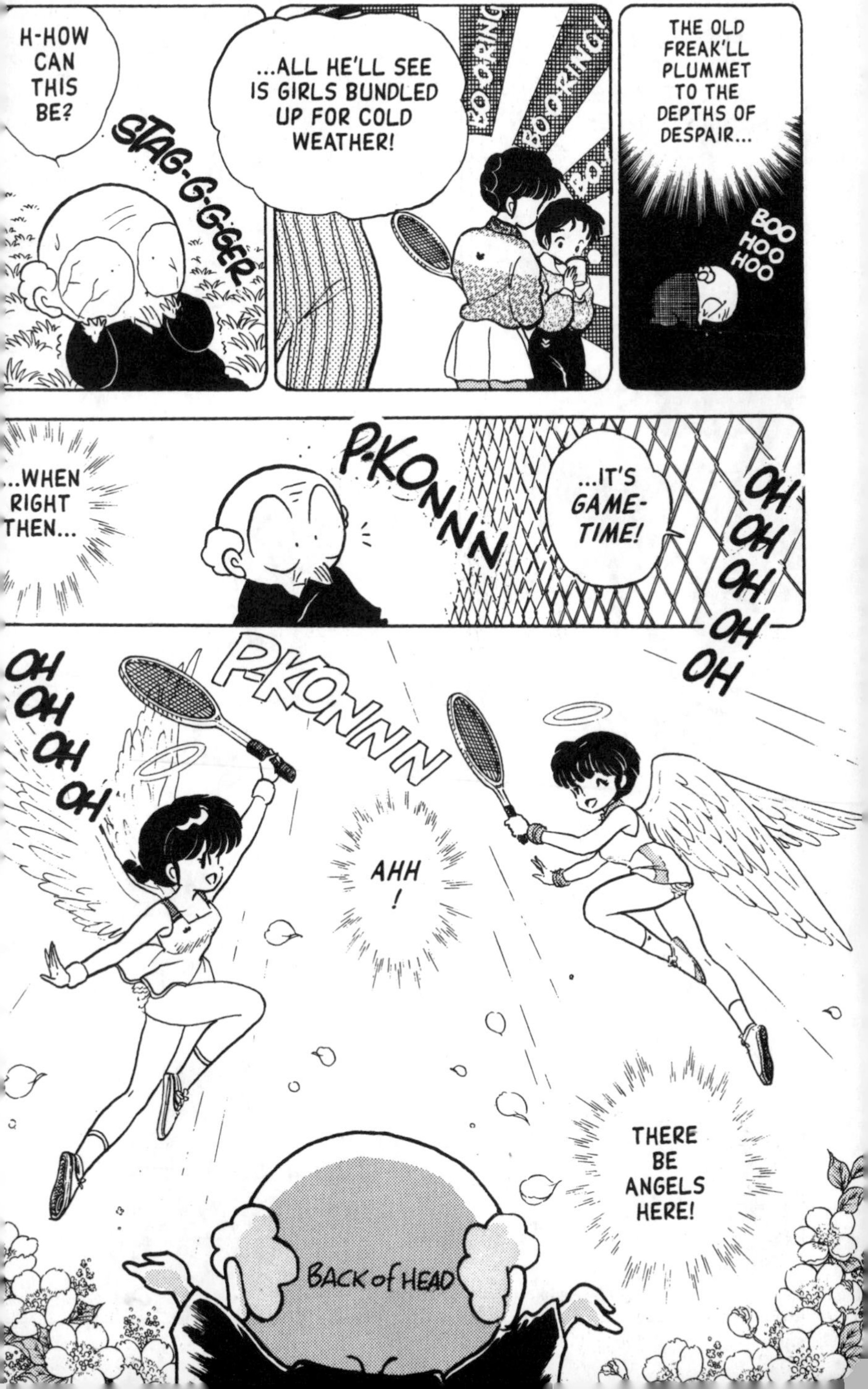
H-HOW CAN THIS BE?
STAG-G-G-GER
...ALL HE'LL SEE IS GIRLS BUNDLED UP FOR COLD WEATHER!
BOORING
BOORING!
BO...
THE OLD FREAK'LL PLUMMET TO THE DEPTHS OF DESPAIR...
BOO HOO HOO
...WHEN RIGHT THEN...
P-KONNNN
...IT'S GAME-TIME!
OH OH OH OH OH OH
P-KONNNN
OH OH OH OH
AHH !
THERE BE ANGELS HERE!
BACK of HEAD

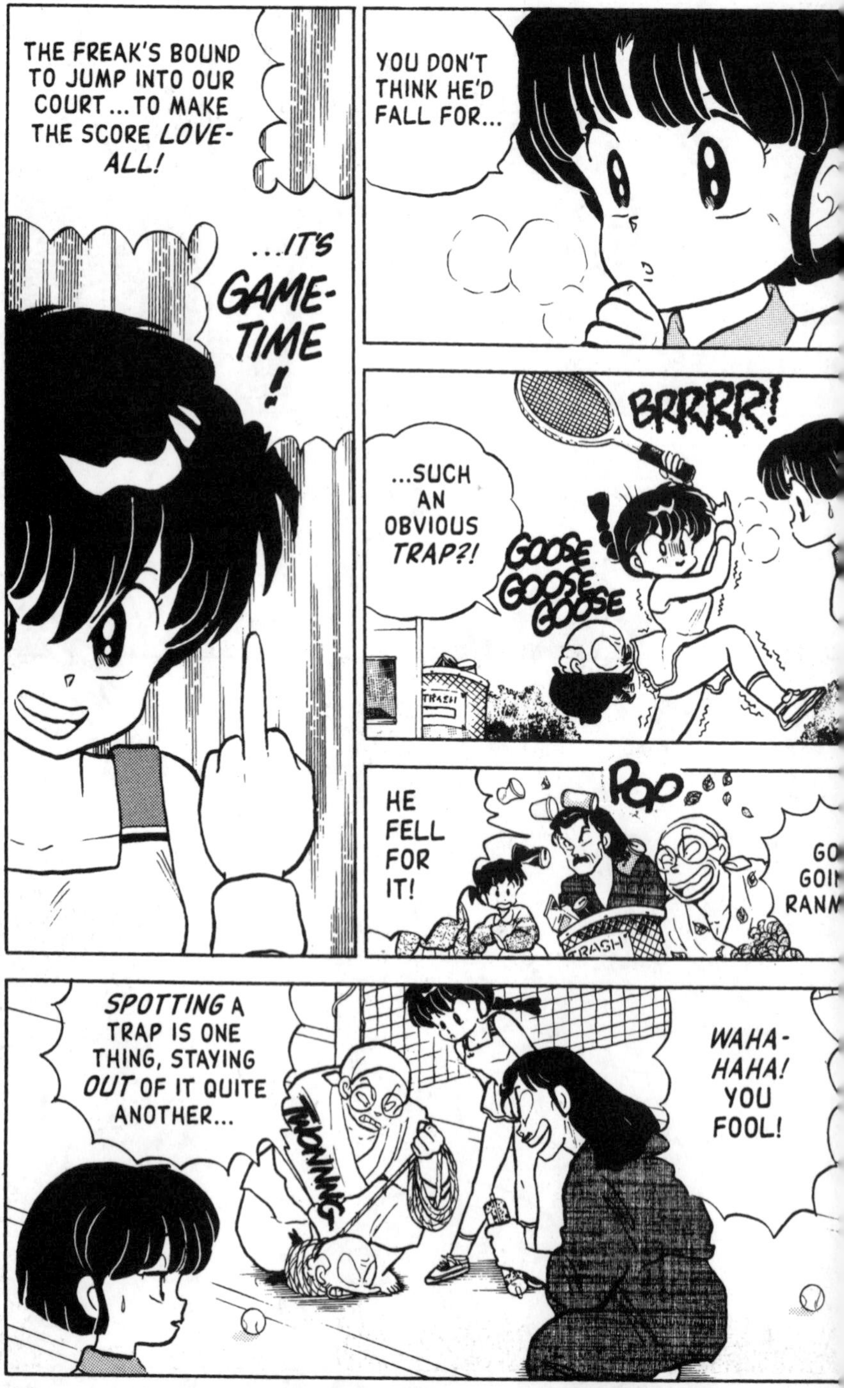
THE FREAK'S BOUND TO JUMP INTO OUR COURT...TO MAKE THE SCORE *LOVE-ALL!*
...*IT'S* GAME-TIME!
YOU DON'T THINK HE'D FALL FOR...
...SUCH AN OBVIOUS *TRAP?!*
BRRRR!
GOOSE GOOSE GOOSE
TRASH
POP
HE FELL FOR IT!
TRASH
SPOTTING A TRAP IS ONE THING, STAYING *OUT* OF IT QUITE ANOTHER...
TWONNNG
WAHA-HAHA! YOU FOOL!

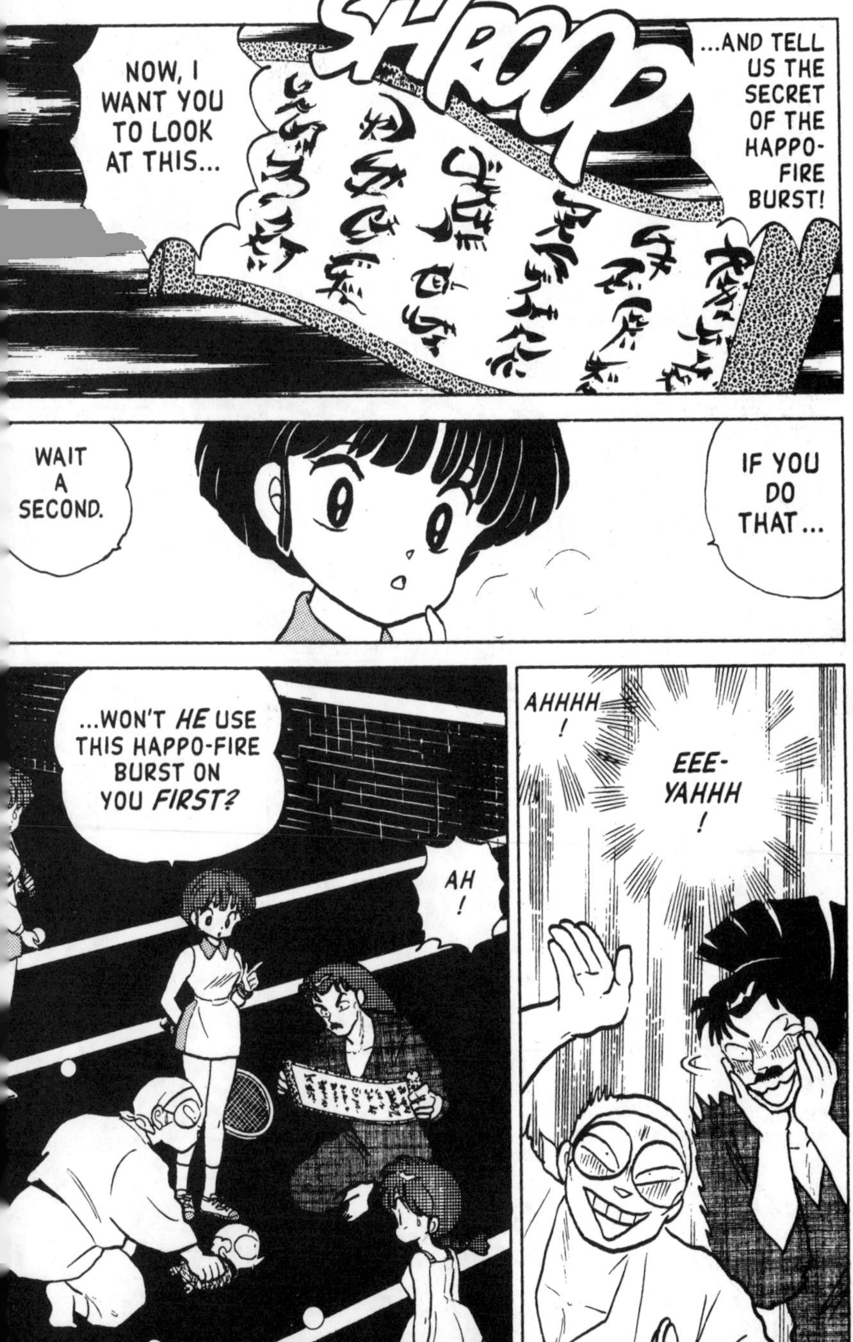
NOW, I WANT YOU TO LOOK AT THIS...
SHROOP
...AND TELL US THE SECRET OF THE HAPPO-FIRE BURST!
WAIT A SECOND.
IF YOU DO THAT...
...WON'T *HE* USE THIS HAPPO-FIRE BURST ON YOU *FIRST?*
AH!
AHHHH!
EEE-YAHHH!

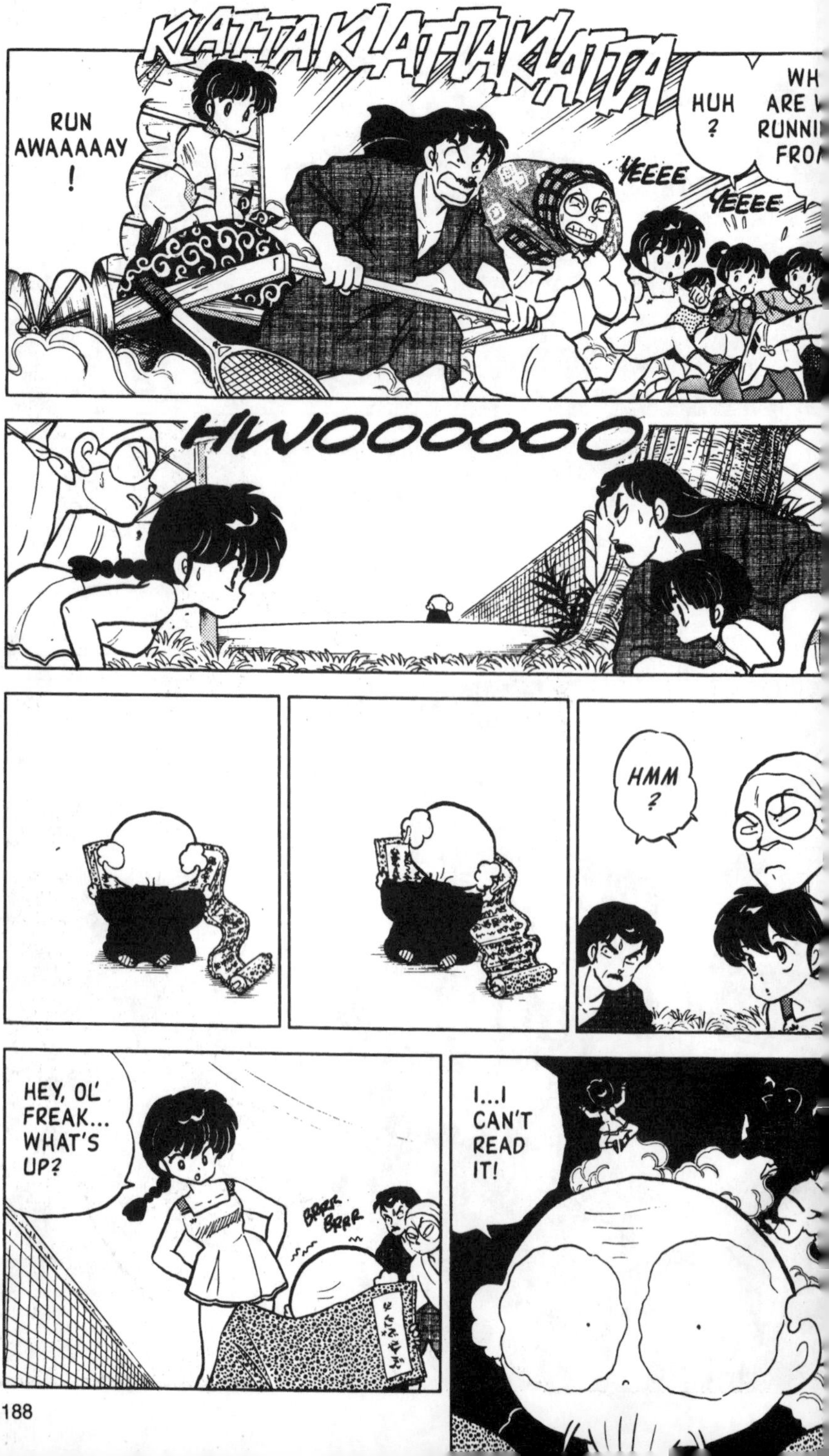
KLATTAKLATTAKLATTA
RUN AWAAAAAY!
HUH?
WH ARE W RUNNI FROM
YEEEE
YEEEE
HWOOOOOO
HMM?
HEY, OL' FREAK... WHAT'S UP?
BRRR BRRR
I...I CAN'T READ IT!

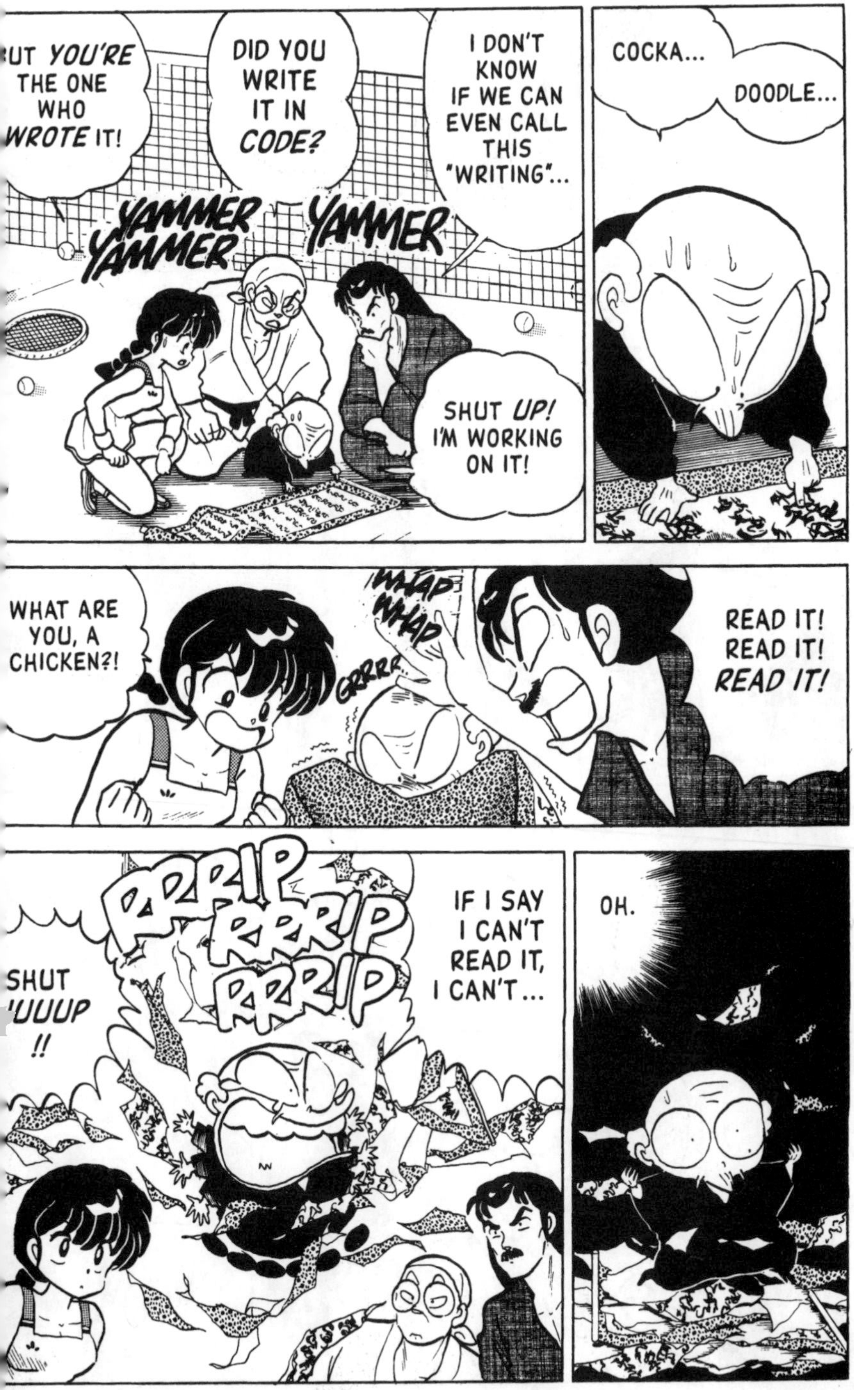
BUT *YOU'RE* THE ONE WHO *WROTE* IT!
DID YOU WRITE IT IN *CODE?*
I DON'T KNOW IF WE CAN EVEN CALL THIS "WRITING"...
YAMMER YAMMER
YAMMER
SHUT *UP!* I'M WORKING ON IT!
COCKA...
DOODLE...
WHAT ARE YOU, A CHICKEN?!
WHAP WHAP
GRRRR
READ IT! READ IT! *READ IT!*
SHUT UUUUP!!
RRRIP RRRIP RRRIP
IF I SAY I CAN'T READ IT, I CAN'T...
OH.

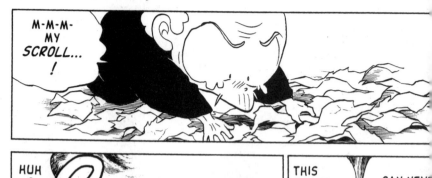

M-M-M-MY SCROLL...!

HUH?

OOOOM

THIS MEANS... THE MASTER...

...CAN NEVE USE T HAPPO-FI BURST (US EV AGA

WE HAVE NOTHING TO FEAR FROM HAPPOSAI!

MURMUR MURMUR

BIFF BIFF

BOOM BOOM

POW POW

TAKE THAT! TAKE THIS! TAKE THAT!

HWOOOO

HFFF HFFF HFFF

HUH?

HE AIN'T MOVIN'.

RRRMBLE

POKE POKE

ALL RIGHT! THEN LET'S FINISH HIM OFF!

DAD, DON'T YOU THINK THAT'S A BIT MUCH...?

IT'S ALL RIGHT... AKANE DEAR...

HUH ?

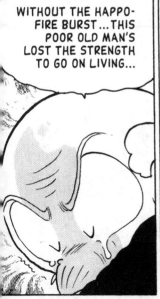

WITHOUT THE HAPPO-FIRE BURST...THIS POOR OLD MAN'S LOST THE STRENGTH TO GO ON LIVING...

POP.

GLOMP

SO WHY DON'T I JUST GET RID OF...

...WHAT LITTLE LIFE YOU'VE GOT!

KA-BLONK!

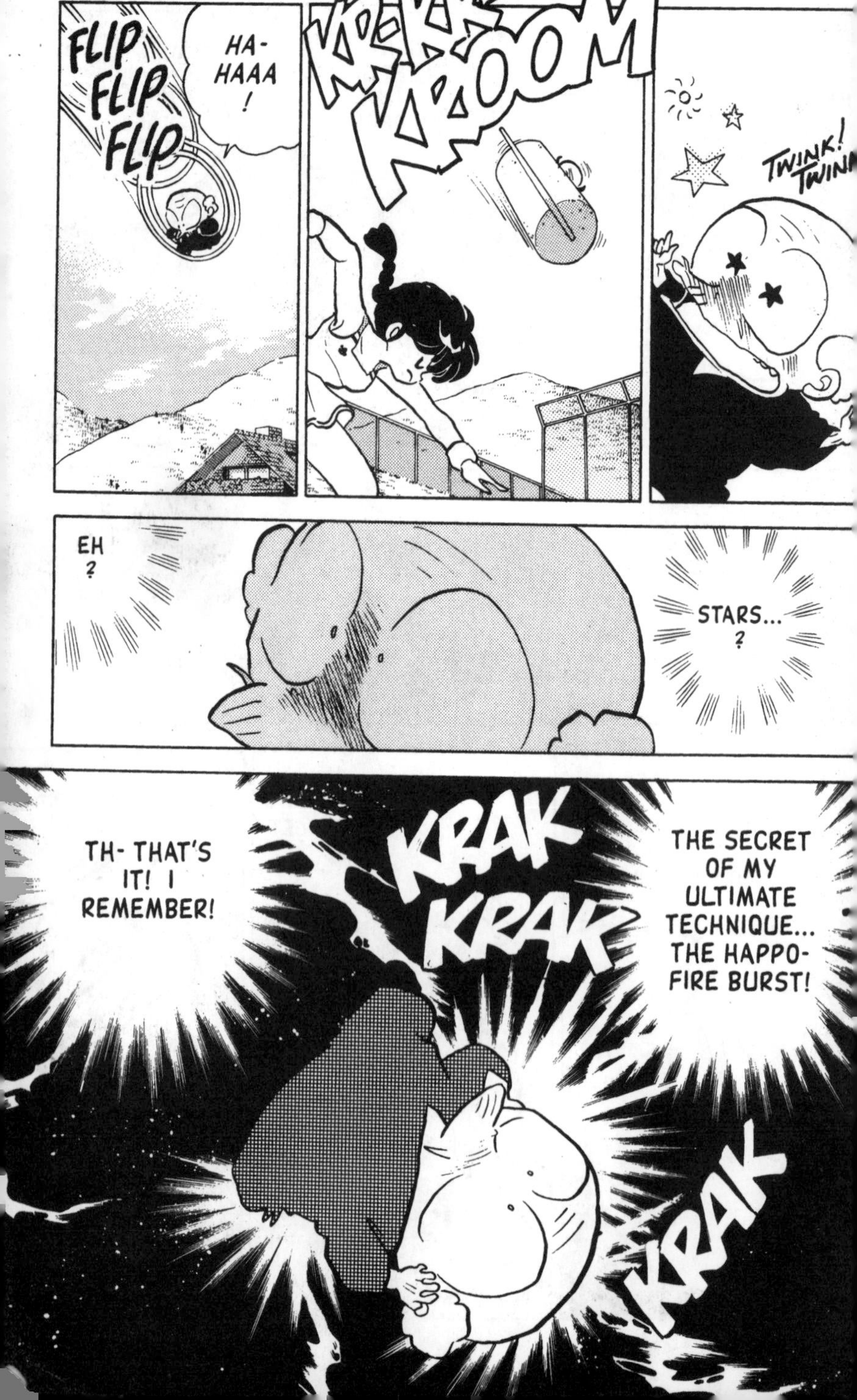

FLIP FLIP FLIP
HA-HAAA!
KR-KR-KROOM
TWINK! TWINK
EH?
STARS...?
TH- THAT'S IT! I REMEMBER!
KRAK KRAK
THE SECRET OF MY ULTIMATE TECHNIQUE... THE HAPPO-FIRE BURST!
KRAK

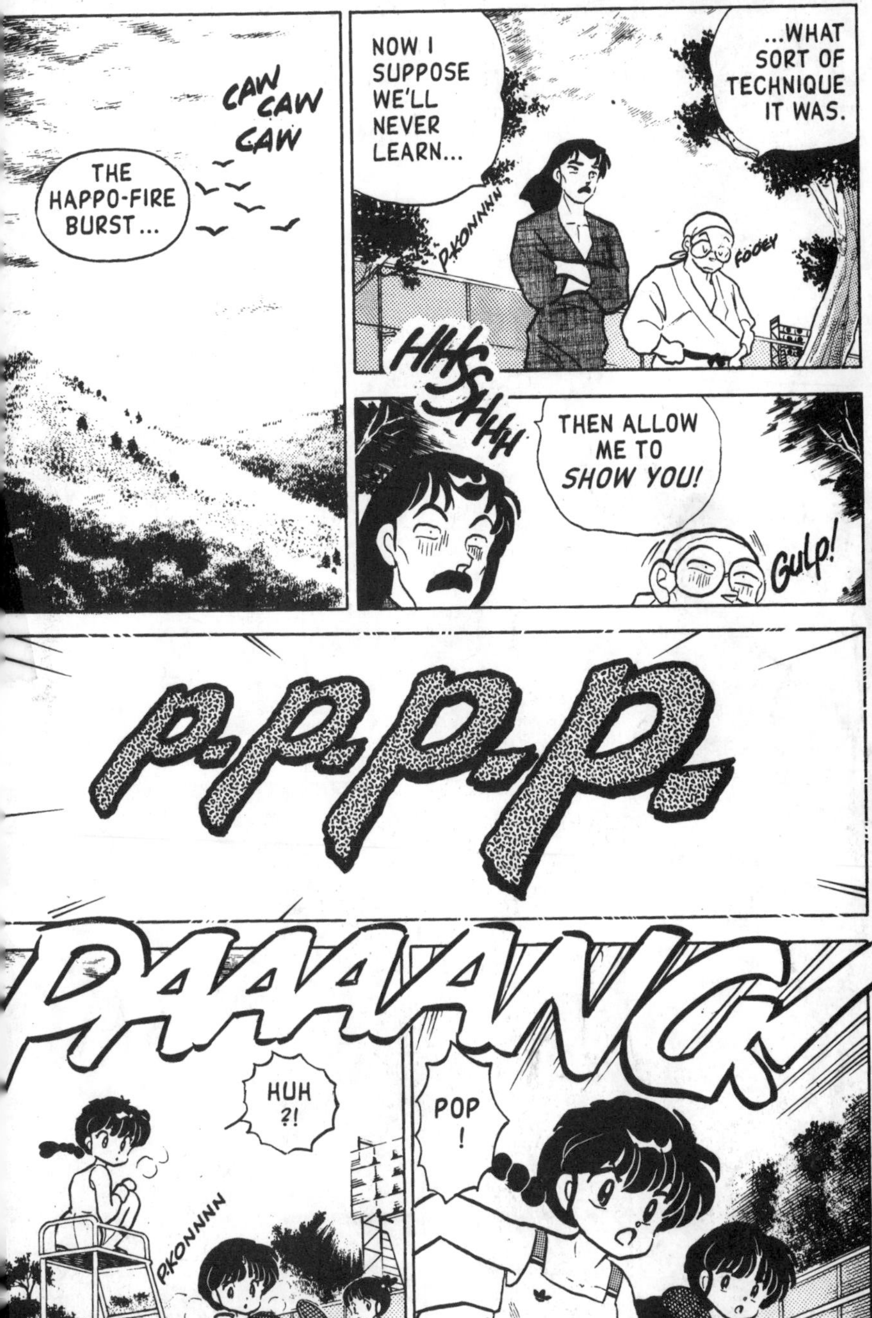
CAW CAW CAW
THE HAPPO-FIRE BURST...
NOW I SUPPOSE WE'LL NEVER LEARN...
...WHAT SORT OF TECHNIQUE IT WAS.
P-KONNNN
FOOEY
HHSSHHH
THEN ALLOW ME TO *SHOW YOU!*
GULP!
P.P.P.P.
PAAANG!
HUH ?!
P-KONNNN
POP !
AKANE

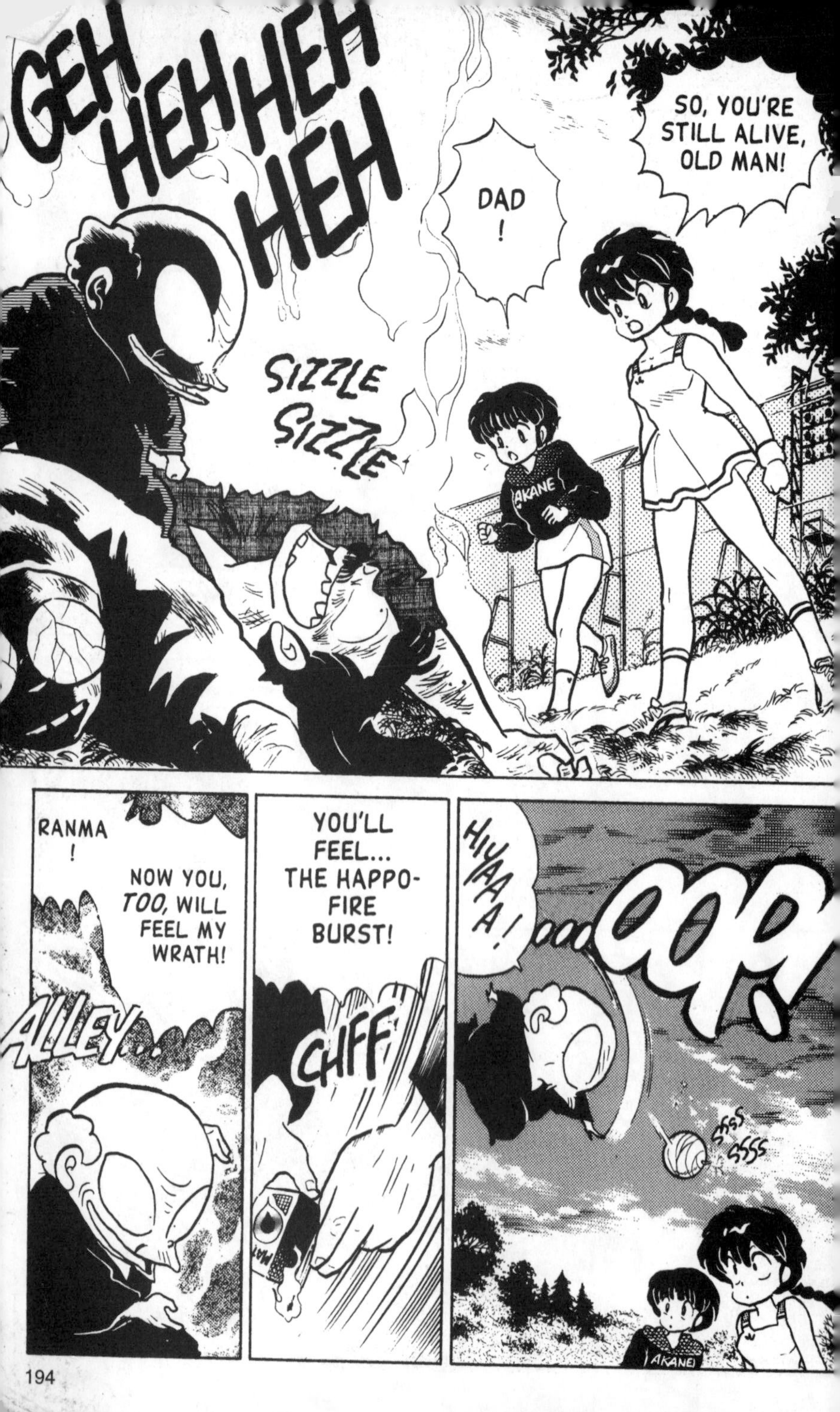
GEH HEH HEH HEH
SIZZLE SIZZLE
DAD !
SO, YOU'RE STILL ALIVE, OLD MAN!
RANMA !
NOW YOU, *TOO,* WILL FEEL MY WRATH!
ALLEY...
YOU'LL FEEL... THE HAPPO-FIRE BURST!
CHFF
HIYAAA!
...OOP!
SSSS SSSS

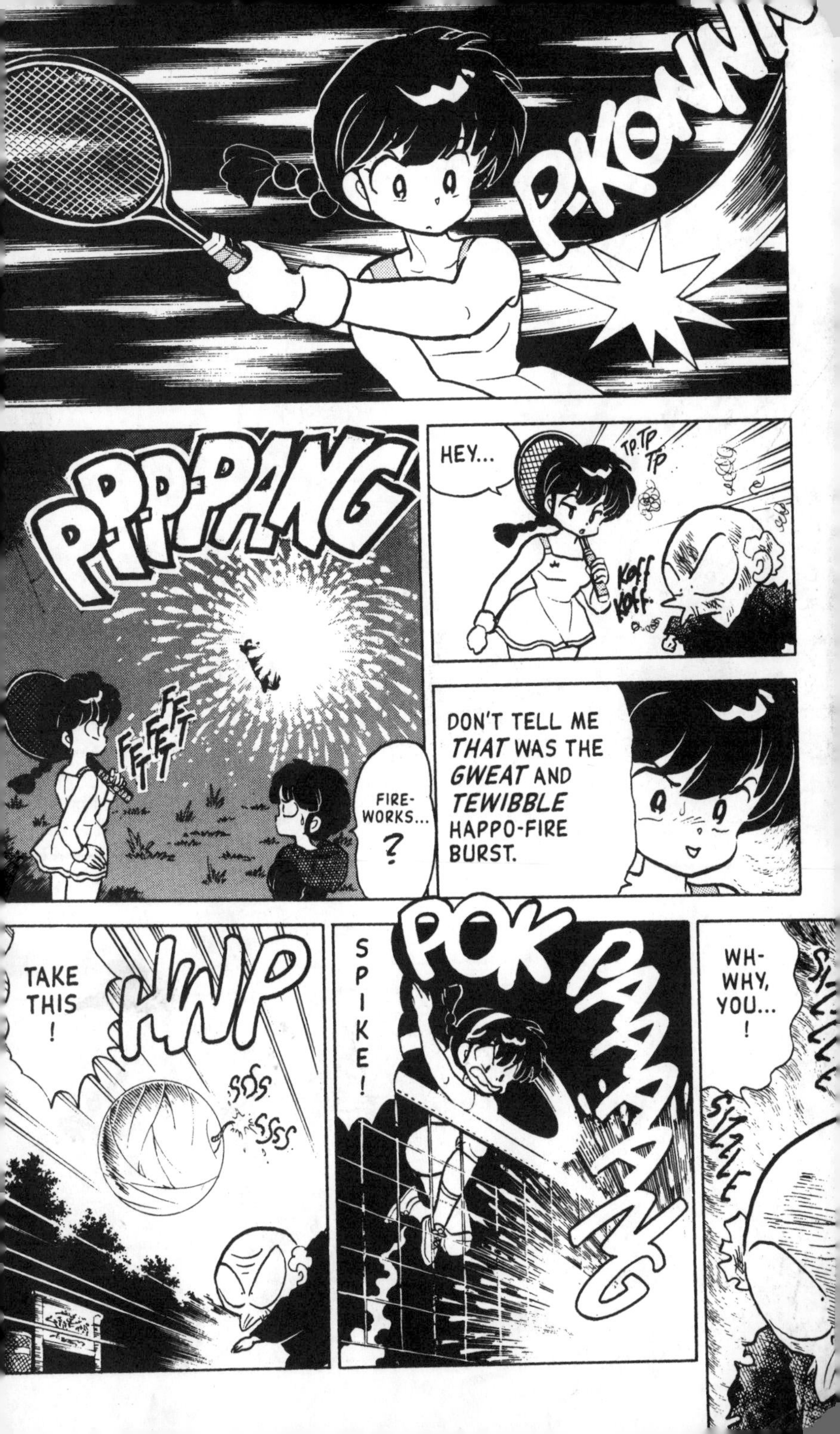
P-KONNA
P-P-P-PANG
FFFFFFT
FIRE-WORKS...?
HEY...
TP TP TP
KOFF KOFF
DON'T TELL ME *THAT* WAS THE *GWEAT* AND *TEWIBBLE* HAPPO-FIRE BURST.
TAKE THIS!
HWP
SSSS SSSS
SPIKE!
POK
PAAANG
WH-WHY, YOU...!
SIZZLE
SIZZLE

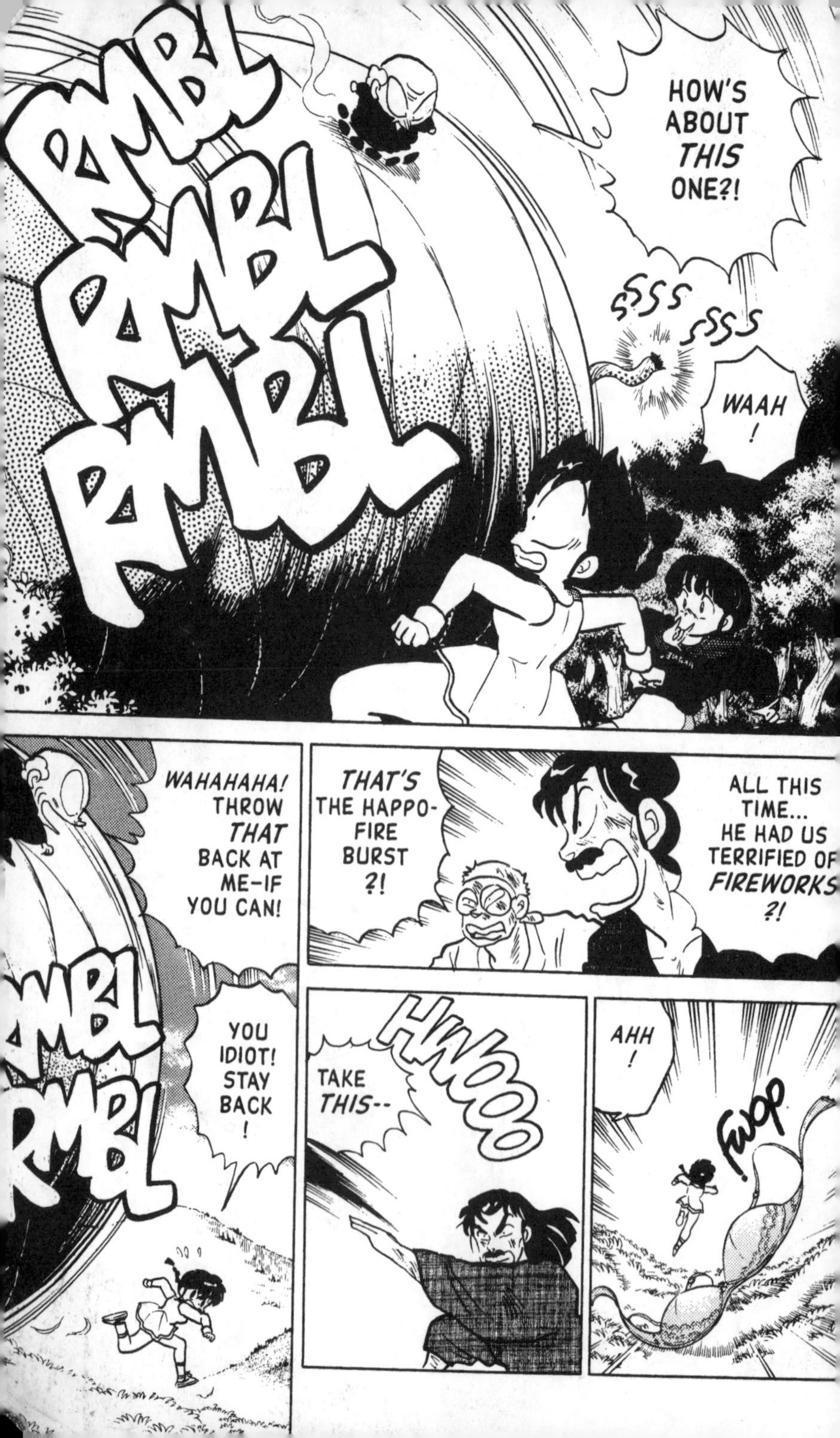
RMBL
RMBL
RMBL
HOW'S ABOUT THIS ONE?!
SSSS
SSSS
WAAH!
WAHAHAHA! THROW THAT BACK AT ME—IF YOU CAN!
MBL
RMBL
YOU IDIOT! STAY BACK!
THAT'S THE HAPPO-FIRE BURST?!
ALL THIS TIME... HE HAD US TERRIFIED OF FIREWORKS?!
HWOOO
TAKE THIS--
AHH!
FWOP

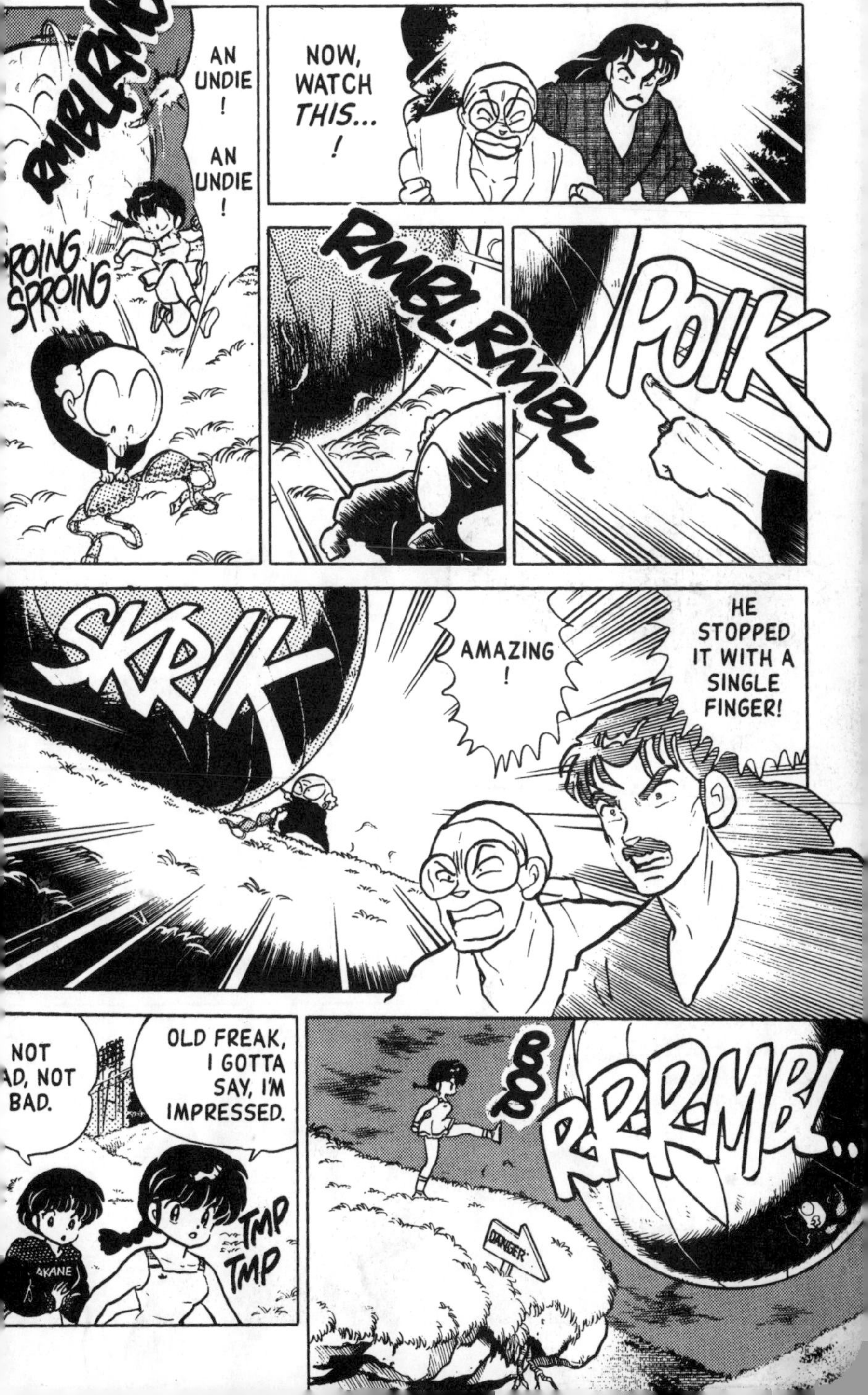
RMBLRMBL
AN UNDIE!
AN UNDIE!
SPROING SPROING
NOW, WATCH *THIS...*!
RMBL RMBL RMBL
POIK
SKRIK
AMAZING!
HE STOPPED IT WITH A SINGLE FINGER!
NOT BAD, NOT BAD.
OLD FREAK, I GOTTA SAY, I'M IMPRESSED.
TMP TMP
AKANE
BOOO
RRRMBL...
DANGER

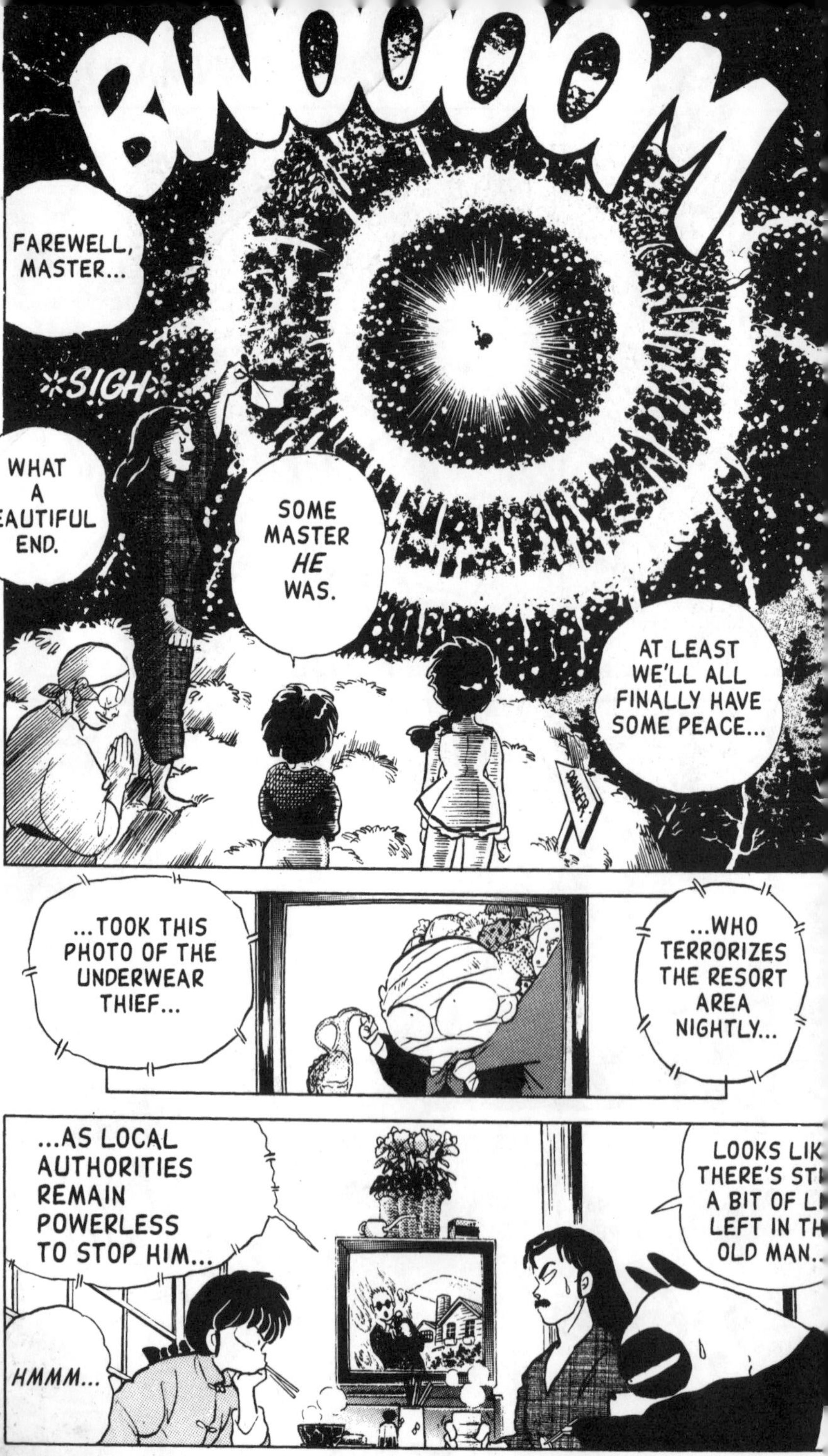
BWOOOOM
FAREWELL, MASTER...
SIGH
WHAT A BEAUTIFUL END.
SOME MASTER *HE* WAS.
AT LEAST WE'LL ALL FINALLY HAVE SOME PEACE...
...TOOK THIS PHOTO OF THE UNDERWEAR THIEF...
...WHO TERRORIZES THE RESORT AREA NIGHTLY...
...AS LOCAL AUTHORITIES REMAIN POWERLESS TO STOP HIM...
HMMM...
LOOKS LIK THERE'S ST A BIT OF L LEFT IN TH OLD MAN..

END OF RANMA 1/2 VOLUM

Rumiko Takahashi

umiko Takahashi was born in 1957 in Niigata, Japan. She attended women's college in kyo, where she began studying comics with Kazuo Koike, author of *Crying Freeman*. In 8, she won a prize in Shogakukan's annual "New Comic Artist Contest," and in that same ar her boy-meets-alien comedy series *Lum*Urusei Yatsura* began appearing in the weekly nga magazine *Shônen Sunday*. This phenomenally successful series ran for nine years and over 22 million copies. Takahashi's later *Ranma 1/2* series enjoyed even greater popularity.

kahashi is considered by many to be one of the world's most popular manga artists. With publication of Volume 34 of her *Ranma 1/2* series in Japan, Takahashi's total sales passed one hundred million copies of her compiled works.

Takahashi's serial titles include *Lum*Urusei Yatsura*, *Ranma 1/2*, *One-Pound Gospel*, aison Ikkoku* and *Inu-Yasha*. Additionally, Takahashi has drawn many short stories which been published in America under the title "Rumic Theater," and several installments of a known as her "Mermaid" series. Most of Takahashi's major stories have also been animat- and are widely available in translation worldwide. *Inu-Yasha* is her most recent serial story, first published in *Shônen Sunday* in 1996.

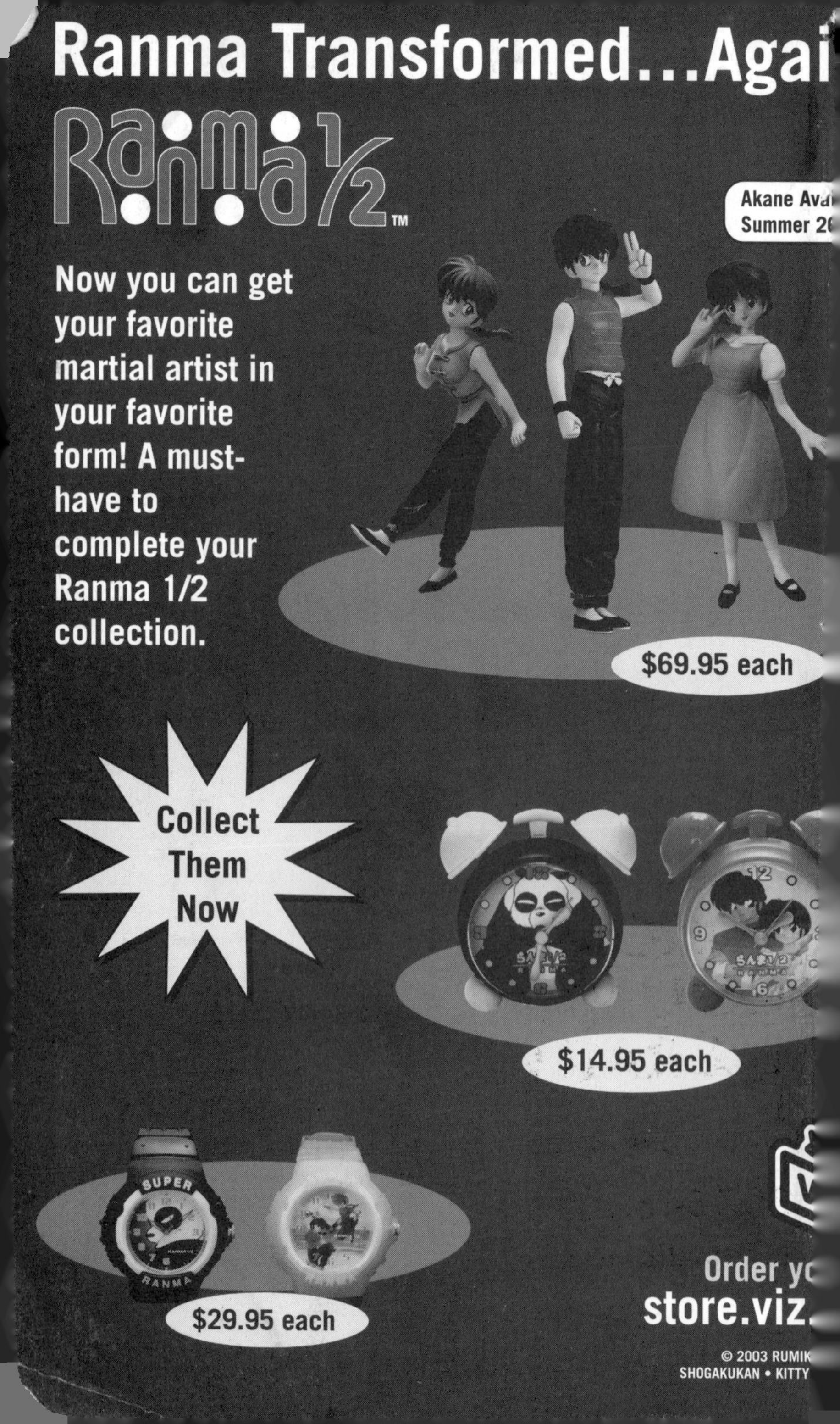

Ranma Transformed...Agai
Ranma 1/2™
Akane Ava
Summer 2
Now you can get your favorite martial artist in your favorite form! A must-have to complete your Ranma 1/2 collection.
$69.95 each
Collect Them Now
$14.95 each
SUPER
RANMA
$29.95 each
Order yo
store.viz.
© 2003 RUMIK
SHOGAKUKAN • KITTY